# THE *Gene* POOL

# THE Gene POOL

E. C. Hiatt

iUniverse, Inc.
Bloomington

# The Gene Pool

iUniverse books may be ordered through booksellers or by contacting:

iUniverse
1663 Liberty Drive
Bloomington, IN 47403
www.iuniverse.com
1-800-Authors (1-800-288-4677)

ISBN: 978-1-4759-5356-5 (sc)
ISBN: 978-1-4759-5357-2 (ebk)

Printed in the United States of America

iUniverse rev. date: 11/09/2012

This book is dedicated to my bibliophile wife, Ellen,
and to Tiny, a retired marine who gave me some technical
support for my story.

The dictionary reads,

"A novel is a fictitious prose narrative of considerable length and complexity, portraying characters and usually presenting sequential organization of action and scenes."

*The Gene Pool*, by E. C. Hiatt, is a novel . . . more or less.

# Chapter
## 1

I T's unusually cold in the mountains of southern Wyoming this December of 1959, even for Westriver. Saturday after Christmas, Casey White is readying himself to pick up his waitress girlfriend from the restaurant where she works.

He bundles himself in heavy flannel-lined denim jeans. He jams his feet into his insulated high-top boots. He likes the snow and cold. The rest of the weenies can just stay inside.

Casey is unusual by most standards. At six feet two, he weighs only 120 pounds. He has his father's ice-cold blue eyes and a generous haystack of blond hair he keeps cut in a flattop. It is a standing joke that he can play hide-and-go-seek by hiding in the shadow of a clothesline.

Aside from that, since his graduation from high school, he has been employed in a job that requires some rigorous work. He's physically toned, and he can press two hundred pounds. This is a feat most other high school kids cannot attain. The coach pressed him to work out with the wrestlers and be on the team during his junior year of high school, but he and the other kids have differing ideas.

It's his lot in life to be the son of a professing Methodist, who is a Christmas and Easter Christian. Casey is growing up in a town that is 90 percent Alfeta. The kids won't let him forget who and what he is, or that his dad is the school's lowly janitor who works at their pleasure.

The history of the Alfeta church starts around 1800. An itinerant drifter with no formal schooling, taught his numbers, the alphabet, and the rudiments of reading by his grandmother, dreamed of starting his own church. Unknown to his family, he was born with extremely high intelligence and a split personality that would emerge later, with some other unsavory proclivities.

In his late teenage years, he came up with his own interpretation of the Bible and was disciplined by the pastor of the Methodist church he attended sporadically. He was finally kicked out for disagreeing with the pastor and for his inappropriate advances toward the young women of the congregation.

He insisted that one night he had a conversation with God. God told him the Christian church in its present form was dead and that, like the original creation, he would create his own version of the Bible. Because it was to be based on the seven days of creation, the church would labor for six days and keep the Sabbath holy. The church was to be named referencing the original Hebrew scriptures from which it was researched. The first and the seventh characters in the Greek alphabet became the name of the church. Alfeta is the name he chose for his new religion, although he didn't realize at the time that Alpha was spelled with a "ph," not an "f." He told his followers that God had told him to spell it that way. To further distinguish it, he named his churches precincts to separate them from the mainline religions.

He became founder and head until such time as enough converts could be trained. The best, richest, and most educated among them would be his apostles. He would continue to have conversations with God as God brought down from heaven a gold sword with the scriptures inscribed on the blade. Each time he turned it, a new verse was revealed.

He was thus inspired as to how and what to write in the new Bible he was producing, although he stole liberally from the Protestant King James Version, utilizing and rewording the passages to suit his purpose. None of his followers ever saw the golden sword, as God took it back up to heaven. He promulgated the religious, moral, social, military, and political mores of the Alfeta religious community.

This religion was deemed a perversion, a threat, and a cult by established religions, since its inception was a source of controversy in the religious and political community of the Northeast, where it was conceived, to the Western territories, where it was driven.

\* \* \*

Naomi Stryker is the girl Casey has been dating since his freshman year in high school. She's the daughter of Arthur Stryker, an alcoholic but skillful bulldozer operator. He's an Alfeta slacker (one who ignores the dictates of the church hierarchy and doesn't pay his apportionment or follow the church disciplines), who imbibes Old Rooster on the weekend and manages to make it to work sober on Monday morning at the local road construction company site.

Naomi doesn't fare well in the eyes of the Alfeta church or with her peers as a young woman who has chosen to date someone outside her faith. Her church laws state that it's a sin to go inside the church of another religion. The dozen times she'd gone with Casey, it hadn't appeared to harm her, and she was always welcomed by a friendly congregation.

"Mom, don't wait up for me. I'm going to pick up Naomi. She isn't sure whether she'll get off at midnight or one." Casey gives his mom a peck on her cheek.

Child labor laws restrict minors from working past midnight, but Naomi gets away with it because the local cops have more serious things to look out for in this little, supposedly religious town with over a dozen bars and three package stores. She likes her job because she makes good tips from the late-night customers as she cheers them up.

"Are you planning to go to church tomorrow?" Bella asks him, hoping he will say yes.

"I don't think so, Mom; we're hunting early," he tells her. It's a non-answer; he knows she wants him to go.

His dad, Walter, meets him at the front door.

"Casey, how are you doing on cash? I can loan you ten until payday."

"Dad, I'm good." Old Dad isn't above slipping him a ten to carry him over until payday. On paydays, Walter would never accept the money back. Casey knows he's his dad's favorite, as he doesn't have a curfew. He's one of a family of six, including two older sisters who graduated from high school, married, and moved on with their lives, and a younger brother, Gene, who is in the sophomore year of his high school trial. The ages of the White children span ten years.

Few of the younger generation remain in town after graduation, because there is no place to seek real employment. They can apply to work for the railroad, hire on with some sheep or cattle farmer, perhaps pump gas, or stock shelves in a grocery store. *Real jobs with a future, like mine,* Casey thinks wryly. *One day I'll blow this town.*

Right now, the primary thing on his mind is the 1949 Ford Custom he drives. *Will old number sixteen start?* He calls the car number sixteen because the first license plate he was issued was number 1916.

The thermometer on the front porch indicates eighteen degrees Fahrenheit. The snowbound Ford looks forlorn, its rear tires encased in the chains he installed nearly two months ago. He brushes aside some snow, finds the electrical connection to the block heater, unplugs it, and then carefully pulls the extension cord back to the porch and tosses it inside.

The car door's hinges complain with a chalkboard shriek as he opens the driver's side and gets in. The compressing springs make a cracking sound as the ice lets go, and they settle with the load. He inserts the ignition key, pulls the choke all the way out, pumps the gas pedal, and presses the starter button and hopes.

"Come on, ol' sixteen, do your thing." There's a slight hesitation, and then the motor starts turning over. He gives a couple of quick pumps on the gas pedal just to make sure. The old flathead V8 comes to life. He breathes a sigh of relief and allows it to run for a few minutes; then he adjusts the heater defroster and the choke. He steps back out to remove the two inches of snow on the windshield and rear window.

With the car in reverse while slowly letting the clutch out, he can feel the vibration of the chained-up tires digging to pull the car through the snow. He makes it onto the iced-over street and heads downtown to pick up Naomi.

Driving past the school gymnasium, Casey is surprised to see basketball practice letting out after midnight. Several of the jocks gather up snow and throw it at him.

"Hey, White, go to the city dump and die!"

It's far too cold to make a snowball. Another one shouts an obscenity at him, and he turns to look back to see who it is. *Ass holes*, he thinks, making a mental note of it, knowing he'll extract some small act of revenge—if not on the man, then most certainly on his car. He's good at that.

Most of the guys who can afford a car have them leaded, lowered, add fender skirts, moon hubcaps, and glass pack mufflers to sound so cool. Casey steadfastly rejects the notion, knowing ground clearance is more important than coolness. He's at present running an exhaust pipe purchased from the local junkyard, from an equally aged Lincoln, which also contains a resonator. He likes the extra quiet it affords him, so he can be sneaky.

While he was working on it the first summer he owned it, he drilled out the rivet in the release handle for the hood latch and attached a piece of cable, ran it through the firewall, formed a loop, and fastened it inside the interior. Now he's the only one who knows how to get under the hood to the engine.

Removing the screws from the glove box and carefully filing the sharp edges of the sheet metal down allowed him access to the area behind it. He stores his booty along the welded ridge of the car that connects the firewall to the interior trim and the heater radiator box. He's added a piece of sheet metal formed to hold his Ruger .22-caliber auto pistol.

The first summer he owned the car, right after his sixteenth birthday, the older brother of a classmate of his was drafted. He came by one night and showed Casey how to sneak past the cashier guarding the entrance to the truckers' showers at the truck stop. They pushed damp paper towels up the delivery chute of several of the rubber machines; they then went back an hour later, pulled the paper towels out, and collected the ones the truckers had abandoned, thinking the machine was empty.

Casey now has a side business of sorts reselling them to guys who want or need them. As a benefit, he knows who is doing whom, or at least hopes to. He utilized some of his products for his own personal use in early fall, after he turned sixteen and lost his innocence to an older woman.

When Casey arrives at the Chinese American restaurant and Naomi isn't outside waiting, he knocks on the door. The elderly Chinese man running the place makes note of his presence, lets him in, and goes back to his count of the till.

Naomi comes from the back, throwing her coat on and pocketing her tips. Seeing her pleases him because she is always so "up." As usual, she gives him just a quick peck on the cheek. She smells slightly of stale cigarette smoke, old french fries, coffee, dirty dishwater, and lipstick.

"Hi," she says in greeting.

Casey only shrugs. He wishes she could find another job doing something less tiring. When they discuss it, she refuses to change; she likes the money her job brings in. She knows how to work the tourists who overflow from the bus stop and hotel restaurant next door to get them to leave a larger tip.

"Some of the jocks gave me some crap when I came by the school just now," he tells her. "They're pretty late getting out of practice tonight."

"Was it little Marvin?" She cuts her eyes back at him.

"Yeah, that rectal orifice was one of them." His voice has an edge to it now.

Naomi is a svelte five six; she weighs 110 pounds and is well rounded out in the front and the back, fully a woman. She has pretty honey-brown hair, a generous smile, and a Nordic complexion. The only thing detracting from her appearance is her slightly oversize nose.

"Do you need to go right home?" Casey asks, giving her an appreciative once-over as she sits down and scoots over beside him. "I can stay out a little, but my feet and legs are awfully tired. A double busload of passengers from the valley ended up over here. Crystal didn't show up until late; then she had to go home early to take care of her brothers and sisters. I had to work ten booths, but it's okay, because I made a lot in tips tonight," Naomi says to him.

"That's still a lot of work for one person to have to handle."

"Crystal's folks are having another knock-down, drag-out. Why don't they just divorce?" She pouts, turning toward him. Before driving away, she looks up and down the street and, seeing nobody, kisses him fully on the mouth. He holds her briefly, opens the button of her coat, slips his hand inside, and cups her breast.

\* \* \*

Arriving at her home, they park in the driveway beside the house that runs back to the single-car garage.

"Pull up farther; we can park there as long as we want. Donnie should be in bed already." Her brother is two years younger than she. He's the product of another reconciliation period her folks endured when her father promised to stop drinking. He's since slipped back into his old habits.

Casey pulls into her driveway, ahead of them; the family Buick is parked. It's a black '57 Buick Roadmaster. They bought it new when he was working steadily and there was more money.

Casey's car is warmed up now. Naomi opens her coat, shrugs out of it, and drapes it across her legs as she turns in the seat and cuddles against him. She offers her lips to kiss, and he pushes the seat back as far as it goes.

Naomi is what the guys consider a "nice" girl. She'll neck but won't allow any sex. Casey has managed to get her naked to the waist several times, but she has become more cautious the longer they dated. She knows the consequences if she doesn't. There will

7

be no trip down to the valley to have an unwanted child to be given to the church's adoption program—or worse, an abortion.

"Are you coming by tomorrow after church?"

"I'm not going. Ron, Ken, and I are going to go deer hunting early."

"What time are you going? It's almost one now; do you ever get any sleep?" she asks, not really surprised.

"I guess I'd better be going. We're going to be up on the eastern ridge behind Ken's pasture about daybreak." He nuzzles her neck, reaches up, cups her cloth-encased breast in his hand, and kisses it.

"Would you like to feel that without all the cloth around it?"

He reaches up and releases the buttons of her blouse, and she pulls it open. He has to fumble to release the three small hooks of her brassiere but manages to get it unfastened.

"Kiss my nipples, Casey." She's getting damp between her thighs and stops him. Casey knows the evening is over. His body is fully ready, but he knows she will just give him a quick kiss and disappear inside.

He gives her one last kiss, and then she gets out, shuts the door quietly, and dashes toward the back door. When things get too bad, there's a local woman anxious to help him.

Naomi starts through the door and then turns and steps back out. He can see her smile, bright blue eyes, and goose-pimpled pink breasts as she turns the light on and does a pirouette to exhibit her.

"Call me tomorrow and let me know what you get hunting," she says, and he takes a long, appreciative look.

"I'll bring your dad a front quarter," he replies while starting the car. He looks back to check the driveway and then forward again. She's gone, and the light is out.

He drives home and backs into the tracks he made previously. He pulls out and backs in again just for good measure, making the track a little wider. Then it's inside, up to his room, set the clock, and go to bed.

* * *

Casey doesn't allow the alarm to ring more than a single beat before he shuts it off. He can smell the coffee and knows that either Mom or Dad is up making it for him.

Bella is sitting in back of the table with her back against the wall, allowing the heat vent to blow upward beneath her nightgown. She stands, pours him a cup of coffee, and pushes the sugar bowl to him. He drinks it, and she pours him another.

"Where are you going today?" she asks him, sliding the sugar bowl back over.

"We're going up back of Ken's property along the ridge into the county. He worked the cattle this fall and saw some nice racks up there," Casey replies.

"Will you be gone all day?" He knows it worries her every time he walks out the door carrying a gun.

"We'll be gone all day, or just as long as it takes to get a deer." He looks at her knowing exactly what she's thinking, but he's responsible with guns.

Casey returns to his bedroom and slides out the gun box from under the bed. His choices are the Remington 780 .30-06 and the M1 Garand military, which he and his dad bought in a questionable legal exchange with a gun dealer after they joined the NRA and the junior shooters club.

He selects the M1 and puts two clips into his coat pocket. He decides on two more for the opposite pocket and adds them to his arsenal. He's sharpened his hunting knife and ax to as fine a hone as possible, and he straps them on his calf with the special harness he constructed just for the purpose.

"Bye, Mom," he says, and he kisses her cheek.

"Be careful, and if you get a deer, don't forget about the organs." He doesn't need reminding; his dad loves the heart and the liver.

Casey starts out and then realizes he hasn't reinstalled the extension cord to the block heater. Apprehensively, he tries old sixteen.

*Damn, how did I screw up like that?* he thinks. *I hope ol' sixteen will start.*

## Chapter 2

T HERE'S enough heat left in the engine from the previous night to do the trick even though it is only sixteen degrees. Casey arrives at Ron's house and finds him waiting on the front porch holding his father's .30-30 saddle rifle in the crook of his arm. He slides in while stifling a shiver. Ron Phillips is a childhood playmate from the fourth grade.

"Sheeeat, it's cold out here!" Ron leans forward to where the warm air is starting to rise from the floor vent. He slumps down in the seat and grabs a few more precious minutes of sleep as they drive the ten miles to Ken's house.

Casey breaks a new path through the fresh snow up the gravel driveway. They step out and see Ken's mom waiting for them on the porch. She hears them coming, and they plod through the accumulation, up to the steps to the porch stoop, where she hands them a broom.

Ken's dad is a county agent and is always interested in their activities. He's standing at the stove, and as they enter the kitchen, he turns around and sets before each of them a plate of bacon, eggs, and toast.

"Kenny will be down in a minute; go ahead and eat." He sets steaming coffee cups before them and pushes the cream and sugar over.

"Are you coming with us?" Ron asks.

"I'm getting too old to go stomping around the hills now. That's why folks like me have fine young men like you to do our going." Casey looks down and sees his deer license lying next to Ken's on the table. Kenny joins them at the table and starts fixing his coffee.

"How's the weather out there?" Ken asks as his dad places his breakfast in front of him. Ken is a smaller version of his dad in size and appearance, sculpted by ranch work. They both have the appearance of folks that work long and hard for a living.

"Cold enough to freeze the—" Ron doesn't have a chance to complete "balls" before Ken's mom steps in.

"Don't be using bad language in here, Ron; I'll have to take the broom to you," she says, scolding him.

"To freeze the icicles off the porch," Ron continues, trying to cover his first outburst.

"That's not what you were going to say." She takes his cup, pours him a refill, and smiles slyly down at him. As they finish breakfast, Ken steps out and starts the stake-body Studebaker; they'll be driving to where they'll hunt. It has dual rear wheels, and both are chained. It rides hard, but it will get them where they want to go.

They all three jump in the cab, and Casey beats Ron to the center seat. He knows the cowboy rule: if you get to sit next to the door, you have to open the gates.

They pull across the highway and drive down the short off-ramp. Ron struggles with the barbed-wire gate loop for a minute, and after it releases, he drags it through the new snow and out of the way.

"Leave it open; Dad moved the sheep to the shed, and there are none in this pasture." Ken knows every wrinkle in the lay of the land, and they pull up to the next gate.

Ron dutifully opens that one too. The road from here is a windswept upward grade. It will be a climb of about a mile to the ridge. The sky in the east behind them is a cloudless golden pink, starting to lighten. Before they crest the hill, Ken kills the headlights, stops the truck, and sets the brake.

"I think we should just have a look-a-see," says Ken. They take out their magazines and shove them in place. They all look at one another and know the drill.

They spread out about ten feet apart and slowly inch up to the ridge. The light wind is blowing the powdery snow from off the drift into their faces, but it isn't strong enough to deter them. Ron stands up behind several almost intertwined, naked aspen trees as Ken suddenly freezes in his tracks and drops to a squat. Something is out there.

Casey squats down and crawls. He checks the safety and then works his way behind a huge growth of sagebrush. He looks out, and there, almost a short thirty yards in front of them, are more deer than he can imagine. There are three bucks and about a dozen does working their way up to the ridge.

One or two of them look their way, and Casey freezes. He looks over at Ken and then Ron. Ken holds up one finger and points right, indicating that the buck on the right is Casey's. He shows Ron two fingers, indicating the center one.

The countdown begins as Casey aims for a head shot at the buck. Ken fires, Casey and Ron fire, and three deer collapse. Casey sees the does flash and run. The sun is rising directly behind them, and the deer couldn't have seen them had they wanted to.

Casey jumps up and away from the cover of the sagebrush and places the rifle butt against his body. He hip shoots three times, and three does in midflight go down. He looks over at his buddies, who are staring open-mouthed at him in disbelief.

"What the hell! How did you do that?" Ken is shouldering his rifle and is about to get off another shot when Casey fires. Ken slowly lowers his gun, the surprised look still on his face.

They both ask, "How?" astounded at what they just witnessed. They look at him and then back toward the deer, which made it about another ten yards from where the initial rounds found their marks.

"I've been practicing that a long time; I can take a duck out of the air if you want me to." Casey bends down and searches for his spent brass. His dad wants him to return them for reloading.

It isn't an accident he can shoot. In his free time, he takes one of his guns out to the hills and practices. He knows how to hip shoot every gun he has. He shoots down the barrel because he knows it's important to be able to hit something far away. The adjustable iron sight on the M-1 fascinates him, and he's fired enough rounds at distance that he feels confident he can hit anything he can legally hunt.

The three of them stand and walk to their deer. Casey's has a small hole in the front and no other marks. He walks farther and looks down at the fallen does. Two are dead, and the third is paralyzed. She can move her head and nothing else. He places the muzzle of the M1 about a foot from the underside of her head and pulls the trigger.

The chore now is the field dressing. He releases his rounds, clears the chamber, and props the rifle against the fence. He judiciously cuts the scent glands away and opens the carcass.

He carefully cuts away, removes the heart and liver from the rest of the organs, and sets them aside. Ken is just as fast, and he puts his tools down and goes back for the truck.

"What are you going to do with the other three?" Ron asks Casey.

"It's one apiece," Casey replies.

"I can't take another. I already have a deer in the garage from earlier, and it's a two-deer season."

"I have Dad's license with me if we need another. If we don't see a game warden before we get them home, then I won't pull the stub off. Mr. Stryker wants some deer meat, and I'll just give him one," Casey says.

It takes them the better part of half an hour to load the six deer onto the back of the stake body. Ken doesn't want his hearts or livers, so Casey cuts them away and keeps them for his dad. *There,* he thinks, *I've got five. Dad should be happy with five hearts and livers. Mr. Stryker can feed the family deer for a while, and it will help out on the groceries.*

Casey drops Ron and his deer off and helps him hang it in the garage. He decides it's prudent to take his home first. His dad is elated at getting the extra hearts and livers. They hang the two deer in the shed behind the house. Casey still has one in the trunk. He won't pull the stub off the license, but he keeps it along with him as he drives back to Naomi's house.

When he arrives, there's no one home. He backs into the driveway and finds the garage and house locked, but he knows the secret way in. He knocks the snow and ice from the slanted basement doors and reaches under to release them. Once inside, he descends the steps, locates the house key on the top of the door trim, opens the basement door, and returns the key and steps inside.

There are several quilting frames set up in the open area beyond, and a small kerosene heater percolates quietly in the corner. Upstairs, he opens the back door and unloads the deer in the garage. It's a trick to get the limp body of the deer to hang up, being still warm. He finally has to throw a rope over a rafter, pull it up, and tie it off.

It's cold enough that the deer will freeze in the daylight hours, and Mr. Stryker will have to make arrangements to have it butchered and packaged.

He then goes back into the house and downstairs to Naomi's bedroom. Casey takes two shell casings from the .30-06 from his pocket, finds her underwear drawer, and places them in the pair on top. They can be felt but not seen. She'll know he paid her bedroom a visit.

He's about to lock up when he hears a crash from another room. He returns to the kitchen, looks in the living room, and turns the light on to investigate further.

He cautiously looks inside the front bedroom and sees a scene reminiscent of an old-fashioned barroom brawl. The noise he heard was the dresser lamp falling from the bed to the floor. The corner of the dresser is covered with matted hair and dried blood. Someone had rapped his head against it. Casey decides he'll just lock up and leave. He doesn't want to get involved in someone else's troubles.

He encounters the black Buick two and a half blocks from the house. He slows as he sees Mrs. Stryker doing, likewise, and rolling her driver-side window down with a somewhat surprised look on her face.

"I put a deer in the garage," he says to Althea. Her face lights up in a smile.

"Why, thank you, Casey. That should help out on my meal planning for some time to come."

He looks over and sees Arthur sitting with his head bandaged, and his eyes closed. He's still in his bed clothing and offers no conversation. There's no one else in the back of the car.

"The kids are at the precinct, and I need to get Arthur home and go and get them," she says to him.

"Okay, tell Naomi I'll call her later. I need to go and help Dad with our deer." He rolls his window up and pulls away. Apparently, Crystal's family isn't the only one having marital troubles. If the old man can just keep off the booze, everything else will iron itself out.

At home and after conferring with his dad about the short day's hunt, Casey decides to take a nap.

\* \* \*

His mom is shaking him and telling him to get up to eat. He looks out the window and sees the sky growing pink along the western hills. He knows it must be late in the day, and they've allowed him to sleep completely through lunch. She's awakening him for supper.

"You must have been really tired. I do wish you'd come in earlier. You know I worry about you." His mom sits on the side of the bed and runs her fingers through his short-cut hair. She has the far-away smiling look a mother always has when she is in close contact with her own.

"That's a nice young buck, Casey, and the doe is about three years old. It was a warm fall, and she's still a little fat, so I guess she weighs as much as the buck," his dad says as he sits down to eat.

15

"Yeah, we found them right at the edge of the ridge. We didn't even have to go down into the lower valley where we hunted two years ago."

The phone rings two long and a short. It's their ring. They don't like being on a party line, but at this end of the town, there're only so many wires run, and that's the best the phone company will offer without them investing some of their own money in the new wires.

"Can you come and get me out of here, Casey? I need to get completely out of the house now." It's Naomi.

"I will; I have to finish eating supper. I'll be there in about thirty minutes."

"Thanks, Casey. Please hurry," she replies.

He finishes his supper but doesn't hurry. He isn't in the mood to have to listen to someone else's problems, even if she is the woman he loves. When he arrives, she is waiting on the porch for him. She runs through the snow and gets in.

"My parents are at it again. The hospital told them to go to the big hospital down in Salt Lake because Dad was throwing up blood. Mom just shoved him in the car and left. I can't go down and see him, and Mom is being a bitch. All I want to do is just go somewhere and talk." The car is warming nicely. She allows her fur-topped boots to drop to the floor and is in stocking feet.

They drive aimlessly for a while and talk, and Casey pulls up into her driveway, stops, moves the seat back, and tunes in the local radio station. She changes her position and offers herself to him. They neck for a while, and he checks his watch. She has to go to work tomorrow, and he has to be in early to unload grain.

"Come inside a minute and get warm," she says as she buttons her blouse. They step out of the car and realize it's much colder now. He locates the thermometer on her porch and notes the temperature has dropped to fifteen degrees in the last hour. The wind has a real edge to it.

They go tiptoeing inside and sit down on the couch in the almost darkened living room after Naomi unplugs the Christmas tree. There is some quiet noise in the back of the house, and Casey assumes it's the refrigerator or freezer coming on. She comes into his arms again, and they neck on the couch.

"Help me." He pulls on her blouse at the waist, and she releases the pants button as she sucks her tummy in. Naomi sits up, pulls her blouse up over her head, and snuggles back into his embrace. She kisses him again and removes her brassiere. It's quicker than Casey can do it.

She wriggles in delight as he stimulates her, and then she makes him stop. She reaches up to unbutton his shirt. He pulls it up over his head and drops it on the floor beside hers. He places his elbow down between her thighs, and she squirms and pushes her thighs together.

"Just press down."

He thinks, *Enough of this,* and reaches down and pulls both garments off her legs. She lifts her hips to facilitate their removal. *If I can get her going, it will be a sweet end to a beautiful day.* Casey feels her squirm. This goes on for only a moment as Casey notices she's moved and kicked her slacks off the couch. He pushes her over onto her back, kisses her breasts, and feels down her tummy.

They return to kiss, and there is a click and a near explosion of light as the overhead fixture in the room comes on. They both look up, and standing not five feet from them is Mrs. Stryker, Naomi's mom. She's completely naked save for a towel wrapped around her head. She's supposed to be down in the valley with Naomi's father at the hospital.

"What!" is all she can come up with? She has the same deer-in-the-headlights look Naomi has but does not move to cover herself. Naomi reaches to cover her own body, but there is nothing she can grasp.

"Naomi, go to your bedroom now!" Her breasts make a little bobbing motion as she points to the rear of the house. Casey takes a long, careful look at Naomi's mom. *It's what Naomi will look like in about twenty years,* he thinks. *Not bad at all.* But he wonders why she isn't attempting to conceal her nudity. He can't tell if her redness is from embarrassment or anger.

"Casey, you go home now!" Naomi gathers her wits and rises from the couch. She stands up in front of him and bends over to retrieve her clothes. Her mother watches him watching her and then watches her daughter disappear into the back hallway.

"What were you planning to do to my daughter?" she asks. Casey hears Naomi slam the kitchen door and then hears her footfalls on the basement stairs.

"I don't know, Mrs. Stryker. We never got this far before," he says to her.

"You'd probably gotten some of Naomi tonight if I hadn't fallen asleep in the bathtub. You thought I was still down in the valley with Arthur. I enjoyed listening to you two making out, but I stopped you. Naomi needs to be a virgin." She remains standing tall and straight in front of him, displaying herself. It seems to Casey that she is deriving some kind of pleasure from him looking at her.

He gathers his clothes, and his hand finds the front doorknob, turns it, and pulls. She's right beside him, and he feels her breast brush him. He reaches up to push her aside. Her hand is quick, and she holds his hand on her as she simultaneously leans against him and the door.

"What's the matter, Casey? Am I not as good as my daughter? You go ahead and get a quick feel."

Now Casey is getting seriously worried. She's naked and really coming on to him. It's all he can do to slip through whatever opening the door allows and drag his coat behind him. She gives a vicious laugh as he vacates the door.

What in the world is the matter with the woman? She isn't drunk. Then it hits him. Naomi's dad is an alcoholic and probably not taking care of his homework. She's casting about for someone to help her with her sexual frustrations.

# Chapter
# 3

CASEY tosses fitfully until, at last, the alarm clock arouses him. He dresses, eats his breakfast listlessly, and drives to work. The place boasts that it's been in business for over a century. God knows the buildings look the part. All are turn-of-the-century construction.

Westriver Wholesale Retail Supply is a glorified general store; they sell groceries, men's and women's apparel, home furnishings, appliances, bedding, and livestock salt and feed. They also wholesale and retail cases of cigarettes, cigars, snuff, and other tobacco products, all of which are despised by the Alfeta church. The owners and operators of the store are all Alfetas.

The company owns a storefront on the corner along with a lot. Two-thirds of the lot had been demolished and paved over for parking. The back third of the lot contains the rest of the building and currently serves as a warehouse for kegs of nails, readymade horseshoes, and sacks of feed, salt, and grain.

Mr. Herman is Casey's boss; he's a squat, chunky man who stands about five feet four. He is balding with a bad comb-over, wire-rim glasses, and acne scars. Sometime in his youth he lost a fistfight, and he never had his nose repaired. He always wears one of three sets of the same type of pants and suspenders, long-sleeve shirts, necktie, and boots. He keeps a pocket full of pencils and a small spiral tablet pad of paper.

Mr. Herman is waiting for Casey as he steps inside the back door at ten minutes before the hour, but that doesn't matter; if you're here, you are at work, as far as Mr. Herman is concerned. Casey knows not even to mention overtime. "We only work straight time," Kurt had often told him.

"Morning, Casey, it's already a busy day. The church is holding a building program at the new precinct building, and we need volunteers to help out tonight. Would you like to come down and join us?" he asks.

"Sure, what does it pay?"

The older man throws his head back, puffs his chest out, grins, and replies. "If you do the Lord's work, Casey, you get the Lord's pay. Just look at the church, Casey; we are growing by leaps and bounds. Soon we will be richer, stronger, larger, and more powerful, be in more countries, and have as much control as the Catholic Church. We're already closing in on the attendance of the Methodists. Now is a good time to join us. Our founder's vision of the new world is coming true."

Casey hears this sort of talk repeatedly, and it repulses him. *Isn't the aim of the Christian church to bring the lost, unwashed, and unbelieving to Christ?* he thinks. Alternatively, it is all about money, influence, and power. Casey also knows what "busy day" means—there already are feed orders to be loaded from the boxcar on the railroad siding. "Will Lloyd be helping me today?" Casey asks, already suspecting he knows the answer.

"He pulled a muscle in his back moving the Christmas display and won't be able to unload bags of corn for a while until he gets better. Here are six orders, and Mr. Gates is on his way down to the railroad siding right now." Mr. Herman switches from religion to work with a flick of his hand. He gives the receipts to Casey.

"Can I get something to take with me for lunch? I didn't bring one, and it looks like a long day today."

"Yes, but you'd probably better drive your car over instead of walking. We need to get going." Casey knows that Lloyd, the ne'er-do-well that's worked there since he graduated from high school twenty years ago, is putting on his usual "oh, my sore back" routine. He doesn't care. Casey paces himself, and it will be a good workout.

Up front, he selects an assortment of junk and a couple of drinks for lunch. He's surprised when he steps up to the register to pay for them; Belinda, the boss's daughter, is at the machine, checking people out.

Belinda is pretty, agile, and smart enough to have been chosen as a cheerleader during her sophomore year of high school, but she gave it up because she didn't like the way the jocks mistreated them. However, she keeps dating the team captain to preserve her position in the pecking order.

She has her mother's generous breasts, wide baby-maker hips, and a narrow waist. Her long legs are a little heavy, but shaped nicely, and end in a small foot. Her brown hair and slightly green eyes make for a pretty package. She doesn't look anything like her father, Mr. Herman. Her mother's biology must predominate in the gene pool.

"Good morning, Casey." She's professional, not friendly, but she gives him a big smile. It's almost a victory smile, and it makes him wonder what's going on now. Years ago, when she was just a freshman, she offered to date him. It didn't happen; her parents rebuffed him because he wasn't an Alfeta.

Casey pays her and she offers a bag, but he sticks the goodies he selected in his pockets on one side of his coat and the drinks on the other. He walks out thinking that for sure nepotism is alive and well in his little town. As he looks back, he notices that she's watching him leave.

The first rancher backs his stake-body truck to the side of the boxcar, gets out, and hands Casey the receipt. It's for thirty one-hundred-pound sacks of corn.

The old farmer steps back into his cab, indicating to Casey that he'll be loading the truck by himself. It takes a little while as he takes a break after every fifth bag. When he is finished, Casey closes the truck's gate and hands the receipt back to the farmer.

"Through already? It takes old Lloyd about a half hour longer." Casey just smiles back and waves him on while looking at the next truck waiting to be loaded.

It's an all-morning endeavor, and Casey deliberately stops at twelve. He sits down, eats his candy bars, and drinks his soda. He relishes his Twinkies, milk, and doughnuts, although there is a customer waiting.

About three in the afternoon, the last truck comes, and Casey returns to the store. It's become overcast, and the temperature is going down again.

At five each evening, Casey is detailed to break off from whatever he's doing and start the evening cleanup. He works his way down one aisle and reaches the end. As he pushes the broom out, he hits a shoe and very nearly knocks Belinda off her feet. She gives him a dirty look while hurrying along but says nothing. *Well, that's one in the negative column for me,* he thinks.

A few minutes after six, and just before Mr. Herman can lock the door, Johnny Stephenson steps inside. Johnny is the son of the overseer of the state's experimental cattle farm. His father, Bishop Stephenson, also heads one of the three Alfeta precincts in town.

When Johnny sees Belinda throwing her coat on, he pulls himself up to his manly, six-foot-two, 170-pound stature and tries to look regal. He's the captain of the football team and plays basketball. The back of his head just hints at his coming baldness, and his face, his fight with teenage acne.

Casey has little respect for him. Johnny thinks he is God's gift to women. His father acts the same way, so it's easy for Casey to see where he gets his attitude.

When Johnny sees Casey, he scowls but says nothing.

"Are we locked up in the back, Casey?" Mr. Herman asks.

"Yes, sir, I jammed a piece of two-by-four in the top of the broken window they repaired and never replaced the lock." Casey sees a look of surprised concern cross Mr. Herman's face. He's usually good at remembering things like that.

"You kids go on. I should go and have a look for myself." He turns the lock, and Casey deliberately steps out in front of Johnny before he can reach to hold the door for Belinda. *There, that should give him another reason to want to beat on me,* Casey thinks. He wants another go at the pompous bastard.

He obviously won't be dating Naomi tonight and plans to let that rest for a while. He pauses for a moment and decides to go down to the local soda fountain and dance hall. A few of the kids his age hang out there. He thinks of contacting his "reserve" lady, but it is a "don't call me; I'll call you" situation for a few days.

That evening, as he gets to his car, he discovers the headlights are broken out. He looks around to see if anyone is watching. Seeing no one, he pulls into the alley behind the medical clinic two blocks away. He parks where no one can see him from the street. He unscrews one of his broken headlights from its holder and places the rim on his backseat. After tucking the sealed beam under his arm, he goes looking for a little payback.

He finds one of the jock's cars, looks it over to confirm the owner, and punches the tip of a screwdriver through the headlight. He removes the other headlight and replaces it with the broken one he brought with him. That satisfies him, and he begins to look for more cars. *If the headlight game is what they want to play, I will give them game.*

A car beside a hydrant is the one owned by the kid who cursed him as he drove by the gym. He looks around to affirm he isn't being watched and quickly pops the hood open. He forces the screwdriver between the mounting and the Bakelite distributor top and jerks hard. He hears it crack. He reaches into his pocket, takes out a cough syrup bottle of used motor oil, which he keeps with him for just this kind of occasion, removes the radiator cap, and empties it on top of the antifreeze.

He closes it and quietly bumps the hood latch shut. Now the car either won't start, or if it does, it will run rough. A quick look into the radiator will show the oil slick, and the obvious conclusion will be a blown head gasket or a cracked head. It will be a major engine teardown that will still require a distributor cap replacement to make it run. *Be careful whom you curse*, Casey thinks as he steals away.

The following day at work, the first opportunity he has, he stops at the automotive store and buys a replacement headlight bulb to replace the other one broken out of his car. He goes across the street and makes out a vandalism report at the police station.

During the afternoon, he catches Belinda watching him. He wonders if she isn't acting as a spy for her father.

That night, just after they finish dinner and Casey's dad is drawing the drapes, the phone rings. Casey picks up, and Naomi is on the line, trying to keep from crying.

Chapter
4

" **C**ASEY, I'm home now, and Mrs. Fields is babysitting both Donnie and me. I desperately need to talk to you. Mom is back in Salt Lake with Dad, and she won't be home until late tomorrow. Please come and pick me up; we've got to talk. Oh, please hurry."

"Okay, I'll be there in just a couple of shakes." Casey gathers his snow gear, bundles it under his arm, and puts it in the car.

"You be careful, Casey; you don't know what the bastard Alfetas are up to," his dad says to him.

"I'll be careful, Dad; right now, Naomi needs me."

\* \* \*

Naomi is standing in the snow beside the porch and doesn't even allow Casey to turn into the driveway before she runs and gets in.

"Get out of here; Mrs. Fields thinks I'm pouting and have my door locked so she can't get into my room."

"What's the emergency, Naomi? What's going on?"

"Just drive us somewhere we can talk and be alone." Casey thinks a minute then heads out of town to one of the fields where they hunted rabbits. *I can park behind the barn, and will at last have an opportunity for her to tell me what's troubling her so.*

On the way out there, she lays her head in his lap and begins sobbing. He pulls into the farmyard and notices a light still on in the house, but he continues on and backs in behind the barn.

"I'm not a virgin anymore, Casey," she tells him between sobs. "He had me last night. Mom knew he was coming and didn't even tell me anything that's happening. I know Dad is going to be hospitalized for a long time down in the valley, but they didn't say anything about me. I feel like a whore. I've been sold to the highest bidder."

*What the hell is happening?* he wonders. She continues crying, and all he can do is hold her and hope she'll stop soon and explain. "Who had you? What is going on?" he asks.

"The man they've contracted a marriage agreement with. I'm to be his wife. I won't even get to graduate from high school with my class. I'm going to be enrolled in some private school and get my diploma. I have to get all my things packed by the end of the week." Her words come between breaks in her crying.

"Slow down a minute; I'm still digesting you're not a virgin," he says, trying to think this through.

"I thought we . . . you and I . . . we were going to be married and have a family. If you'd only ask me before—"

"Naomi, I graduated less than a year ago. All I have is a little piece-of-shit job. I need time to get situated. I love you; you know that."

She manages to compose herself a little more. "He came up from the valley. He's some kind of lawyer for the church. He brought legal documents, and Mom signed them. Mom allowed him to go through all my things. He pulled all my keepsakes out from under the bed, dumped the box, sorted it, and told her how much I could keep.

"He found the two empty .30-caliber cartridges in my underwear drawer. I told him that I had them there as a reminder to separate one week's laundry from the next. I put four .22 casings in the one I chose as me. It was to represent the four children we were going to have.

"My brother Donnie is going to be schooled at some kind of commune. Mom will be there with him until he gets started, and then she'll be moved into a home on the property with some more women her own age. I don't know what she will be doing.

"One of the documents was for the sale of our house. Mom and Dad will get the settlement for it and put it into their bank account. I don't know how long Dad will be in treatment."

"How can we stop this? Did you sign anything?"

"No, he said that since I was a minor, all my legal responsibilities still rest with my parents. Casey, it's like I've been sold to someone."

"How did the sex thing go down?"

"Mom came over to me and introduced us. He didn't say anything for a while, and then Mom said that I must submit to him because he's claiming me for his wife according to the ancient Alfeta church law.

"Another man, a doctor—or at least he said he was—examined me. I've never been so embarrassed in my life. I dressed right after he went out of my room. He went upstairs and told the other guy, the one I was supposed to marry, and said I was okay.

"Mom and Donnie went out and got into his Cadillac, and they drove away. He took my shoulder, and we went to Mom's bedroom. I was really afraid then. He's a big man. He looks like Johnny Stephenson, only broader in the shoulders.

"He told me to undress. I got down to my underwear and stopped. He locked the bedroom door, disrobed, picked me up, and put me on the bed. It hurt when he pulled my panties off and put his forearm against my throat. Then he started talking crazy as he was getting on me. 'We are to be married under the rules of the ancient church,' he said. 'A man chooses a wife, and she is subservient to him. She follows his instructions directly and does not cause him trouble. You must know that I am a direct descendant of the founder of the church and in that capacity have the first choice of the virgins.

"'When we arrive at our home, you will clean it and prepare our meals as I have directed. I will inspect daily and note any infractions you make, and you will correct them. I will father our children, and we will bring them up in the church. I feel I am as good a disciplinarian as any other man, but I will be gentle until you learn my ways.'

"He went on and on. I was stunned."

"Did he use a rubber?"

"Yes, there was something about not impregnating me until the day of our wedding. All he did was claim me like the original Alfeta pioneers did." She broke down again.

"My God, I thought all that Alfeta history was done away with back in the last century. Now you're telling me your brother is going to be sent to some commune to be indoctrinated into thinking like them. Your mom is likely going to end up there too. That will be at least until your dad gets out of the hospital. What do they intend to do with him after he's released with no home to go home to?"

"Casey, I don't know. All I know is that I want you. I want to have your baby, and I want it now." Casey isn't ready for this, but deep down, he knows it's what he wants too. It will at least be a small way to strike back at the people who are about to destroy his future happiness.

Naomi sits up and begins disrobing, and he joins her. There is a real intent in their actions now, and she waits for him to disrobe. She climbs over the back of the seat, lies down and beckons to him. She is as beautiful as he imagined, there in the moonlight. She just holds him for a moment before they begin to make love. It is as though they have to hurry to consummate their relationship, and Casey doesn't have to work for long. They lie panting and grinning at each other as it ends.

"I'm just going to lie here with my legs up and make all the little tadpoles swim up inside me like the slide presentation showed."

"I think we should go kill some rabbits now so they won't be coming out here to see what's going on."

"Okay, Casey, but this isn't over yet."

He dresses and starts the car while she gets prepared. After he opens the gate to the pasture, she volunteers to hold the spotlight for him as he gets back in. Casey has four boxes of ammunition with him and plans to use all but one. He has learned always to save the last one.

It takes them over an hour to use up the ammunition, and then Casey has another trunk full of rabbits to be frozen and cashed in for the bounty the following day. *Money is so easy to make this way.*

"I want to do it again tonight, Casey, to make sure," Naomi says. Casey backs in behind the barn and watches her remove her clothing. As he turns the light on, she removes her blouse. She hasn't bothered to don her underwear from before and just removes her jeans and retreats to the backseat.

They take their time now, and she revels in his attention to her. They make love like two committed souls, and when it ends, they are panting and out of breath. This is Casey's first real venture into the gene pool.

"I hope it took, Casey. I love you, and I will love you until the day I die," she says to him.

"I love you, Naomi. Let's hope this is all just a bad dream, and we can find some way out of it." After he dresses, he makes sure she's ready to go and pulls the car to the front of the farmhouse. "I took 186 rabbits out of the back pasture for you" is written on the note he drops inside the screen door.

They drive back to town with Naomi's head on Casey's lap, and she cries softly. He accompanies her to the outside basement door and helps her open it. They unlock the door, and he holds her for a long kiss. He kneels in front of her and pushes her blouse up as she unfastens her brassiere, and he kisses her breasts.

"I love you. Naomi, maybe something will work out for us. Try to reason with your mom."

She kisses him and walks to her room. He returns the way he came in, wondering what the future holds for them. Many thoughts are whirling around his head as he drives home.

\* \* \*

A car roars around him, almost sideswiping him, and he has to pull over while avoiding a snowbank. *I need to be more alert,* he thinks. He slows, and when he looks, there is another car a ways behind him. The first one hurries to the intersection, spins around, and comes toward him. He stops; it's better to have a slow-speed wreck.

Casey opens his door and steps out as the other car stops. He's not about to be attacked sitting defenseless in the front seat. Why tonight of all times to challenge him? He sizes up the two men who emerge from the car. It bears Utah plates, but he's never seen them before. The one looks older than his buddy and is holding a baseball bat in his hands. The two getting out of the car behind him he recognizes as locals with bad reputations. Casey is silently sizing up his chances of coming out of this in one piece.

The four are approaching him, so they'll get to his car at the same time. He looks down and realizes the two from the Utah car are not wearing overshoes. They are dressed quite nicely in suits and leather-soled Florsheim oxfords.

He takes off, running toward them; the man with the baseball bat braces himself as Casey lowers his shoulder for a tackle. Gaining speed, he suddenly alters his attack by leaning back and sliding like a baseball player crossing home plate. He slides between them, knocking both off their feet. He hears a head strike the iced-over road.

Casey makes a grab for the bat and catches the end of it. The man holding it isn't ready to let go, so Casey rolls over and kicks the other downed man in the face and gains his feet before the two locals can join the fray.

He kicks out viciously and catches the man with the bat in the gut just below his ribs, and he screams in pain. He kicks again into his thigh. He finally wrests the bat away and uses it on the other man, who is struggling to stand. Casey hammers him on his ankle with the bat, knocking his feet from beneath him again.

The two locals are almost on top of him, and he raises the bat to strike. The first anticipates the blow, but it doesn't come. Casey reverses the bat and uses it like a pool cue to flatten his nose.

The other one grabs him, and they go down in the snow, kicking and slugging at each other. Casey finally manages to get hold of him in the crotch and the back of his hair, lifts him up over his head, and slams him onto the frozen earth. There is a bone-shattering thud, and he lies still. The man from Utah is yet again trying to get up, and Casey catches him right above the ankle with the bat and knocks his feet from beneath him.

Now there is near silence, with only the sound of heavy breathing and one of the men crying. The cold wind punctuates the scene. Casey sees one of them trying to stand. His nose is gushing blood, and he spits it out, trying to get his breath.

"Who put you up to this?" Casey demands of him, spitting blood from his own mouth.

"Screw you, kid." Casey thumps him on his lips with the bat, breaking teeth. The man recoils in pain.

"I'd like to know what I did that is so terrible that someone would send four hoods to beat me up." He brings his balled-up fist back, and the guy puts up his hands to protect himself.

"The council, you dumb-ass; we work for the council."

"Whose council?" Casey demands.

"The local one. The Utah men are only up here to report back to whoever sent them. They bring the instructions. I ain't got nothing against you, kid. I'm just following orders."

"How much did they pay you?"

"Nothing, it's what we do."

"You have a job that pays you nothing; you go around beating up people for the so-called council? Who is behind this council?"

"The church," he says from between his bloodied lips.

*Oh shit*, Casey thinks. *What have I gotten myself into this time? Why me, and why now?* He returns to his car and carefully navigates around all the bodies still in the street and pulls to the end of the block.

He steps out of his car and walks to the Utah car which at this time is on the wrong side of the road, accelerates just enough to bend sheet metal, and crashes into the front of the local car. There's a satisfying cacophony of bending metal and breaking

31

glass. He emerges and looks at his handiwork. The radiator spews a ribbon of steam into the frozen air.

"I'm going to get the cops here now, and what they'll find is a fight between a couple of local hoods and a couple of Utah bangers. I have your license number, and if I hear anything from the cops, I'm pretty good at payback." He rolls the almost-unconscious man over, flips his coat up, and feels for his wallet. He finds it and extracts his license.

"Tell David here that I have his address and that if at any time anyone else jumps me, he will be the first one I will come gunning for, and I do mean gunning." He slips the wallet back into his pocket. He returns to where the man remains sitting on the frozen street.

"Do you understand where I'm coming from?"

"Yeah, I got ya, kid; no more fighting." With that, Casey picks up the bat, steadies himself on his feet and swings for the bleachers, so to speak. The bat leaves his hands and streaks across the front yard of a nearby house and crashes through the picture window. A light comes on immediately in the back of the house as Casey climbs into his car and carefully drives away.

He watches the scene, for as long as he is able, and just as he turns, he sees the overhead bubble-gum-machine light of the local police cruiser as it turns onto the street. It takes him a long time to get to sleep that night.

\*     \*     \*

The following morning, before he goes to work, he fills his parents in on the attack. That day at work, Mr. Herman acts almost like a kid, joking and carrying on. He does not, however, let up on Casey; he keeps him busy all day, allowing him only a short lunch. Casey steps out while eating his sandwich, walks to the phone company building, and calls his mom at home.

"Has anyone called for me there, Mom?"

"No, honey, but earlier this morning, a lot of traffic came by. I didn't think anything of it until I realized that they weren't turning to go up Little River Road, but were going back down Sixth Street. Oh, Casey, Dad missed the mail yesterday; can you pick it up before you come home?"

"Sure, Mom," he replies. It isn't long before he has an order to fill from the boxcar at the siding. Belinda personally brings the slip back to the rear, where he's working. She seems different now, almost sweeter, and apologetic. It only takes him the better part of an hour to fill the third truck that materializes. He accepts when the man inside offers him a ride back the six blocks to the store.

Casey is dropped off behind the store, and he cuts through the alley and goes into the post office. When he opens the little letterbox, he finds a pink slip the postal clerks put there when customers have a parcel post. This time it's scratched through, and his name is scribbled on it. The message reads, "Casey, come to the window and ask for the postmaster."

*What the hell have I done now?* Casey apprehensively knocks on the window. In a moment, the window shade goes up, and there is Mr. Lynch, the postmaster, who has been there as long as Casey can remember. Casey played with his kids at an earlier age and had even sat in on several catechism classes with them at the Catholic church.

"Casey, my boy, it's good to see you." With that, he leans out the tiny window to see if there is anyone else in the lobby. "Come down to my door."

Mr. Lynch opens the door and beckons him in. He follows him to his office and is served a cup of coffee. He motions at Casey to sit down and pours coffee for himself.

"Casey, I have some news you need to know, and I don't want you to let anyone know how or where you found out about it. The draft board is meeting, and you, Ron Bates, and Ken Collins are the first three on the top of the list." Casey feels as though he's just been sucker punched.

*That son of a bitch! No wonder Old Man Herman is so happy. He's the head of the draft board, and he's found a way to ship me and my friends out of town for good.*

"Aren't all the names rolled up and put into little capsules to be drawn at random?" Casey asks.

"That is the illusion the board wants everyone to have, Casey," Mr. Lynch replies, smiling. "Unfortunately, some influential Alfeta mommies don't want their little Johnnys to get drafted and have to go off to the military. They get to go on a mission for the church, and by then other Protestant or Catholic boys have come of age to take their place in the draft."

"How soon will the induction letter get to my home?"

"They're sent to the draft board headquarters, where they're typed up and mailed. I suppose you have a week or so before you receive yours. It depends on how many young men are in the call-up this month."

"I don't know how to thank you, Mr. Lynch."

"It's okay, Casey. You were the only one who would befriend my boys back when they needed someone to play with. I appreciate it, and now I'm returning the favor." With that they stand and shake hands, and Mr. Lynch opens the door. He pulls the accumulation from Casey's mailbox and lets him out the back door. Casey carefully looks at the mail, folds it, and puts it into his coat pocket.

That evening Casey can't get away from work fast enough. When he finishes, he drives directly to Ken's house, where he finds him sitting at the supper table. Ken's family invites Casey to eat, but he is too nervous, and he and Ken go to look for Ron.

They find Ron at home and sit down to discuss what's happening. None of them knows why it's happening, but they are all angry that it is happening to them, and at Christmastime. They decide to visit the navy recruiter on Monday morning. None of the three of them want to become a ground pounder.

# Chapter 5

A T five that afternoon, Casey finishes the case of canned beans; he has scrubbed the old prices off and stamped them with new ones. He takes the broom and decides to start sweeping in the grocery section. At five minutes to six, Mr. Herman is picking through his keys to lock the front door when a woman slips inside.

Casey sees it happen, and he knows what it means. She pulls a lined notebook page out of her purse and hands it to Mr. Herman. He looks around and nods to Casey. It will be a longer night. She pulls this trick about once a month. It will take the whole crew about an hour to get her order together.

"There are a lot of things to come up from the basement. Take the list, go down, and get started." Mr. Herman hands it to him. Thankfully, the freight wagon is empty and on the freight elevator. Casey works his way down the row of boxes, pulling the wagon and loading it as he goes. Partway through the order, he hears something behind him and turns around with a start.

Belinda is there, grinning and eyeing him, leaning on the stack of boxes on the cart with the top two buttons of her dress undone and her breasts pressed down, giving him a visual almost to her tummy.

"I've been watching you, Casey; you know how to sling those boxes around. Or is it that you're really trying to impress me?" Belinda says with a smile as she stands up.

"I impress you? Does Mr. Herman know you're down here?"

"Yes, he told me to take the list and help you along so we can get out of here tonight." Casey hands her the list. He knows Mr. Herman gives explicit instructions to all the girls employed there never to go down to the basement. *Perhaps it's okay because she's the boss's daughter,* he thinks.

It takes them about twenty minutes, and in the end, Belinda has to help push the now heavily loaded cart to the elevator. Casey turns it around so that the tongue end will come off first, and she pulls, backing into the elevator. Now she's pinned there and cannot get around to free herself. Casey planned it that way.

"Hey, Casey, wait," Belinda says in a panic.

"Just stand there, and as soon as it gets to the first floor, I'll pull it out, and you can take the list back to Daddy." He reaches between the bars of the gate, feels for the button, and gives it a push. He quickly removes his hand, and the elevator begins to rise. He takes the steps two at a time and meets the elevator when it stops at the floor. He pulls the gates open.

"Casey, please hurry and get me out of here," Belinda says.

Behind him, Casey hears Mr. Herman's voice. "As soon as you get these loaded, go to the men's department and get the big box beside the back door. Bring it back here and we can load it. Have you seen Belinda?"

Belinda ducks down behind the load of goods on the wagon. Casey knows she's been gaming him and wasn't supposed to be in the basement.

Casey hesitates long enough to make Belinda squirm before he says, "I think I saw her going up front by the cheese display when I went down." Mr. Herman turns and walks toward the front of the store. Casey pulls the cart forward far enough so that Belinda can snake between it and the wall of the elevator. The color returns to her face as she smiles at him.

"I owe you one for not ratting on me, Casey. Gosh, I wish you were one of us," Belinda says as she moves away.

"I'll collect later," Casey replies.

Belinda just grins and disappears toward the ladies' powder room.

Out of the corner of his eye, Casey sees Mr. Herman unlock the front door, and Johnny Stephenson steps in. He looks Casey's way as Belinda strides by him with an air of superiority while slinging her coat on. When Casey finally gets to his car, he finds that his other single headlamp lies broken. Luck smiles on him as a police car approaches just at that moment. He steps out and waves the officer down. Luck is really running his way; young Officer Peters is at the wheel.

"Hi, what's going on?" Officer Peters says while lowering the window of the cruiser.

"What's going on is that I've been working all day, and now, when I come here, I find both my headlamps broken out." The officer pulls the cruiser into the parking lot and looks at his broken lightbulbs. Whoever broke them had taken a large piece of the glass, placed it in front of Casey's tire, and tried to cover it with snow.

"I'm sorry, Casey, I'll just add it to the report you filed with me. I don't have any more forms, and I'll be darned if these little rodents are going to get away with it."

Casey drives toward home with a plan slowly forming in his mind. He drives up the street that goes by the gymnasium. There is basketball practice tonight, and most of the jocks' cars are parked there.

At home, he relates the day's happenings to his folks. He's tired of the hassle, and for the first time in a long time, he chooses to go to bed just after eleven that night. His body isn't used to it, and it takes him some tossing and turning to get to sleep.

When he wakes, he hears someone moving around, probably making breakfast. As soon as he steps into the kitchen, he startles the daylights out of his mom.

"Yikes, Casey, what are you doing up so soon?"

"I went to bed too soon last night, and now I'm about two hours ahead of myself. You can bet I'm not going to work early, though."

His dad comes out of the bedroom wiping shaving lather from his face. "Something happened last night and the night before. I looked out, and people kept coming by and looking for you or your car. They didn't give up until late."

"Probably the local idiots planning something to do against me or doing something they think they can get me blamed for. It's okay; I'll be on the lookout for them."

Casey goes out to the shed, picks out some tools, and drops them onto the backseat floorboards, where they rattle around during his drive to work. He gets there almost a quarter hour early, and Mr. Herman corners him in the back of the store.

"Casey, we're having a building party at the precinct tonight, and we need anyone who can swing a hammer. Do you want to come and join us? It could be your last chance."

"Sure, Mr. Herman, how much does it pay per hour?"

The man pulls himself up to his full, self-important five feet four. "If you do the Lord's work, Casey, you get the Lord's pay. Just look at the church, Casey; we are growing by leaps and bounds. Soon we will be richer, stronger, larger, and more powerful, be in more countries, and have as much control as the Catholic Church. We're already closing in on the attendance of the Methodists. Now is a good time to join us. Our founder's vision of the new world is coming true."

The words repulse Casey once again. *Let me guess who believes the scriptures in the phony Alfeta Bible*, he thinks. He turns his head and mouths the man's little speech along with him.

After work, Casey has just stepped inside at home when his dad motions for him to sit down with him.

"Mrs. Stryker called and wants you to call as soon as you get home. Now what's up with her?"

"Dad, I don't know what she wants. Naomi and I had a little fight the other night, and we decided not to see each other for a while. I can only assume that's what she wants to talk about."

"Don't let her put anything over on you."

"I won't. I need to eat supper, and then I'll give her a call." It is a nearly silent supper; none of them says much. His mom picks up on the problem and doesn't press him for any details.

After dinner, Casey decides to go downtown somewhere to use the phone so the party line won't be listened into. He'll use the free phone in the telephone company lobby. The operator smiles and waves him through the glass door. He picks the receiver up, and there is a click on the line.

"Who do you want to talk to, Casey?" she asks him.

"The Strykers."

The line rings twice before Mrs. Stryker picks it up. "It's Casey, Mrs. Stryker. Do you need to talk to me?" he asks her, dreading the worst.

"I've gathered up all your things, and I want you to come and get them. I have them in a box for you to carry out of here. Come as soon as possible, preferably now."

"I'll be there in a little while." He knows his baseball glove, fishing equipment, and the scrapbook he and Naomi had been putting together are there. He can't think of much more, unless she wanted him to pick up the personal things he'd given Naomi.

He thanks the operator, and she blows him a kiss. She apparently knows of the arrangement that he and Arlene, one of the other operators, have.

Back in his car, he thinks about it for a while. *This is really it.* He wonders if he's supposed to know Naomi is getting married to the man in Salt Lake City. He decides not to acknowledge it.

The street is clear when he pulls up in front of her house. He goes ahead and pulls into the driveway. There is no Buick. *Maybe Mr. Stryker is sober enough to drive now.*

He tries the back door but finds it locked. *She must still be really mad about catching us together on the couch.* He goes to the front door, and just then she pulls into the driveway in the Buick. She moves it forward and parks it tightly behind his car.

"Go in; I'll get the box of things." It takes her a few minutes, and he chooses to stand rather than sit and wait.

She comes out of the back hallway carrying a box high up against her chest. She walks over to him and sets it down. He sees her breasts jiggle and notices that her dress top is open.

"Mrs. Stryker? I—" He's unable to complete his sentence before she reaches out to grab him. She tries to kiss him. He ducks, and her lips hit him on the cheek. He puts his hand between them but only encounters her breast. He pushes back in panic and amazement.

"Mrs. Stryker, why are you doing this?"

"Casey, you get naked or I'll scream my lungs out and the neighbors will come running, and you'll end up in jail for trying to rape me. Go ahead; I told them you were coming to see me tonight."

The evening becomes a blur.

"Go ahead, shower and get cleaned up. I wouldn't want anyone to see you leave here looking like you just screwed me." She laughs a very vicious laugh. Casey takes his clothes, goes to the bathroom, and showers.

Mrs. Stryker is still lying on the bed when he returns. "I wish there was more time to explain things to you, Casey, but for now you'll just have to go on thinking and trusting me and believing all things work out for the best."

"Will you let me out of the driveway, please?"

"Damn, I forgot. Yes, wait a minute and I'll get dressed and move the car out of the way."

"Wait, don't move if you're comfortable, Mrs. Stryker. Just stay there on the bed and give me the keys; I'll move it for you."

She reaches over to the nightstand and throws him the keys.

"I'd get up and move it myself, Casey, but I'm still enjoying my last screw. Don't forget to take your box of things with you." It's her angry, sarcastic attitude again.

He picks up his box from the middle of the living room floor and goes out the front door. He starts the Buick, backs it from the driveway, and runs it backward at full throttle into the snow that was pushed up along the street by the clearing equipment. It would require some vigorous shoveling to free it.

He opens the front door and throws the keys onto the seat of the living room chair. Mrs. Stryker was still lying in the bed with her legs propped on the pillows.

"Bye, Casey. Have a nice life, and don't come back and bother us or look forward to seeing Naomi again."

Casey pulls the door closed and quickly runs down the driveway and sneaks in through the basement door. He quietly goes to Naomi's room, draws a "What, me worry?" face on the mirror in lipstick, and remembers she hides her important jewelry in the cigar box in the bottom drawer. He finds it and looks through it.

He takes her class ring and the birthstone ring he gave her this Christmas. It has a matching ankle bracelet, which he finds as well. He takes her little pearl earrings, which had been a gift from him after they first grew serious about each other. He finds their scrapbook and her gold-inscribed, personalized book of Alfeta, which he decides he will hollow out to hold the things he's taken. Beside it is her two-dollar bill collection, which he adds to his pocket.

He sneaks quietly up the steps, walks down the driveway, and looks into the window. Althea's there, asleep on the bed. He wonders what her kids will think when they come home and discover her like that. He decides he has to go somewhere and think. *How did my life get so quickly and disastrously turned around?*

# Chapter 6

CASEY leaves a half hour early for work because he first wants to check out the Strykers' house. It's still dark, and after circling the block twice, he pulls up in the alley. He crosses the backyard and looks in the glass of the garage door. It's empty.

He can see into the side window, and there is no furniture in the house. He goes under the exterior sloping basement door and feels his way to the bottom, hoping the key is still there. He steps in after listening for a minute and walks the entire house and finds nothing. It's completely empty.

He locks up and thinks about the trash. He returns to the alley and finds a large pile of discarded items thrown beside the full trash barrel. Using his flashlight, he looks through it and finds many of Naomi's things, which he picks up and puts into his car. Most of her keepsakes are here, and he intends to preserve them with the slim hope that he will see her sometime in the future.

\* \* \*

When he arrives at work, Casey encounters Belinda at the back door, breaking down a cardboard box to go into the trash. *No problem,* he thinks, *she always leaves the small stuff for me.* She looks at him through reddened eyes and tousled hair. Her face is puffy, apparently from crying, and her usually perfect lips lack lipstick. He's his usual ten minutes early and wonders how long she's been working to have already put a box of beans on the shelf, or—looking farther—several boxes.

"You're getting an early start this morning, aren't you?" he asks. She turns toward him, and he sees a red mark on her neck and a bruise on her collarbone. There's another on the side of her arm. The scarf she didn't usually wear isn't covering her collarbone bruise.

"Yes, as a matter of fact, I've been here quite a while. I came in about five thirty this morning." There's jagged sarcasm in her voice now, and he wonders what happened. It has to be Johnny Stephenson. He probably got too frisky with her, and she hadn't wanted to play his game.

"I'm sorry, Belinda; it's none of my business." He steps back and tries to get around her to start work.

"Don't you want to know how I got in the store at five thirty in the morning?"

"I suppose not, but I'll bet you're going to tell me," he replies while stepping back farther.

"I took Dad's key off his ring, came down here, and opened up. I hoped the store would just fill up with people, and I could somehow make it through the day and not have to think about ever going home." She almost hissed her words at him.

*Wow,* he thinks, *that just about blows it out of the water.* "Do you need someone to bounce it off of and help you work through whatever's wrong?" he asks.

"Yes, but first I need more time to work off my anger and frustration." She turns, and he follows her inside and is amazed that Mr. Herman doesn't meet him at the door with a handful of things to do. He walks to the front looking for him.

Lloyd Granger is standing in the middle of the aisle in front of the cash register, looking self-important. "Kurt isn't here, and until he shows up, that makes me the boss," he says.

"Sure, Lloyd, I suppose it does." Casey waits for instructions but never receives any. Belinda steps from behind the shelf display and walks up to his face.

"That doesn't include me, Lloyd, and don't you forget it." Lloyd steps back with a look on his face as though she slapped him. It's all Casey can do to keep from laughing out loud. *The pompous bastard needs to come down a peg or two.* He turns around and retreats down the aisle, grinning. He knows a few things that need to be restocked. When he comes up the aisle again, Lloyd is recovered enough to have assembled the feed purchase receipts, and he hands them to Casey. There are as yet no receipts for feed from the siding. He again encounters Belinda at the back; she looks almost confused.

"Can I get you a drink or something? You look like you really need one."

"I'm not supposed to drink Coke, Casey, but right now I want something—anything—to clear my head and settle my stomach." He interprets that as a request for a Coke.

"I have to go to the warehouse; I'll sneak into the IGA Market and get a couple on the way. Have you eaten anything for breakfast?"

"No, but it's okay. I'll steal a danish from the bread rack and then look out for you when you get back," she replies while looking around for Lloyd.

Casey checks to see what Lloyd is doing and then slips out the back door and down the alley. The little grocery also has a door used by customers entering from the back alley. He darts in, pulls two Cokes and two orange drinks from the cooler, and pays for them and a small tin of aspirin. The checkout clerk gives him the usual "What is the competition doing shopping in my store?" look.

He pockets the drinks and walks to his car, where he carefully pries the top off one Coke. He takes a swig and replaces it with vodka from the bottle in his hiding place under the dash. He presses the top back on, puts the two orange drinks under the seat, and goes to the warehouse. Once there, he shoulders a bag of grain and carries it up the alley to the store. *When you plot revenge, you have to be ready to strike at the first opening,* he thinks. Belinda is waiting to meet him at the back door.

"Lloyd is watching. Go upstairs, and I'll meet you in the furniture over by the mattresses," she says.

"Okay." He drops the bag of grain on a hand truck along with a couple of cases of canned goods to be taken out when the customer arrives. Lloyd is busy with a customer, and Casey quickly mounts the stairs two at a time after he hangs up his coat.

Belinda is there, waiting for him at the two five-foot-high racks of mattresses. He pushes them aside wide enough for them to slip between the stacks, and then he uses them to form a V with the wide end at the back, giving them room to sit on the floor. They sit down and now can't be seen from anywhere on the floor except directly in front of the racks.

The plan germinates in his mind, and he makes a production of pulling out his Scout pocketknife, opening the bottles, and handing Belinda one of them. She surprises him by tipping it up and taking a long belt, swallowing several times, and then grimacing as the gas from the bottle comes out of her nose. She accepts the aspirin from him, takes three, and pockets the little tin as she belches the gas away.

"What is it, Belinda?" he asks her.

"I can't talk now, Casey; just sit and keep me company for a minute or two before we have to go back to work."

She produces two cellophane-packaged sweet rolls from her dress pockets, gives him one, and rips into hers and eats it before resuming the drink. She's eying him, and several times looks to him like she wants to say something. He waits, but she remains silent. He can see the tears she's controlling.

Belinda turns around and leans against the stack opposite him. They're sitting flat on the floor, and she has her legs pulled up. Casey can count the five petticoats she's wearing and the clips of her garter belt holding her stockings. She begins rolling her eyes and straining to keep the tears from coming.

"When you're ready to talk, let me know, and I'll be there for you," he says.

She reaches out and takes hold of his hands. He helps her stand and then holds them for a minute. She steps up to him, encircles him with her arms, and holds on for long minutes. He cuddles her and nuzzles her neck.

"Casey, do you know where the reserve key to the back door is hanging in the business office?" Belinda asks.

"Yeah, it's on the second hook, along with the reserve warehouse key and old man Milner's house and garage keys. Why, what do you want me to do?"

"If you can get it, let me know, and I'll tell you what I have in mind for later."

They finish and go back to work after she thanks him for the drink. He wonders how the alcohol will affect her, as tired and beat as she looks.

It turns out to be a weird day. Mr. Herman finally shows up about four in the afternoon, and Casey notes that he walks favoring his right leg. What the hell is going on? When he comes in, Belinda grabs her coat and leaves in a huff.

*This isn't Johnny; this is a family thing,* Casey thinks, and a plan forms in his mind.

An hour before the start of the cleanup, Casey stops stocking shelves and goes upstairs. If they check on him, all he has to say is that he looked at his watch wrong and started too soon. He gets the broom and sets it where it will be handy.

Back up front in the bed display, he checks to see if anyone is watching. When he finds that the area is clear, he makes the bed with a pad, both sheets, and matching pillowcases. He adds a design spread as well.

In the dinette section, he pushes a table and two chairs to the front of the bed and turns the wardrobe sideways, effectively blocking any view of the bed from below. It's not visible from the stairwell, but it doesn't matter anyway; the Christmas tree on the other side of the entrance creates a great diversion.

He picks up the bedding wrappers and puts them in the trash, which he will dump after sweeping the floors. When he cleans down to the main office, he looks across the hallway and sees Mr. Herman sitting in the main office, immersed in conversation with Mr. Milner, his boss.

They see him looking, and Mr. Herman stands up to close the door. *Yes!* Casey sweeps down the hallway and out of the office. The next office is where the business machines and all the money are handled. He reaches in, selects the key hanging on the second hook, slips it into his pocket, and places the spare warehouse key where the first key had hung. He takes the trash out to the big container and carefully goes about his usual locking-up routine, finishing up the day. When he gets to the door, he meets Mr. Herman, who is pulling on his coat. "See ya in the morning, sir."

Kurt only nods and he starts checking on Casey's locking-up routine.

Casey slips out the front door and walks down the windless street to the parking lot. It isn't terribly cold, and he doesn't have his coat buttoned all the way up. It's already dark as it's near the shortest day of the year. His is the only car in the lot, and he sits down for a moment to think.

He's about to start the car when a cold hand reaches up and grasps his neck. It scares the shit out of him, and he jumps out the door. Belinda is there, crouching on the back floor, suppressing a wicked smile and chuckling at her ambush through still reddened eyes.

"What the hell are you trying to do?" he demands.

"I'm sorry, Casey; I didn't mean to scare you that bad. I need a ride, but not necessarily home. Would you like to buy me a burger?"

*Well, I'm not going to be seeing Naomi tonight,* he thinks. "Sure, but you'd better keep down in the car so that no one sees you. I don't want a fight with Johnny right now, although I'd like to kick his arrogant ass."

"You two can settle things between yourselves later. Right now, I need someone to talk to, and it can't be him."

"Why is it me? Doesn't your church have counselors to help their young people over rough spots in their lives?" Casey asks, digging at her a little.

"Yes, but unfortunately, Kurt is on the council, and right now he is the last one I want to talk to. As a matter of fact, he told me to report to the second precinct bishop, and I told him it will be a cold day in hell when that happens."

That little disclosure completely blows Casey away.

She wants a hamburger, which means they have to head to the drive-in; they obviously can't go to the drugstore. Casey reverses, heads back up the alley, and pulls out onto the street leading to the drive-in.

"Belinda, reach down and pull up on the back of the seat, and it will fold forward. You'll be able to climb over the seat back and get into the trunk. Pull the blankets around you, because there isn't any heat in there." She follows his instructions. The trunk has a musty odor to it, and he knows it's from all the rabbits he's thrown back there. *She'll just have to grin and bear it. This is too good to be true.*

Casey knows she has one of the two keys to the store, and he has the other one. He drives through the underpass to the little soft ice-cream stand and parks in the next-to-last spot at the rear of the building. The carhop comes out and hands him a menu.

"I don't need it, Karen. I want two burgers with cheese, two large fries, and a vanilla and a chocolate malted."

"Who's helping you eat that, Casey? I get off at ten," she says flirtatiously, as she knows no one is watching her.

"I'm a big boy, and I didn't get time off for lunch, so I think I'll be able to eat both by myself. How about a date tomorrow night? I have no plans for then."

"I'm sorry, but I won't be available tomorrow night. By the way, I'm sorry about Naomi," she says casually.

"What do you know about Naomi?"

"Not much, just the gossip going around." She turns and goes back to the door and disappears inside.

# Chapter 7

PERIPHERALLY, Casey catches a car pulling into the drive-in, and when he looks the other way, he sees another coming in through the exit. The two cars park, one on each side of him, and he slowly reaches down, pulls his pant leg up, and releases the hunting knife from its scabbard.

He rolls his window all the way down, folds his arms, and holds the knife just under his arm on the windowsill.

"We're going to kick the shit out of you, White, inside your car or out. Then we are going to wipe up the blood with your beaten unconscious body and throw it in the Dumpster. Do you understand me, you retard?" It's fearsome Freddy Folsom, the two-hundred-twenty-pound offensive center and bully for the school football team.

"No, perhaps you should explain it in English in small words, like dumb fucking Alfeta, or 'I'm from the ACA, better known as the Aborted Confused Assholes church.'" Freddy steps to the window. Casey braces himself; he knows a punch is coming.

He sits leaning slightly forward with a smirk on his face. When the fist comes through the window, he jerks his body back and drops his arm down. The fist misses its target by inches, but when its owner withdraws it, Casey's knife, with the blade turned upward, slices the underside of his forearm, even opening his wrist and the palm of his hand. His coat is neatly sliced open and flapping freely. At first, he doesn't realize what's happening, and he turns his arm over to look at it. It's then that the pain and bleeding start, and he screams and jumps back, looking at the blood.

The unwritten code is to fight fair. However, when there are two carloads of enemies, and it is five against one, you go by a different standard. "You'd better go to the hospital so you won't bleed to death," Casey says to him. His buddy, who is watching to see Casey get pounded, looks at the blood gushing from his arm and blanches.

Freddy's younger brother advances and takes a stance as Casey gets out with his hands down beside him to fool this adversary. He kicks him across the knee. He sees the kneecap move completely to the side. The color drains from his aggressor's face. "I'm sorry, idiot; I know it's a hard lesson to learn, but if you come back at me, I'll put you all the way down."

This one also screams out in pain, and he falls to the concrete as his knee bends the wrong way. These clowns finally realize how seriously Casey wants to be left alone. They hurriedly help their wounded and broken friends back in their cars and start out in a hurry.

Casey stands next to the retreating car, gives it a healthy kick, and watches some of the body putty crack and disassemble. It disappears in the direction of the hospital.

Casey sits back down, puts his knife in its sheath, shuts his door, and catches his breath. Almost miraculously, the carhop appears with his bag of food. He gives her a tip, tucking it inside the top of her uniform, and she smiles and retreats inside.

The entire encounter lasted only minutes, and she hadn't seen any of it. There's a small puddle of blood slowly freezing on the concrete. He pulls out of the parking lot and wonders where he should go. A muffled voice comes from the back: "Casey, what's going on?"

"I'm going to park at the library lot behind the hedge." He has to break open a track in order to pull into the lot. It hasn't been cleared from the previous night's snow. He steps out and into the backseat and pulls it forward.

"Casey, what in the world is happening? I've never heard anyone curse you like that before." Belinda looks more disoriented now than before.

"That's mild compared to what I've had to endure, Belinda. It's just the regular treatment I get from all your Alfeta friends."

"You can't mean that, Casey. Nobody treats you like that all the time."

"No, you're right. Since I graduated from high school, it's gotten worse." She just looks at him in wonder. "Open the sack and get our hamburgers and fries out. Here's a malted. Do you want chocolate or vanilla?

"Vanilla. Chocolate makes my face break out."

"You drink chocolate sometimes?" he asks teasingly.

"Oh, stop. I try to live by the church commandments."

"Is this a good place to have the talk you wanted with me?" he asks, looking around.

"No, Casey, we can't talk here. Now I'll be telling you a lot more than I was going to tell you before," she replies, a slight question in her voice.

"Do you have your dad's key?"

"Did you get the reserve key to the back door?" She replies while looking into his eyes, trying to see if he's joking. She sees that he isn't.

"Where do you want to go from here?" he asks.

"We'll just slip inside, lock the door behind us, and have the whole store to roam around in. You're really going to do it for me, aren't you?" She reaches into her pocket, searches through several used tissues, finds the key, and hands it to him. He puts it in his pocket with the other one. She has surreptitiously given him her permission.

Casey drives to the telephone equipment yard next to the phone building, pulls the car into the yard, and parks between two work trucks.

"We're really going to do this. Kurt will be furious," she says with a bemused smile on her face.

51

"You're not as mad at him as you were when I first saw you this morning. I have to go inside and talk to one of the operators." Casey steps out and goes to the lobby. The eyes of one of the operators smile a bright hello when he walks in. He motions for her to come to the lobby.

"I have a huge favor to ask of you, Arlene. I have someone with me who is having trouble with her father at home, and she needs a place to sleep tonight. I mean she needs a verifiable witness to cover for her for all night." The woman's eyes brighten up.

"I'll do it, but only if you promise to come over to my place and keep me company one evening," she says.

"Okay, it's a deal." Casey gives her a quick kiss on the cheek, and she pats him on the butt as he leaves.

"What was that all about?" Belinda asks him.

"You need a place to sleep tonight," Casey replies.

"Yes, I plan to go back inside the store and sleep on the bed upstairs."

"You can't do it, Belinda; the store gets too cold overnight, and you'd have to be real quiet when old man Milner gets there. The only reason you got inside this morning is that he gets to work so early. He opens the top and bottom lock, and you just opened the bottom one. If he had not been there, you wouldn't have been able to get in."

"I could have possibly gotten the key myself, but I don't know how to work the lock," she says.

"We can do it, and then afterward, I'll put the reserve key back in the office and put Kurt's key on the nail where he hangs his coat. He was so confused tonight that he won't remember whether he did it or not."

She nods in agreement. Casey sees what he thinks might be a slight smile on her lips, but he can't be sure.

The snow is deeper than the fur tops of Belinda's boots, and some snow works inside the boots as the two break a trail out of the yard and down the alley. They pause in the last place they have cover and look around. There's no one there, and they run across the alley.

Casey puts Belinda's key in the lower lock and then works at the top one. He pushes the door inward, and they quickly duck inside. He locks the door, and they are in almost total darkness. Instinctively, her hand seeks his out.

"Good God, Casey, I'm shivering all over with fright. I've never done anything like this before." She's hugging him.

"Take your boots off, empty the snow out of them, and carry them to the second floor so we won't leave a telltale track the cops can trace to you. Sit at the dining room table, and we can have the little talk you want." They grope their way to the back stairs and go up and find the dining room furniture. He pulls a chair out for her.

"No, Casey, I want to sit next to you."

"Wait a minute." He pulls her up and directs her to a couch, where he sits down. She sits beside him and pulls her feet up under her. "Does this have anything to do with the red bruise I saw on your neck this morning?"

He reaches up and tugs her scarf down, and she pulls it the rest of the way off. "It's too dark for me to see it."

"I'll show it to you later, Casey; right now, I need to tell you what happened." Belinda turns to him.

"What's the big deal?" Casey asks her, his interest further kindled by her mysterious tone.

"Dad tried to have me last night! It's only by Mom's intervention that he didn't. I didn't know he was that strong. He kept saying something about it being his right to claim me. He had me almost naked before she could intervene." Belinda diverts her eyes from him.

*Wow!* Casey thinks while looking and seeing how earnest she is. It's apparent to him that she's telling the truth. The bruises stand for something.

"I found out some things about our family that have been kept secret too long. First of all, you have to understand some of the history of the old church, Casey. If a man is an elder bishop in the church, he can choose any unmarried female he wants for his wife."

"Even a daughter?" he asks.

"No. He cannot pick a blood relative. Last night I found out that he's not my biological father. My mom is my mom, but he isn't my dad. The woman I thought was my oldest sister, Clara, is really his second wife. I don't know who my real dad is; Mom won't tell me, and I don't know how to find out.

"Constance, the next oldest, who I thought was my sister, is my half sister by his second wife. That is, she would be if he were really my father. The next one of the younger sisters, Mary Jean, is my half sister too. The two youngest ones, Rose and Della, really are my sisters by my mom and Kurt. I think my real dad is somebody close to the church and maybe in my extended family.

"It's all so confusing. There are some people married to each other that shouldn't be. Everything is such a secret, and no one will tell."

"Isn't polygamy against the law? Didn't the church outlaw it when the federal government threatened to take over all the Utah territory halfway through the 1800s?"

"Not according to Dad. He insists that he's only following the old Alfeta biblical law and that the laws enacted by the gentiles don't carry any weight at all. He says he can marry anyone he wants to. In fact, he needs a third wife as his station in the church allows it.

"They don't even recognize the border of Wyoming and Utah as being where the government says it is, and they claim some of Idaho too. They say that the federal government has no right to it and that they will reclaim it when the church comes to power after the gentiles are defeated, and the US becomes our theocracy."

"So your mom stopped it because she didn't want to have to compete with you as the third wife?"

"Yes, that and what he was doing to me, and having the whole house torn up about what was going on. Maybe she's just tired of everything being so tenuous and would like to end it all so we can live normal lives."

"You do realize he's in a lot of trouble if the authorities ever find out. I guess the whole family can be."

"Yes, I know. But Casey, the church controls the council, the city council, the police department, the sheriff's department, the courts, and everything else in this town. All the important people in the county buildings are Alfetas, so the influence even extends there. All the lawyers in the law office downtown are Alfeta.

"I wouldn't be at all surprised if there aren't another ten dozen families in town as badly screwed-up and inbred in a similar fashion as my family is. The marriage records at the courthouse are closely guarded, and you need approval from the church to view them."

Chapter
8

" **Y**OUR feet are cold, aren't they? You need to take your shoes off, and any of your petticoats that got wet in the snow," Casey says, looking down at Belinda's feet. He has to change the conversation for a minute to give him a chance to mull over what she just told him.

"I'm wearing nylons. You're right; my feet are wet and cold." She stands and hikes her skirt, and he watches as she releases the garters and loosens the stockings. She starts them down, and he reaches to help remove them.

He feels her petticoats and knocks some snow from them. He tugs down on the ones with frill and pulls them from her. "Hold on to them so you don't lose them. We don't want to leave any incriminating evidence up here."

"Casey, I feel kind of funny. I've felt weird all afternoon, and a little sick to my stomach. Maybe it's the fight with my parents last night, or having gone for almost two nights without sleep. I probably need a good night's sleep to think this out."

"I don't know about yesterday, but I know what we're doing now is a tremendous rush, and you're probably responding to it that way." He reaches down and pulls her feet up into his lap, turning her toward him. He then opens his coat and places her feet in the warmth against his stomach. He rubs her ankles and calves. "Where are you going after today?" he asks.

"Casey, I don't have anywhere I can go. I think my dad reasons that my rejection of him is a denial of his position. He's punishing me and thinks that I can't find anywhere to go, and that I'll apologize and come around to his demands. He doesn't respect my mother's opinion."

"That's pretty cold on his part, but I have a place for you to stay."

"Casey, I can't go home with you. If anyone ever finds out, I'll be excommunicated for sure. What would your parents think if you brought me home with you?"

"You won't be going home with me. I'm going to take you to Arlene's house. She'll vouch for you. Arlene is in control of the town dispatch tonight, so we'll know if anyone is coming here. The phone will ring three long rings as a warning, and if that happens, we'll have to get the hell out, and fast. We'll use the front door because they always respond to the back on a burglary call."

"Casey, have you had sex with that woman and every other vulnerable woman in this town?"

"Now let me see, there are still you, the librarian, the lady behind the bus ticket counter, Mrs. Cable, the Alfeta choir, most of the senior class—"

"Oh, stop! I know you have a reputation, but I've never actually heard anyone say they did it with you." She looks hard into his eyes. "Casey, I want revenge for what Kurt did to me last night and all the lies he told me about my family. I want to go and get some new clothes."

"Why don't we start downstairs, then, and pick out some pretty things for you. I know your dad gets most of your clothes here. He probably won't be able to differentiate between the new ones and the ones you're wearing right now."

"You know that if anyone sees us, and we're caught, it's stealing and we go to jail."

"What do you call what he tried to do to you last night? Just leave your boots here. Come on; we'll come back and get them." He pulls her across the darkened second floor to the front stairs.

There are people on the sidewalk, so he leads her to the little dinette just beyond the display and directs her into one of the chairs. He takes the orange drinks out of his coat pocket and offers her one. "Let's just wait here a few minutes and let more of the people going to the movies get by." He hands her one bottle and then takes one for himself and drinks from it.

She takes her bottle, withdraws the tin of aspirin from her pocket, and pops three. She draws in a short sip and then continues to nurse it as they watch people passing by. Finally, the street clears and he takes her by the hand. They quickly run down the front stairs and disappear into the darkened aisle in the ladies' apparel area.

"We'll never get away with this, Casey. They'll come looking for you," Belinda says to him.

"Why will they come looking for me?" he says, almost knowing what she's about to say.

"Because the church council voted you in disfavor, and you are to be driven out. I heard Kurt tell Mom that. The only thing worse is a shunning or an excommunication, and they can't do that because you're not an Alfeta."

"I know. Kurt made sure. I'm about to be drafted into the army. What I'm doing tonight is my last strike, my revenge against your church, this town, and Kurt," he replies while looking straight at her. She makes no reply, but only accepts what he tells her. "What kind of underwear do you wear?"

"Casey, please."

"No, seriously, how old is the pair you have on right now?" He knows he's hit on a sore spot.

"They're kind of old and torn. I had them on last night when Kurt attacked me," she says, reddening.

Casey leads her down the aisles, and she starts in the lingerie area as Casey hands her items. In the ready-to-wear area, she selects several outfits and looks further to the jeans. She finds her size and adds half a dozen pairs. Back up the aisle are pajamas, and she takes two sets. She looks in the bottom of the cabinet and finds a shorty set left over from last summer.

"Isn't this a hoot?" Casey says with a laugh.

"Yes, Casey, I can honestly say I've never been so petrified in all my life. How do you know my sizes? You've hit them right every time?" she asks him.

"I have to move all the receipts up to the third floor monthly. I remember stock numbers, as they reflect sizes. I looked at your family's records and found yours. Now sit down and pile all of our booty on the table." He reaches under the bottom of the shoe rack and finds the fifty-pound burlap potato sack he had hidden for something else he was going to do. He stuffs clothing and garments into it.

"I think we need to go and finish up our orange drinks where there's more light." He gathers up what she can't carry, and they go to where he arranged the furniture earlier.

"What's this? I didn't know anyone rearranged the floor display. You can't even see the bed from the first floor now." Belinda is surprised at the change. What with the lack of sleep she experienced the previous two nights, she isn't thinking clearly.

"If we sit back, no one can see us from the street. Do you want to get dressed now? I'd like to help you if you'll allow me."

"I need to try this stuff on to make sure it fits," she replies meekly, still trying to form the thoughts she wants to converse about with him.

"Belinda, turn around and try the pajamas first. They're the only things I don't know your size for." She doesn't stop him when he gently pushes the garments from her hand and starts disrobing her.

This is her chance to tell him what she wants from him. She stands with her back to him as he wipes their fingerprints off the drink bottles.

He completely undresses her as she faces away from him, and then he lifts her foot as he slides the pajama bottom up, reaches around her, and buttons them. He opens the top and places it around her shoulders, and she slips her arms inside. They're a little loose, but then pajamas are supposed to be.

"Belinda, can I please kiss you?" he whispers, and he nuzzles her neck as she leans back against him.

"Casey, I don't want Kurt to be able to claim me, and I know you can't, because you're not an Alfeta. Maybe if we just hold each other and make believe you're Johnny, I can tell Kurt I was claimed, and he can't have me."

Casey slips his arms around her and holds her to him. He doesn't have his coat on now, and he can feel the warmth of her body. Belinda slowly turns, and their lips come together. "You're cold." Casey reaches down and pulls the covers of the bed back. She's momentarily surprised that it's made, but she bends down and rolls into it. He throws the covers back over her, tucks the pillow under her head, and sits on the bed beside her.

She reaches up, pulls him down, kisses him, and watches as he calmly unlaces his boots and removes his socks. She continues watching with unemotional eyes as he disrobes.

"Casey, it's like everything is in slow motion now; I can remember every move you've made."

"That's good, Belinda. You'll remember every little detail of tonight. Let me help you now."

He reaches under the covers and gently pulls her pajamas, sliding them down. He releases the buttons of her top, undoing the last of the three, enjoying contact with the softness of her breasts. He slowly pulls the covers from her.

"Belinda, we're going to make believe I'm Johnny now." He can hear there's no conviction in her voice; it's just something she says as she waits to see what happens next. "Are you still a virgin after last night?" She nods as he leans over, whispering and kissing her. Her eyes are wide and apparently sleep disoriented as she looks at the colored lights of the Christmas display reflected by the metal ceiling.

"Yes, but it doesn't matter anymore. I just don't want Kurt to try to claim me again." She watches Casey intently as he joins her on the bed.

As their union ends, Belinda gives a surprised little shudder and lies passive. Once again, Casey has altered the Alfeta gene pool.

They continue to cling together, and Belinda begins to ask questions. "Casey, how many like me have you ever had?" she asks, lying there, holding him against her with her eyes closed. "The one thing I guarantee is that no one will ever find out, unless it comes from the girl. I never tell; all it does is shame the girl and make the boy look small for telling."

"Casey, I just want to lie together here and cuddle with you for a while." He accommodates her, reveling in her softness and wondering what she's thinking. They watch the lights playing across the ceiling. "I want you again, Casey, please."

He's ready again, and it takes longer this time. Belinda is more animated in her response. Afterward, they lie panting and shivering from the growing coldness of the room.

"Casey, you know what we're doing now is wrong. It feels good, but I know I'm going to be pregnant. You know the church established the clinic down in the valley to do genetic testing and make sure the baby's not deformed because of all the intermarrying.

"No matter whom I marry now, at least I've interrupted the gene pool sequence of incest and intermarrying. My child will be free of that threat. I don't care if they think I'm a fallen woman.

"I wonder how hard it is to raise a child alone. I realize you picked me for revenge against my dad and the church, and I can't blame you for that, because I've been a little bitch toward you ever since I first met you. Apparently, all the girls love to hate you, but then when they need someone to go crying to, it's always you. Do you know why?"

"Sure, I'm a Protestant, a gentile, and no reputable Alfeta girl dares to date me or tell me anything personal. If anyone accuses her of those things, all she has to do is deny it. Who will anyone believe, her or me? I'm deniable. My best move is to be very discreet, and so far, it has worked.

"As for your fear of being a single mother, you won't have to, Belinda. Don't you realize how crazy Johnny is over you? He has your initials carved on the dash of his car, in the metal. You can't see it because he has them covered with a metal Chrysler emblem.

I saw his annual three years ago, and he had taped a frame around your picture. Didn't he ask you to sign it?"

"Yes, but the frame wasn't there when I signed it for him." She studies Casey, wondering if it's true, wondering how to answer the question, and wondering how she missed all this.

"Don't you have a standing deal with him to come to the store every night he doesn't have practice and pick you up and take you home? Go out tomorrow night and let him seduce you. I don't know if he subscribes to the old 'claiming' theology, but I can almost guarantee you a husband. You know he's already employed part time by the state. As soon as he graduates, he'll have a steady job. Come on, now, we have to get out of here." Casey arranges the covers so it will be seen by anyone passing by the bed. "I need to get you some overshoes."

"They're size six," Belinda replies while dressing.

"I know. Wait for me here." Casey stops back in the women's area and selects a pair with buckles. He thinks further and selects a pair of saddle oxfords and patent leather shoes. Now she'll have all new ones. He looks at what she's wearing and wonders why she doesn't have better. He adds a half-dozen nylons and more anklets from the display.

Upstairs, he finds her walking toward the back, looking sleepier than before. He carries the burlap bag down and places it by the back door. It's larger, fuller, and heavier than he imagined it would be.

"Belinda, we have one more thing we need to do." He takes her down the hall to the office and kicks the door, breaking the jamb. They go inside. "We need to make it look like a burglary gone sour—really mess the place up. Put your gloves on your hands."

She doesn't need any encouragement and starts pulling things off the shelves. As a final gesture, Casey picks up the adding machine and ferociously slams it against the dial of the safe, effectively jamming it.

"Are you about through venting your anger?" he asks.

"There's just one more thing." She systematically removes all the cards from the Rolodex and slips them into her coat pocket.

Casey steps into the back office and pulls the two-by-four from the repaired window. He then reaches out and pulls a huge armful of snow inside to the floor.

He places the key on the hook in the second office, thinking he will just replace the other one when he returns to work in the morning. They peek out to see if the coast is clear and have to duck quickly back inside. Casey locks the door. Old Cotton Trot the cop is coming back down the alley, shaking doors.

They stand together behind the door, listening to him test to see if it is locked. Casey feels Belinda's hand grip him tightly as the cop shakes it from the outside and walks off down the alley without even looking in the back window, where he would have seen the disarray left in the office. They duck out, and Casey makes sure the door is locked. He goes to the window and pushes it wide open.

They dash across the alley to the back of the telephone building. Casey looks into the window of the exchange and sees that there is a different operator sitting down; Arlene is just getting up to leave. He knows then that it must be after two in the morning. He stands by the side of the building and tries not to startle her.

"Arlene, do you need a ride home?" Casey whispers.

"You betcha, big boy. Are you alone?" she replies.

"No, Belinda is with me."

"Darn, I could use a little nookie tonight."

Belinda comes around the corner of the building, and Arlene takes one look at her and immediately knows what's going on. "You just get us girls to my place, and I'll take care of the rest," Arlene says. Casey helps Belinda into the rear seat beside her bag of new clothing and starts toward Arlene's home.

"Help me get her inside, Casey; she's exhausted." Arlene says when they arrive. The two of them move the almost-sleeping Belinda inside and deposit her on the couch. Arlene goes to the bedroom and pulls the covers down. When she returns, Belinda is asleep, slumped over on the cushions. Arlene pulls her shoes off, puts her

63

legs up, and throws a cover over her. Casey returns to the car and brings her bag of clothing in.

"Casey, she's asleep, and I've got the bed turned down. We can go for a quickie if you have the time."

He looks down at his watch. "It's a quarter after two in the morning."

"Oh boy, it's nookie time," Arlene says, disrobing on her way to the bedroom. He quickly joins her. Casey went slower with older women. He would take his time and allow her to enjoy his youth; and he, her maturity.

All at once, Casey becomes aware of someone standing beside the bed. It's Belinda, holding the coverlet. "I'm cold," she says. Casey pulls the rest of the covers down, and Belinda climbs in and pulls them up around her neck. She rolls over with her back to Casey and Arlene, and in minutes, she is sleeping again.

"Casey, what in the world is her problem?"

"She was up late two nights ago and all night last night and most of tonight. She's afraid to go home because her father tried to have her."

"That son of a bitch." He can feel Arlene's body clench him. "I always knew there was something wrong with him. Somebody should shoot his balls off." Having said her piece, she slips out of the bed, and they go down the hall to the second bedroom. She quickly picks up the rhythm of their lovemaking. Afterward, Arlene lies there breathing hard and grinning up at Casey. "I'm glad I don't have the baby factory anymore."

She gets up and heads down the hallway. Casey waits for her to return from the bathroom. When he returns to the original bedroom, Arlene has the covers pulled down and is disrobing Belinda. "She's beautiful, Casey; all the younger ones are. I was once." Arlene says wistfully. She searches through the bag and finds Belinda's nightie.

"When does the poor thing have to be at work tomorrow morning?"

"I think I'll just let her sleep as long as she can, and then she'll be in a position to make decisions." Casey turns to leave, and Arlene follows him to the door.

"I heard what happened to you and the guys. How much time do you have left until you have to leave?"

"We have less than a week. I hope to make it a week of revenge on this little dump of a town. I plan to burn my bridges."

"Please come back here at least one more night before you do," she asks him earnestly.

"I will, Arlene; you're good people. You are one of the few who hasn't ever given me grief." He wonders what the following day will bring.

# Chapter 9

CASEY'S questions as to what the future holds are quickly answered as he pulls into the store parking lot. Old Cotton Trot the cop steps out from his cruiser and shouts to Casey: "Stay where you are." He reaches inside and honks the horn three times. The police chief comes swaggering around the corner of the building.

"Step out of the car, Casey. I need to search it." He pulls the door open, and Casey steps out and away. The chief gets in and does a perfunctory search.

"What's in the trunk?" Casey opens the trunk for him. The only thing there is his rifle, a carton of .22 shells and his winter survival stuff.

"Can you tell me what this is all about?" Casey asks.

"There was a break-in last night," the chief says.

"Someone broke into the feed warehouse?"

"No, they broke into the store. They vandalized it too. Where were you last night, Casey?"

"Home. It's too darn cold to be out in weather like this." He knows that his dad will come through for him at a time like this.

"Can you prove it? Do you have an alibi?"

"Just call Dad, or maybe you could go there and see the paper we kept the score on. I beat him three times straight in cribbage before he trounced me, and we listened to the *Hallmark Hour* program on the radio." Casey knows the chief will never call; he just wants to act like the big shot.

"Do you know anything about all the headlights being broken recently?" the cop looks at him directly.

"Look at the front of my car." The chief walks to the front and sees there's a headlight missing. "If you want to find out who's doing it, search the basketball team's cars and look for something with a square shaft, like a screwdriver or a file. Have you searched the cars of the other employees?" Casey asks him.

"You can go now," the chief says, arrogantly dismissing him. Casey closes his car door, locks it, and walks down the alley. He has to have the right amount of concern on his face when he walks into the store. Mr. Herman is standing there talking to a man in a suit.

"Casey, go upstairs and clean up the bed display in the front," he says.

"What do you want me to do with it?"

"Just make it look like it did yesterday. Someone vandalized the store last night and stole some things. We'll probably have to do inventory."

He had spoken the dreaded "I" word. Inventory didn't usually start until about the middle of January. It will be earlier this year because of him. Inwardly, he chuckles.

When he gets up there, he sees used flashbulbs all over the floor. He pulls the furniture back from where he placed it and pulls the sheets off the bed. The mattress cover has a stain in the center. He hears Mr. Herman approaching.

"Casey, do a quick sweep up of the whole store. It needs it," Mr. Herman says.

"What shall I do with this mattress and the bedding stuff?" Casey asks him.

"Take it somewhere and burn anything that has any blood or whatever on it," Mr. Herman says, seemingly exasperated. "I have a list of what was vandalized." He then walks away.

Casey carefully folds the sheets and mattress cover, wondering how accurate the list is and how much will be added for insurance purposes. He adds the blanket and the spread to his accumulation to go out. He strips the cases off the pillows, which are the only things he plans to return to stock. He thinks, *What the hell, the pillows are used too.* He reaches up and adds another sheet set to the box he's making up to carry them out. *She'll need a change.* He includes the pillows and the cases along with the rest of the merchandise to be destroyed.

He feels almost liberated carrying the mattress and box spring down the freight elevator. He carries them, then the box, to his car.

He's being watched by a tired Old Cotton Trot the cop as he ties the mattress and springs on the top of his car.

Casey knows he should have noticed the break-in while checking out the alley, and figures he's probably being made to stay on duty by the chief as a punishment.

"Where are you going with that?" the cop demands of Casey, approaching him with his hand hovering over the handle of his revolver.

Casey can only smile in amusement. "My boss said to burn it. If I can find enough dry stuff at the dump, I'll do it there." The cop returns to his car and huddles before the heater. Casey takes the box to Arlene's front door.

"Are you coming back for a quickie already?" Arlene asks facetiously as she opens the door for him.

"I have a new mattress and spring that Belinda can use. Here's the bedding that comes with them."

"What happened over there today?"

"Someone broke into the store and had a wild drinking party. They stole a bunch of things but didn't break into the safe—apparently because they didn't know how."

"I wish I'd been at the switchboard this morning. I could have listened in and found out all the juicy details. Do you know any juicy details?"

"I'm not allowed to discuss the break-in until after the police conclude their investigation. Mr. Herman is trying to put out a missing-person report on his teenage daughter, Belinda, but he can't until twenty-four hours have elapsed. She needs to call in sometime later in the day and let the authorities know she's okay

and has not been abducted—ravished, possibly, but not abducted."
He goes out and brings the rest of the things in. "How's sleeping
beauty?"

"Great, want a look?" He follows Arlene through the house to
the bedroom. Belinda is there on her back, partially uncovered,
and snoring. He pulls the blanket up over her and gives her a little
kiss.

"Is this your new girl? I'm sorry about Naomi."

"No, she isn't my girl; I'm just her sperm donor. She wants a
baby who is not inbred among the Alfetas and reaches outside the
gene pool. I donated the baby batter. She'll be marrying Johnny
Stephenson, as soon as she can convince him that he's the sperm
donor of the baby whose cells are dividing in her even as we
speak."

"You know more about it than I do. I never had one after
my accident and don't want one now. All I need is an occasional
quickie, and afterward, I'm good to go."

"What do you mean, sorry about Naomi? What have you
heard about her?"

"There was a flurry of long-distance telephone calls from Salt
Lake about three weeks ago. They all went to the second precinct
church and to Kurt's residence. I think she may have been forced
to do something she didn't want to."

Casey feels revulsion rising in his gut. His time is getting short
at home, and he has to do something to make them all back off.

"Ask Belinda if she knows anything about Naomi, after she
wakes up," he says to Arlene.

\* \* \*

Casey works the morning stocking shelves and trying to look
concerned for the customers. About noon, he needs to go to the
siding for feed. There's another railcar; it is one of the new long
ones. He takes the customer's receipt and loads the bags of corn.
Tonight will be a good time to modify the access to this railcar.
Lloyd will have a difficult time unloading it.

Inventory has officially started when Casey returns to the store. He has the responsibility of counting the basement. He knows it's an all-day job, and they are just getting started. Mr. Herman's two youngest girls are in the cigarette storage area, tax-stamping the packs. He hears them giggle. He looks and sees that one of them is standing at the edge of the elevator.

"Hey, Casey, do you need a woman to marry? I'll be available in about ten years, but then you'll be gone and Dad will have to find me someone else."

"Don't let anyone but you choose the man you marry," Casey says. They look at each other and apparently don't know what he's talking about. *What the hell's going on? Do even the boss's kids know what's happened to Naomi and me? Why can't I find out something?*

He continues counting up case goods and straightening the stock. He makes an effort to get the list finished and by late afternoon, Lloyd comes down to help.

"I don't know why we have to inventory the basement stock," says Lloyd. "I don't think they stole any case goods. Do you?"

"No, Lloyd, but the quicker we get done, the faster we can get back to normal, and we won't have to do it later this month. Whoever broke in here definitely wasn't after a case of beans." When it's time to go and sweep up, Casey hands the remainder of the forms to Lloyd.

Casey knows Lloyd hates to do inventory, but also knows he hates to sweep even more. Casey goes upstairs and starts. There are little spirals of black powder everywhere they have dusted for fingerprints. *That's okay,* Casey thinks. *Mine will be all over the place.* There isn't a single piece of furniture up there he hasn't had to move at least twice. He also knows they'll not find his fingerprints on file, because he's never been arrested.

When he goes past the office once again, the door is shut before he gets to the end of the hall. Mr. Herman looks out the door and tells him just to finish the locking up and go ahead and leave. He meets Johnny Stephenson trying to get in the front door. He turns the lock and steps out.

"Johnny, I don't think this is a good time to go into the store. We had a break-in, and everybody's suspicious. They're looking for a goat to pin it on."

"What happened to Belinda?"

"They haven't heard from her. Something serious is happening at her home that apparently upset her to the point that she cursed her father out and just disappeared." Casey can see the surprise and alarm rising in Johnny's eyes. He almost feels sorry for him—almost.

"If you love her, you better claim her, Johnny. You could lose Belinda like I lost Naomi." Johnny doesn't respond; he only rolls his eyes, pivots, and turns and walks away with his shoulders lowered and his hands jammed into his pockets.

Casey goes to Arlene's and pulls beyond the property line, where he cannot be seen. He gives a secret knock to see if she's still there. After the curtains move, Belinda answers the door.

"Hi, how are you doing?" Casey asks her.

"Great! Arlene is my hero. She's invited me to live here with her and help with the food. I have my own double bed thanks to you. How did you get the matching box spring?"

"Kurt told me to burn anything soiled. I was to take it to the dump and set it on fire. Nobody noticed the springs were not stained, or that no smoke came from the dump.

"Now you need to check in with someone, Belinda. Call the cops, call your mom, and please call Johnny. He's really worried about you. Pick up the phone, and after Arlene comes on the line, tell her to connect to whomever you want to speak with first. Tell her that they should think you are down in Salt Lake or some other place long distance." They go together to the phone, and Belinda picks it up. Arlene answers on the other end of the line.

"Go ahead and connect me to the police, and I'll tell them I'm okay," says Belinda.

Casey listens to her talking to the officer and repeatedly refusing to tell him where she is. She talks to her mom next, and it's short and to the point. Her mom says she is to come home, and that her new bedroom is in the basement. Belinda hangs up the phone, and Casey can tell she is agitated.

"What if I arrange a place where you can meet with Johnny and have a talk?" asks Casey. "It will have to be tonight, and he'll have to trust me."

"I'd like that, Casey. Go ahead and set something up with him if you can." Casey picks up the telephone, calls the agricultural farm residence, and asks for Johnny. There's a long silence, and then he comes on the line.

"Johnny, I know where Belinda is, and she wants to talk to you," Casey says to him.

"If she's there, put her on!" It's a panicked demand on his part. Belinda takes the receiver from Casey, and when the conversation between the two becomes intimate, Casey leaves the room to give Belinda privacy. He looks in and sees her holding her hand over the speaker and beckoning to him.

"What did Johnny have to say?" Casey asks her.

"You're right, Casey, he's beside himself with worry. He wants to meet with me somewhere before I go back home," Belinda replies.

"Johnny, it's me, Belinda. Please listen to Casey and do exactly as he says." She hands the phone back to Casey.

"Go downtown and park in the library lot and leave the keys in the ignition, then walk over to the Texaco and wait for me to get there," says Casey. "Go around the alley side, and after I get the car on the lift, I'll let you inside."

"If this is a joke, White, I swear I'll—"

Belinda takes the phone from Casey and speaks angrily. "Johnny, you listen to me! He's on our side; just do what he says."

Johnny immediately calms down. "I'll do it. I hope nobody knows I'm past curfew."

Belinda hides under a blanket on the floor in the back of the car. Casey pulls up to the pumps, and Stephen, the high school dropout night attendant, comes out.

"That's a cool car, Casey. When did you change?"

"Fill it. I haven't bought it yet. I'm test driving it." He steps out, and as Stephen starts the fill, Casey approaches him. "I really need to use the rack tonight."

It's the same routine as many times before. Casey backs the car in and then watches the lights go out. Johnny appears at the door, and Casey slides it up to let him in. Johnny is beside himself with apprehension, wondering if Casey is setting him up to get back at him.

"Now let me explain how this works," says Casey. "You have to pay Stephen five dollars for the use of the rack. You have to keep low in the seat, probably in the back, so that the cops don't catch you in here. They will be around shaking doors again, so if you get out of the car, always look to the front first and see if the town cop is anywhere around.

"I'll lock the door on my way out. Now get in the back, and don't get caught. When you're done, look and see if there is any traffic before you pull out, and be sure to lock the door."

"I understand, but where is Belinda?" Johnny asks.

"Go on and get into the back. No, don't open the front door; use the back." Johnny looks embarrassed, mad, out of options, and a little confused, but he reluctantly follows Casey's instructions. When he gets in the back, something moves, and Belinda pokes her head out from under the blanket.

"Oh my God, Belinda, I've been so worried." They're immediately in each other's arms. Casey raises the overhead door only enough to get out, puts it down again, and locks it. He walks back to pick up his car. He goes home to sleep, planning to get up about four and catch Arlene coming home so she can entertain him until he has to be ready for work.

\* \* \*

The following day, he's called into the office and meets with a young man in a black suit with a badge fastened to his belt; he is with the State Bureau of Investigation. He interviews Casey at length. There apparently is more going on than Casey suspects, but he gives the man satisfactory answers.

The man places some papers on the desk that are covered with red ink. There are two sets of columns of numbers, and at the bottom one is in red and the other in black.

The man stands up to sharpen his pencil, and Casey quickly looks at the figures. There is over eighteen thousand dollars' difference between the two columns. Someone had been really ripping the place off or using it to launder money.

"Casey, can you think of any way to shed some light on my problem?" the officer asks him.

"Is any of this being recorded?" Casey stands and makes sure there's no one outside the door.

"I assure you it is not."

"You can start by quietly looking at marriage records in the town courthouse and determining where the plurality is going on. I know it takes a lot of food to feed a big family, especially if there is only one wage earner. I don't know if you can get into the records of the church, but that will be another place to look." The eyebrows of the officer arch higher. "You need all the old purchase records for our stock. Compare them against the sales records."

"That is what this represents, Casey. That is a major difference to mark off as loss."

Casey looks at the papers again and notes the figure. "You might check store bank accounts—not here, but down in the valley somewhere—find out what bank they use, maybe a bank backed by the Alfeta church. I know that about once a month, a courier from the valley brings some kind of package up here. Mr. Milner has family there, and they are financially well-off. I think a couple of them do run banks or at least work in one. You can't hide money in a small town like this one."

"And you infer all this because . . . ?" the agent asks.

"Because, sir, I'm not an Alfeta. I'm their whipping boy. They don't trust any Protestant. Can I go now?" He pauses briefly in expectation of an answer. "Wait a minute; that isn't quite accurate.

I'm considered by them to be a gentile—as are you, sir—and for that reason, they will not be forthcoming with the whole truth.

"You should call the feds in too. The draft board is phony. I know it's a supposed to be a lottery, but look at the records. You'll find who's drafted and who's on a religious mission."

"What you've told me is pretty profound, son. I'll look into your allegations—quietly, of course—and then get back to you," the officer replies.

"You'd better have a plane ticket in your back pocket, then, because in just a short while, I am to become part of the US Navy. They drafted three of us into the army over the top of about three dozen of their own, and we made an alternate decision."

With that, Casey rises and goes back to work. *This place became a dump when Belinda left*, he thinks. His future is a blank, and if not for the ongoing investigation, he'd just quit. But to quit now would only make him look complicit in what's happening, and he doesn't want that to happen.

# Chapter 10

INSTEAD of going home, Casey ends up at Arlene's house. She fills him in about the Belinda saga. Johnny proposed marriage after the night in the garage. He and Belinda plan to elope, and it will happen as soon as Johnny can get all the arrangements made. Belinda and Johnny plan to take Arlene with them when she finishes work one night and go to the justice of the peace and wake him. They'll use Arlene as one witness, and the justice's wife will be the other. Casey secretly wishes he could be one of the signatories on that document.

"I've heard all the stories about you, Casey. How soon are you going to be leaving town to go to the navy?" Arlene asks him.

"I've got less than a week. However, I plan to burn a few bridges before I go."

"Don't you get careless and screw up and get put in jail for some stupidity. You're too good a kid for that to happen to."

"I'm careful, Arlene. It's just that I've been putting up with their crap for so long that I think it is time they have to pay me."

"Well, I know I can't talk you out of it. If you need a hideout, my place is always available."

"I know, and I appreciate it. You're the only older woman I feel comfortable with. You don't act like some controlling old—"

"Whoa, stop, I'm only thirty-six." Her eyes soften. "Casey, I'm on duty alone tonight. Why don't you just stick around, keep me company, and then go home with me after my shift is over at two?"

"Well, right now I can't think of anything I'd rather be doing." They walk to the telephone exchange arm in arm, and she goes in while Casey makes a trip to the drugstore for drinks and snacks. When he returns, she tells him to sit at the supervisor's console, where he can't be seen from the lobby, and put the headphones on. She shows him how to listen in on conversations. When Arlene has about fifteen minutes to go, she lets him out of the building. He waits around for her relief to arrive, and then, after Arlene comes out of the door, they walk back to her house.

Belinda is surprised to see them come in together. She heard the sound of someone unlocking the door and got up to make sure it's Arlene.

It doesn't take her long to put two and two together, and she closes her door as they go to Arlene's room. Casey sees Belinda's door open just a crack as he and Arlene make their way toward the other bedroom. They turn the lights off as they go. Finally, they fall into the bed and make love.

When they are finished, they hear the slight squeak of the door as it slowly opens. The hall lights are still out as Belinda comes into the dark room. The bed dips as she sits.

"Casey, it worked," says Belinda. "Johnny and I are going to be married. He didn't even want to use protection. He claimed me for his wife. We did it twice in the back of his car. It's just a matter of time until we can elope. I'm sorry I treated you like such a shit. I'm the one who is, and I should have known better."

Arlene gets up and opens the curtains. There's enough soft light coming from outside to illuminate the room. Casey feels the bed dip down as Arlene comes back and sits beside them.

"Is there anything you'd like to tell Casey, Belinda? I think he needs to know," says Arlene.

"If it gets out, I know they'll come and get me, maybe even kill me," Belinda replies, concerned about her safety because she knows what's going on.

"Don't be afraid to tell Casey. He won't let anyone know where or from whom he gets his information."

"Casey," Belinda says, "what you don't know about is that in the old church, the hierarchy can choose anyone they want for a wife."

"That's not news to me," he replies.

"Nowadays, they interpret it differently. The man claiming Naomi is a lawyer for the church, and a pretty high-ranking one. He's remained unmarried for a period exceeding three years after achieving his calling, and the church thinks he needs a wife and children.

"What they do is send out a call to all the surrounding regions for the local bishops to submit a list of young, available virgins for him to pick from. He narrows the list down to a dozen or more, and extensive histories are prepared for each of them. It's a very exhaustive search of their pasts, including a family history, a background check, and a physical exam to ensure that they are indeed virgins. The church has an extensive section of scholars who do nothing more than work on family histories and genealogy to rule out those you shouldn't marry and those who they don't have a complete history for.

"Naomi became the top choice of the lawyer, and that sealed her fate. They've prepared documents that will force her to marry him. They have promised her parents financial help and hospitalization for Arthur to get him dried out.

"They have to furnish housing for the family for as long as there is a minor child of the parents in their care. In this case, it more or less exploded in their faces. Arthur has cancer and will be dead in a year or less, but Althea is pregnant like me!"

Casey wonders if he is responsible for this change in the gene pool, or if he was just an interim stud for Naomi's mom until she had to leave town.

Belinda continued. "Her mother demanded an account of the proceeds of the sale of her home. But there's no actual sale; the church takes over the mortgage. A financial document in her and the church's name is deposited in the church-run bank. She may never see a penny of that money. Naomi will have to sue the church to get her mother's money for her.

"Her younger brother, Donnie, is a hard case. They had to take him to a commune and do a food deprivation and isolation program on him to make him fearful enough to follow what they want him to do. They'll get him brainwashed into the little follower they want him to be."

"Why didn't Naomi just tell me this?" Casey asks.

"She didn't know or understand what was happening to her. They moved so fast that her mom barely had time to make arrangements. All the household furniture is still in a moving van parked out in the desert on the road to the commune, although it might be inside the barn by now."

"Damn! Isn't this the twentieth century?" Casey responds. "How did you find out all of this?"

"I'm aware of it happening once before because Dad—oops, Kurt, that son-of-a-bitch—submitted a name to the district. I heard him tell Mom about it. I think it's how he got his second wife, who I thought to be my oldest sister.

"Another thing you should know is that not all Alfetas know about this so-called inner sanctum of disciples. They operate as an autonomous unit. They are entirely separate from the main church, though they use it as a home base and a cover for their operations.

"They are the radical militia, and only the twelve apostles and the Stead, who is the god-father of the Alfeta church, have control of them."

"Unbelievable!" says Casey.

They all talk well into the morning, and both women are astounded at some of the things Casey endured while growing up. The bullying, the harassment, the fights, The arrogance of the Alfeta classmates because he was not an Alfeta and their scorn because his dad was a lowly janitor.

"Casey, I'd better drive you home," Arlene announces finally.

They dress, and Belinda comes to the front room, her pajama top still unbuttoned, and gives him a good-bye kiss.

"I don't know how or if I'll ever be able to make it up to you, Casey. I want you to know that I'm truly sorry for all the grief I've caused you over the years."

He holds her and kisses her again. "Thank you, Belinda, that means a lot to me" he says to her as Arlene and he step out into the chilly night air. Her car starts on the third try, and she drives him home while he lies down on the seat with his head on her lap, enjoying the accommodations.

He hops out and gives her a good-bye kiss, and she pulls away as he makes his way to the house. There are only two hours of the night left for him to get any sleep, but he's used to it. He'll have another night without Naomi to recuperate.

\* \* \*

When Casey arrives at work, he's given a list of things to bring up from the basement. It takes him an hour to get all the stock items up to the elevator. Lloyd carefully takes all the smaller cases to work on.

Casey takes several orders for feed and enjoys the respite getting out of the store offers. He takes his time unloading and walks slowly going back to the store. He stops and finds an old unfired shotgun shell in the trunk of his car. He cuts off the end of it, pulls it in two, and dumps the shot into his pocket.

When he returns to the store, he goes to the basement, unscrews the top of the platform scale weight balance, and adds a small handful of the tiny lead shot to the container. He reassembles it and goes back to work. Now anyone buying goods weighed on the scale will be getting a bargain.

At the start of the evening's sweep-down, Mr. Milner stops him and asks him if in the future he will please sweep his part of the store just after noon if at all possible. Casey does a quick sweep-down as Mr. Milner watches.

The next day at work, the harassment really begins, in earnest. Mr. Herman finds the most dirty, disgusting jobs he can for Casey to complete. Casey goes about them in a casual manner, never complaining.

Toward the end of the day, as he sweeps down, he stops by the cooler, takes two packaged fish out of the display, and throws them into the trash can he is pushing along.

He goes to the women's area, pulls the bottom panel off the radiator cover, and places a fish under it. He forces the cover back on so that it will take a Herculean effort to get it open. While he is there, he surreptitiously slips packages of rubbers into several pairs of women's panties.

He slips the second fish under the steel reinforcement for the cash register stand. It is a permanent part of the front checkout counter. The whole counter would have to be unbolted and lifted in order to remove the rotting remains of the fish.

Upstairs on the third floor, where the pipes to the steam radiators run through the floors down to the basement and the boiler, he upturns a gallon glass bottle of bleach with a small hole poked through the lid, and ties it upturned with the hole right over the opening in the floor. Now when the bottle becomes warm as the steam turns on, a portion of the liquid in the bottle will expand and be expelled out where the chlorine aroma will permeate the air in the area and make it untenable.

He pulls the now heavy trash container back and bumps it down the stairs, where Mr. Herman is waiting for him. "Carry it, Casey; don't mark the floors. You'll be varnishing them before you know it if you keep that up. I think you need better discipline, Casey. You move too slowly."

"Oh, I don't think I'm moving too slowly. I think a message is being transmitted to me today by someone who thinks he is so superior to anyone else that his shit doesn't stink. I think that if you can't tell me in your retarded self-important English what I've done wrong, and you've been all over my ass for, then perhaps there won't be another tomorrow."

"You can't use that kind of language to me!" Mr. Herman says as his face flushes.

"I just did. Are you afraid that if you fire me, you'll have to pay me unemployment?" Casey asks.

"That's only an idea in some politician's head. There is no law requiring us to do so."

"Why did you pay Lyman's salary for a month when he quit under mysterious circumstances?" Casey asks him.

"He was a valued employ . . . How did you know that?"

"You're transparent. Your motives are transparent. Your reasoning is transparent, and your phony religion is transparent. Everything you stand for is transparent."

"Go to the office, collect your last paycheck, and get out," Mr. Herman says in a huff, pointing to the office.

"No kisses good-bye?"

Now Mr. Herman is red in the face and clenching his fists. Casey puckers his lips.

"If you were a man, I'd—"

"Get your arrogant, transparent ass kicked up between your arrogant, transparent ears. That would make the little transparent inbred Alfeta bald spot on your head glow like the phony gold-plated sword that supposedly came down from heaven."

"Get out of my sight!" he fairly shouts at Casey.

Casey calms himself down, goes to the office, and knocks on the door. Mr. Milner is behind his desk, working with a new adding machine.

"Yes, what is it?" he answers, looking up, surprised to see Casey standing there.

"Kurt and I just had a meeting of the minds. He thinks it will be better if I find employment somewhere else. Will you make out my pay? He said to compute it to the end of the month just to make it fair."

"He did?" The man obviously hadn't heard the previous exchange.

"Yes, sir, he was very emphatic about it."

Mr. Milner pulls out his new Rolodex and turns it to Casey's stub. He turns around, keys the figures into the adding machine, stands up, walks to the cash box, counts the money on the counter, and pulls out the tax form to go with it. He puts the cash box away, recounts it, and hands it to Casey.

"I'm sorry to see you go, Casey. You could have been a valuable asset to the company. You're a good worker."

"You mean better than ignorant little impotent Lloyd? He's done a twenty-year stretch in a dead-end job right out of high school, scraping by on minimal wages like you pay me, while bowing down to an arrogant nobody? He has no future, no past, no wife, no kids, and no one to go and have a beer with; a little cracker box house just big enough for him and his aging mom. He'll grow old and die there, and nobody will remember him. He's a valuable little ottoman for the church. No thank you. I'll just go."

"Just leave before I call the authorities and have you arrested," the man says when he overcomes his shock and finds himself angry.

"Be careful who is arrested. I know where most of the eighteen thousand went. It isn't where the authorities want to find it!" Casey says over his shoulder. He actually has no idea where the money is, but judging from Mr. Milner's reaction, he knows he's close to finding as raw a nerve as possible.

He turns and goes out of the room, unlocks the back door, dumps the remainder of the shot from the shell he disassembled into the frame so that the lock won't engage, and goes out that way. *They can lock it up*, he thinks. *I'm no longer an employee of the company.*

"Wait for a minute, Casey White!" Mr. Herman hollers. He steps out into the alley acting like he's spoiling for a fight. It's what Casey thought might happen. He's puffed up and looks like he's about to unload on him.

"I can see right through you, young man, and I demand respect, and I demand an apology," he says in an elevated, blustery voice.

"Well, you see, you ignorant old fart, you don't understand, do you? Respect is *earned*. You can't buy it, and no one gets respect by demanding it. You're the one who is transparent. Your phony religion is transparent. Your way of life is transparent, and your family is transparent. I can see what you tried to do to your daughter, and that is really transparent." When Casey says the last bit, Mr. Herman's eyes widen more, and he continues to grow angrier.

"It wouldn't surprise me that you've tried something with your younger daughters, judging from what they've told me goes on in your household," Casey says, further baiting the man.

"If you were my son, I'd beat the living hell out of you right now for being so unappreciative," says Mr. Herman. "Listen to me, you ignorant little bastard, I'm the one who broke up your little love nest. I couldn't let you rape a perfectly good Alfeta girl. I submitted her name to the council, and she is the one they picked. It was me. Do you understand? Me!"

"Yeah, that's old news. You win that one, you impotent little half-breed bastard of a man. Let me give you some news. I screwed your wife; she really begged me for it. She says she doesn't like you just jumping on, getting your jollies and jumping off." He continues raising the level of torment he is directing at Mr. Herman.

Casey is leaning forward and can see the man clenching his fists. He doesn't know how much it will take to provoke the man to attack him. Out of the corner of his eye, he spots Officer Peters working his way down the alley toward them.

"Listen to me, you insolent little son of a bitchin' bastard. You haven't been anywhere near my family. If you had, I'd know it and have you arrested for rape."

"Rape?! Oh, you mean like the charges that you could be facing even now. Your own daughter is afraid to go home and is in hiding. I think, O transparent one, you're the one who doesn't know I looked up the marriage records in the courthouse. You know, the ones that Miss 'The Widow' Howell guards so closely for all the phony grand Alfeta Pooh-Bahs of this town.

"All I had to do was go over, shovel her walks, and go inside for cocoa and sweet-talk her. I had to shower with her and help her make the bed after I banged her. After that, we went right over to the courthouse.

"As I was turning pages, she pointed out to me the despotic, inbred marriage history of this town. It is incredible. I think the Alfeta gene pool is fatally polluted. She wanted to breed again right there on her desk, on your family page, in honor of the occasion." The last part is another fiction, but Casey has to keep the pressure on Mr. Herman to get him to attack.

"You'd best watch your mouth, Mr. White. You might not live long enough to make it to the army." Suddenly, Mr. Herman takes a stance, and his haymaker comes around. It misses Casey's face, but he jerks his body back and falls backward as though he's been punched.

Mr. Herman comes right at him, kicking. Casey lifts his foot up and turns the bottom of it toward him. There's a steel horseshoe tap on the heel of his boot, and it contacts Mr. Herman's shin as he kicks out at him. Mr. Herman pulls back, grimacing in pain.

Casey enjoys every second of the action as he watches the young officer make a takedown, kneel on the man's back, pull his arms around behind, and lock them in handcuffs. He steps back and lets the man stand but keeps him under his control.

"What's going on here? Why did you strike him?" Officer Peters asks, directing his questions to Mr. Herman.

"Officer, thanks to the Lord you're here. I want him arrested and charged with attacking me."

"I saw you punch him, sir. He didn't even have his hands up in front of him."

"Get these damn things off me! Do you understand who you are dealing with here? Do it now!" He turns and stands with his back to the officer.

"You are under arrest. Do you understand me? I saw you make an unprovoked attack on this young man. Now you are going to have to come with me and cool down. Would you like me to call your home or somebody you can talk to?"

"Let me out of these handcuffs now!" He turns and tries to kick out at the officer, who deflects the blow the same way Casey did. The old man grimaces in pain again.

85

"Are you all right, Casey? I'll have to make out assault charges against him. Do you want to press charges?"

"Yes, I think so," he says, just to see what reaction it will produce in Mr. Herman. "This kind of hooliganism shouldn't be permitted in the community."

"What's this all about?" Officer Peters asks while pushing Mr. Herman back from where Casey is standing.

"I think Mr. Herman is somewhat overwrought. He's worried about an incident of fraud in the store, and he might be behind the break-in to cover up what's been going on here. I know he's having family problems and is worried about the upcoming breakups of his marriages.

"His daughter left home after fighting him off in a rape attempt. She's hiding out somewhere, waiting for a chance to go home to pick up her belongings when her parents aren't there. He needs time to sit down, pray to the golden sword, and mull over all his problems. He probably needs a lawyer." Casey looks right at Mr. Herman and smiles and winks.

"Please come with me, sir." Officer Peters takes the still fuming man and leads him away down the alley, toward the police station. As they cross Tenth Street, a group of citizens going home from downtown stand open-mouthed, looking and wondering what's going on.

*The grapevine will be alive tonight,* Casey thinks. *Tomorrow, it will be all over town, and there's nothing Mr. Herman can do about it.* Sometimes the grapevine works in the little man's favor. Casey follows at a respectable distance to see if they do indeed make it to the station. He watches as they disappear through the door.

Instead of driving home, he goes directly to the railroad siding, drives a square horseshoe nail into the bottom of the lock, and beaks it off.

Since it's a brand-new freight car, he knows the brake system won't be all rusted up. He takes an adjustable wrench up to the top of the roof of the boxcar and loosens the setscrew holding the brake wheel on the shaft. A few good blows with the wrench, and he manages to pull it off. He hurls it discus-style across the tracks and watches as a shower of snow comes up where it hits the ground and disappears into the snowbank.

He doesn't know how long it will take them to find out what's happened, but he knows that Mr. Herman usually waits to call for a car movement until the last day before the railroad starts charging demurrage for cars left too long on the track siding. *Poor old sore-backed Lloyd will have to finish unloading this car. That is, after they get the door open.* Casey comes down the ladder, takes a second, smaller nail, and pounds it into the shaft of the wheel that the door moves on, making it almost impossible to move. *This small revenge is completed. On to the next one.*

# Chapter 11

CASEY lies in bed until late morning. His bladder and stomach finally move him. He knows it's the last time he'll be able to sleep in for a long time. He goes downstairs, and his mom warms up the leftovers from the breakfast she prepared earlier.

She tells Casey that she can sense there's something wrong, and she wants to talk. He sits down and replays most of the week's happenings—but not the bad stuff he's done, which would upset her, and not the sex parts, which would offend her more. He tells her of the incident triggering his firing.

"It's just as well," she says. "You need a little more time than you're allowing before going into the military. I don't think you realize how big a change this will be in your life."

"Mom, I sometimes wish we never came to this godforsaken place where we ended up. I'd rather be in Laramie, Boise, or Las Vegas—anywhere away from any of the Alfeta religion. I know that you and Dad both have good jobs, but there's nothing for me in this town. I should go thank the draft board for forcing me to decide about my future."

Bella lets his curse go unrecognized and continues what she's doing.

Later, Casey works at putting his things away in boxes. He wonders whether he will ever use most of them again. The final drawer of his dresser is the top one. It's what his mom calls his junk drawer. It's the accumulation of all the things he kept while growing up and never threw away.

He pulls it open and starts looking through it. Caught in the back, there is another knife to be put away with his hunting equipment. He gives the drawer another tug, and all at once gravity takes over. A shower of junk and collectables hit the floor. "Shit."

"Did you say something, Casey?" His mom comes into the room and looks over the scattered remains of his boyhood. He resolves to just sweep them up together and put them in a box to be sorted out later. His eye catches something under the side of the bed. He picks it up, turns it over, and looks at it.

It's the ring his first love gave him in the fourth grade when they pledged their love forever. He looks it over, slips it on to his pinkie, and continues picking up the scattered remains. The ring is nothing more than a cheap, thin band of gold-plated metal with an expanded area at the top. At some point, he tried to scratch his initial into it, but the W looks more like a K.

His mom returns with yet another boot box, and he fills it with the drawer items. Everything is more or less done for now. His dad comes home after work, and they drink coffee together and reminisce. They eat supper, and then the telephone rings. Arlene is on the line.

Once again, Casey drives to Arlene's house and parks up the driveway, behind her car. He gets out, rings the bell, and waits for her to answer.

"Casey," she says in a lowered voice, "please come in and take your clothes off."

"Do you mean my coat or my clothes?"

"You make the decision," she replies, and she unbuttons her blouse and walks toward the bedroom. Casey follows her instantly. She hushes him as they walk past Belinda's bedroom. Casey hesitates and listens. Whatever is going on in there is causing some really heavy breathing. He closes the door behind them.

Their lovemaking has a more leisurely tone to it than the times before. They realize it might be the last time for them to be together. When finished, they return to the kitchen, where they find Johnny and Belinda.

Belinda is sitting in Johnny's lap at the table; they are holding hands and looking like lovers.

"What is going on, Belinda? You look like the cat that just ate the canary," Casey says.

"Johnny and I are married. We went to the justice of the peace and were married instead of having to put up with the church ritual."

"Well, congratulations. Are you keeping it a secret?" Casey looks at Belinda's hand and sees no wedding ring.

"It's no secret, but we are so broke we couldn't afford a ring," says Johnny. "I promised Belinda we would get one, as soon as we can afford it."

Casey reaches into his pocket. "I can help." All their eyes follow his hand, and he pulls out the ring from his junk drawer, polishes it on his pant leg, and slips it on Belinda's finger. Instantly, there are tears in her eyes. She turns the flat side down and looks at what, for now, is her wedding ring.

"I think it's time for me to go home," says Casey. "It's getting late, and I have a lot of things to accomplish in the next two days. Johnny, can I give you a lift somewhere, or are you spending the night?" Casey thinks he could almost get to like this guy. He certainly likes his bride.

Arlene gives Casey a long good-bye kiss. "Keep me informed about you before you go," she asks Casey.

Casey and Johnny leave for Johnny's home at the cattle facility to keep Arlene from having to drive him.

"Casey, I owe you an apology. I'm sorry I've treated you like I have all this time. You're not so bad. I know Belinda thinks the world of you. She wouldn't be where she is now if it hadn't been for you."

Casey reaches over and extends his hand; they shake and continue driving as Casey smiles inwardly, thinking of where Belinda is right now. "Johnny, will you promise me something tonight?" Casey asks.

"I will if I can," Johnny replies. Casey notes that he seems somewhat perplexed by the request.

"Will you take a family picture every year, perhaps around Christmas, and send it to Dad? I don't know what my new address will be, or if I will be settled right away, but I'd like to keep some contact with home."

"Sure, Casey, I'd be proud to do it for you." Johnny directs Casey through the grounds to the residence, and when they arrive, Casey lets him out.

Casey gets a feeling of nostalgia as he goes back home past Naomi's house.

\* \* \*

Two days remain before Casey is to leave for his navy physical. He decides his plan must be put into operation. After he finishes breakfast and tells his mom he will be leaving a day sooner than originally planned, he heads downtown.

He stops at the bus station and buys a round-trip ticket to Green River and another one-way to Denver. He sits in the restaurant to study the schedule so that he'll get on the correct buses. Afterward, he finds his dad at work and tells him he's decided to go a day early because the navy recruiter told him that if you show up first, you have a choice of schools. His dad buys it.

Upon his returning home, he tells his mom the same thing. He calls Arlene and tells her to get the grapevine going: the Protestant boogeyman would be leaving town on the next morning bus. He talks with his mom the remainder of the day and stays home with his parents that night.

\* \* \*

His mom and dad rise early to drive him to the bus depot. His dad is his usual stoic self, and his mother tearful. There is quite a gaggle of people there. Johnny and Belinda show up, as does the preacher, his wife, and a couple of the people from church. Officer Peters is the last to shake his hand and say good-bye.

He has to explain his reason for leaving early, and when they ask why Ken and Ron didn't elect to go, he tells them that they decided against it because they already had plans.

There are two men in a car with Utah plates watching from across the street in front of the bus station. Casey wonders what they will report, and to whom. He gets on the bus holding his small suitcase. He masks his true emotions as the door closes, the brakes hiss, and the Greyhound Senicruiser rolls out of the lot.

The bus is sparsely populated, and Casey claims the backseat and sleeps most of the way. He walks to the YMCA carrying his bag and asks if he can just sleep for an hour or two in the lobby; he tells the attendant that he is a navy veteran returning home on leave. The old man behind the counter tells Casey he has a room he can use free of charge and takes him upstairs. About noon, he wakes, and the elderly man offers him a sandwich and a drink.

His bus back to Westriver arrives just as it's getting dark. He steps off and quickly dashes to the rear of the lot to conceal himself in the bushes. He takes his white garb out of the suitcase, dresses, and conceals his baggage in the foliage. He walks to where he knows Mr. Herman will soon be arriving home. Mr. Herman never altered his habits; he was as punctual as a German officer in a World War II movie.

Casey stands partially concealed by the bushes lining the walk. After a short wait, he hears the sound of footsteps. He braces himself, and as the man passes by, he steps out behind him, balls his fist around the roll of quarters, and gives him a solid shot to the back of his head, right behind his ear. The man is momentarily stunned, and Casey hits him again. He goes down to his knees, and Casey hits him and kicks him in the back.

Certainly, Mr. Herman seems hurt or at least partially incapacitated, and Casey is stunned, when he turns to identify his attacker. Casey catches Mr. Herman's coattail and pulls it up over his head, across his face, and down, effectively blinding him.

Mr. Herman makes a lunge at him, but Casey sidesteps, and his wrestling training comes into play as he leverages the man's strength and flips him into a snowbank. Casey punches him in the side of the neck to keep his head from turning.

There is a stream of vulgarity coming from Mr. Herman's lips like Casey has never heard. Mr. Herman tries to get into his coat pocket, but he can't, because his suspenders are caught on his coat and are keeping him from finding it. That means only one thing to Casey—the man has a gun. Mr. Herman finally finds it and pulls it out. Casey grabs for his hand and covers the gun. He can't believe the little man's strength.

The gun barrel is forced toward him, and now he can see the front of the cylinder. It is an old nine-round .22-caliber revolver, and it's empty. If a shell is under the hammer, it will not fire until the trigger has been pulled nine times.

Mr. Herman gains his footing and rises up on one knee and one foot. Casey whirls him around, and the verbiage continues, with Mr. Herman condemning him and his ancestors and his descendants forever after.

Casey still has his head covered and is not about to give up that advantage. Casey knees Mr. Herman in the face, stunning him as he holds his head down, reaches over him, and catches his fingertips under the little metal levers that lock his suspenders in place.

The struggle produces results. As they work against each other, Mr. Herman's pants begin to fall and hamper his movements. Casey gives him a solid punch to his kidney, which stuns him. He then moves behind him and pulls his drawers down.

Casey moves his hand up the grip of the pistol, but the man refuses to let go. *The bullet—it's the last one that you keep "just in case,"* he thinks as he locks his foot, stands on the pants, and feels inside his coat pocket. He finds the cartridge near the bottom. He thumbs the cylinder open and, after several tries, manages to get it into the cylinder. He closes the action and yanks hard, trying to get the man to let go.

Casey has Mr. Herman bending over, and he gives the pistol another hard jerk. The hammer falls, and there is that ominous split second of silence, and then the pop as the gun fires.

Mr. Herman's body jerks like he's been struck by lightning. The night muffles the shot. There are no lights on in the house, and Casey is silently thankful for that. The man collapses in front of him. He looks like someone kneeling deeply in prayer, and his nose is bleeding.

Casey hurriedly looks around and sees Mr. Herman's wallet. It's worked its way out of his pocket. He picks it up and looks inside. There is a half-inch-thick stack of one-hundred-dollar bills. The wallet is so full it cannot fold.

He takes the banded cash, leaving sixteen dollars, and pushes the wallet just under the edge of the snow along the walk.

Casey looks and sees the bullet wound in Mr. Herman's scrotum. It nipped the end of his penis as well before stopping somewhere in the snow. Casey quickly pockets the gun and the cash, turns, and runs.

Casey realizes his plan just to beat the shit out of the man got a little out of hand. He has to dive into the snow as a police car comes by, its bubble-gum-machine light twirling in the night.

Casey is sweating profusely and breathing audibly. He takes his white coat and trousers off as he approaches the downtown area and places them in the grocery bag he's carrying for that purpose. He checks his watch; it's almost an hour before his bus is to arrive.

He walks a block to the train depot, where there's a steam pipe he knows is hot. He sits on the platform, and his ragged breathing returns to normal. He drops Mr. Herman's driver's license down a storm drain.

Casey sees the Greyhound bus coming through the underpass, and he hurries to the lot to be one of the first in line to get on. He fishes his suitcase out of the snow-covered bushes and goes to the door of the bus.

"Can I please go aboard now, driver? I'm almost frozen to death."

"I'm not supposed to, but yeah, I guess so." He takes Casey's ticket and allows him to board.

\*　　\*　　\*

When the bus pulls into the station in Denver, Casey walks in, finds a booth in the coffee shop, and orders. He takes his time eating and reflecting on what he's done. He decides to change his attitude and be responsible. He watches as a brown bus labeled "US Navy" parks nearby. A crusty old navy PO first class comes in, looks around, and pegs him. He orders coffee and, without asking, slips into Casey's booth with him.

"It's going to be a few hours before we can get downtown to the armory," the PO says. "That's where you'll be getting your physical." They talk, and Casey asks him every question he can think of that has occurred to him since he found out he'd been drafted.

"Will we be able to send our clothes home from here?" Casey asks him.

"Sure. If you pass your physical, you'll be sent on to 'Diego, and its welcome to the hurry-up-and-wait navy," the sailor replies sarcastically.

Casey worries about the gun and wonders if he shouldn't just get rid of it. But he soon decides it's a trophy for all the crap he put up with for twelve of the most awful years of his life. He opens the suitcase and rearranges the clothing so the white suit with the pocket containing the pistol and cash is on the bottom. He hopes no one will expect a volunteer joining the navy to bring a pistol with him to the physical exam.

They finish many cups of coffee and a breakfast, and when the bus arrives, Casey watches Ken and Ron step off.

"Where did you go to, Casey?" Ron asks him. "We thought you missed the bus or at least chickened out."

"I didn't want to get involved with that gushy, teary good-bye stuff, so I took the early bus," Casey replies.

"You missed all the fun. Somebody shot old Herman's balls and the end of his dick off and then shot him in the foot so that he couldn't chase whoever did it. The guy left him to die in the cold."

Casey isn't too amazed at the accuracy of the report. He does, however, manage to fake a look of surprise and ask all the right questions.

They board the navy bus, and the driver delivers them downtown to the armory. Once inside, they're told to strip down to their skivvies.

They're herded into a huge room and greeted by five lines that have already been set up. The doctors and nurses urge them quickly to disrobe and get into line. It's embarrassing for some of the recruits to be naked in front of several hundred other men and have a nurse walk down the rows, giving instructions.

Casey chuckles. The woman standing beside him winks and smiles. He sees her insignia; it contains two snakes, so he knows she is a doctor. She takes a half-dozen folders from the men at the head of the line and allows each in turn to step behind a screen. It affords very little privacy.

He watches the man in front of him start to get an erection. The doctor quietly takes the unsharpened pencil from behind her ear and gives him a gentle whack, and it deflates as quickly as it started.

Casey, Ron, and Ken are through before some of the buses unload. They're addressed by a corpsman standing at the door, who tells them that they can kill a little time sightseeing but should not wander far as they have to be back by four in the afternoon.

The three of them come across a little coffee shop, go inside, and order food and large coffees. They arrive at the auditorium to find a huge assortment of men standing around. One of the corpsmen steps out of the door and blows a police whistle and waves them back inside.

Each recruit is handed either a red or a blue card with his name on it as he finishes with the physical. After finishing, he gets dressed. The three of them meet in the corner near the same door they came in through. The head doctor takes the PA system mike, bumps it against the table, and addresses the room.

"All you recruits have either a red or a blue card. I want all the blue cards to the west side of the auditorium and all the red ones on the east side." There is a general shuffling, and the doctor waits.

"Now then, all of you who have a blue card have failed this portion of the physical. You will be sent back home, and in two weeks, or less you will be inducted into the US Army." Casey's astounded that about half of the recruits have failed to pass the basic physical. Ken and Ron and he slap each other on the back; they will be together through this. "The rest of you, go out the door and board the buses. Give your card to the driver as you board."

There are several buses ahead of them as they disembark at Stapleton airport. They have to wait for the first group to form up.

Casey looks out the side window and sees a US Navy R5-D Skymaster, a large aircraft powered by four radial engines, waiting. The door opens, and the first group boards. The door closes, and one by one the huge radials crank and come to life. The roar is deafening. Their group is herded down the concourse, and when Casey looks in front of him, he sees a brand-new Braniff Airways Boeing 707 aircraft. They board, and when the doors close, his ears pop. The plane is pushed back, and his new adventure begins. They will beat the first group in the R-5 to San Diego.

The engines whine, roar, and blow black smoke. They taxi to the end of the runway, and the aircraft starts to whine more deeply. He can feel the front slowly being forced down. All at once, there is a rush of air as the brakes are released, and he's forced back into his seat. Welcome to the new age of jet aircraft.

The men board three buses that drive across downtown San Diego and through the main gate of the navy base. They divert and go through another gate to the recruit training center. The recruits are told that they can't go to sleep, as reveille is at four hundred hours and is about to happen.

The loudspeakers roar a bugle call, and all at once, the place seems to spring to life. They have to sign in again and are given a card to hold. This one is white and contains only their name.

# Chapter 12

THE men from the three buses are herded into the back of the open-front building, where strong lights shine down. A short, stocky, beaten-up, and mean-looking master chief in an immaculate gold-striped uniform steps out of a black Cadillac and stands, assessing the assembled men.

"My name is Master Chief Engineman C. R. Saltzman. I am your new company commander. I am just one step short of God as far as you are concerned. I want you to form up in six rows starting from the tallest to the shortest. Now move when I talk to you! I don't want to see anything but elbows and assholes. Move, damn you, move!"

There's general confusion as he starts moving men around like he wants them, in columns.

"Now stand with your hands clasped behind you with your knees slightly relaxed. It's called parade rest. You probably won't be standing much at parade rest, as my company always moves. Do you hear me?"

There's a general muttering of "Yes, sir."

"You will answer in unison, 'Sir, yes, sir,' and I will hear it."

The next time there is a full chorus of "Sir, yes, sir."

"I see one hundred men here. I think there will be some of you who do not have the fortitude, the endurance, or the intelligence to graduate in three months. My last company had a 40 percent dropout rate. I hope this one can do better." He walks down the length of the six rows, looking at each man. "Now I am going to teach you how to march. You start out on your left foot when I say forward march and continue until I tell you to halt. Do you understand?"

Once again, there is a chorus of "Sir, yes, sir."

"Atehen hut!"

The men in the columns straighten their backs and assume what each of them thinks is attention.

"For'ard march." The group struggles to get in step, but once going, most of them do.

"Pick up the pace. My company is never outpaced by any other." The pace quickens at the voice count of the chief, and those of shorter stature at the ends of the columns have to almost race to keep in step. They march past rows and rows of old World War II barracks.

"Company halt. Fall out."

Casey sees that some of the recruits are already out of breath. He wonders who will be the first to leave and be pushed back. They're allowed to go inside the barracks and are assigned a bunk and an old .30-06 bolt-action Springfield rifle to carry. They place their personal things on the bunk and form up outside, where they march to the chow hall. They hurriedly eat and march back to the barracks.

Casey looks at the floor. It is spotless. He looks at the rest of the place too; the windows and the toilets are spotless. He wonders who cleans them. He soon finds out the answer to that question. The barracks are never quite clean enough to satisfy the chief or the officers who come by on inspection.

They take their personal belongings, form up outside, and march to the clothing issue. They're only given a rudimentary start for their sea bags and a pair of boots that the chief refers to as boondockers. They're the shoes the recruits will wear out during the three months they are under the tutelage of the old chief. He herds them into the next room to get the primary measurements for their dress uniforms.

"Now, most of you brought personal items with you. If there is something you need to send home, put it into your suitcase, and it will be sent back to your home. You won't be able to wear the clothes you wore here, so I'd volunteer to give them to the navy relief."

Casey thinks about the pistol and wonders how much trouble he'll be in if it's found. He opens his suitcase, and inside with his snowsuit and coat are his changes of clothes. He pulls his clothes out, except for the suit and coat. He turns around to find that the chief is standing behind him.

"What's the trouble, recruit? Can't you make up your mind what to send home to Daddy?" He looks over his shoulder at the contents of the suitcase.

"Sir, no, sir, the suit is my daddy's," Casey replies. "I had to go out and help him dig the car out of the snow, so he could bring me down to the bus station to get here."

"You poor thing. Look here, everyone; he has to send his things home to Daddy. Everyone say aaaaaaww."

There is a torrent of aaaaaaww's.

"Go ahead and mail it back, but you are going to donate the rest of it to the navy relief, aren't you?"

"Yes, sir." He keeps the suit and his winter coat.

"What?" The chief jumps back.

"Sir, yes, sir." The storekeeper behind the counter is stifling a grin. He's already gone to a typewriter and typed out a label; he affixes it to Casey's little suitcase. "Sign here," he says. Casey takes the pen and signs.

"What are you waiting for, White? Do you think the whole company can wait around for you to get nostalgic? Drop and give me twenty-five push-ups now!" Casey drops to the floor and quickly does his push-ups.

"Too soon, White, give me twenty-five more."

Casey again does his push-ups.

"Too soon, White, give twenty-five more."

Casey continues on and sets the record for five hundred pushups before the chief allows him to stand. He could have done more with a little breathing room, but he chooses to slow down to see whether the man will get off his back. He feels the chief grab him by the collar. The chief lifts him and herds him around to the front of the now assembled men as he catches his breath. "Recruit White has set an impressive mark for the rest of you to attain. He's done five hundred. That will be the mark for the rest of you to attain. Company, atehen hut! For'ard march. Now double time."

\* \* \*

The first week melts into a tightly structured regimen of marching, eating, cleaning, and going to classes. On Friday of each week, a recruit is called into the company commander's office for individual counseling. The whole unit never sees the recruit who's sent back for whatever reason. When the company comes back into the barracks after one of these counseling sessions, they find an empty rack.

The next Monday morning, they go to health and personal fitness classes. The teacher is a corpsman. He holds out a package and asks the class what it is, and he then points to a recruit. The man responds by telling him that it's a rubber. The corpsman corrects him by telling him, "This is a condom, and we will from here on refer to this personal item for the prevention of transmittable social diseases as a condom."

Casey sits listening and remembers his supply hidden under the dash of his car, which is still parked in a snowdrift in the front yard. He makes a mental note to himself to remove them when he's home again.

The next week they learn some other things, but there's always marching and physical training, Casey loves it. The chief sometimes gets down on someone personally, and sometimes he gets down on the whole company.

During the fourth week, Casey is called into the office for his counseling. The chief closes the door, steps up to him, and closely scrutinizes his face. He's covered with scabs where he has tried to scrape off his peach fuzz with his navy-issue safety razor.

"Son, you don't even have peach fuzz. Are you sure you're the age stated on your paperwork?" the chief inquires sternly.

"Yes, sir, I was drafted." He forgets the second "sir" in his reply, but the chief lets it slide.

"White, I'm going to go out on a limb and tell you I'm concerned that you are going to cut yourself and bleed to death some morning. What I order you to do is to let no other man in this outfit know what we are about to agree to.

"I will require you to continue to shave every morning just like the rest of the company, but you won't have a blade in the razor. I will continue to inspect you closely, and if any peach fuzz shows up, I will make you shave it off. When this happens, there will be some punishment also. Be a good actor, White."

"Sir, yes sir," Casey replies quietly. Chief Saltzman then leans back in his chair and assumes a more casual attitude.

"Tell me, White, where did you learn to do push-ups? I look at you and can tell you don't meet the outward appearance of an athlete or weight lifter."

"I worked in a feed store unloading grain. I unloaded about two rail cars a week during the winter and probably one every other week in the summer. I worked at the store for five years. I heard the wrestling coach say once that I was an ectomorph. I didn't know whether to be mad or not.

"It doesn't matter, because I didn't like any aspect of wrestling anyway. If I'm going to smell someone's armpit, I want it to be a young lady's."

With that remark, the chief stifles a grin. "I like an athlete, White. Now go and keep your part of our bargain." Casey walks out of the office with a newfound respect for the man.

\*   \*   \*

The next Friday, the company is taken to the rifle range. It's almost noon when they arrive, and scores of other companies have already fired the M-1 Garand. They assemble in rows, and the man at the front of the row takes the weapon lying on the pad in front of him, inserts a clip of ammunition, and fires prone.

The proctors have already adjusted the weapons with the correct elevation and windage. After an individual fires the rifle, he is moved up to the butts to pull the target for the man behind him. Casey assumes his station and waits as the group fires. The targets drop, are marked with patches put over the holes, and are raised for the next man.

When it's Casey's turn, he stands at attention. At the command, he reaches down and picks up the M-1 to load. He allows his hand to touch some of the barrel, and it's immediately burned and blistered. He cannot cry out, so he grits his teeth and continues. He loads and fires at the target.

On the way to the butts to pull the targets for the next group, the men returning are all asking, "Who is number sixteen?" He doesn't know why they're asking about his number. He sheepishly admits he's number sixteen. All at once, every one of those returning want to shake his hand.

He pulls that target for the next man, and when he returns to the line, he asks the corpsman for a Band-Aid. The man looks at his hand, gives him a square of cotton gauze covered with ointment, and tapes it to the side of his hand.

That night at mail call, the chief unexpectedly shows up and takes his turn distributing the company mail. He usually went home after four in the afternoon. When the end of the alphabet comes and Zymenski receives his mail, Casey can't imagine why there are no letters for him. His mom had been religiously writing him at least twice weekly.

"White, front and center!" The chief stands up with two letters in his hand. "I want to know why you screwed up on the range today."

Casey is dumbfounded. He thought he had done very well. He looks, and the chief is suppressing a grin. He hands Casey his mail, and Casey turns to leave.

"White! I told you front and center!" Casey quickly returns and stands at attention in front of the chief. Now the whole company is looking at him and wondering what is going on.

"White had only a single round outside the bulls-eye today, and it was close. I want to know why they weren't all in the bulls-eye, White."

"Sir, I must have misjudged the first round; I picked up the weapon, and it was so hot it burned my hand." The chief looks down and, for the first time, notices the bandage on Casey's hand.

"Let's see that." Casey extends his hand, and the chief carefully removes the bandage. The quarter-sized blister has popped, and a piece of dead skin hangs loosely. "Why didn't you report this, White?" he asks.

"Sir, the corpsman told me not to, sir." The chief looks him in the eye, stands up, and turns to leave.

"This man is a credit to the company, but don't you go and get a big head now, White. Gunnery is only one little aspect of your training. Now it's almost lights out." Men scurry to their bunks.

\* \* \*

Casey is sitting in the barber chair on his two-month anniversary of being a recruit. He watches as a car pulls up and an officer takes Chief Saltzman aside and talks to him for a minute. Casey makes a mental note of it as he continues to get his hair cut with the rest of the company.

The next morning after chow, they're marching to an academic class on naval history and tradition. The company files into the room, but Casey is stopped from entering by the chief. The chief says, in a lowered voice, "Go get into that navy sedan and let me know when you get back." The chief points to a sedan parked next to the curb.

*What now?* Casey thinks. He gets in as instructed and doesn't ask questions.

The sedan leaves the base with him and two more recruits in the backseat. They drive back to the rifle range. Marines are firing when they arrive, and they have to wait for a portion of the range to become available. Casey is handed an M-1 that is cool to the touch and a bandoleer of cartridges.

"Follow the lieutenant out to the far side of the range and await further orders," the range officer says.

Casey does as he's told and joins a group of about a dozen men.

"You men exhibited exceptional marks in your initial round of training with the M-1. Now it's time to find out if it was a fluke or not. You will all fire eight rounds from each of the primary positions: sitting, standing, and kneeling. You will be given three tries to achieve your best score. That is seventy-two rounds, sailors. Ammunition is expensive, so make every round count. Now take your positions, one position apart." The three of them assume their positions, stand at parade rest, and wait.

A Marine Corps weapons carrier pulls up. Four marine recruits jump out and double-time up to their positions. Casey doesn't recognize the shoulder insignia of the Marine Corps officers waiting there, but he knows they are high-ranking. They wait for a little longer, and two black navy sedans appear.

A captain, a commander, a lieutenant, and a CPO driver step out of each of them. They mount the hill to the firing positions. There is an air of festivity among them, and Casey sees some money being exchanged. The two chief petty officers stand, each holding a wad of money. He watches the bravo flag being raised, and a siren sounds.

"Ready on the right. Ready on the left. Commence firing." The range officer yells into the mike.

Casey thumbs the clip into the rifle, draws in a slow breath, and wiggles his ass and fires. He fires from all positions and returns to complete the next set. The range master clears the range, and the second set of firing commences, and then a third. He notices that after each round, a new target is applied to the lift. They wait, and in a moment, several marines come running with the targets in hand.

"Step back and relax, White," a voice says from behind Casey, startling him. "I'm sure you did your best." He turns to find the chief there. Casey assumed the chief deliberately had not told Casey he was coming to keep the pressure off him; he wanted his company personnel to shine.

All at once, all eyes turn to Casey. One of the navy captains comes toward him, and Casey automatically comes to attention when he sees his company commander doing so.

"Chief, who do you have here, Annie Oakley in drag?" the captain asks.

That's all it takes; a broad grin breaks out on his chief's face. The officer holds the targets up and shows them to him.

"We have never in the past ten years had a recruit shoot a perfect score. Now we have a man do it three times in a single day. Is there anything else you'd like to show us, recruit?"

"Sir, I like to hip shoot, Captain, sir."

"One sir is enough for me, son. I'm impressed. What do you mean hip shoot?" Casey looks around and sees the other recruits getting back into their vehicles and departing from the range.

"May I have a fifty-yard target, please?" As soon as he says this, two of the men pulling targets run off down the side. They disappear into the butts, and a new target appears.

"Ready on the right. Ready on the left. Commence firing." Casey thumbs the clip into the M-1, relaxes, wiggles his ass, places the weapon at his hip, and fires. He feels the reassuring bounce and counts until he hears the metal clip make its ping as it ejects out onto the ground. After the whistle blows, he lays the weapon on the ground as he watches the target drop from sight. One of the target pullers comes running with it in his hand and hands it to the captain.

"Damn, son, you really are Annie Oakley," the captain says.

Casey looks at the target and sees that he has put two of the rounds right at the ring on the inside of the bulls-eye and the rest well inside the black. His chief turns around, and the chief behind him hands him another bill. The lieutenant standing beside him is still in awe of what he's just done.

"Son, is there anything else you'd like to impress us with?" the range officer asks. Out of the corner of his eye, Casey spots three gulls in flight heading in their general direction and holds his hand out.

"One more clip, please?"

The officer hands him one, and Casey takes the rifle from the ground and waits. There's an air of expectancy as they have no idea what he's up to.

The gulls continue in and then switch course and fly parallel midway behind the range in back of the fifty-yard butts. They look small to the casual observer, but to Casey, each one is just another white target.

He thumbs the clip into the weapon, places the rifle against his hip, and fires three times. There are three explosions of feathers followed by dead silence, shocked expressions, short breaths, dropped jaws, and the realization that he got all three of them.

"Christ, son, we don't shoot seagulls!" The range officer reaches over his shoulder and takes the weapon from him and then continues watching the feathers floating to the ground. There's nothing but surprised expressions looking first at him and then back at the falling feathers.

"You hit a bird in flight, with a bullet, at that distance, without aiming? I could just make them out, son. How the hell do you do that?" the range officer asks.

The only one whose jaw isn't dropped is his chief, and he just stands there grinning. "I think it's time to get back to the training center," Chief Saltzman says. The navy captains are still looking at the men running out to where the birds fell. One turns and nods to the chief. Casey knows he's impressed someone. He doesn't know why he's out here, but he knows they got their money's worth.

When they sit in the chief's Cadillac and both doors are closed, the chief laughs openly without explaining himself. Casey sees several bills wadded up and stuck in the chief's pocket.

\*      \*      \*

On the last Friday, just before graduation he's called to medical and his hand is checked again. He finds a scale in the hallway, steps on it, and realizes he has put on twenty-five pounds in three months. The dress field is all pomp and ceremony. Colors are presented, and men march as about a thousand proud parents who found a way to attend observe the field.

Casey draws a school at the Great Lakes training center and has a week of leave. They're assigned to a bus that will take them home by the most direct route. It only takes about fifteen minutes, and the bus is as silent as a tomb. Casey's mind is racing, and he doesn't know how long it will take, but soon he'll be able to tell his parents all about his adventure. He watches as row after row of orange trees flash by like rows of corn in Iowa.

# Chapter 13

THEY have to change to another bus in Salt Lake, and as they leave the city, they head south, cross the city, and then go up a long, sweeping curve into the mountains. It is the same boring ride up the canyon, but this time, he is excited to be coming home. It's a bright sunny day when the bus pulls into the Westriver bus station.

Casey is the last of the three of them to use the phone in the bus station to call home. When he picks up, the voice at the telephone exchange isn't Arlene's, but the woman who answers recognizes his voice.

"Hi, Casey, I thought you went to California?"

"Yeah, it was for boot camp. I'm home on leave now. I have a week before I have to go to Illinois for school," he tells her.

She connects him, and Casey doesn't hear the second click, so he knows the operator is still listening. His mom is really happy to hear from him. She doesn't drive, so she can't come get him.

All at once, there's a reunion in the bus station. Ron's mom must have broken all the speed limits coming to get her boy. She offers Casey a ride home, and he readily accepts. He tells his mom he has a ride and will be home shortly.

When Casey arrives home, he pulls his sea bag out of the car and walks to the front door. His mom starts to hug him but then steps back in amazement at the change in her little boy. He's a man now, and her eyes glaze over looking at him in a repeat of the scene that plays out that day when Casey's dad returns home from work. Casey hasn't seen his dad cry but once before, and he's genuinely impressed it is happening now. His dad disappears upstairs and returns with the suitcase Casey sent home.

"I didn't know if I should open it, so I just waited until you came home. What do you want to do with it?"

"No, Dad, it's just the white outfit I wore sometimes going hunting." Casey remembers the gun and the money. There's no way he can resolve that little dilemma now. "Just go ahead and put it back with the rest of my stuff." He wonders how he'd ever be able to explain it to them.

Casey's dad returns the suitcase to the attic. They sit down, and as his dad is pouring him a cup of coffee, there's a knock on the door. Casey answers it, and there stands Arlene. Now there are more tears and hugs.

"Come in, gal, and have a cup of coffee." Casey's dad pulls up a chair for her, all the time looking and wondering who she is.

"I'm sorry, Dad. This is Arlene Spencer. She's a telephone operator at the exchange."

"Mr. and Mrs. White, your boy Casey has done me more favors than I can count. He's shoveled my walks, mowed my grass, raked my leaves, and cleaned my gutters. When he worked at the general store, he'd go pick up something for my lunch if I couldn't get away from the switchboard. He's a good boy, and I sure miss having him around." It's clear what she wants, and Casey knows he'll have to make an excuse to see her.

"Dad, Mom, I need to go and see my friends. I sure miss them. Is it all right if I just go and—"

"Yes, Casey, we know you're just bustin' to tell all your friends about what you've been doing," says Casey's dad.

"I've got to get back to work soon, Casey. Come and see me before you leave town, okay?" Arlene asks him.

"Sure, Arlene, I'll stop and talk after I go and see the postmaster to thank him for what he did for us."

Casey finds a pair of jeans and a shirt to change into, but they're too small. There's no way he'll wear those again. The old chief was right.

"Dad, I need to borrow—"

Casey's dad is standing in the doorway to his room, holding a pair of jeans and a shirt with a sly grin on his face. "I don't know if they'll fit you, but I know you aren't going to get into the ones you left behind."

Casey tries them, and they're a little high water but fit him in the waist. *It's only for a couple of days,* he thinks. He kisses Bella good-bye and jumps into his old Ford. The motor grinds once and then clicks; the battery is dead. He thinks, *Maybe I should just sell it.* He lets the decision hang, goes inside, and borrows the family car.

Arlene is waiting for him on her front porch. He pulls into the driveway so that the car can't be seen from the street, and looks around to see if anyone is watching. He runs onto her porch, and she almost melts in his arms. They hurry to the bedroom, discarding clothing as they go. They make love and finally have to come up for air.

"Casey, I know our lives are going separate ways. You'll be gone, and I won't have my little stallion any longer. However, all isn't lost. My ex-husband contacted me. He's been celibate for a whole year and wants to go to marriage counseling and get back together. We think we can rebuild our marriage. I think it is a good thing, and I'm going to go for it."

"Good for you, Arlene. I've always wanted life to hand you something besides leftovers. Why don't you do the same thing Johnny promised me and send me a Christmas card each year to let me know how things are going for you? Send the first one to the folks, and they'll forward it to me."

"Casey, that's a darling idea. Now let's see if the navy taught you anything; you need to mow my grass again." He sits on the side of the bed and touches the skin and body that fascinate him. She wiggles in anticipation. They make it last as long as they can, and afterward, they just lie there and talk.

"The police conducted a lengthy investigation into the attack on old man Herman and came up empty," Arlene tells him. "The final thinking is that there must have been a sexual pervert hobo on the train that stopped who picked him as a target of opportunity. I listened to the surgeon telling the sheriff that Mr. Herman lost his left testicle, the end of his penis, and the big toe on his right foot. I guess my thinking someone should shoot his balls off almost came to fruition.

"There's something going on at the store that the town can't find out about either.

"Officer Peters and his wife pulled up in front of the police station in his pickup one Friday evening to collect his paycheck and drove off with all their belongings behind them in a trailer. Someone else had to work the night shift.

"Belinda still comes and visits occasionally and spends the night when Johnny has to be out of town for some kind of schooling or training. He's taking some kind of off-campus course and will, over a stretch of time, earn his degree in veterinary medicine. It's a heavy load for a graduating senior to be taking college courses, but he's doing well. They're living in a little cottage on state property. The high school is allowing Belinda to finish and graduate. She and seven other girls have been told to wear loose clothing and not to make a big deal out of being pregnant."

They give one another a final long kiss, and Casey decides to go talk to the postmaster. He catches him leaving the post office, and the two of them go to the drugstore and order Cokes. The postmaster tells Casey that the justice department is investigating the town's selective service board, and that he has given them all the information he has. There should be some major changes coming.

Casey returns home and spends the night talking with his family. His brother seems almost like a stranger. For the last two years of their lives before Casey was recruited, his brother had worked a schedule opposite Casey's, and Casey hadn't seen him except on rare occasions when they met at the table for a meal. They would have been closer if Casey hadn't been the wild one who ran the streets all hours of the night.

His brother asks questions about the navy. He tells Casey he knows the same thing that happened to Casey could happen to him, and he wants to be ready. Casey tells him to go and make friends with the postmaster and have him keep him abreast of the draft board's actions.

Casey sleeps in for the first time he can remember since joining the navy. The next morning, he drives his car to the service station after his dad gives him a jump, and he has Stephen install a new battery. He leaves the garage still feeling like a stranger in his own hometown. He knows why and also knows that he can't do a darn thing about it. He thinks that perhaps in time he'll find something that will help.

Casey eats supper with his folks and announces he isn't going to stay in town any longer as he can't stand it. His parents both give him the "we understand" look. That night he goes to the bus station, cashes in his ticket, and then goes on to the train station, where he purchases another, more expensive, one—but this time, he'll ride in style.

There's only one change of trains, and he'll be in Chicago. His brother comes to see him off this time, and it turns out to be only a family affair. He calls Arlene, and her soon-to-be husband is visiting. He calls Belinda and tells her good-bye, as he does to Ken and Ron. He can't think of anyone else he needs to call.

The train car lurches as the engines strain against the load, and the train begins moving forward. He takes his carry-on and moves to a seat. *At least this time I'll be seeing a different part of southern Wyoming.*

When they cross the back of the state cattle facility, there is a station wagon parked almost against the crossing gate. The horn of the train blares a warning, and the horn of the car answers. Casey sees Belinda and Johnny sitting inside, waving and yelling good-bye. That helps pull him out of his melancholy.

Time and vistas pass, and he becomes nostalgic. He wonders if he'll ever see Naomi again or find out about her and their baby. He knows Naomi's mother is pregnant with what is probably his child. Belinda is carrying his child as well.

Casey counts on his fingers and comes up with a count of women who are carrying his offspring. He decides that a long way from Westriver is where he will settle.

*Perhaps, if it's good to me, I might just make the navy my home for the next twenty years.* Thinking back on what he's done, he wonders if he could, in fact, be a faux Alfeta, what with all the changes he's initiated in their gene pool.

He waits for his sea bag to materialize and then walks into Union Station. Inside is a huge sign over the stairwell: "All Naval personnel going to the Great Lakes Naval Training Center go to lower level." When he goes down, he finds the floor filled with more sailors going to the same place. He buys a ticket and boards the subway. After it reaches the city limits, it becomes a surface train. It stops in Waukegan, and he begins a new chapter of his life.

"Welcome to Great Lakes Naval Training Center, sailor; now get a cover, and don't let me catch you uncovered again, or you'll be placed on report," the gate sentry hollers, and Casey is quickly brought back to reality. He's just a lowly E-2 machinist's mate fireman apprentice on his way to school.

When he checks into the modern four-story brick-and-block barracks, the first-class tells him to sign in for the watch. He's early and they're the ones who stand colors instead of watches. This means he will be bringing the flag down in the evening and putting it up in the morning.

* * *

The fourth weekend after arriving, Casey has the duty. He can go anywhere he wants on the base but can't leave it. He decides to do a little sightseeing. He takes his camera and heads out, wandering around the base and the lakefront. He finds a pier with a submarine docked alongside.

Above his head is a sign posted warning that no photography is allowed. He looks for a long time. It appears to be like any other World War II submarine he's ever seen in pictures. Perhaps it's a little smaller, but for the most part, it's the same design. He wonders why in the world the navy needs a World War II submarine here in 1960. He knows it is active because it's flying a Union Jack.

\*   \*   \*

On Sunday, Casey decides to skip chapel, and after the library opens, he approaches the woman at the desk. "Do you have any reference books on submarines?" he asks.

"Specifically the one tied up at the reserve piers?" She smiles at his question. Apparently, he isn't the only one who's seen the boat.

"Go pull the red book from the center of the naval history reference section and look it up." He finds the volume she indicates, takes it to a table, and opens it.

In the back, in a well-thumb-printed section, he finds what he's looking for. The United States was worried about the German navy sneaking a submarine into the Great Lakes during World War II. Subsequently, three smaller freshwater submarines were built and kept almost unknown to the general public. At one time, all three patrolled from here. After the war, all but one was decommissioned, and the remaining one is still manned by reserves. It is the USS *Mero* (SS 378).

These submarines were diesel electric, but now all the new boats are nuclear and are massive. They are large enough they couldn't even think of coming into the lakes. But why would anyone want them to? Casey closes the reference book and looks for something else to occupy his time.

Back at the barracks, there is a note on Casey's bunk asking him to contact the duty chief. His mail has caught up with him.

He scrutinizes the last letter; there's no return address on the envelope, and it's stamped in red several times by the post office. The sender didn't know his correct address, and the navy postal service has tracked him down. He leaves it for last. The letter from his mom is long and newsy.

115

Eventually, Casey opens the last one. Belinda's neat, long handwriting says,

> "I hope all is well with you. Thank you for everything. The university accepted Johnny's full-time application, and we will be moving there just as soon as we graduate."

> As ever,
> Belinda

\*    \*    \*

During the final week of school, Casey opens his envelope and finds he's been assigned to the Naval Auxiliary Air Station at Kingsville, Texas. *What in the world does a seagoing sailor, a machinist's mate, do at a naval air station?* It causes more questions than answers. *Now the hard part; I have to choose to take leave or proceed directly to my next duty station.*

Against the advice of the crusty old chief in command of his class, he declines to take leave. He'll proceed directly to the air station. It's one more trip on the rattler train, another on a bus to the airport, and a wait to be allowed to board the aircraft. He's happy to see it's another 707. It's a first-class way to fly.

\*    \*    \*

Finally, the door opens and the passengers are allowed to board. It's the same euphoric takeoff that he's grown to enjoy, although some of the passengers are white-knuckled until after the aircraft levels out.

He naps and eats lunch, and later, the aircraft is the first to land at the brand-new airport in Houston, Texas. What awaits him is almost impossible for him to comprehend. It's still ninety-two degrees and 89 percent humidity. It's after nine in the evening.

He can't believe he's traveling in dress blues—wool dress blues, to top it off.

After he changes planes and arrives in Corpus Christi, Casey learns his ticket includes a bus ticket to Kingsville, and he'll have to find his own way out to the air station. Sitting and sweating in the non-air-conditioned bus terminal in Kingsville, he encounters three other sailors going to the base. They pool their funds and ride together in a taxi to the main gate.

\*　　\*　　\*

While standing next to a desk in the administration building the following morning, he looks at a mystified personnel clerk waiting for an answer.

"What the hell is a machinist's mate doing at an air station?" He looks up at Casey.

"I think I'm supposed to be going to public works and work in the garage there." Casey lies, hoping that it might at least let him work with his hands around equipment. A chief at the rear of the room speaks up.

"All unassigned lower-rated men are going to the crash crew for now." Casey knows what that means; the "for now" thing means he is being given a shit job nobody else wants. The second-class aviation electrician at the terminal spots him, and his eyes light up.

"Oh man, another warm body!" He's allowed to take his things and get settled in the non-air-conditioned WWII barracks.

\*　　\*　　\*

The following morning, dressed in dungarees, he heads back to the terminal, where he's introduced to his section leader and the chief responsible for the crash section.

Life dissolves into days of cleaning the trucks, drilling, sitting on the hard stand, and watching the boot camp aviators pull some of the most stupid things man can imagine. You really have to have it mentally on the ball to pass all the courses to become a naval aviator, but it doesn't mean you have any common sense.

An exciting break comes when an occasional pair of Marine Corps F8U Crusaders put in an appearance to do a touch-and-go just to impress the boot camp aviators who are out there. It's a beautiful after-dark takeoff that really impresses, what with twenty-five feet of fire coming out of the back on afterburner.

\* \* \*

Casey reports to work the following morning and is called into the office of the chief.

"White, I just lost one of my men, and the command allows me to replace him. Would you like to join the maintenance group?"

"Does a bear do it in the woods? Yes, sir!"

"Okay then, you'll have to work with your group today just like normal, and tomorrow you'll be part of my men," the grizzled old chief says to him.

He's the only man who has been picked out of the crash crew in the past months. Usually if the chief wanted a good man, he would go and beg one from one of the squadrons.

\* \* \*

The following morning after reveille, the maintenance chief shows up in the crash shack to pick him up. The chief purposely had not told anybody because Casey and he knew the section leader would go crying to the division officer, and usually he won. He didn't win this time.

Casey finds himself officially on the maintenance group. The nice part of the deal is that he doesn't have to stand a watch overnight at the crash shack. He has his nights free. During those odd weekends, he can get off, he goes to the little Methodist church in downtown Kingsville.

It is a lively group that readily accepts him, and best of all there are no Alfetas around to give him grief. He strikes up personal friendships with several girls and quickly finds out which ones can set aside any remaining abstinence issues. Southern women can be so accommodating.

A week later, in the afternoon, the secretary of the air boss delivers a priority envelope to his chief. It has Casey's name and "priority" written across it.

"White, look inside and let me know what's going on." He hands Casey the letter and waits for him to read it.

"I'm supposed to report to the Special Warfare Training Building at Naval Air Station Corpus Christi in the morning, Chief. It says I'm under TAD orders and not to discuss my orders with anyone."

"Damn, just when I get a team I can rely on, they tear it down. I'm sorry, Casey; I guess it has priority. Go ahead, check with admin and see what they know."

Casey makes his way to admin. What they know is that Casey has to be ready to go to Naval Air Station Corpus Christi the following morning, or as soon as he can get there. It's up to him how as administration isn't sure they have to provide transportation. He decides he will just catch the first jitney bus from the base and go by Greyhound to Corpus Christi.

*Chapter*
**14**

THE Greyhound bus to Corpus Christi is lightly loaded early in the morning, and after waiting for the bus to the air station, Casey finds himself showing his orders to a gate sentry.

"Wait here a minute." The sentry steps inside the little booth and uses the telephone. When he hears the voice on the other end, he seemingly comes to attention and listens attentively. "Just wait right here, and there will be a vehicle here to pick you up," he says to Casey.

True to his word, a marine lieutenant dressed in camouflage uniform stops his jeep only long enough for Casey to load himself and his AWOL bag, and they roar off toward the far end of the base. The officer drives them around the south side of the air station and stops at a gate, and they have to produce identification.

Casey's name is checked against a list. They're waved through, and they proceed to a small compound comprising five buildings pretty well dispersed in the overgrown mesquite. He stops the vehicle and dismounts.

"Sailor, I'm sorry for all this, but we have top-secret orders, and we're a little spooked by anyone new to the group. Come in and meet the rest of us."

Casey dismounts and follows him into the largest of the buildings, where several men of various ranks sit around looking at him as he enters. A Marine Corps captain is standing at the front of the room. Casey chooses a desk and sits down.

"We've done in-depth background checks of all of you. What I want is for all of you to stand and hold your right hand up and swear. Repeat after me: I swear that none of the information imparted to me by this activity will ever be divulged based on national security."

They all follow the order.

"White, I have your range results. If you're as good as you promise to be, I think you'll make a very nice addition to us."

The mystery is compounding now, and Casey's really getting interested in finding out just what they're asking him to do.

"Perhaps we need to clear that up right now," the captain says. He motions the group out, and they follow him to the edge of the area where they're looking down a cleared path about one hundred feet wide and about two hundred yards long. There are various silhouette targets and animal cutouts set up all the way down the length, and it ends up in a huge earth berm with a windsock on it.

"White, shoot me a deer." The marine captain tosses Casey an M1 Garand from where he's standing in the back of a pickup truck.

"Out there?" Casey looks down the corridor, his hands still smarting from catching the rifle.

"Yes, there is a deer out there."

Casey is momentarily overwhelmed. He spots the silhouette of a deer and thinks about the distance. He can see a windsock at the far end, and he adds slight windage to his estimate.

"Now?" he asks the officer. The assembled men are all watching him.

"Yes, you go ahead."

He raises the rifle to his shoulder after checking to see if it is loaded, takes aim, and fires. There is a *whang* as the bullet contacts a heavy metal surface.

"I'm impressed," says the captain. "Go ahead and find something else to kill out there."

Casey looks at the silhouettes of men and various other animals, large and small. He knocks them over one by one until he's shot up about half of the length of the range from the deer. He reloads the M1 and continues hip shooing. One by one, the targets topple. He quickly uses fifty-six rounds of ammunition.

The wide-eyed captain seems to be pleased with his shooting skills. The man is sitting on the hood of the vehicle now. He slides down and reaches into a cooler. He pulls out two beers and heaves them into the air while saying, "Don't let them hit the ground."

Casey hurriedly jams a new clip into the breech and hip shoots the beer cans. They explode in a frothy white haze.

"I think you probably qualify," says the captain. "Most of these bozos didn't even come close to the beer, and I got to drink it on the way home. How many rounds do you have left?"

"Six, sir. I only fired the two after I reloaded."

"Find something else out there to shoot; I don't want to take a partial clip back to the armory."

Casey steps to where the officer is standing behind the vehicle and places the M-1 over the hood. He takes a moment to orient himself and picks out some targets at the far end of the range. He fires up to his three last rounds and then carefully takes aim at the slender staff holding up the windsock.

He fires twice and hears the rounds contact the pole. He fires again, and the windsock does a slow bend and is blown over to the ground. Behind him, he hears the captain curse softly under his breath.

"Damn, two hundred twenty-five yards and open sights; this kid is something else." They then return to the classroom.

"I'm going to give you the skinny about why you're out here," says the captain. "As sworn into the military, we promise to defend the Constitution with our full vigor. Now what I want to find out is if you want to go to one step further and help your president. The reason you've been picked is that you are not participants of any existing department, covert group, Special Forces, army or navy intelligence, UDT, FBI, CIA, or anything like that.

"The president wants a small elite group of men who have no ties to Washington or any political or other military security or intelligence group. You're what he wants. There is a need for us to accomplish quickly a certain mission for the president, and for now only he and a very small handful of men know of our mission."

Now he has Casey's ear. It's the thing kids dream about but never get to see or participate in except in their fantasies or the movies.

"We have another week to prepare before we deploy. We are on rather short notice. If any of you do not want to or think he cannot accomplish this mission, you're allowed to back out now, and nothing will be held against you."

He looks at the room of men, and silence rules with all the men looking at each other. "I take it, then, that we are committed to a mission." He stands and shakes the hand of every man.

\* \* \*

The following week consists of a morning run of five miles, calisthenics, and target practice with a variety of weapons, basic hand-to-hand fighting and a trip as a group to the galley to eat. They don't talk to anyone while there and leave as soon as they finish. They are, however, allowed to eat all they want. Casey notes that like him, none of them smoke.

Back at the compound, they study maps, including the topography of Cuba, a quite detailed map of downtown Havana, and maps of several other large Cuban cities. When the map first opens, there are a lot of questions. It will be a quick in-and-out to rescue a hostage, and then they'll all return to their former duty stations. The officer presents information about conditions in Cuba.

"There is major infighting still going on between the revolutionaries and the remnants of the old Batista regime. The hills are full of bandits, attacking the peasants as quickly as they will attack an armed column of soldiers. Communism has taken over there, and most of the world's countries have cut staff in the embassies to a bare minimum, if they remain open at all.

"The Russian embassy is fortified and has been expanded, and it is a popular gathering place for the Cuban soldiers of the

Communist revolution. The American government does not know from day to day where Castro is, but they know he's controlling things. Recently, there have been reports of shiploads of Russian soldiers and their equipment being unloaded at the piers."

The morning of the day they're going to deploy, Casey is pulled aside and told he is going to have to do something about his blond hair. A young Spanish woman carrying a heavy suitcase steps out of a sedan, and he is directed to follow her into an auxiliary building. The rest of the group continues preparations for deployment.

"Please be seated in the chair," she tells him in heavily Cuban-accented English. He sits, and his hair and eyebrows are dyed black. Another kind of dye is applied to his scalp and skin, and he instantly turns brown where she applies it. *Instant suntan,* Casey thinks.

"Disrobe, and I will do the rest of your body."

*I don't believe this is necessary, but who am I to question.* He quickly drops the rest of his clothes and sits up on the table. She starts applying the dye to his skin.

"Lie on your stomach and let me do your back first." He complies. She applies the dye and works down over his body, even doing the bottoms of his feet. "Now please turn over." Again, he complies. He's okay until he begins to rise to the occasion. She looks down at him and smiles.

"I do not have an opportunity like this often," she says. She quickly locks the door and disrobes almost in one swift move. She's on him in a minute and moves herself against him, trying for her own pleasure. She remains there for a moment, enjoying her accomplishment. Afterward, she wipes his sweaty body dry.

Casey wonders if he has invested in someone else's gene pool as he wore no condom. It took her only a few minutes—talk about a quickie. She doesn't get dressed until she completely dyes all of his body. She has to turn him back over and reapply.

"Thank you, and that's for good luck, please," she says, smiling. "Here are some pills; take them if you become nauseated or sick from the side effects of the dye." They dress, and Casey returns to the group in the assembly building.

The group makes fun of him for being the only blue-eyed brown-skin among them. They're issued green camouflage uniforms. The collars contain a flap under them to affix uniform insignia.

After they dress and close up their personal gear, they load aboard a weapons carrier, drive to a waiting US Navy R5D, and fly to an air force base somewhere in the Northeast. It's cool, but they aren't issued any cold-weather uniforms. They're held in a remote area overnight and loaded onto an air force EC-121 Super Constellation. They wake up when the aircraft lands somewhere in Switzerland where they are shuttled off to a small nondescript building behind the main terminal.

They are given food and drink but have to wait. In time, another vehicle comes and picks them up. Now Casey can say he's been to Switzerland, if only for a few steps from one aircraft to another. The next one is a Swiss Air Boeing 707.

They're placed in the very back rows of the aircraft, and no one sits near them. The stewardess serves the same meals the other passengers are eating, but the military team members have to consume them from behind a hastily erected curtain. At the end of the trip, the captain comes on the speaker and in perfect English announces that they're about to land in Cuba. He then repeats it in Swiss and French.

As the rear door opens, they're directed from the aircraft into a waiting limousine and are driven to the French embassy. They're quartered in what Casey determines must be the attic of the huge, old building.

\*     \*     \*

The following morning, after breakfast, they assemble in what appears to be a ballroom and wait there. A Marine Corps captain comes in and introduces himself.

"I'm Captain Harold King, USMC. I will be your commanding officer during this exercise."

*How long has this little exercise been planned and why is it only now being implemented?* Casey thinks, knowing he'll never find out.

Captain King is a tall, athletic-looking marine of Latin descent with the neck of a linebacker. Casey wonders if he played academy football.

The captain continues. "We're down here to escort a VIP out of the country and return him to his home. This may or may not be a difficult mission. You have been selected for this mission according to various skills you have. I need to have each one of you stand and give me your name and a brief description of the skills you bring to this group. I've read most of your information sheets, and I need to get to know each one of you personally." He then points to the chief.

"I'm Master Chief Ordnanceman Dale Gordon. I deal in explosives, ordnance, gunnery, and handheld weapons. Anything naval that goes boom, I've probably dealt with it. This is my fourth mission of this type."

He was the only other one of the group that had to get his hair touched up with black dye after the woman did Casey. For a man of his age, the chief is in surprisingly good shape. He worked out with the rest of them during the fit-up for the exercise.

"I'm PFC Larry Brown, USMC. I'm a specialist in map reading and have signal skills in Morse code. I'm qualified on most models of the radios, the navy and the Marine Corps use. I'm qualified with most handheld firearms used by the military." He takes his seat. Brown is exactly that—he looks almost like an American Indian, perhaps mixed with some Caucasian blood. He is as muscular looking as the rest of the marines here.

"I'm PFC Albert Mendoza. My family immigrated to the USA, and I am a third-generation Cuban American, although you can drop off the Cuban part of that. I speak Spanish, English, and Russian. I have qualified with the M1, the service .45 ACP, and revolvers used by the military. I have a basic working knowledge of Russian weapons." Casey suspects he was picked because of his Cuban heritage and knowledge of the island. He had found out in conversations with him that he visited Cuba several times with his family before the embargo.

"I'm PFC Clay Bennett, USMC. I'm qualified in map reading and have also qualified with the M1 and the service .45 ACP. I've been trained on Russian weapons and studied their tactics in warfare. I understand some of the language, and I understand some Spanish, although I do not have a fluent usage of it. Brown and I were in the same boot camp company." Bennett is almost as tall as Casey.

"My name is Casey White. I'm an E-2 machinist's mate fireman apprentice. That's a seagoing rate. I guess you could say I'm a sharpshooter. I'm surprised to be in on this operation, considering the others' qualifications. That is the only real talent I bring to the group." He sits down, not being able to think of anything else to say.

"Son, don't ever devalue yourself," says the marine officer. "If you weren't valuable to the group, you wouldn't be here. Have you had any infantry training? Is all yours strictly navy?"

"It was strictly navy, sir, except for the training we had at Corpus; I can hit where I aim." He sees the officer turn and look at the chief.

"Yes, sir," says the chief. "He can do it, and in spades."

"Okay, I guess that clears up any question I may have had. I know the navy doesn't indoctrinate the same way the Corps does. Now, this is the reason we are here." He pulls several photos out of a folder. "Diego Francoise Du Bois. He was almost picked up—or should I say captured—by the Cuban revolutionary army. The CIA down here managed to get him to a safe house, but they are being picked to pieces by traitors and desertions. A few pesos or a piece of meat to a starving family is known to sway allegiances. There are only a few of the original group left."

"Who is this guy Du Bois and why is he in Cuba?" Chief Gordon asks Captain King. "Couldn't his own country get him out?"

"We don't know why he went to Cuba in the first place. We only know that the Cuban government put a price on his head and half of the population of Cuba is looking for him. He was on his way to his embassy from some club when the Cubans snatched him off the street. It's only by a stroke of good luck that two of our men saw it and took counteraction," Captain King says.

"Counteraction?" Chief Gordon asks.

"They had to kill the guys," he replies.

"So now I guess the whole place has an ax to grind about this guy? How did they get him away?" Now every man in the room is listening very carefully.

"I don't know about the actual incident, only that he was held in a private home with the occupants at gunpoint overnight, then hustled into a produce truck, and later hauled out of the city to a safe house. I'd like to say that's where he is now, but they've had to move him at least three times in the past two weeks, and he's been hiding for six."

"How are we going to get inside and rescue this guy if the locals and the CIA haven't been able to get him out?" Chief Gordon asks.

"We've come up with a different approach. We'll pick him up, transport him south across Cuba to a place called the Bay of Pigs, and have a boat waiting for us there. If all goes smoothly, we'll be taken into Guantanamo Naval Base and will turn him over to the authorities," Captain King says.

"What kind of guy is he? Will he be someone we'll have to handle with kid gloves, or is he any kind of a man?" the chief asks.

"His bio says that he's the son of the French government's ambassador to Spain. He comes from an old French political family, and you know what kind of playboys they are. He isn't in Cuba on any official mission for his government, and his government isn't telling us any more than that."

A silence follows as the men digest this information and formulate more questions.

"Why don't the frogs go and collect their own? Why is it always the good old US of A that has to do the dirty work?" Chief Gordon asks.

"The only one who can answer that is the president, and as of now he isn't talking. He's promised personally to reward each of you for a job well done as soon as the mission is successfully completed," Captain King replies.

"Do you know if the guy is in any physical condition to go across Cuba undercover? Do you have a description of him?" Chief Gordon asks.

"Here's a picture of him." The officer takes the picture from the folder he carries. The man in his mid- to late-twenties and has a light brown mop of hair. He is somewhat bucktoothed with a prominent nose and a high forehead. He stands about six feet tall and is slightly skinny. He's pictured wearing a yachting outfit and canvas shoes."

"I sure hope he wasn't dressed like this when he came down here," the chief says. "Clothes like that won't last any time in the countryside."

"No, as far as we know he's in jeans, a polo shirt, and leather shoes. I have a pair of boots for him to change into."

"How are we going to get across the width of Cuba? Is there transportation, contacts, and food?" the chief asks.

"We've made contact with some of the remaining assets, and we will be met outside this embassy and transported to the safe house where he is currently hiding. We will then drive across the country making the best time possible. We will meet up with our contact in the little town of El Jiqui north of the Bay of Pigs. From there we will go directly to the pick-up point."

"Why can't we go straight south across the country. Isn't there a huge bay there?" the chief asks.

*He must be mentally reviewing his map reading,* Casey thinks.

"We have to rule that out; there is considerable Soviet construction going on in that area. The Cuban assets looked into it and found Communist infantry activity engaging the rebels, and a column of Soviet vehicles working or headed in that direction.

They are very restrictive of the personnel coming in and out of the area."

"How are we going to be armed? We've been training with American military gear. Do you have those kinds of assets down here?"

"So that you won't be tempted to engage any Cuban units in a face-off, you are going to be armed only with a couple of M1 carbines, and each of you will be issued a 9mm auto. You are already armed with a personal combat-type knife.

"If you need ammunition, you will be able to utilize the existing ammunition being provided. If necessary, you may take more from the Cubans or the Russians."

"I thought we weren't supposed to engage them."

"That's just in case something goes wrong. This shouldn't take more than the three or four days we've planned for."

"Why do they call it the Bay of Pigs? Do the locals wash pigs there before taking them to market or something?" the chief asks, continuing his line of questioning.

"No, the pig reference is about the presence of some kind of fish in the bay. They make grunting noises when taken out of the water. Apparently, this is the primary place around Cuba they inhabit. There's a pretty good fishing industry there with lots of boats and a little boat-building or repair business inland."

"What kind of transportation are we talking about getting us down where we need to go?"

"I think you'd call it a cattle truck if we were back in the States. I'm sorry, but things down here are a little rustic right now."

"I'm still a little concerned about this guy we're supposed to get out. How do we know he isn't working with the commies and will turn us in?" Casey asks.

"Like I said, he comes from an old and well-respected family in France. If anything is wrong, I think the French would have told us. They are genuinely anxious to get their son back out of here."

"Are they paying us or the government anything to do this?" Brown says.

"No, this is just a commitment made by the commander-in-chief. I think after it's all settled, he or someone in his family will come and give us the complete story."

"Where is our food, and how will we get to it?"

"You're probably not going to like what I'm about to tell you. There are several cases of C-rations here at the jump-off point. I know they're nothing to laugh about, but they are better than the average rebel down here is eating right now. Drink all the water you can hold, and refill your canteens. The city water is so polluted that this embassy is either chlorinating or using distilled water to drink."

"Can I have a shot or two of vodka in mine?" Chief Gordon asks.

"I don't see why not. I'll ask that they do it for you."

"We've been issued a brand-new combat radio. It has a crank that generates all the electricity the radio needs. Our call sign will be Kilo Charley. The radio also receives standard AM radio signals."

He picks up a carbine and hands it to Casey, and he gives another to the chief. They are all issued handguns and ammunition. A case of ammunition and extra magazines is passed around. They are allowed to take all they think they personally need.

Casey looks through the backpack given him and sees the standard-issue toilet pack, a poncho, mosquito netting, a folding shovel, C-rations, a flashlight with spare batteries, a compass, and a tightly rolled sleeping bag. They don't contain the standard utility belts so the men won't look too military. Casey drops his extra ammunition and rations into the pack and folds it shut.

"If anything goes horribly wrong, are there any plans to get us out of here?" Brown asks.

"I can't answer that, marine. I think it's in the works. I hope everything will go as planned. A lot of people have been looking into all facets of this, and we think we have the plan well developed. We will be checking in twice a day for the maximum three or four days they think it should take."

131

"How are we supposed to contact this boat that will take us to the Naval Base?" the chief asks.

"We have already buried on the beach at a place noted in the map a package containing flags and reflectors, a radar target, an audible float, and a couple of lanterns. There is included more ammunition, food, and water also.

One other thing: the air force is conducting high-altitude flights over the island daily now. If the operation goes wrong, we are to do a signal layout so that we can be photographed, and we will get further instructions."

They all know that this little adventure has become deadly serious.

"You know," says the chief, "we were told that there are only a few people who know about this mission. Now we even have the air force in on it. Why doesn't the president go ahead and just invade and get it over with?"

"The answer to that is that we are not at war with Cuba, and invasion would be a violation of international law. Are there any more questions now?" He pauses, but no one speaks. "Let's get our gear and get ready to move out."

# Chapter
## 15

J UST as the men are preparing to head out, the door opens. A
staff member comes in and motions to the captain to speak
privately with him. They confer for a minute, and then the captain
turns and speaks to the group.

"The embassy guards are reporting an increase of local
military activity just outside the walls. Apparently, we've been
made, and they're going to make it a whole lot more difficult to do
this rescue. Wait here and let me find out what's going on."

The team sits back down where they are and drinks from
their canteens and refills them. A steward comes through the
door and offers them canapés and food items left over from some
kind of party. Under other circumstances, they would have been
delicacies; now they are just food, and the team divides them up
and eats them like they are the last things they will get to eat.

After a short wait, the ambassador's aide comes back in the
door and tells them to assemble in the parking garage. They're
told to get into the limo parked there and lie down so that they
can't be seen from the street.

Casey notes that this limo doesn't have tinted windows. That
doesn't seem too smart.

"I hope we don't end up heaped like this before the operation
is over," one of the marines says as they pile in and lie down
perpendicular to the car. The six of them end up piled like cord
wood on the floor of the limousine. The driver shuts the door and
starts the engine. *Good old Mercedes quality.*

From somewhere outside the walls, an explosion reverberates and is followed by gunfire. The embassy guards open the gate, and immediately three Cubans carrying AK-47s approach the car and look at it. They don't see anyone except the driver, note the French flags flying from the front fender staffs, and hurry off to join their companions, firing on whoever set off the explosion.

The limo turns left just as a burning vehicle slowly rolls across the opposite intersection, bumps up the curb, and is stopped by the corner of the building.

At the next intersection, the driver turns again.

"Load your weapons," the driver tells them. Casey doesn't have to, all he has to do is to pull the action back and jack a shell into the chamber and safety it. They remain there for a somewhat tortuous trip through downtown and then the local residential area, although now they are sitting up and peeking through the bottoms of the windows to see what they can see.

The limo turns onto a four-lane road and starts to leave the city. The roadway is jammed with military vehicles and lined with the remains of burned-out vehicles. They slow down and mingle with more traffic going the same direction. They soon approach what looks like a more upscale residential area.

"Get down and stay down until I can see if we are being followed." The driver turns off, stops, and watches the vehicles that pass by him. They sit there for almost ten minutes until the driver is satisfied that they are not in any kind of trouble.

He backs up the limo and pulls into the driveway of a rather large-walled compound containing a stately house and then continues around the back.

"It's the end of the line for me, fellows, good luck." Captain King holds the door for them to get out. They look around and see an old Chevrolet stake-body truck with a hayrack on it, filled with hay.

"Brown, Bennett, pull the back of that truck open and let's see what kind of accommodations we have." The two marines unlatch the back, and it leads to some kind of door lined with hay that hides an empty interior.

"Get in, men, we don't have much time." They watch as two figures come out the back door of the house, look around warily, and hurriedly walk to the truck. One is stooped and older, and one is a young man dressed like a tourist.

The younger of the two comes and gets inside the back of the truck with them, and the older man closes and fastens the back. It is too dark to see what he looks like; the men inside know only that he is now finally with them.

"No talking back there; the patrols are out like ants tonight," the driver says in heavily accented Cuban English. "They are looking everywhere for our passenger."

The young man has no luggage, only a bundle under his arm. He sits silent and tries to make out the men's features just as much as they are trying to make out his. The truck starts up and begins to move. It stops hard at the street, and several vehicles come roaring by. One is diesel powered, and Casey knows it must be some kind of military vehicle.

"Everyone sit in line with the man just behind you. Captain King's orders. If we have to stop like that again, we'll be braced for it. Chief, see if you can look out the front and give us any warning if traffic is coming toward us." Chief Gordon gets up on his knees and pushes some of the hay aside so that he can look forward.

The rear window of the cab is missing. The Cuban pushes the lighter in, and when it pops out, he lights a cigar. The smoke wafts back to them. In the primitive surroundings, Casey is reminded of some of the vehicles that came into the store to be loaded with grain. He can look down and watch the roadway going by. He assumes it's a good thing, as they probably won't die of carbon monoxide poisoning.

"Hey, Yanks, how is it going back there?" the driver says, hailing them in broken English.

"You speak English well. Where are we, and where are we going?" the chief replies, striking up a conversation with him.

"My name is José Jesus Hernandez. I am Cuban but educated in Florida, USA, by the citizens' council to take back Cuba. I volunteered to come and help the CIA when we learned of so many defections.

"We have to look out for the Cuban people's army faction, and the hills are full of bandits, but the worst are the Russians. They don't care who they kill. The bastards wiped out my family one afternoon. They came and took all our sheep and killed my brothers and sisters after they were through with them."

"Where are your mother and father now?" Chief Gordon asks.

"I do not know. The Communists came and told us that the state was taking over our land, that it was being sold to the Russians. We were relocated to another district, and they came with their machines and moved into our valley. Now we cannot even go there. It has a fence around it, and the guards watch it from towers, and they have dogs."

"How far is that from where we are now?"

"It is a few kilometers south of us. This road runs southeast, and we will have to go near to it when we pass. I have to turn now; get down."

Abruptly, José turns onto a dirt road leading into a sugar cane field. It is a bumpy ride, and the team has to hold on so they won't be injured. At a break in the cane field, he again turns sharply, proceeds up the lane, turns again, and stops. He turns the motor off and releases the catch on the back of the truck. It is an absolutely black night. Casey can look up and see a thousand stars. The rest of the team is on the ground, stretching their legs.

"I have to turn off the road," says José. "There are Russians coming from the south." That little tidbit of information grabs everyone's attention. The chief and the captain walk back down the road to see if they are being followed. There is only darkness. In a few minutes, the faint sound of trucks can be heard. They aren't coming from just the south but from both ways. The squeaking sound of a tracked vehicle echoes in the distance. By instinct, everyone feels their weapons and double-checks it to make sure they are at the ready.

"How did you know they were coming, José?" Captain King asks the driver.

"I listen with my ears and with my heart. I can tell when they are near. If they are really close, you can also smell them." That's quite a disclosure from the man who is driving them. Casey can still smell the recently extinguished cigar he is chewing and his heavy body odor.

"Men, go on and eat," says the captain. "I don't know where we are, or how long we will be here, but we should be ready to move at a moment's notice."

"Am I going to be able to eat also?" It's the disembodied voice of Diego Du Bois, speaking for the first time. He has a decidedly French accent.

"Yes, come over here and join us. Let's get acquainted." The chief takes a C-ration out of the backpack and hands it to the young man.

"How do you open it?" he asks the chief.

"Here, give it back to me, and I'll do it for you." Chief Gordon opens the ration and hands it to him.

"This smells like the food we prepare for the poodles at the country estate. I can't eat this. I want real food." A chuckle passes through the team.

"I'm sorry to disappoint you, Mr. Du Bois, but it is what your country sent with us to eat as we rescue you from the Communists," Captain King says to him.

"Someone else will have to eat this, or I will throw it into the field."

Casey reaches up, takes the food from him, and shares it with Brown, who happens to be seated beside him.

"Suit yourself, Diego," says the captain. "Maybe tomorrow we can find you something more to your liking."

"I will help," says José, who steps up, takes a machete, and whacks at several of the canes close to them. He peels a stalk down and hands it to Diego.

"What is this?" Diego demands.

"The life blood of Cuba; bite it and see." José insistently hands it to him.

Diego cautiously takes a bite. "It's sweet. It's sugar cane. We ate this on our vacation out here when I was a boy." Another chuckle passes through the team, and then José cuts more and hands each one of them a stick to chew on.

Suddenly, a vehicle comes up between the rows, and they hear the sound of the tracks again. Everyone jumps aboard the truck.

"No, there isn't time. Just go into the cane and be prepared," says the captain. The truck is about fifty feet up the road from where they turned the last time, and the tracked vehicle is coming up the same way they came from. It goes past the place where they turned, illuminates the lane, and then continues on.

They listen in silence. Everyone is managing their own breathing, so they will not make a sound. Casey thinks he hears Diego crying.

The next thing they have to worry about is whether there is any infantry following the vehicle. They stand there in the darkness for about fifteen minutes after the sound of the vehicle returning down another lane goes back on the main road and continues on to where it was originally headed. The thing Casey takes from this little scare is that it's almost impossible to move very far into the cane as it grows so densely.

"José, you are a wonder," says the captain. "If you hadn't heard the vehicles coming, we would be goners now." José just smiles.

"Do not give me all the credit; Jesus is watching over us now."

"I'll give both you and Jesus credit. Now, are we going to get underway, or do we have to wait some more?"

"I am thinking of some other way to go, because I think the Russians are out on patrol tonight. If we stay here, the sun will give us away in the morning. It rises in the east—that direction. Anyone in the hills can see into the cane fields. Let us get into the truck and drive to the south, so we can find somewhere to hide in the trees until tomorrow night."

The team and Diego get back into the truck, with José behind the wheel. The engine barely turns over, and then nothing. He has a dead battery.

"Come on, men, let's push start this thing," says the captain. The team gets out and takes a position behind the truck. Casey knows it will not be easy, but there are six of them, and with a little luck, they might get it to start.

It is all they can do to get the truck rolling, but as soon as José pops the clutch, the engine fires.

The team eagerly jumps in the back, and the truck continues down the long row of cane. Jose turns and pulls back onto the road after carefully listening for any more vehicles. He continues down the road, going southeast. It's a slow, bumpy, nervous ride.

They encounter another side road, and José, with Captain King riding in the passenger seat, decides to take it. The road quickly becomes a trail, and the landscape starts to go upward. Ahead of them in the single headlight, they can see trees.

"Brown, Bennett, Mendoza, White, take the machete and get to work on those trees, so we can get under cover," says the captain. José passes the machete from the cab, and they take turns cutting away at the saplings until they are fairly well into the forest. José turns the truck around so it will be headed downhill in the morning. He takes the cut saplings and props them against the front of the truck.

"We must be alert and cover the truck. When the sun comes up, the light will reflect from the windshield," José says to them.

Here in the cover of the trees, it's damp, and the trees block out the stars. It is absolutely black. No one dares to turn on a flashlight for fear of being seen from the valley they've just come from.

"Men, make it as well as you are able with sleep," says the captain. "White, you have the first watch. Wake Mendoza in a couple of hours. I don't want any one of you to stay up all night. We all need our sleep."

## Chapter 16

"**T**HIS is the most miserable I have ever been in my life; where am I supposed to sleep?" Diego says in a strained voice, wondering where he will get to bed down.

"Just be patient, Diego. We need to think about security before we get comfortable," Captain King says. "There is a pack for you in the back of the truck. It has a sleeping bag and a poncho in it. Put the poncho on for warmth if you need it. Get into the back of the truck, take some of the hay, and make a bed. Tomorrow morning you will put the boots and heavy cotton socks on and leave your shoes here."

Casey drops to his knees, feels the softness of the forest floor, and then decides against sleeping under the truck and takes up a position in the trees away from it.

He intends to be far enough that if someone finds them, he can use the distance to his advantage. He pulls his sleeve back, looks at the glowing hands of his wristwatch, and sees that it's after two in the morning. About three thirty, he wakes Mendoza. He's sitting on the back of the truck when Casey dozes off.

The sun coming up over the hills wakes Casey. If it weren't for his poncho, he'd be soaked; everything in the forest is covered by heavy dew. He pulls his shirt and his T-shirt off and uses the T-shirt to bathe in the collected dew. The coolness of the water is invigorating. *What I wouldn't do for a hot cup of coffee,* he thinks. He spreads his T-shirt across a rock and waits for the sun and its warmth to dry it. Mendoza watches him and mimics what he's done. It's going to be a long, boring day in the forest, waiting for night to come.

"Men, gather around here," Captain King orders. They make a circle and look at the maps. José quietly opens the hood of the truck after making sure his cover is intact, and he works on the motor. "I've been talking to José. He thinks we're here." He holds up one of the maps and references a point on it. "If he's right—and I think he probably is—we are not making the progress we should be. We're trapped here until it's safe for us to travel, and we should be making good use of the time.

"White, Mendoza, take one of the carbines and go straight north and recon the area up there. As soon as you get back, Brown, you and Bennett go along the bottom of the stand of trees. Don't get out so far that someone is going to see you. Where is Diego?"

Casey takes the carbine, adjusts the sling, and puts it across his back. He looks up in the truck and sees that Diego is still asleep. He motions to Captain King and points to the truck, and then they leave the group and start up the side of the hill.

It isn't a high mountain—more like the large rolling hills on the back of the mountains surrounding Casey's home. He thinks about Naomi and then chastises himself for not concentrating on the job at hand. They soon come to the top of a rise, and the land continues down toward another small valley. Everything in the area looks the same. *We could be miles from where we think we are, and probably behind schedule.*

The view is of a row of demolished or burned huts and a sugar cane field. They rest a minute before continuing back. They take another way back about one hundred yards from where they came up just to cover more territory. When they return, Brown and Bennett take off to recon. Casey and Mendoza open their C-rations, eat breakfast, and joke about not having coffee. They learn from Chief Gordon that their French man held his nose and voluntarily ate his breakfast. Afterward, he didn't complain too vigorously. Hunger can be a great modifier. *With a little luck, he might turn out to be human.*

Brown and Bennett take one of the carbines and return to the top of the hill. They come down about noon, and Captain King has the radio out and is attempting to contact the group waiting for their call. He knows it will have to be a quick message because they don't know if the Soviets have radio interception set up.

"Sweetwater, this is Kilo Charley, over."

"Kilo Charley, I'm reading you loud and clear. Sorry to hear you didn't make it out of Havana. We are sending another team to relieve you. Hunker down and wait further, over," says the voice over the radio.

"Sweetwater, we'll be moving at sundown or after the night lights come on and wait for further orders. Over and out."

"Sometime today I'll go to the top of the hill and try to find a clear spot to get a sextant reading. If I can't, then I'll try again tonight with the north star," Captain King announces.

"Sending another team means the boat should be waiting for us when we finally get to the Bay of Pigs," says Captain King. "The original schedule means they will start looking for us every night just after sundown after the third day. They will continue to be there every night after that until we are picked up or until something happens, and we cannot be picked up. We have the equipment to signal them buried in a watertight box in an area designated here on the map." He reminds them of the marker on the map.

Diego sits with a bored look on his face as if it's some sort of game they're playing. Captain King gives the radio another wind, tunes the AM band, and adjusts the frequency.

"Mendoza, what are they saying?" Mendoza listens intently for a while and relays the content of the conversation coming out of the speaker. The station abruptly goes off the air and then comes back on a minute later.

There is martial music, and the announcer reports that criminal elements started a fire in a millinery shop downtown, and one of them was killed. The group doesn't know how accurate the report is, but there was at least one dead Cuban who gave his life to free the man-child they are escorting to safety.

Around noon, Captain King comes up to where Casey and Mendoza are sitting beside a rock, watching the activity in the field below them. There are about a half-dozen men cutting cane and piling it in the back of a cart. Another pair is digging what look like vegetables from a plot next to a burned-out hut.

"What do you make of it, Mendoza?" Captain King asks, looking in the direction of the men working.

"I think they might be bandits getting food for another larger group. If the cane was being harvested, they would just torch the fields to remove the leaves, and then a whole crew would come in with harvesters and clean it out."

The drone of faraway aircraft to the east of them catches their attention. They look, and way up in the sky is a Piper Cub aircraft making slow circles in the sky. It's apparent the group of men in the field is aware of the small plane also as they keep looking up at it.

Captain King walks back from the edge of the trees, climbs onto a small rock, stands with a little sextant, and tries to determine where they are.

"Mendoza, stay here and keep an eye on things, and let us know if anything changes. White, you come with me." Casey follows Captain King back to the truck. "Men, we have company across the hill. They're cutting cane, and there's a small plane overhead east of us. Make sure that the glass of the truck is covered so that no reflection can be seen."

"I will do it, Mr. King." José stands up, goes to the cab, pulls a canvas tarp from under the seat, and fastens it across the windshield by shutting the ends of it in the doors. He rolls down the side windows as well.

They hear the sound of vehicles; several trucks and two tracked vehicles, like the one that came through the cane field, are coming down the road. Mendoza comes running back to the camp.

"The men who were down there took what they had and disappeared into the trees," he says.

"Which way did they go, toward us or the other way?" Captain King asks.

"They went the other way," Mendoza says.

Two of the trucks and one of the tracked vehicles turn off the road and make their way toward the cane field. The group watches as the vehicles round the lower point of ground, and then they go running up the hill to see where they will come out on the other side. They get to their vantage point about the same time as the vehicles reappear from around the bottom of the hill.

The vehicles stop where the men were cutting cane. One man, possibly an officer, climbs up onto the tracked vehicle, sits on the coaming of the hatch, and scans the hillside with his field glasses. A man comes out to operate the gun mounted on top of it.

The sound of heavy machine-gun fire fills the valley and reverberates off the hills as several small trees and limbs fall. There is a second volley, and then they stop shooting. None of the men deploy. It is just a show of force for the benefit of the bandits.

The unit turns around, goes back across the cane field, and continues down the road. This is an enlightening experience for the group as it is the actual first offensive gunfire they've experienced.

"Live and learn, guys. The Russkies don't necessarily need a target to use their guns," says the chief, who is standing there with the rest of them.

They make their way back to the truck, and Diego is just getting down. José has a grin on his face. "I wonder what he will do when the gunfire is directed at him," he says to the returning men.

"He'll probably crap in his pants," Bennett says.

"It's getting about time we eat something and bury the evidence, then get moving," Captain King says.

Each man takes his food out and starts eating. Casey digs a shallow hole with his spade. He thinks about it and then walks off into the woods a few more yards and digs another, deeper, hole. He drags a half-rotten log across one side of the hole, relieves himself, and finds his toilet kit. He returns to the group and invites everyone to use his contribution.

Everyone except Diego does. He thinks it's too primitive. He is noticeably upset when Captain King throws Diego's two-hundred-dollar Bruno Magli shoes into the pit, and they're covered up with its contents. He'll have to live with the combat boots.

They cover up their camp as well as possible and put their things on the back of the truck. José gets in the cab and preps it to start. Together, the men get it to move down the hill. It takes two tries, but it finally catches and runs, coughing and spitting until José can smooth things out.

The sky is partially overcast, and there is a slightly larger slice of the moon than there was the night before. It's just light enough that you can see the ground. They all pile into the truck, go to the road, and turn south. José is not using his headlight since he can see where he is going, but he is going slowly. About midnight, they stop to take the jerry cans out of the back and fill the truck's tank, and they then continue. The sky is beginning to look cloudy, and there is the promise of rain in the air.

Ahead of them is a fork in the road. The one turning south bears the telltale ruts of heavy military vehicles turning that way.

"We'll take the other road so that we don't run into the Russian soldiers," José says. He pulls the truck across the newly turned-up dirt and stops. He carefully uses a broom to brush over the tracks they made on the fresh dirt, and then they move on. They go past several peasant huts, one of which has a light showing. José shakes his head. "Not good, they hear the truck."

They go down a lane bordered on both sides by tall growth of sugar cane. To the right is a lane going off to the side, and he takes it. He drives until there is another and turns that way. Farther along is another turn. They cross a small ditch that rattles everyone's teeth, and the truck just quits.

"You take all your things and go now," says José. "Continue south out of the cane field. There is a stream you can follow. It has good water to drink. Do not hide in the cane; they know of that deception. Do not go down the west side of the road; it is the swamp. Stay on this side until you find the road to the bay. Go now, and God help you to get home." He gives them directions.

The group members pick up all of their things and dismount from the truck. They go to say good-bye to José, but he is not to be found; he has simply vanished. Behind them, they can hear the sounds of vehicles passing.

"Everyone make a single line and step in the boot print of the man in front of you, so they can't tell how many of us there are. Follow me." Captain King leads off through the cane field and manages to get them back to the road. There are no vehicles on the road, so they decide to use it. They are three paces apart and running. Captain King takes Diego; he holds his hand and makes him run. Since Diego is not carrying but a light load, he can keep up for about twenty minutes.

They soon find themselves in a small open area, and there is no apparent cover to conceal them if anyone should come along. The captain gives the men five minutes to catch their breath and then continues on, setting a pace as fast as Diego can move.

They finally come to another cane field. On the opposite side is what looks like the continuation of the swamp. Across a field partially covered by water is a stand of trees.

"Come on this way," Captain King says. They work across the field as quickly as they can, toward the far side. The water is almost as deep as the tops of their feet. They move into the trees and find that the land is a little higher and, thankfully, free of water.

Casey looks at his watch; it reads almost five in the morning. *Where in the world are we?* he wonders. Then a new menace attacks them in hordes—mosquitoes!

Captain King again gives orders. "Get your ponchos on and put the mosquito netting over your head and hold it on with your hats. Each one of you check your buddy and make sure his netting is tucked into his shirt collar. Now get down wherever you can find a dry place and make a shallow foxhole. Don't dig too deep and find water. Put repellant only on your hands and wrists and save the rest for later."

Casey helps Diego put his poncho on and then slathers his hands and wrists with mosquito repellant. As dawn approaches, Casey catches himself dozing. He looks around and sees that the only one awake is Captain King. Casey signals him of his alertness, and the man nods to him. As it becomes light, they can see that the path they made across the water has been mercifully reclaimed by the green slime on the top of the water.

Each man has a shallow hole to hide in, and he surrounds it with foliage from the area. They can see the road from where they are, but they are well hidden in the growth. They lace grasses into the mosquito netting, which allows them to sit a little higher without being seen.

During the early-morning hours, vehicles begin coming and going on the road, and Casey starts keeping track of what kind and how many by marking the back of his shovel. During the slack periods, his mind wanders back to the ones he left at home.

The sound of more vehicles coming down the road brings his attention back to the present, and he resumes counting. Late in the afternoon, the last of the vehicles rumble off toward the north.

Captain King speaks up. "Men, I've been studying the map. I think there's another road just to the south of where we are now. Let's move on through the swamp and see if the road is there, or if I am totally disoriented."

The group responds, and the first thing they hear is the high, whiny voice of Diego, saying, "I am higher born than you; I should not have to endure this torture." If he's trying to win the favor of the men who are risking their lives to get him out of Cuba, then he's beating the wrong drum. The men just ignore him.

Captain King uses his flashlight several times during their trek through the alternately wet and then soft, boggy soil. All at once, the land slopes up, and they find they are standing on firm, dry ground again. In the distance, they can make out houses. They make a wide detour around them and continue. They eat their C-rations on the run and put the remains in their pockets to be buried later.

They are back in an area of low, rolling hills and find a small stream coming out of a forested stand. There are no roads around, so Captain King decides to go into the trees and try to make it to a safe place to hole up for the day. The stream seemingly is coming from a natural spring. The Captain takes a handful of it and samples.

"I guess it's good enough to drink. Let's fill our canteens here. Spread out and look around to see if we are alone." Each man walks a different way and reports back soon. They find the trees run only about one hundred yards to the north and about twenty yards wide.

"Bennett, Brown, go past the tree line and see what's beyond that little rise," says the captain. Casey hands him the carbine, and they sprint away. Not much later, they return.

"Captain King, there's a place over the hill we can probably get down into and sleep. It's a ditch that's overgrown with weeds. There is a second large hill of dirt about halfway across the valley that will afford us visual coverage."

"Come on, let's check it out."

They go over the hill and find the ditch. It looks like someone started some kind of irrigation project and then abandoned it before going much more than twenty yards. It's five feet deep and runs parallel to the hill with the removed dirt thrown on the side.

The captain takes charge. "Go in the far side and try not to knock down the natural grass cover. Each man will space himself about ten feet from the next, and we will spend the day here." They all dismount into the ditch, and at some places they have to cut the grass and vines away in order to make it down the full length.

Captain King takes the radio out and starts contact again. "Sweetwater, this is Kilo Charley, over." There is a long silence, and then Sweetwater answers him.

"Kilo Charley, this is Sweetwater, go ahead."

"We've eaten about half the melon and will continue the picnic. The chariot race is over. The horse died. Over."

"Kilo Charley, the gods of Africa are about to cry for you. Please look out for their tears. Find a temple to pray in. Over and out."

"Men," says the captain, "We have an approaching storm. It may be a hurricane. This is the season for them. I hope it goes up the eastern seaboard instead of entering the gulf. We have enough on our plate to worry about."

# Chapter 17

THEY fill their canteens, and Bennett busies himself digging a deeper hole to bury their trash. The sky is just getting light when the sounds of heavy engines alert them. Captain King and the others look out and see the field below them slowly filling with vehicles and men. It doesn't appear that they have been found out.

"Bennett, Mendoza, listen to see if you can make out what they're saying," says the captain. It's as though the whole group is holding their breath.

From the far side of the field, a vehicle drives to the front side of the earth berm midway in front of them. They can't see what's going on, but it doesn't look good. The vehicle pulls off to the side, and a group of conscripts with rifles take a position and begin firing. They can hear some of the errant rounds impacting the dirt bank in front of them. They realize that in choosing their shelter, they have inadvertently chosen the backup berm of the rifle training grounds used by the army troops.

All the men hunker down and wait. There is another round of firing, the sound of machine guns, and then the sounds of heavier weapons. The other sound is the crying of Diego. Captain King has a very firm grip on him and is not allowing him to move. In the afternoon, the firing continues, and more weapons are brought into the fray. Several times a heavy round from a horizontally fired weapon goes astray, and they can hear it impact in the dirt in front of the berm where they are hiding.

Above them, something pops, and there is an almost blinding white light emitted as it burns itself out. It manages to set the grass on fire near Bennett. He crawls toward it and throws sand over it, and then he pats and smothers the embers. They breathe a sigh of relief.

Diego suddenly jumps to his feet and begins screaming at the top of his lungs. "I'm a French citizen, and I demand that you let go of me. I wish to surrender to them. They will have to take me back to the embassy in Havana and turn me over." He manages to crawl away from the captain and is starting to stand up when both Casey and Brown tackle him.

"You little frog bastard, do you want to get us all killed? If they catch you, they will torture you, and they will find out how many of us there are. Then they will hunt us down and kill us too. We didn't come all the way down here to get our asses shot off for somebody who should still be in a nursery school," says Casey.

Diego's face is almost ashen in color, but he continues to try to stand. Brown punches him once, then again, and the fool just looks at him in apprehension as he tries to get his breath. The whole exchange takes place in less than a minute, and the sound of firing nicely covers his screaming voice.

In the distance, Casey hears the howl of jet aircraft and pulls the cover over him. Brown is now lying on top of Diego as the jets approach from the north. Overhead, they dip their wings in recognition of the group and do a ninety-degree pull up, stand on their tails, and disappear back to the north. Casey can see the contrails of the engines condensing in the sky above them.

The soldiers start dismantling their equipment, and after another hour, the whole area appears to be clear of anything Russian. The sound of silence is overwhelming, and each man sits sorting out his own thoughts.

Finally, Chief Gordon speaks. "Diego, tell us the truth now. Why in the world are you down here? You don't work for your embassy, and your parents didn't know where you were when they started looking for you. Your friends are free just to ride out of the embassy, go to the airport, board a plane, and go home. Who the hell are you, anyway?"

"We were playing the nightclub game the four of us made up. Each one decided on two each—countries to go to nightclubbing in. We went to the Rivera, to a club where there are topless dancers—and if you wait around later at night, it became bottomless too. Next, we pulled my choice of Cuba out of the hat. We came down here to see El Toro. We knew the government had outlawed that kind of act, but my brother told me he could contact someone and get us in to see him, and he did."

"Who is this El Toro?" the captain asks, and Chief Gordon interrupts.

"Captain, when I was young and dumb on my first deployment down here, I went to see him. It's a disgusting display, and I got sick to my stomach and had to leave before the act finished. The guys I was with made fun of me for years."

"Well, what the hell is so unusual about this EL Toro?" Captain King asks again.

"It's an act where they advertise he will have live sex on stage with a virgin. They find some young peasant girl and drug her and haul her out on the stage, and he rapes her in front of the audience," Chief Gordon says to the captain.

"That's an act?" the captain asks incredulously.

"Yes, sir. Apparently, he's done it for years. He only stops when Castro takes over and threatens him. He's in hiding and still has an audience of creeps who come down here and look him up."

"Is that right, Diego? You came down here to watch some creep do a rape job on some young girl?" the captain asks.

"Yes, I guess. We wanted to see if it was true."

"Well, that doesn't say much for the French, does it?"

"No. Apparently not for the Cubans either; it is they who allow it to take place," Diego replies, trying to deflect some of the criticism from him.

"Men, get your things ready to go. We'll move just as soon as I make contact." He takes the radio out of his pack and cranks it up. "Sweetwater, this is Kilo Charley, over."

"Kilo Charley, short and sweet, the tide is coming in, and if you want to get any fish, you should get the trawler moving before the rest of the competition's boats arrive at the good fishing grounds. Over and out."

"Okay, men, apparently someone thinks we are in the area, and they are looking for us. We've got to get moving."

"Which way do we go, Captain?" Chief Gordon asks.

"Let's go back to the road and head south to see if we can make up for lost time."

The men stand to get out of the ditch and, amazed, find that in front of them is some kind of ordnance still burning out. Brown is first on the top of the berm.

"Oh shit, down!" yells Brown.

They all dive for the protection of the ditch once again.

"What is it, Brown?" Captain King comes crawling to see what startled Brown.

"They left a couple of guys down there. They must be watching something, because we know there wasn't anything there when we came in this morning."

"White, take your carbine, Brown, the other one. Bennett, you go with them. Mendoza and I will circle around and see if there are more of them. Diego, you stay here with the chief. Keep down, and keep quiet. If I even think you are going to give us away, I will personally write your parents and tell them how you died."

"Yes, sir!" Diego says whiningly. Chief Gordon grins.

The three of them climb up the end of the ditch and start moving down the field feeling alone, excited, and exposed, and wondering who or what they will find. They're walking through a field of grass and weeds with a soft texture, and they can move almost silently.

When they get to within about fifty feet of the two figures sitting on the cases, they can see their outlines. They also see the glow of their cigarettes and smell the acrid smoke of the Russian brand. They stop and listen. All at once, one of them suddenly stands up and brings his rifle to bear.

Casey and Brown fire almost simultaneously, and they can hear the rounds impacting the two soldiers. Then there is silence.

A whispered shout comes from the darkness. "You guys okay?"

"Yes, Captain, we got both," Brown replies. All at once, it occurs to Casey that yes, he can take a life.

They move to where the two men fell and see they were watching a stack of crates of ammunition.

"Get the weapons and whatever ammunition you can carry and let's get the hell out of here."

"Captain, I've a suggestion, sir. Let's carry them up to the ditch and throw them in. It should take the Soviets a while to find them, and it might add a few minutes to our time."

"Good idea, Brown," Captain King replies.

Without being told to, Casey picks up one of the AK-47s, three bandoleers of cartridges, and four extra magazines taped together in pairs. These are the full-stock infantry weapons, not the pistol-grip models shown off by the Cuban troops patrolling in Havana. He winds the rounds around his chest, picks up one of the dead soldiers, and carries him out the same way the captain came from. He doesn't want to add any more trails for the enemy to follow and hunt him down.

Brown has the other soldier over his shoulder and is close behind Casey as the rest pick up additional bandoleers and magazines. When they arrive at the ditch, the chief climbs out and attempts to pull Diego up. Casey drops the body he is carrying into the ditch and jumps down. He grabs Diego by the butt and the back of his shirt and throws him out. The captain and the chief turn their heads away while grinning.

"Wait a minute, let's strip them and lay them sixty-nine in the ditch. The old guard of the Russians will go out of their way to shoot a queer." The chief says. "Maybe we can throw them off a little longer. Take all their clothing." It takes them five minutes to cut the uniforms off and arrange the bodies together in an intimate fashion, as well as they can.

"Captain, can I go down there and have a look around?"

"Sure, Chief, what do you have in mind?"

"I'd like to see what kind of ordnance is there; maybe we can leave them a surprise for in the morning."

"Okay, go. Mendoza, go with him and keep a lookout. The rest of us will be going back behind the hill, and we'll wait for you to catch up."

Chief Gordon and Mendoza come up behind Casey and are snickering.

"What did you do?" he asks them.

"The chief put a grenade under a box of warheads so that when the top box is moved off, it will trigger the whole thing. I hope we are miles away from there when that goes up."

It's getting foggy. The mosquitoes have quit following them, and they make good time to the wet area where they crossed before. They then walk alongside the road in the ditch for an impossible fifteen minutes.

"Okay, get rid of the clothing, and let's get a good cadence going." The two rolled-up uniforms are unceremoniously thrown as far as they can be into the stagnant water. All at once, there is a flash and a roiling of the water. Two large things dart out of the growth about ten yards from where they are standing and rush into the water. Out where the clothing fell in, it is deeper than where they crossed, and apparently the local alligator population is bargaining for the remains of the blood-soaked clothing. They all stand amazed for an instant.

"White, give your carbine to Mendoza to carry. Give him enough ammunition, so he can use it if he has to. They are really going to be looking for us now." The moon is getting larger with a light, hazy circle around it, and tonight there is very little cloud cover. They run and walk fast for almost half an hour. They only quit when Diego collapses on the road, gasping for breath.

The captain looks around as they go past a little rise, and there is yet another little valley off to the right. In the middle is a sugar cane field. A road leads off to the side of the cane field.

The sound of approaching vehicles makes them choose to run toward the sanctuary of the swamp. Two trucks loaded with men appear. This time, no tracked vehicles accompany them.

One turns off the road and continues on toward the direction of the huts. The other one continues toward where the first one left the road.

They can hear someone in the truck talking on a radio. Bennett listens closely. "They're checking out the area to see if the bandits are hiding there. It seems as though they caught a bunch of them here a little while ago and smoked them good."

The truck going down the far side of the field stops. All at once, there is a chorus of automatic gunfire. The volley that starts from the hill is answered from the truck. Men jump down and take cover behind the vehicle.

The driver of the truck in front of them turns off the road to turn around, drops the front axle into the ditch, and stalls the truck. An officer swears and then chews the driver out.

"White, Brown, Chief, get over there." The three of them go across the swamp as quietly as they can. *Maybe the soldiers will think we're alligators,* Casey thinks.

The driver manages to get the truck to start again and backs it up and tries to turn around. One of the soldiers sitting in the back sees them approaching and attempts to warn his comrades.

He raises his weapon, but Casey has already raised his. He sprays down the side of the truck using an entire magazine. He quickly flips it over and reloads. Across from him, Brown accomplishes the same thing. The chief moves to a vantage point and unloads the carbine into the front of the truck.

It bucks once and again stalls. From inside the back of the truck, Casey hears the ping of a falling hand grenade spoon. He and Brown dive to the ground, and in the next seconds, there is an accompanying explosion and then silence. He sees Brown get back up, and together they cautiously look into the back of the truck.

It's a bloody mess. One of the men in the trucks tries to throw a grenade but drops it. The chief is on the running board, emptying the magazine of his 9mm into the cab. He looks and confirms that all of his rounds have accomplished what he started to do.

Across the field, the skirmish continues, and Casey sees several dark forms maneuvering to flank the truck. There is another exchange of gunfire. One of the forms goes down. Seconds later, a tremendous explosion sounds, and the top of the truck seemingly disappears in the air. Casey sees two of his group up in the truck. They look through the carnage, and each finds an AK-47 and ammunition.

"Now we've really got to move, men," says Captain King, who is standing beside Casey, who hadn't even heard him approach.

"Wait a minute, Captain, I have an idea." The chief climbs under the truck with a hand grenade and pulls the pin. He jams it against the shaft of the shift mechanism so that when it's moved, it will explode. If the enemy is not able to move the truck, it might give Casey's group some valuable time to keep moving ahead.

They alternately run and walk until an hour before daybreak, when they start looking for a suitable place to hide out. They will need to go a long way across an open field where the land starts up into the hills; they have no other choice.

They individually step off the road, making sure to cover their tracks for the first twenty feet or so, and they then walk in a zigzag manner, so they won't leave a trail for an acute eye to pick up on. It takes them twenty minutes of feeling very vulnerable before they manage to get to the cover of the trees.

This hill is a little higher than the last one, and they continue to the top of the rise so that they can command a view of both sides. They find several rock formations coming out of the ground about ten feet high, and this affords them a chance to pick some sanctuary to rest in.

Some of the rocks contain splits that go back about twenty feet. Casey and Mendoza check them out. They report to the others that the crevices will be good places to bed down, although the men will have to maintain a watch and not get caught in there. The captain agrees.

Casey takes a long draw from his canteen and notices that it is less than one-third full. He'll have to conserve until they find good water. It's gourmet C-rations for dining again this evening. Casey looks at Diego and wonders how much longer he'll be able to keep up the pace. He looks skinnier, more pale, and more frightened than the first time he saw him.

The only bad thing about the place they choose to hide in is that someone has to go partway down the hill to see out. They decide to post two men on watch. One will be perched on top of the rocks, and the other one in the trees.

Casey finds his shovel and steps off to where he feels comfortable and starts digging a trench. He makes it long and narrow and throws the dirt far and wide so as not to create a barrier to his vision. It will be a good defensive position. His rounds will not go inside the rocks but will cover most of the approaches to them. The captain comes over to see what he's doing.

"Dammit, White, why aren't you a marine? Be sure to give it a good brush cover."

Casey takes the machete, walks away from their area, and takes the limbs out of several trees to use for camouflage around the top of his creation. He tells the others that whoever has the watch can utilize the trench along with him.

The moon that started earlier as a medium slice is now a thick slice, gaining size every night. Before Casey settles in for the day, he takes one last trip to the edge of the trees and looks out for the coming dawn.

When it's Casey's turn up on the rock, he is there for only minutes before he hears voices. He drops a small rock on the chief, and there is an instant shuffle for weapons.

The voices continue to get closer, and Casey takes the safety off and points his AK-47 in their general direction. They grow louder, and then he can hear footsteps in the soft earth. The tension in the air is almost palpable. The glow of a cigarette gives away the actual position of whoever is coming. The smoker comes within several feet of the rocks, and Casey crouches to not create a silhouette or a target.

The men continue, fatefully choosing to go around the back side of the rocks, not knowing that they almost stumbled into what surely would have been their final walk thought the woods.

Casey listens carefully for a long time afterward as Chief Gordon and Brown follow them for a while to make sure they don't turn around.

When they return, the captain is up again. "What were they talking about, Mendoza?"

"Captain, it seems as though they were in on the raid last night. They killed a whole truck full of conscripts and captured their weapons. There was more than they could carry, so they took the newer weapons and then torched the truck. It exploded and killed one of their men."

It's beginning to grow light, and they look at their food supply. Each man is down to three meals and most, like Casey, have only the bottom of their canteens left. They take three of the ponchos and spread them between the rocks, forming a funnel. They place a canteen underneath, and it is about full by the time the morning becomes hot and unbearable again. Playing connect the dots with the remaining dew droplets garners another half canteen for them.

There is the unspoken word again, and each man knows what has to be done. They take different directions and go as far as reasonable to reconnoiter the area and report back. Casey looks north and notices there are several small aircraft, probably Piper Cubs, flying over the area.

In the afternoon, boredom overcomes the captain, and he cranks the radio and turns the AM band on. Mendoza listens. The Cubans promise a bounty for the criminals who caused the explosion and killed the soldiers in their training grounds. That causes a grin on Chief Gordon's face. Contact with Sweetwater makes it plain that they are not to engage the enemy in any fight. They are to get to the pickup point as soon as possible and transmit when it's accomplished.

The night turns out to be a cat-and-mouse game of hiding from the vehicles, getting up, and running after they pass. The men don't make much distance and are worn out when the sky begins to get light.

The next hill over is about a half mile away, and they decide they'll keep off the road and just walk through the field. They travel through where the cane has been harvested, and the ground is full of random pieces of cane that fell off the trucks, and the men begin picking them up. Casey finds several nice ones. He takes his knife, carves down the side of one, and sucks the juice from it. He puts the other pieces in his pockets. The only bad thing about this is that it leaves his face all covered with a sticky residue.

They make it to the top of the hill and look down. Below them are peasant huts. Several have been burned, and those closer to the road have been run over by tracked vehicles. The sound of vehicles brings them down as every one of them tries to become one with the land.

There are enough small boulders around the area that they can hide between them. They will be hard to spot from the air as their uniforms are about the same color as the ground. Casey hears a faraway rhythmic humming sound.

# Chapter 18

A LL at once, the roar of radial aircraft engines fills the air. They are close and closing fast. The first one clears the top of the hill by only one hundred feet, and the second is slightly higher. They bank, and the air is filled with the staccato roar of .50-caliber machine-gun fire.

The first aircraft takes up a path parallel with the edge of the cane field, and the second one strafes slightly in from where the tracers of the first one show. They pull up sharply and turn. There are several areas of the cane looking like a new-mown lawn.

Casey listens. "They're coming back for another run!" he shouts. Every man hugs the ground a little closer. The planes are higher on this run. One continues farther in the field, and the second focuses on the row of huts. They pull up, gain altitude, and continue off to the north.

In time, a dozen men emerge from the cane field and run toward the cover of the woods. It's a poor decision on their part; as soon as they've covered half the distance, both aircraft come over the top of the hill again.

The roar of their eight .50-caliber machine guns almost cancels out the drone of the radial engines. Hot empty casings shower around the rescue group. The dozen men running in the field are mercilessly chopped to pieces. The aircraft make a low turn and return to see the results of their handiwork. This time they do not fire. Captain King's group, thankfully, is not seen.

"What the hell was that?" Bennett and Brown ask simultaneously.

"They're B25-J Mitchells," says Casey. "I studied a lot of aircraft recognition while I was stationed in Kingsville. They are twin-engine bombers modified during the Second World War to become ground attackers. Apparently, the Communists have a couple flyable again. They must have captured enough ammunition to keep the guns going for a long time."

"Men, I hate to interrupt this love fest," says the captain, "but we are exposed out here. Crawl toward that big boulder."

They do as the captain instructs, and once there, they dig a foxhole between some of the rocks. It takes almost two hours to get enough dirt moved fully to conceal every one of them. Casey picks up some of the expended .50-caliber casings and puts them into his pack.

"Men, if they come back, don't look at them," says the chief. "They're looking for the whites of your eyes, and they can pick you out every time." His advice is well timed, as almost as soon as the B-25s roar off, several Piper Cubs appear and move closer. They crisscross the area for about fifteen minutes and then withdraw as several trucks of soldiers arrive. The soldiers dismount and go to the center of the field, where the bodies of the freshly killed bandits are shedding their last drops of blood. The soldiers look around and pick up what weapons they can find. They're satisfied they've won that one, and they remount and leave the area.

The men watching from the top of the hill give a collective sigh of relief. It's been a long day, and they still have most of the afternoon to weather. They discover that the soil is cooler where they dig into it, so they resume digging. Soon everyone will have a trench deep enough to sit down in with his head above the ground to look out.

Toward the afternoon, women begin to appear as the men watch. They're looking for lost loved ones. Casey watches intently as one or two find someone they knew or loved and wail. He looks off toward the north, and to his chagrin, he sees the outlines of the B-25s again. They had been waiting all that time to see who would show up. They never bother to sweep in from behind the hill. They fly in low and level up the valley, the guns roar, and the women join their loved ones in death.

A stunned silence falls on the men, and Casey sees Diego crying. No other attempt to remove the bodies is made. They are simply left to rot in the field. It is a harsh lesson for the bandits to learn.

It's not hard for the group to get moving this evening as every one of them wants to get as much territory as possible between them and the massacre. Now the road has some gravel on it, and they take the chance and walk down the middle. Every one of the men is aware of his thirst.

They come upon a small village that has been flattened. They are excited to find a well behind the large foundation of a church destroyed here. Some glass beads from the stained-glass windows still rest among the burned remains. One side of the well is caved in, and the bucket is unusable. Casey volunteers his boot. They secure it to the rope and use it to retrieve the precious water below.

It takes the better part of half an hour to get everyone's canteens filled. Each man has his own joke about drinking champagne out of a slipper. Casey claims the last two boots full and dumps it over his body; the coldness of the water is invigorating. He jams his T-shirt down into the boot to dry it, puts on his sock, and ties the boot up.

This alleviates the need for water, for the time being, but it doesn't do anything about the food supply. They move back to the road, ever watchful for oncoming vehicles. In another half hour, the captain calls for a rest and the men scatter into the cover of some tall brush.

They hear one shrill, pleading voice and two more voices heavily laughing just across a little rise. They disperse to check it out. There is a Russian military vehicle pulled off the road in the front of some huts, one of which has flickering candlelight in it.

Loud, boisterous voices issue out as they quietly cross the road to get the advantage and try to see what is going on. Fifty feet behind them is another hut, this one darkened and seemingly abandoned. They cautiously enter it and make sure it's uninhabited.

"What do you think, Mendoza?" Captain King asks.

"It sounds like a couple of drunken Russian officers. They must have cornered the peasant and are torturing him or his wife." A soldier comes out of the hut, gets into the vehicle, and lights a cigarette. The sound of a woman's scream brings everyone's attention to the front of the hut to watch what's happening. The man in the vehicle snuffs his cigarette and goes back inside.

Casey brings the carbine around from behind him, checks the load, and takes a position to fire. The woman continues to scream and cry for mercy. Something has to give.

Casey goes out from the back and around to one side, where he has a commanding view of the front of the hut as Captain King points to where he wants him. Casey then hears the sound of a breaking bottle and a struggle. An older, naked, bleeding woman suddenly bursts through the door with the officer right behind her.

He's holding an AK-47 loosely in his hand. The woman's eyes are filled with terror as she runs. The officer raises it and fires the entire magazine. The front of the woman's body disappears in a pink haze of blood and body parts.

Just as the Russian fires, a second man appears in the doorway, and then a third. Casey fires, and the third man falls, bumping the second, who falls against the officer. He turns to find out why he's being pushed from behind, and Casey's third bullet enters his ear. He's dead before his body hits the ground.

Mendoza, Brown, and Bennett charge the house. They take opposite sides of the door and then go inside. They wave all clear to the group and beckon them to come ahead.

Diego has to be forcibly brought through the carnage. He throws up as soon as he sees the woman. There is little in his stomach to throw up, so he dry heaves.

The chief quickly checks out the vehicle. "It's got gas, and we could get some distance between us before anyone finds this," he says to the captain.

Captain King steps inside and looks around as Casey looks from behind him. Anything worth using is broken. The mutilated corpse of the woman's husband lies in the corner, covered with cigarette burns and blood. The whole area reeks of death.

They hear a rustling. It's only slight, but it's noise, nonetheless.

"Quick, cover the outside," says the captain. Two of the men rush out to take a cursory look around. All of the men see a slight movement under a pile of sugar cane against the side of the hut. Every gun is pointed at the pile.

"Come out from under the cane," says the captain. There is no answer. "If you don't come out from under there, I am going to empty a whole magazine into it." He kicks at the pile.

The pile begins to move, and the dirty face of a girl in her late teens or early twenties emerges. Her eyes are filled with terror when she sees all the guns aimed at her. Bennett deliberately tips the remains of the table over to block her view of the murdered man nearby.

She speaks in Spanish, and Mendoza interprets, saying, "Please do not shoot me." She just remains there, panicked and pleading not to be harmed.

"Get her up out of there," Captain King says to Casey. He leans over, takes her hand, and pulls her from under the pile of cane. It appears to be a hideaway for just the purpose she was using it. She stands and looks at all the men around her. She is filthy, dust covered, and she looks like she needs a good meal.

"Mendoza, tell her we're Americans, and we are not going to hurt her," Captain King says.

"Who are you?" Mendoza says to her in Spanish.

"My name is Sereta," she replies in almost perfect English with a Spanish twang.

"What are you doing here?" he asks while looking her over.

"This is where I live. It is my home," she replies.

Chief Gordon comes into the hut and is surprised by their find. "Captain, we've got to get moving. It's getting lighter all the time, and we need cover."

"I can hide you. We have dug a place to get away from the bandits, but the soldiers surprised us, and we were not able to get into it," the young woman says.

"Show me," says Captain King, and he stands aside for her to pass, blocking her view of her murdered mother. She leads them out of the hut to a rise in the hill where a road has been cut for the cane trucks to travel down to the fields.

She goes across the road to just before the turn on the overgrown side, kneels down in the drainage ditch, and begins pulling at the brush and vines.

"It is here, but we need to not give away the entrance for the Communists to find it." It unveils a cave entrance about four feet high that goes back into the hill for about ten feet. At the end of the opening is a room roughly fifteen feet in diameter and higher than the opening.

"The ones who harvest the cane left the tools many years ago, and we have been making this to go into when the storms come and to hide from the bandits," she says.

The men gather around and know that Captain King has a painful decision to make. They can take the truck and see how far they can get, or they can do something to hide it and conceal themselves in the cave.

"I checked the truck; there are explosive packs in the back plus a whole lot of ammo and grenades, and a couple of RPGs," Chief Gordon says.

"Let's set up a little welcome for whoever is looking for our dead officer, his aide, and his driver. Chief, can you rig some kind of land mine out of the explosives?"

"Yes, what do you have in mind?" The two of them leave the room, and the men wait for their instructions.

"Someone wait here with Miss Sereta, and the rest of us will make war on the bad guys."

"I will watch to see that she doesn't run," Diego says, surprising the rest of them. The others begin work on the vehicle.

It's a simple plan. They carry the body of the officer to the front of the truck and put his hat on his head sideways so that the bullet hole doesn't show. Chief Gordon takes his knife, slices off one of the officer's epaulets, and puts a grenade under him. He pulls the pin carefully and backs off. Now it will detonate when the body is moved.

There's a tow cable in the back, and the chief ties it to the officer's foot to make it look like someone had been preparing to extract him. About thirty feet ahead of the end of the tow cable, they dig a pit in the roadway and place two satchel charges in it. A grenade is placed directly on top and packed with earth around it so it will trigger when the dirt is disturbed. They are working against the daylight now, and everyone hurries. They take the weapons and ammunition from the vehicle and put them into the cave.

Chief Gordon again takes an epaulet from each of the fallen soldiers. They never move the other bodies, just step over them and remove their footprints from the road. They look around, and the last thing they find is a goat, slaughtered and cleaned by the Russians. They take it with them.

They cross the road, and they erase their footprints and carefully replace the foliage concealing the entrance to the cave. Casey knows that if the captain is wrong, then this could be a disaster for the team; they would surely die right there. The others know the odds as well. Brown sits at the entrance as a watch.

"Sereta, how did you learn to speak English so well?" Captain King asks her.

"The padre at the mission teaches us; he was educated in the US. We go to mass, and then he teaches an English class. I have been learning since I was little. We take turns reading from the English Bible he hides under the statue of the Blessed Virgin. We learn Spanish too, but he says it is important that we learn English so that when the war is over, we can go and work at the big hotels in Havana. He says that I can make as much working at the hotel as my father can." She moves to the side of Diego and still has a worried look on her face.

"Why does everyone have a gun?" she asks.

"We are US marines, Sereta. We are down here to rescue Diego and take him home to his parents. He is from France. Do you know of France?"

"Is that why he does not have a gun?"

"He is not trained to shoot one, so he does not have one," Captain King says.

"Is there anything here to eat?" Captain King asks her.

"There is only the goat. The soldiers killed it and the cow we shared among our families. The other soldiers took the cow with them when they left. The chickens are afraid, so they went to the forest to hide."

Sunlight filters through some of the covering greenery. It is a carefully thought-out hideaway. It is deep, and high enough above the valley floor that it can be used to ride out a bad storm. Above them is some pretty solid rock. Each man finds a spot on the floor and makes himself as comfortable as possible.

Casey looks at Sereta as he is lying down and sees she's not wearing underwear. "Where is the rest of your clothing?"

"What I am wearing is all I have. The soldiers take everything else. I am happy to keep my shoes. The soldiers kept asking my father where I was, and they torture him because he would not tell them," she replies.

They wait, each man taking an hour watch at the entrance of the cave. It is almost noon before they hear the sound of motors. They hear men deploying from some kind of vehicle and running around. Several of them come up the road past the entrance to the cave, but they don't stop.

From the vantage of the front of the cave, the side and the front of the house can be seen. A tracked armored personnel carrier and a heavy truck pull up. Men deploy from both. They look at the body of the dead officer, and one of the men spots the grenade. They look at the tow cable attached to his foot and surmise that someone thought about pulling him off the grenade so that the explosion would not kill whoever moved him.

"Mendoza." The captain motions to him to come to the mouth of the cave. "What are they saying?" he says in a hushed voice.

"It's something about the body being booby trapped, sir. They think there might be a second grenade under him and that the first one is only for show."

The two of them watch as the men who came on the tracked personnel carrier reenter it and close the back hatch. The tow cable is attached to the clevis on the back of the vehicle, and it slowly moves forward.

The line grows tight, and just as the body starts to move, the track of the carrier presses down just hard enough on the buried grenade to move it. The noise the motor is making covers the sound the handle of the hand grenade makes as it flips away. A tremendous explosion lifts the tracked vehicle up in the air on a column of fire and flips it over on its back to land on the top of the truck.

The Russians standing close enough are killed. Others are showered with shrapnel and wounded. The two men in the truck cab and the officer who ordered the dead man pulled out from the truck dies in the explosion as do all the men in the tracked vehicle.

Almost immediately, the ammunition inside the overturned tracked vehicle begins to cook off as the vehicle blossoms fire. Burning streams of fire pour out of it, and it ignites the truck on which it landed.

The men in the cave take turns looking through the small opening. The explosion shakes loose dust, and they have to put their T-shirts over their noses to keep it out.

Captain King, always the gentleman, offers Sereta his handkerchief. Diego just pulls his shirt up and puts it over his nose. The little hut is completely blown away, and the whole scene is visible through the opening of the cave. Bits of the blown-up hut and the one behind it burn. A second explosion of ordnance in the truck quickly kills more of the Russians.

The team retreats to the back of the cave. Mendoza maintains a watch. An aircraft soon flies over the scene, and then a second follows. In about an hour, two more tracked vehicles and two troop trucks stop where the hut used to be. More men deploy and spread around and secure the area.

The stench of the burning vehicles and the bodies is almost overwhelming. One truck that the first group of troops arrived in is also burning, but the new group manages to get some of their things off of it before its diesel tank explodes and burning fuel spreads down the road.

What looks like a staff car arrives, and two senior officers emerge and look at the carnage. The officers look at the bodies and have a pretty good idea of what transpired. They have no way to extinguish the burning vehicles, so everyone makes a wide berth around the heat and smell.

The force of the first explosion moved Sereta's parents' bodies across the clearing from the back of the house to against what had been the vine fence for the cow and the goat.

The charred outlines of one of the two other soldiers lie smoldering halfway across the area behind where the hut stood. The second is in the depression in the earth where Sereta had been hiding beneath the sugar cane stalks. The dead officer still remains beneath the burning truck.

The burning diesel fuel from the second truck runs down a rut in the road and puddles around the unexploded grenade that was placed under the officer. The heat makes it cook off and explode. The two officers on the scene are caught in a blast of shrapnel and gravel from the road.

One is killed, and the other goes to his knees. The troops quickly help him to his feet, drag him across the road in front of the cave opening, and continue to the top of the hill above them. The wounded are put in one of the troop trucks, and it leaves with its cargo of men.

The second truck is turned around, and all the bodies that can be retrieved are loaded onto it. The second tracked vehicle and five men are left to guard the remaining ruins. The rest have to get on and ride wherever they can. Soldiers end up with their feet on the dead bodies of their comrades. The wounded officer is hurriedly placed in his car and driven away.

It begins to grow long in the day, and Captain King asks if anyone has anything to eat. None of the men have any rations left.

"Bennett, didn't you bring the Sterno pack along with you?" Captain King inquires.

"Yes, sir. I have six small cans in my pack." He begins digging them out.

"Pass them out among the men. Brown, put the goat here on the big root in the middle of the room."

"What are we going to do, Captain?"

"We're going to have an old-fashioned cookout. With the stink the burning vehicles and bodies are producing, they won't even smell the goat being barbequed."

Captain King uses his knife to make a deep cut in the back of the goat, and he slices off some thin pieces. He then puts some dried roots over one of the cans of Sterno to make a support. He lights the can and proceeds to cook one piece of meat. The rest of them follow suit.

After Casey eats his first piece, he offers the second to Sereta, who takes the meat and eats like she hasn't eaten in quite a while.

"Thank you. What is your name?" she asks.

"I'm Casey," he replies as he puts another piece of meat over the flame and holds it to cook.

"What about me?" Diego says, complaining again. "Am I not allowed to eat also?"

"Come over here and share our fires, Diego. We will take turns and perhaps get to know each other," Captain King says. Diego reluctantly joins him and Chief Gordon and watches the progress of his meat slowly turning brown.

Mendoza is on watch in the front of the tunnel, and after Casey and Sereta eat what he considers a fair amount, Casey relieves him, so he can come and eat. Mendoza continues to cook for Sereta and him.

Mendoza relieves Casey, and he continues to listen for whatever snippets of conversation he might hear. Casey continues to cut thin slices and cook them until the little flame exhausts itself. Just before twilight, Casey wonders if his stomach is going to rebel, but he manages to keep the contents down. Through the afternoon, they take turns sleeping and watching the entrance of the cave.

The sound of a truck grabs the men's attention. Mendoza is still sitting and watching the burning vehicles. The Russian soldiers are relieved by five more.

The officer on the truck calls them to attention and gives them some explicit instructions. They salute, and he leaves with the five men they've relieved in the tracked vehicle. They leave a truck there for the soldiers who are left guarding the scene.

# Chapter 19

"Is that a radio the guy next to the fence is holding?" Captain King asks Mendoza.

"What do you want to do, Captain?" he asks.

"We'll slip out of here and snake our way up the ditch and go behind the hill to get as close as we can. White, you get in the entrance of the tunnel and take out the man with the radio. Your shot will be the signal for the rest of us to open up. Give us a little time to get out there."

They bend down and snake through the brush covering the front of the tunnel. The chief is the last one out, and Casey begins subconsciously counting the minutes. The sky is darkening faster than he likes. He needs a little light for a clear shot. He hopes it isn't too late.

When Casey thinks it's been long enough, he moves to the front of the tunnel. He looks around, and Diego and Sereta are just barely visible in the darkness of the cave.

At the front of the tunnel, he kneels and puts the barrel of the carbine across the top of the branch that's holding the heavy overgrowth. He makes sure it's loaded and ready, and he takes sight.

*Now this little war is personal again*, he thinks. The man in his sights is looking away at something across the road. Casey is afraid that one of the other men is over there. The man stands and says something to his comrades. Casey fires, and the man drops.

In the next second, AK-47s open up. It's not a firefight; none of the soldiers are fast enough to bring their weapon to bear.

"Diego, Sereta, gather up all our things and come on," Casey says. He pushes a portion of the cover away, and the three of them and whatever items the rest of the men left behind exit the cave. Casey makes an effort to push the enclosure closed to keep it hidden.

Of the items the soldiers had managed to unload from the burning truck, two were Soviet versions of the jerry can. The men quickly search the fallen soldiers.

"Please, Captain, can I take some of the uniform parts to make something to wear for what they took from me?" Sereta asks Captain King.

"Yes, but hurry!"

Casey cuts through the belt of one soldier and throws it aside. He pulls his shirt off and moves on to another. He gets the second soldier's shirt with Bennett and Brown helping. He, Bennett, Brown, and the chief throw the bodies up into the back of the truck. The chief plunges his knife through the top of the jerry cans and tosses one on top of the bodies along with any weapons left, and the second he lays down inside the truck. Now all of them have an AK-47 and ammunition. Casey keeps the little carbine on its sling behind his back, as does the chief.

Chief Gordon finds grenades and rolls a body over one of them. He carefully places another grenade and pulls the pin. This one will be indistinguishable from the others, and when the body is moved, it will take all of them with it. That and the diesel fuel will make a roaring fire.

"I carry the big stick, the club thing for you," Sereta says, and she picks up one of the RPGs. "Diego, you carry one too." Diego reluctantly picks it up, along with a belt of ammunition that he wraps around his chest.

"Let's go, men. We have to put a lot of distance between here and wherever we spend the next day."

It isn't an easy night. It is alternately almost moonlit by the filling moon, but when the clouds close in, dark enough that they have to hold hands. Sereta can keep up with them easily and looks disparagingly at Diego because he is so out of shape. The soil is alternately hard and then almost swampy. When they encounter water, they go east a little and continue. They skirt around the next small settlement.

At the edge of the next town, there's a small church, and behind it, a well. They very quietly use the bucket to refill their canteens. The first turn of the crank gives a squeak, so they unwind the rope and haul the water up by hand. The road coming into the town is fairly well traveled, and Captain King decides there is enough cover on both sides that they can use it if vehicles or humans come along. They can just disappear into the side foliage.

They come upon a burned-out truck blocking one branch of a fork in the road. They can see that the heavy traffic uses the road going southwest. The one blocked goes southeast. The captain decides to take it as there won't be vehicular traffic on it to threaten them. It's then that the clouds part and Captain King and Chief Gordon can read the map.

"Let's move on and see how much time we can make. We're getting closer, men. Another couple of days' travel at this pace and we'll be close to the bay where the boat will pick us up."

They see something or someone coming up the road, and they jump into the brush to the right. They wait, and soon two old men leading a cow and pulling two goats along the side of the road pass by without knowing about all the weapons being trained on them. The group waits until the old men are a long way down the road before coming back out of the undergrowth.

"Captain, if we keep on in this direction, we'll go completely past the turnoff point," Chief Gordon says.

"Are you sure, Chief?" Captain King replies.

"I think so. When we read the map the last time, it looked like the fourth small road from the cave."

The captain pulls the map book from his pack, and the two of them sit down on the road, shielding their flashlights as the captain flips the pages. The map book has been used enough times that the top three or four pages have come loose. A puff of wind catches the top pages, and Captain King pulls his automatic out and uses it for a paperweight. With another, stronger, gust of wind, they blow off, and the wind takes them down the road.

"Here, Chief, hold this." The captain hands the map book to the chief and hurries down the road after the torn pages. He traps one beneath his foot, goes after the second and catches it, and heads after the third. When he steps down hard to capture it, there is a huge explosion, and he disappears in a reddish-pink cloud of fire, smoke, and flesh.

They all stand there open mouthed, not quite wanting to acknowledge what just happened. Casey realizes then why the animals were being herded down the side and not on the road. Casey comes out from where he was standing, steps up to the road, and looks for the chief. When he finds him, he is a fetal ball at Casey's feet, clutching his head with blood streaming from his face. A projectile from the explosion struck him. The four of them quickly pick him up and carry him into the brush. Bennett is first to see the rock impaction in his eye.

They field dress the wound as best they can and continue into the brush. They finally hit dry ground and top a small hill. In the valley below are several peasant huts. They know the enemy usually searches them, but this is an emergency; they need shelter.

Now there is more wind, and a light rain begins. The only saving grace of the weather is that the mosquitoes completely quit bothering them. They go in, check out the first hut, and find no roof. They move on to the second and then the third. It is the only one that is habitable.

A fallow field is about forty yards in front of them, and a small stand of trees is about twenty behind. They find morphine, but the chief declines. He doesn't want to become so drowsy that he can't walk or help out in a fight. They put powdered sulfa from a first-aid pack in his eye.

"It feels like it's just rattling around in there. Can you pull it out?" Bennett tries, but it won't move. They figure that if it comes out, he will probably bleed more. They leave it alone and put bandages over the top of it.

The chief's eye rolls back and he slumps to the floor. Diego approaches and drops the captain's pack on the floor in front of them.

"Thanks, guy, that's the first real thing you've done for us." Casey looks behind him to get someone to help lift the chief to a small pallet.

Casey sees a red stain coming down Sereta's leg, and it soils her dress also. *My God, did she get hit too and not say anything?* he thinks. He studies her for a moment and realizes that if she had been hit, she would be in pain. He knows what it is. He takes the uniform shirts he removed from the soldiers, holds them out of the front of the hut, and allows the rain to wash the blood from them. He wrings them out several times and goes to Sereta.

"Stand in the doorway and lift your dress and allow the rain to wash you. Here, take this shirt, put it between your legs, and tie the arms around your waist. Put this one on over your head, and then you can wash your dress." She complies. She knows every eye in the hut is on her, and it's not easy to put on a cold, wet shirt.

"Diego, take this last shirt and replace the one you are wearing. Your odd colors give us away." Diego doesn't move. Casey whirls around and bores his eyes into him just to make sure he complies. "You will, or I will take your shirt off you with my knife, Diego. Now do it!" Diego jumps up and begins removing his shirt. He gets the one with only one bullet hole in it.

Casey knows Sereta is cold, so he helps her back into the Captain's poncho and sits down. She hangs her dress beside the wall, in the only available space where there isn't rain coming in. She goes back and sits beside Diego. She seems to be more secure with someone who doesn't have a gun.

The other weapons they garner from the trucks are piled against the inside of the hut. This morning it doesn't get light. The wind increases, and the rain comes in torrents. They pull the poncho out of Chief Gordon's pack and put it over him. The men take turns alternately checking him and looking out the doorway. If it isn't a hurricane, then it's a close brush by one. It is one miserable day.

They can feel the little hut shaking, and they're afraid it will be blown away. The wind and the rain increase. The roof quits trying to shake off the water, and it pours through in several places. Whoever is sitting in those places just moves over and finds a drier place to sit.

They drink from their canteens and refill them from the water pouring through the roof. They share their water with Sereta and Diego.

Casey reaches into his pocket, takes out a handful of dry cooked goat meat, and offers it to anyone who wants it. It isn't exactly beef jerky, but it is edible if you chew it long enough. It's a diversion, and they use it to help time pass.

"How did you manage to get enough of this stuff cooked to hide some of it away?" Bennett asks him.

"I just cooked two pieces every time I put it on the fire and then put one of them in my pocket." Sereta takes another piece. She apparently thinks nothing of the consistency of the meat. She's probably eaten worse. Diego, on the other hand, eats his like he's swallowing poison.

Casey remembers the extra sticks of cane and searches his other pocket. It's a sticky mess. He pulls the short sticks out and offers them around. Once again, they partake of his offering.

When Casey looks into the weather, he cannot see the open field. He stands there with his pocket turned out and lets the rain wash the stickiness away. It grows darker, and the rain and wind increase. He returns to the only other dry place.

Suddenly, Sereta jumps up, comes over, and sits down beside him. He cannot see what's going on, but he can tell she's cold.

"Casey, I sit with you now." He wraps her dress around her and rearranges her poncho, and she leans against him. Perhaps the two of them can keep warm together.

"Sereta, why is the field not growing sugar cane like the rest?" he asks her.

"The field is where they grow the rice, but this year, there are no plants, so they never flood the water. There will be less food to harvest."

It grows late, and the wind and rain lull them into a troubled sleep.

No one is on watch for most of the night, but it is an unusual situation. Casey stirs when he feels something hit him in the face. When he feels it again, he slowly opens his eyes and sees the chief across from him, holding a small handful of pebbles. He immediately becomes alert. The chief drops the pebbles and motions for Casey to come over to him.

He wakes Sereta, and she moves off his lap. The volume of the wind and rain make conversation hard, so Casey leans close to the chief.

"Casey, put more sulfa on my eye and redress it. I can stand the pain if I can just get it to stop oozing water and blood." Casey finds the medical kit and removes some bandages. He hands them to Sereta, who's by his side. They administer the sulfa powder and redress the wound.

"You got anything to eat?" Chief Gordon asks him.

"We dined on gourmet jerky last night. Here, have some." He reaches into his pocket, finds the remaining eight pieces, and gives them to the chief. He makes sure the chief has all the water he wants.

In the morning, the rain and wind won't let up. They figure that if they don't want to move, the enemy surely doesn't want to either. If they go, they will have to face the storm. They decide just to wait it out, but it also means another day lost. Casey returns to his place, and Sereta joins him.

"What happened last night to make you come over to me?" Casey asks her.

"Diego touched my body and tried to put his fingers between my legs, and I am afraid. The father told us not to do such things until after we are blessed by the Holy Virgin and are married in the church. After that, we will be blessed with children."

Hell flies in him. Casey stands, picks up his AK47, thumbs the magazine release, and lets it drop down just far enough that it won't pick up a round. The men are all awake but don't realize what he's doing.

He walks directly to Diego and kicks his shin to get his attention. He pulls the action back and releases it and then points the weapon at him.

"If you ever put your hands on Sereta again, I'm going to shoot your balls off, Diego," he says.

"I didn't! I wouldn't touch her; she's—"

Casey pulls the trigger, and there is a sharp click as the firing pin strikes nothing. Diego clenches his closed eyes, expecting to be shot. He opens them after realizing he's unharmed.

"We're not going to mention this again, are we?" Casey asks.

Diego mutely shakes his head. Casey can see the cold sweat coming down his face. He returns to where Sereta is seated. He looks over to see the chief smile for the first time since being wounded.

\*    \*    \*

That night, the storm continues, and they take inventory of what they have. Their all-important radio was vaporized in the explosion, and there's nothing they can do about that. They still have at least two more days to go until they get to an area where they can be picked up. Once again, the storm lulls them into a sense of security, and they sleep.

\*    \*    \*

Casey's leg is asleep from Sereta setting on his lap for so long. He looks at his watch and realizes that it's almost noon and that his bladder must have awakened him.

He moves Sereta off his lap and goes to check Chief Gordon. They redress the eye and add more sulfa. There are only two more packets of the drug. He hopes it's doing its work. The men take turns relieving themselves and then allow Sereta privacy by turning their backs. Casey realizes it takes her longer than normal because she is rinsing the shirt out, putting it back in place around her, and tying the sleeves to hold it.

The rain falls off to a drizzle in the next hour, and they decide the smart thing to do is take cover in the trees. The little valley is about a foot deep in water. They take the high side of the hill and work into the trees. Everything is soaked, so there is no sitting to rest.

They go across the slope of the hill and have almost come out the other side.

"Wait here a minute and let me have a look over the hill." He puts his AK against a tree, crouches, and then moves behind two trees. He peers around and looks out onto a much longer valley.

Casey hears a sound like he's never heard before and will remember the rest of his life. The air pressure against his head pops his ear. The round takes a tiny amount of flesh from his ear as it passes between it and his head. He instinctively ducks and throws his body sideways, and then he hears the report of the shot. His foot is under a root, and he pitches over and falls to his face. Immediately, Sereta crawls beside him. He reaches up and holds her down.

"The rest of you stand just high enough to be seen for a second, and run back to the forest." The chief motions for the men to go, and they immediately respond.

Casey crawls the short distance to the cover of the hill and makes Sereta do likewise.

The chief says, "Stop now. You men come back real low. We need to outflank this guy."

They hear the sound of an engine starting, and a lightweight vehicle comes straight across the open meadow as fast as the water and the mud will allow it.

"Sereta, Diego, go with the chief," Casey says to them as the chief retreats for the cover of the trees. "Brown, Mendoza, go that way. Bennett, come with me." They split up and crawl to where they can see the oncoming vehicle.

Once it reaches the trees, the vehicle slows, but it's too late. Fire from four AK-47s impacts the heavy glass windshield. The volume of fire overcomes the glass, and the rounds penetrate into the cab. Both men in the front dive over and the vehicle continues, hits the rise, and stalls.

Both men are bloodied, and the driver attempts to return fire, but his rifle catches on the rim of the steering wheel. The force of the two machine guns tears him up.

All at once, the air is again quiet. They advance slowly and see movement from the passenger. Casey is the one closest. He gets on top of the man and pins his gun to the ground by stepping on it.

They never see the third man come out of the back of the truck, and he runs right toward Mendoza. He has a huge knife, and Mendoza sidesteps and turns him. The soldier holds on and is only stopped when Mendoza catches his knife hand.

The man is much larger and stronger than Mendoza. Casey is beside the truck and cannot get a clear shot. Bennett is trying to see if there are any others in the back, and Brown is getting another magazine into his AK.

A combat knife thrown by Chief Gordon ricochets off the enemy soldier's neck, taking a large chunk of flesh with it and distracting him for a second. A shot rings out, followed by another. Diego is standing there looking shocked. He drops the automatic to the ground and returns to Sereta and the chief.

Mendoza turns to sidestep the older man and plunges the knife into him. The man slumps to the ground. Now the only enemy alive is the man Casey has his foot on, pinning his weapon down. He tries weakly to raise it, but Casey holds it tight. There is a deep red stain coming through his shirt and bloody bubbles on his lips. He looks up at Casey and mutters two words. He smiles, attempts a salute, and dies.

"Mendoza, what the hell did he say?" Casey asks.

"'Blue eyes.' Casey, you have blue eyes."

Casey looks down and realizes the weapon he's standing on is a sniper rifle. He picks it up and places his AK-47 into the back of the vehicle. He holds it up and washes the mud from it with rainwater.

"Bennett, what is this?" Casey asks. "It looks old but in good shape."

"Casey, that's an old Mosin-Nagant seven point six two sniper rifle. I didn't think I'd ever see one of those except in a military museum. I'm surprised the Soviets are still using them. Castro is getting all their old World War II junk over here."

Casey gestures toward the vehicle. "Can you get this thing going?"

Bennett reaches in, takes the soldier's hat, brushes the glass shards aside, and sits down to figure out the controls.

From where he's standing, Casey hears a faint, faraway sound he has grown to recognize from his first encounter at the Kingsville air station. "Hey! Quick, all of you get out and follow me! Come on, quick! Sereta, Diego, come on! Run out from under the trees!" There is a general confusion in their response, but they all follow him.

"Lay down right here! Mendoza, Brown, form a *K* with your bodies. Come on, and hurry; we don't have any time! Bennett, Diego, lay down. Now! Form a *C* with your bodies."

The *whooooo* sound is increasing very quickly now, and the men must think Casey's lost his mind, exposing them to an aircraft—especially a jet. "Chief, hold up five fingers. The rest of you, make sure your AKs are not showing." Casey holds one of the carbines up over his head.

## Chapter 20

" Everybody look up. It's one of ours!" he screams joyously.

There's a flash of aircraft as the F8 Crusader with its little windows on the bottom streaks by at five hundred miles an hour. The pilot pulls it straight up, lights the afterburner, and is out of sight in seconds. Casey recognizes the squadron insignia on the tail as one he had seen one night when some of the marine aviators partied at the BOQ at Naval Air Station Kingsville.

"I hope he had all his cameras running. Maybe someone will know we are still alive. Everybody back in the truck. Let's get out of here." Bennett takes a minute and then reaches for what looks like the ignition. He puts the clutch down and tries it. It starts immediately. Apparently, the snipers had better maintenance on their vehicles than the infantry. Casey gives a silent prayer of thanks. The rest of the group climbs in, and Bennett pulls the vehicle into the trees.

"All right, Chief Gordon, where do we go now?" Casey asks the obviously weakened man. "Chief, do you have any idea where we are?"

"Go southeast until you can't go any further."

They wind their way through the trees, and Casey looks through the ammunition in the back of the vehicle. He finds some rounds that look hand-loaded that fit the sniper rifle. They stop after driving in that direction for almost an hour.

"Pull up here a minute," the chief says to Bennett. He stops and awaits further instructions. "The captain is dead, and that leaves me the senior man. I'm a cripple, but my head still works, at least as long as I can keep the blood out of my eye. The rest of you are all E-2s and graduated the same time from boot camp. The only thing different is that three of you are marines, and Casey is a sailor. Do you have any problem with me appointing him as a platoon leader, or whatever designation it takes to be the one to call the shots?"

The three marines look at each other, shrug, and nod.

"We don't have any problem with it," Bennett says. "We know he hasn't had any infantry training, but the way he handled himself back there makes us think he proved himself. The only thing is, if we see something he's doing really wrong, we might have to call him on it."

"I can live with that," Casey replies. *What should we do now? We're out in daylight and should be concealed in some secure defendable place,* Casey thinks.

"It's only two more hours before dark. What with the clouds we have now, it will probably get dark sooner than normal. I think we should stick it out right here for now. Let's get a recon of the area and rest up. I know the rest of you are probably just as hungry as I am. We have water, and sooner or later we'll find something we can eat. If any of you has any input, I'd like to hear it now," Casey says.

They shake their heads and go to the back of the vehicle. They renew the rounds in their weapons, and the three marines take off in different directions. They all return in about fifteen minutes.

"It's a mighty small stand of trees, and there is a little village just beyond the next rise," Bennett says. When they return, Casey finds the remains of the captain's maps.

"There is a pretty big church for such a little village," Bennett continues. "Sereta, go with Bennett and have a look to see if there is anything you recognize." He helps her down from the back of the truck.

They leave, and Casey looks over to the chief. He looks drawn and tired, and his dressing needs to be changed.

"Diego, see if you can get the chief to drink some of the water," Casey says to him.

When Bennett and Sereta return, they're smiling, and she is almost happy.

"It is the Church of the Resurrection at El Jiqui. It is where my father and mother were married. I know the priest."

"Do you think he will help us?" Casey asks her.

"He doesn't like the Communists," Sereta replies.

Casey looks north and sees two trucks and a tracked vehicle heading into the town. Another truck is coming from the south. The two of them are about to meet. The men all instinctively find cover and a place to watch what's happening.

Several people standing outside the church hear the approaching vehicles and quickly step back into the building. The two vehicles stop yards from each other, and the men in the tracked vehicle immediately deploy. The men from the trucks fan out in pairs and begin searching houses. The Cuban and the Russian officers approach each other, salute, and shake hands.

They order several of the men to go into the church. In minutes, the doors burst open and two dozen of the town's people are herded out into the street. The women all have black kerchiefs covering their heads. Four more men emerge carrying a casket. They set it down in the street at the Cuban officer's insistence, and the padre approaches the officers.

"They've crashed a church and broken up a wake. If the Cuban officer has Catholic roots, he won't allow the Russians to go very far," Mendoza says.

Casey feels someone sneaking through the grass at his side. He glances over and sees Sereta looking down with tears in her eyes. "They blaspheme the church," she says. "The people are holding a wake for the dead. Why do they do this?"

"I don't have a reasonable answer for you, Sereta."

She looks up at Casey and shakes her head.

In another minute, a soldier emerges chewing on what looks like a chicken leg. He finishes it and tosses the bone at the padre's feet. The Cuban officer has his men pry the top from the casket, and he looks inside. Satisfied there's a body in there, he loosely returns the top to where it belongs.

Soldiers begin returning from the houses. Some are carrying trophies. When the Russian officer sees what they've looted, he curses them, and they run to put the purloined items back where they stole them from.

"They would have kept them if the Cuban officer had not been here tonight," Sereta says. When she says tonight, Casey notices it's almost dark. Satisfied there's no enemy hiding in the town, the two groups of men rejoin their respective units and, in minutes, pull out of the town.

Casey has a bad feeling about the whole thing but is intent on getting the men some help. The chief especially needs to see a doctor, although he assumes there probably isn't one in the town.

The townspeople pick the casket up from the road and return it to the church. Most of them return inside, and the town becomes quiet again.

"Sereta, can you go down there, find the padre, and ask him to help us? Tell him one is hurt and needs medical attention. Did you see the nun you told us about earlier, when all the people came out of the church?"

"No, I didn't see her, but you can know that she is in town. No one dies in this town and is buried without her." Casey smiles about that.

"Mendoza," says Casey, "accompany her down to about where the drainage ditch runs past that first row of houses." They work their way down the hill, and as soon as they are on the street, Sereta breaks away from him and runs to the church.

The men hold their breath for a long time until she reappears, and the priest accompanies her to the street. The priest and another man disappear behind the church. All at once, different troops come down the street from the opposite direction, and Sereta turns and runs back into the church.

187

Mendoza quickly worms his way into waist-deep water in a culvert under the road where a little stream flows. Apparently, the Russians are unsatisfied with the earlier search and spend more than an hour systematically going through the houses of the town. They leave the church for last and make the people come outside again. The priest puts a torch into a holder on the front of the building and lights it.

One of the people forced out of the church is Sereta. She's gained a black lace cover for her head. One of the Russians questions each of the people who emerge from the church. Sereta apparently gives all the correct answers to his questions.

He notices the bulge around her waist and again steps in front of her. The men cannot hear what is being said, but in a minute, she opens the button at her waist, puts her hand inside, and withdraws it.

When the officer sees the blood, he steps back and orders the men to complete the search. In another fifteen minutes, they load up and leave.

The people left standing in front of the church turn and quietly laugh together. They go back inside, and Sereta walks to the culvert and helps extract Mendoza. They run back up the hill.

"They say they will help us, but we are to wait until someone comes out of the church and takes down the torch."

*There must be some suspicion about the enemy returning,* Casey thinks. They just sit and wait. Killing time is boring, and their minds continue to work.

Brown turns to Diego. "Diego, what is it about you that is so much of a mystery?" The group begins focusing on Diego.

"Yeah, what do you have that makes you so special that the president will get together a covert group of men just to rescue you?" Mendoza asks.

"I am the son of the ambassador. Will you not do as much as that for one of yours?" Diego replies haughtily.

"Yes, I guess so, but still, you act like you're really something special. Do you know the president?" Mendoza asks.

"His father visited with my parents in Europe after he was made your ambassador to France. Mother showed him around our country while my father was gone to Spain on business. It was before I was born," Diego answers.

"Yeah, but one visit does not a friendship make," Bennett says, and now Casey is interested.

"Are you related to him in some way?" Casey asks. Diego almost blanches at the question.

"Truthfully, now, what the hell is going on? Tell us. I promise I won't shoot your ass off if we find out the truth," Bennett says.

Casey thinks about it and focuses on his features. The answer slowly forms in his mind. He has the mouth, the chin, the eyes, the height, the hair color and hairline, and the physique, and he is part of the second generation. "Is the ambassador really your dad? Did someone else slip in the gene pool?"

The color drains from Diego's face.

"Let's see now, that makes you the president's half brother. Is that right?" Casey asks him directly.

"No, please . . ." Diego says, stammering. Casey knows he's hit the nail on the head.

"There's been an American in the French gene pool," he says. The group laughs and once again Casey sees Chief Gordon smile.

"Does your dad know you are really not his blood son?" Casey asks. There's another quiet snicker through the group, and they let him continue his line of questioning. "How does your mother explain you to your dad?"

"They have worked things out. She knows he cheats on her, so she got even with him," Diego says.

"And that produced you. Are there any more little Diegos running around? Your brother, perhaps?"

"I wouldn't know, and it doesn't matter to you anyway," Diego replies.

"No, but it would be funny if there are more Diegos simmering in the gene pools around Europe." A chuckle passes through the men, along with the understanding of exactly why they're here.

*     *     *

It's almost an hour before the trucks reappear, and this time, they come out of the field behind the church. Four soldiers start up the hill.

"Let's move back in the trees. Go to the vehicle, and we can watch them from there." Before the Russian soldiers arrive where the group had been, they've retreated to the darker cover of the trees, but they watch what's going on in the town.

The Russians sit down, light cigarettes, and laugh about the trouble they're causing the townspeople. Little do they realize there are enough guns pointed at them to completely erase any trace of them being on earth.

The air clears, the mosquitoes return, and the soldiers swat, curse, and start back down the hill. The officer approaches them, and one turns, points, and swings his arm around in a wide arc. He's apparently lying to his officer about the area they searched. The second search turns up the same as the first.

The officer motions to a vehicle in the caravan, and it pulls to the front. Casey has a bad feeling about this.

"Everyone take cover until we find out what they are up to," he says. A camouflage cover is pulled away, exposing two mounted machine guns. They immediately start firing and rake the area where Casey and the group had been standing moments before. The second gun is pointed the other direction and rakes the opposite hillside. They haven't been discovered, only intimidated. Sereta crawls to Casey's side and lies curled up beside him. The fire ends and the troops climb aboard their trucks and travel north out of town.

After another wait, a man steps out of the church and puts some sort of container over the torch to extinguish it. They stand and work the kinks out of their bodies and slowly start working their way down the hill. They stop at the road and listen intently. One by one, they run across the street, led by Sereta. As one ascends the steps, the door opens, and he slips inside, and then the next follows.

Casey and Bennett help the chief across the road and up the steps. The man seems intent on going by himself. As soon as they enter the church, they're directed to the rear of the chancel and around the back to a steep stairway only accessible by opening a small, well-disguised door panel in the wainscoting.

Two women immediately begin cleaning up the footprints of the men as the last one disappears down the narrow stairs. Casey looks at all the mourners sitting in the pews, and none look up at him. He descends the steps and smells the aroma of chicken cooking.

There are several small pots bubbling over a charcoal fire in an alcove with a chimney that leads up the back and joins the main fireplace that heats the padre's apartment. Casey wonders how often the Cubans need a fireplace. Perhaps it is used only for cooking.

There are only three wooden spoons, a silver fork, and a silver candle snuffer to eat with. They've boiled chickens and added a large volume of rice to them. Wooden bowls suffice to hold their offering. Fingers and combat knives nicely fill as the missing utensils.

It's the most delicious meal Casey's eaten in weeks. He makes sure Chief Gordon gets his share. The priest brings water and sits down beside him. He motions to Sereta, and she joins them. Mendoza comes over as soon as Casey crooks his finger at him.

"The padre doesn't speak English except for a few words; we'll have to translate for him," Sereta says to Casey.

"The patrols have increased in the past two days, and we know something is going on. The Cuban and the Russian armies search the town every night," the padre tells them.

A trapdoor opens, and in the dim light, Casey sees a tall woman in a nun's habit emerge from the stairwell carrying a rolled-up bundle of cloth. *This must be Sister Victoria, the nun of whom Sereta spoke.* She looks at the rag-tag group and smiles at them.

"The God of our fathers be with you, my friends," she says in accented English as she walks toward them.

"Amen to that," Casey replies, and she steps up and gives him a big hug. Her habit, although old and worn looking, smells fresh and clean.

She turns to one of the women and speaks to her. The woman takes another small pot with a chicken wing in it from the back of the charcoal fire and disappears back up the stairs. The trapdoor closes behind her.

"The Cuban soldiers have returned again. Let us be silent and we will be blessed by the sanctuary of the lord," Sister Victoria says to them.

They hear boots upstairs in the church. Sister Victoria goes to the chief, looks at the bandage, and removes it. "You need penicillin, and we have none."

"Do you think we'll be able to find a doctor soon?" Chief Gordon asks her.

"This is a poor village, and the doctor only comes here once a month," she replies.

"We're going to be picked up by boat halfway down the Bay of Pigs, but we don't know how long it will take us to get to the pickup point," Casey says.

"Do you have a map?"

Casey takes the map container out of his pocket and opens it, turning the pages.

"I don't really know exactly where we are now," he says.

"Let me see," Sister Victoria says.

He hands the map to her, and she looks through the pages until she finds the one that shows the town.

"This map is only partially complete. The area where you get picked up is correct, but you have several things to overcome. This side of the road is a swamp, and the crocodiles and the caimans live there."

"What is a caiman?" Casey asks.

"It is a smaller crocodile, but just as deadly as the larger ones, and it hides better," Sister Victoria tells him.

The sound of moving furniture brings their attention back to the ceiling above them, and they instinctively look up and switch their flashlight off.

"This time they will move the altar looking for you. They will make us move it back when they don't find any hiding places. They will be satisfied just to steal the chicken."

"Do you have a vehicle we might use?" Casey asks.

"No, Mr. Casey, we are poor people. We will send someone with you to show you the way."

"That's fair enough," he replies. He holds bandages for her. She continues to clean the chief's wound but doesn't try to remove the stone.

"I only have two packets of sulfa. I will give you one of them. I must keep one for my people," Sister Victoria says.

"We'll leave you most of the morphine. I wish we could repay you for your hospitality."

"Please do not worry. We do the Lord's work; he will repay us in his own good time." She stands up and looks around. "Sereta, you will now come with me." The two of them disappear through an almost invisible break in the rear wall at the corner. They haven't gone upstairs, so Casey knows there must be another room. After almost half an hour later, they return, and he knows she's helped Sereta get cleaned up.

## Chapter 21

C ASEY looks up, and a piece of paper floats down through a knothole in the ceiling. Sereta is the first to it. "They have left two soldiers in the church and two more outside," she reports. "I guess we're in for a wait."

All the men find a spot on the floor and lie down. Casey looks at his watch, and it's almost half past two in the morning. "Who wants to take the first watch?"

Brown is on his feet in a flash. "I will, Casey. The rest of you try to get some sleep."

"Okay, Brown, but it's the same thing as the captain set up. Nobody stands more than two hours' watch, and then wake someone else." He goes to check on the chief and finds him already asleep on the hard dirt floor.

Diego stands, approaches Sister Victoria, and whispers in her ear. They confer a moment, and she again disappears. She returns with a stole around her neck and places her hand on his forehead. He needs a confession. He is with her for almost half an hour. *Shooting the soldier must be too much for him to handle.* Someone moves behind Casey and Sereta joins the nun, and the process is repeated.

They snuff the candles, and in the total blackness of the basement, there is the sound of furniture being moved. They're putting the church altar back where it belongs.

Casey hears Sister Victoria quietly open the trapdoor, and she disappears through a shaft of candlelight. He takes his flashlight out and checks his watch. He keeps it covered although he's installed the red lens. He doesn't want to take any chances of being discovered.

Three times during the night, he has to roll the chief over to keep him from snoring. He finally goes to sleep after Bennett tells him he'll sleep beside the chief and take care of the snoring problem.

It's possibly the best sleep he's had since after the first night the operation started.

*   *   *

When he awakes, Sereta is curled up against him. He turns over and holds her. She reaches up and holds his hand as he drifts off again. In the blackness, he looks at his watch. It's after ten in the morning.

"Why didn't someone wake me?" he whispers.

"We decided on four-hour watches, seeing as how we won't be able to get out of here until after dark," says Bennett. "Your watch starts as soon as you want it to."

"Do we have access to a privy?" Casey asks.

"Yes, go through the crack in the wall where Sereta disappeared through last night, and there is a hole in the floor for that very purpose."

Casey finds the slender opening in the wall. It's about a foot wide, and he knows that the chief will have trouble getting through it. He relieves himself and discovers Sereta in the room. She is standing only a foot from him. He doesn't know whether or not to be embarrassed, but it is pitch black except for when he uses his flashlight.

"Please, Casey?" She takes the flashlight. "The holy mother gave me cloths last night and told me just to place them in the bucket as I change." She shines the flashlight against the wall and illuminates a wooden bucket. She completes what she needs to do, and they go back to the larger room.

It's quite an effort with two of them on the inside and the other two on the outside, but they finally get the chief into the room and let him use it.

The trapdoor lifts again, and this time the old priest enters. He speaks in Spanish, and Sereta interprets.

"He says he is sorry there is no more food right now, but tonight, when we get ready to go, there will be some to take with us. He will bring water in a bucket, and we are to fill our canteens with it. There will be more through the day if we need it."

The men give him their thanks, and that is a word he does understand. The door closes, and they're in the dark.

"Men, we've got about twelve hours to kill. I think we should all try to get some more sleep. Does anyone have a problem with that?"

"I'll take the first watch, Casey," says Mendoza. Casey moves to the side and checks on the chief. There is a reddening around the eye bandage that he doesn't like, but there is little he can do about it. He shines his light around and finds Bennett, Brown, and Diego already asleep.

He selects a place not far from the chief to lie down. Instantaneously, a small hand reaches out for him. He holds it, and as soon as he is comfortable, she is asleep in his lap.

It seems like he's only just drifted off when someone whispers to him, saying, "It's your watch, Casey." Sereta is not with him. She is standing beside Sister Victoria, redressing the chief's eye. He looks at his watch. It's six. In about an hour they need to get going.

The trapdoor opens, and Sister Victoria goes to the base of the stairs and looks up at the man coming down. She says a prayer for them and introduces them to the man who will be accompanying them tonight.

His name is Horatio Pena. He is a typical-looking Cuban peasant: muscular, short of stature. He smells of cigar smoke, and the wrinkles of the world are etched into his face.

"Do you know English?" Casey asks him.

"A little, but you have a man I can talk to in Spanish much better."

Sister Victoria stands in the group. "Take all your things; leave nothing the soldiers can say is yours. If we are found out, we will die by their hands."

They know that well, and every one of them looks around to make sure he leaves no items or equipment. They queue up at the bottom of the steps, and suddenly there's a stomp on the floor. Sister Victoria looks panicked and motions for the candles to be extinguished. They all wait, holding their breathing to a quiet pace.

An argumentative voice followed by some scraping of dishes indicates that one of the soldiers has returned to the church and is demanding food. After a period of quiet, the pan spins to a stop after he apparently throws it across the room. He shouts an obscenity at the padre, and then the door slams.

In the basement of the church, the men disperse around the sides, waiting for some kind of signal. An hour passes and they settle in for a long wait. "The soldiers are waiting to catch you; you must be content to wait it out," the padre says to Casey.

The chief motions for Casey to come over to him. "Casey, I've been thinking. I don't know if I'm going to make it out of here.

"Yes we are, Chief. All we need is a little time."

The chief holds up his hand to stop him.

"I feel like shit, Casey, and I've had time to do a lot of thinking. I've been sort of a bastard all my life. Both women I chose for wives cheated on me while I was deployed. I divorced both and never had to pay a dime of alimony."

"Why are you telling me this now?" Casey asks him.

"Listen to me, Casey. I want to marry Sereta."

"What?" he replies, astounded.

"Listen to me a minute. She's a Cuban national and won't be very welcome when we get to the base. If she's my wife, they'll have to allow her to stay until they can prove otherwise. Now, I'm Catholic, and if we can convince the nun and the priest to do it, then she will have to be admitted into the US.

"I have no intention of ever touching her, and yes, I know I'm old enough to be her father, but that doesn't matter right now. If I die without a dependent or an heir, then the government keeps all my retirement. I imagine my two ex-wives will end up fighting over the proceeds of my life insurance if there is any way they can lie about the marriages not really being over."

"You think you are really dying, don't you, Chief?" Casey asks.

"Damn it, Casey, don't make this any harder than it needs to be. Go and ask the nun and the padre to come over here, and I'll talk to them."

Sereta looks at him in wide-eyed astonishment. "I don't want to marry you. I want a man I can love and have children with."

"Listen to me, Sereta. This is your chance to get out of Cuba for good. The Russians or the Cuban Revolutionary Army killed all of your family. The government has a price on your head. If they catch you, they will torture and kill you to make an example of you. Please just go along with it. It means your future." He reaches out to her. "Please."

She stands looking at him as Casey goes to the padre and the nun and asks them to talk with the chief. He sits back against the wall and listens as the chief again tells them of his plans and then waits for an answer. They walk off to the opposite corner of the room to confer, and then they return.

"Chief Gordon, we have prayerfully made up our minds," says Sister Victoria. "We want Sereta to have a better life, but you must promise never to touch her. I will say words of a blessing, but not the words of marriage. I will enter her name in the book with her parents while I am removing them from the book of life.

"If any of the authorities come and look at the book, it will say that you and Sereta were here a week ago, married, and just continued on your way. The first thing you must do when you get to the USA is go to a priest and take the vows of marriage. May God have mercy on my soul for putting lies in the holy record book."

Casey hides his amazement. Apparently, the need for a better life surpasses the need for a real marriage. So be it. *If I can get Sereta to the base, I'll deal with things as they work themselves out.* The padre leaves and is gone a quarter of an hour before he returns carrying papers and ink.

"Chief Gordon, you sign here, and Mr. Casey, you sign here." The padre hands Casey a chicken feather, sharpened into a quill, and he dips it into some India ink and carefully signs his name after the chief signs.

"Sereta, you sign on the line beside Chief Gordon." Casey watches her, and it's apparent that she has had very little, if any, preparation for signing her name.

The marks she does turn out, however, manage to look the way her name should be spelled.

"I will allow the parchment to dry and put some of the candle wax on it to help with the ink," says Sister Victoria. "Let it dry as long as you can, and then protect it with this." She gives Casey another piece of parchment covered with a light coating of candle wax. They wait momentarily and then run a candle under the two pages after he has placed them together.

"Carry it carefully, and do not allow it to get wet and wash away the signatures." Casey takes the document and fans the ink dry as the priest hands him another sheet of the parchment. They melt it to the other side of the document. The marriage license is now sealed between two layers of wax-impregnated parchment. Casey tucks it into his shirt.

The priest talks to Chief Gordon, who makes his confession. He's holding Sereta's hand, and shortly they stand and walk to the bottom of the stairs. There are four knocks on the floor, and the priest ascends the ladder. In a moment, he motions to them to help Chief Gordon up to the ladder.

All the enemy soldiers are together outside in the front of the church. They light their cigarettes and curse the mosquitoes as the eight figures slip out the back door.

They run as quietly as they can through the field where the trucks came from before. After a while, they stop and try to get oriented. They have to rest because the chief is breathing so hard. "I'll be okay, as soon as I catch my breath," he says. Casey nods to Brown and Bennett, and they walk alongside the chief and help him go. He insists on carrying his share of the load, so Casey lets him keep one of the carbines.

"Wait here," Horatio tells them. He apparently knows the people of the area.

Shortly, he comes back and tells them to follow him. There is a donkey cart sitting in the yard of the house. The chief protests, but they manage to get him loaded in it along with the heavier weapons. They take off across the cleared land, and the chief tries to keep the extra weapons from bouncing out of the cart.

Mendoza puts the carbine in the cart but keeps his AK-47. Casey carries the sniper rifle and keeps the carbine on its sling behind his back. He deposits the bandoleers, clips, and the AK he's carrying in the cart.

They allow Diego to keep the 9mm he carries, but the RPG is placed with the other one that Sereta is carrying. Mendoza still carries the Russian radio, but his AK-47, like the rest of them, is loaded into the cart along with their extra ammunition. Bennett and Brown take the first watch, pulling the cart while Casey goes ahead with the new guide. Bennett and Brown each have a hand grenade, as does Casey and the chief.

"Hey, I'm useful again. I'll keep all this stuff from falling if the road doesn't get too much rougher," the chief says, experiencing a more lucid moment.

Now they're heading away from whatever it is the Russians are protecting, and perhaps the men searching for them will let up some. Casey looks up and is amazed at the moon. It's either full or only lacks a day or two of being so. That isn't good for them as it probably means they'll have to hide while it is out.

They approach another small settlement. The land around them offers no cover, and it takes them almost an hour to get around it. Twice they have to go off the road and into whatever cover there is and hope that whoever passes is a friendly.

"Where can we spend the next day, Horatio?" Casey asks him as they go down the visibly moonlit road.

"We go to the place of the fish. The Russians don't like to go there, and the Cuban bandits only go there if there is fish to be stolen from the fishermen."

# Chapter 22

C ASEY looks at his watch and notes that it's almost five in the morning. Horatio leads them through a commercial area littered with the remains of boats either under repair or being cannibalized for parts. There's a huge sheet-metal-roofed building leading down to the water and a wharf.

The building is on pilings above the water, and beneath is an enclosed area that can be accessed by pulling some of the boards away from it.

They help Chief Gordon off the cart and manage to get it under the enclosed area. The sound of a motor makes them hurry. Someone recently washed down the decking boards overhead, and the sand beneath the building is wet, all except for a place about twelve feet square in the back where there's sheet metal nailed in place to keep anything from coming through. The evaporating water cools the air, and the shade is more pleasant there.

"You get under there and get settled. If the soldiers come, you can just run down and get into the water and get away," Horatio says. He turns, goes back behind the boat building, and disappears.

The motor sound they hear is a boat, and they watch its shadow come alongside the pier. The sound is soon replaced by voices. *Happy voices*, Casey thinks. He supposes there are some people who can find happiness in their miserable lives.

There's another motor sound, and a small crane begins lifting baskets of fish off the boat. Voices of women and girls soon follow, and it's apparent they're cleaning the catch for market. Not long after, a portion of a floorboard is lifted up and a metal bucket full of glowing charcoal is lowered to them.

They cautiously take it back to the corner and place it in the wet sand to keep it from setting anything on fire.

The floorboard opens again, and three of the largest fish Casey has seen in quite a while tumble down. They are slit down the stomach and cleaned, but not scaled. A bundle is lowered to them wrapped in what looks like an old dress. They open it and find it's steamed rice.

To the starving men, this looks like a banquet. They are just barely polite to one another as they gorge themselves on the rice and take turns cutting steaks from the fish and cooking them over the charcoal. Casey wonders how they can cover up the smell of the cooking fish until he realizes that the people above them are doing the same thing.

The stench in the air is not strong enough to keep any of them from eating, including Diego. Sereta holds out the fish Casey cooks and places it in leaves, and they pick the bones from it and eat. They move to where Chief Gordon is and pick the fish for him to eat.

Another boat arrives and unloads. They sit, contemplating what will happen next. The day is wearing along nicely. Diego and the chief are soon asleep.

Sereta sits at Casey's side and falls asleep on his shoulder. He leans back and she slowly leans over, her head resting in his lap. He looks up, and Brown and Bennett give him big smirking grins. He looks back and shakes his head no. *There is nothing quite like a marine with a dirty mind.*

Casey wonders how long this will go on and then realizes that the tide is going out, and anyone in a small boat can look under the pier and see them. He quickly brings this to the men's attention. They dig down into the sand and make a pile between them and the front of the pier.

The voices diminish, and finally, the last woman walks across the floor toward the back of the building. She leans over, picks up the board, and calls to them.

"Thank you for the food, senora." Sereta goes to where she is looking down. "Sister Victoria tells us to do it. Go to the board with the two knotholes, push it out, and place the charcoal pan there. Dig a deep hole, bury the remains of the fish, and smooth the sand so that they cannot be found if the soldiers come and look." She replaces the board and disappears.

That's easy enough in the soft sand, and it's accomplished in short order. Earlier, Mendoza dug a privy, and they start to close it, but Sereta asks them to wait. She tears some of the dress material from the bundle the rice came in. She wraps her used cloth with a piece of the new cloth.

"Sereta, why do you want to keep the used rag?" asks Casey.

"I do not have a clean one to replace it. When I need another, I will have to clean it and use it."

So okay, he wasn't up on all things female.

\* \* \*

It's twilight, and Casey wonders when Horatio will show up. Finally, there are steps on the floor above them. Once again, the board is pulled up, but a woman, not Horatio, looks down.

"Horatio is afraid and left the town earlier in the day," she tells them.

"Are any soldiers in the town?" Sereta asks her.

"No, none, but they will return soon. You get going."

They thank her again and go out through the opening they came in. The town is mostly dark, and they decide just to go down the road between the houses.

Once or twice when Casey looks, he can discern the eyes of an alligator lying just under the surface of the water. *I wonder how long our luck will hold out.* It's not long before the answer comes.

They can hear the sounds of motors and the squeaks of tracked vehicles. They make it to the road, where they have to turn and run until their lungs almost burst. Mendoza and Bennett are virtually carrying Diego, and Casey and Brown are pulling the cart with Sereta behind, pushing it.

Casey keeps looking at the swamp, and the water still looks ominous. Ahead, it's moonlit enough to see, but he can't make out things in the black water. He looks up at a huge, heavy roll of clouds making their way toward them. He smells something different in the air now. It smells like saltwater, and he makes everyone stop and take a break and listen.

Sereta taps him on the shoulder. "It is the smell of the ocean, Casey." Mendoza agrees, but now they need cover. Ahead of them is another small settlement.

Beside them is a very small stand of trees. They opt to go into the trees and hunker down. They turn the cart over to keep the shadows from outlining it. Casey, Mendoza, Brown, and Bennett open the map case and turn the pages. The others look as they stand in a circle to block out any trace of light from the red lens of the flashlight.

Yes! The two churches and the fish market and dock between them mark important finds. Now they have to get across the swamp to the beach. The mark where the box is buried looks like it's about a mile or so ahead of them. The discovery rejuvenates them. The immediate problem is that in that mile is a lot of swamp and overgrowth between them and the beach.

"Pick up what you can carry," says Casey. "We'll probably have to abandon the cart. Chief, sit on it and hold on to things until we have to let it go."

They all listen quietly for a long minute, and then they go running down the small hill to the road. They hurry along it until the sound of a truck approaching forces them to make the decision none of them wants to make. They help the chief get off and push the cart into the ditch. It bounces in, stops abruptly, and doesn't go any farther.

The ditch is about as deep and wide as the wheels are round. Each one of them walks across the cart, picking up guns and ammunition, and jumps into the knee-deep water. The swamp is deeper than normal because of the hurricane rain.

"Wait up a minute, Casey. I got a grenade I want to plant here," the chief says.

Casey and Mendoza help him into the water, and he jams the grenade into the soft earth beneath the bottom board of the cart and carefully pulls the pin. Now anyone who steps on the back of the cart will free the handle and set off the grenade.

They make it to the cover of the swamp and across to a rise where the land is higher—still wet, but there is no standing water. The trees are larger here.

Two vehicles stop on the road at the cart. Casey hears voices. A group of men dismounts from the truck, and several start across the cart. As soon as the first one tips the balance, the grenade spoon pings off, and they can see the men trying to get back.

There a number of the men are on the cart, and some are behind. The grenade explodes before any of them can get clear. Wood splinters fill the air, and men fall—some wounded, some dead.

"Get down behind anything heavy," Casey says, and they each acquire an intimate relationship with the earth where they stand. They are behind the rise of land and the short stretch of water between them and the Russians. Casey chooses a tree trunk for cover. His order comes only seconds before there is a huge volley of gunfire into the swamp.

They just hug the earth and wait it out. This time Diego doesn't cry. Casey looks behind them and sees that the water is deeper than the water they just crossed. He estimates it to be about three feet deep and thirty feet across. After that, the land is higher and looks dry.

The sound of the tank really brings about fear in them, and they wait, wondering what will happen.

"Keep down now," says Casey. "They're going to show us how bad they are."

"Casey, that's a Russian T-34 sitting on the road," Bennett replies. The sound of the tank's turret turning makes each one of them hug the ground like never before.

The whole swamp shakes as the 76mm gun of the tank fires. The projectile passes overhead with a whistling, rushing sound and explodes where it impacts behind them, where the land slopes up. Crocodiles flash in the swamp, moving away from where they are hiding.

Casey thinks, *It's ironic. The Russians are helping us out by spooking the crocodiles away.* Heavy machine-gun fire comes from the turret gun, and Sereta worms her way over to where Casey is and clings to him. It's very much like the fighting they've already been through, except there is less cover. It's new and terrifying to Sereta, and she grips Casey and trembles. He lies on her for cover.

They see branches being shot off the trees and feel the concussion of the rounds as they impact behind and above them. Casey hears the clanking of the treads of the tank and thinks they have reconnoitered and found a place where the tank can get across the swamp to the higher ground. He follows the sound as the huge vehicle turns across the road and goes into the water. There is a splash and then silence.

*The place we chose to cross at is about the only narrow place along the road. The tank must have chosen another site where the water is shallower.* Casey looks up at the sound of raised voices, and he instinctively knows they have mired the tank in the mud. The engine roars as they try to back the tank out of the ditch. It finally quits, but it isn't time for the group to get up yet.

There is another volley of fire from the heavy machine gun of the tank. One more volley from the big gun, and the tree behind them shatters and slowly falls across part of the swamp they have to cross. This is a blessing in disguise; the last two reluctant alligators swim for it.

From the other direction, another motor sound and lights come through the swamp.

"Casey, it's a T37 amphibious tank. We're refighting World War II," Bennett says.

"Mendoza, do you think you can make use of that rocket-propelled grenade? How about you, Brown? Bennett?"

"Let Bennett have a crack at it; he's studied them."

"Casey, I've never fired one of these. I don't know the range or anything about them other than our Russian weapons-familiarization classes."

"Just wait until you can't miss, and then let them have their play toy back."

Now instead of everyone watching the road, their attention is focused on the approaching tank. The men on the road stop firing once the tank approaches through the swamp, and they watch it and all the soldiers perched on top of it.

Bennett positions himself, and they have to pull Diego away from the rear of the RPG. The tension in the air can be cut with a knife up to the very second he pulls the trigger.

The vehicle is only about twenty yards away, and the impact of the round stops it like some giant hand reaching down and swatting a fly. Fire roars out of every hatch and opening in the skin of the vehicle. Body parts of the men riding on the top fly through the air from the exploding ammunition. A shocked silence from the men standing silhouetted on the road follows.

"Give them what for," Casey says, and he and the rest of them who have AK-47s open up. They can see men falling along the bank of the road. Chief Gordon has the carbine and fires with Diego helping him stand. They kill the man in the turret and the driver of the tank. They hear the hatches slamming closed, and the motor dies.

"Let's scoot!" Casey stands up and wades through the knee-deep water, leaning down to keep from showing his profile. He brings Sereta along with him. They use the body of the burning vehicle for concealment and protection.

"Crap, Casey, what do we do now?" Brown asks.

"All of you go out on the log and get across the water as far as you can. Keep your feet up so you don't tempt the crocodiles. Sereta, wait up, I need something from you."

"What, Casey?"

"Give me your rags—all of them."

He doesn't have to ask twice; she just gives them to him. Casey wraps the rags around a stone and throws the rags out into the water as far as he is able and there is a surge of activity as the crocodiles sense the blood and swim toward where they hit. They generate a roiling of the water.

"Go, guys. Go before they get wise to us," Casey says. They jump off the log into about three feet of water and wade toward the other side. Two of them take the chief and escort him across. Two of the larger crocodiles are coming back to investigate.

That leaves only Casey and Sereta to get across the swamp to dry land.

# Chapter
# 23

"CASEY, what do we do now?" Sereta asks in a panicked voice as she grips him for his attention.

Casey doesn't even think twice about it. He takes her hand, and they go back through the shallow water to where the tank is burning. He looks into the bloodstained water, illuminated by the fire, reaches down, and finds a severed calf and an arm of one of the soldiers.

"Casey, my God?!" she says in protest.

"Sereta, do you want to live?" he asks her.

"Yes, but God forgive us for what we do."

Casey drags the limbs behind him and notices that the blood in the water is attracting crocodiles to the scene of the burning vehicle.

He steps up on the log and throws the two limbs as far as he can. In seconds, the water is again roiling as the two large reptiles rocket past them. He and Sereta take a running leap off the end of the log. As they jump, he feels it let go, and when he hits the water, it's rolling sideways with the shattered end floating toward them. He's pulling Sereta along when he hears "Heads up!" and the sound of a grenade spoon pinging off.

Casey pulls her close and uses the log for cover as the grenade hits the water just feet in front of the returning alligators and explodes. He and Sereta are dragged out of the water by the rest of the group.

"Keep moving, guys, we aren't out of trouble yet," he says. They keep fighting their way through the foliage and cautiously looking over their shoulders. He's thankful they managed to save the machete as it would be almost impossible to go through without it. Ten minutes pass, and Casey can finally clearly hear the sound of the sea. He takes one precious minute again to look at the map.

Behind them, Casey can hear the sound of men screaming and the sound of automatic-rifle fire. Soldiers have crossed the ditch to where the burning amphibious vehicle is, and the crocodiles have found them.

Yes, they are moving in the right direction. They can't make it to the beach yet as the underbrush is too heavy. They continue to struggle through the growth. Casey wonders how long it will take the enemy to realize they're searching in the wrong direction to catch them.

They finally get out onto the beach and run down it and find the three palm trees close together. In front of them, one is growing almost perpendicular to the beach, and behind them is an outcropping of rock with a Cuban flag painted on it. There is a row of stones running back from the beach, pointing toward where the canister is supposed to be. This is it! Casey goes ten feet back into the brush to dig into the sand.

Just beyond one of the trees, he spots the corner of a metal canister protruding several inches above the sand. Anyone coming down the beach in the daytime can see it. The hurricane has unearthed it.

The group members run and hurriedly dig around it. They pop the clasps and yank the top off. Inside is a round, shiny aluminum disc about a foot and a half in diameter. The instructions painted on the top of the flying saucer–looking thing read, "Take thumper into water and swim out one hundred yards and press button." Beneath it are several containers of ammunition, C-rations, and filled canteens.

Casey sees a single waterproof switch on the top of the contraption. Stenciled around the perimeter is "Caution, do not open, protected with an automatic destruct device."

"I don't see any boat, Casey," says Brown. "If I'm going to have to die here, at least I won't go with an empty stomach." They pass around canteens and drink. They look further into the box and find a navy battle lantern and a spare battery. Brown opens a ration and eats it.

"Bury the battle lantern in the sandbank with it pointed outward where I can see it so that I can find my way back from the water. I'm going to take this out like it says and turn it on. Move down the beach over there to that higher sand dune; it has more cover. Take the canister and dig in."

Casey takes one of the ammunition containers, empties the .30-caliber rounds out, and replaces them with 7.62mm rounds. He thinks about it and does the same to a second. He pulls the marriage document from his shirt and places it and the maps inside the second container. He adds the .50-caliber casings and then walks toward the water.

He drops his boots where the waves will not get them. He then shucks his trousers and shirt, puts them inside the other container, and walks toward the water. He knows that carrying both the sniper rifle and the AK-47 will slow him down, but he doesn't want to go out there unarmed. He can balance the sniper rifle on the thumper. He knows his swimming abilities are not great.

"Casey, I want to go with you," Sereta says as she runs down the beach toward him.

"Come on, then, but it might be a long swim. Wait! You can't go out there. The barracuda will smell your blood in the water and attack us."

"Don't worry for me, Casey. I am through with the blood. I come with you." She loosens her shoes. "I will bring the clip things with the bullets for you."

"Everybody get into the brush and wait for me," says Casey. "I have my flashlight, and when I see the boat coming, I'll signal."

They go into the water, and it feels good. He hugs one canister beneath his arm and uses the so-called thumper like a board, pushing it in front of him. Sereta has the other canister and is using it to float along beside him, balancing the two taped-together banana magazines for the AK-47.

When they are about thirty yards from the beach, Casey hears Sereta say, "Casey, wait. I don't swim in my dress. It is pulling me down." Casey turns and is momentarily afraid for her as she disappears beneath the waves. She reappears naked, holding her dress in a heap in front of her. She balls the dress up and puts it on top of the canister she's using. Casey turns back around and accidentally hits the switch.

*Thummmp, thump, thummmmp. Thummmp thump, thummmp, thump.* It almost scares Casey to think about what kind of naval ordnance he might be pushing in front of him. *Thummmp, thump, thummmp. Thummmp, thump, thummmp, thump.* They cycle repeats again.

Casey looks up and sees a monstrous black cloud hovering overhead, moving in front of him. It divides the bay almost in half. The moon is full, and the bay is illuminated beyond where the cloud doesn't cover it. They continue swimming, and he turns and looks back. To his horror, he sees some kind of light tank coming through the brush. It is almost on the beach. It's being followed by another vehicle with a small forest of antennas coming out of the top.

When it is just about on top of the light he's going to follow to return, he makes up his mind that if he is going to die, he needs to take as many of the enemy as he can with him. He slips one of the ammunition canisters between his thighs and rides it, and then he uses the thumper under his arm as a prop for the sniper rifle.

He drains the water out of the barrel of the rifle, and hopes the ammunition is good. He aims toward the light, and as soon as the light is blocked, he fires. There is a satisfying smack and a scream and then silence. At another blocking off of the light, he takes another shot and hears the sound of a projectile finding flesh.

The searchlight on the top of the tank comes on, and his third shot takes it out. His fourth finds the operator. He continues, wondering whether they will get wise to him. He is being concealed somewhat by the light chop on the water.

To his right, he sees his group sneaking down into the water. Two of them are carrying the large canister into the surf. He reloads and continues to shoot at shadows.

Suddenly there's a huge explosion and an erupting fireball as the tank and its ammunition explode. One of the marines has utilized the other RPG. The explosion takes the windshield out of the smaller vehicle and rocks it back.

*Leave it up to good old US Marine intuition, initiative, and guts*, Casey thinks. He watches two shadows running back toward where the rest of the group came down to the water. Now he can make out targets. As soon as one stands up to shoot at the men running down the beach, he takes another name off their roster.

A *Vooooooo* sound approaching from the seaside is one he does not recognize. An older model MiG makes a fast, low pass, pulls up from its run toward the beach, and disappears into the black cloud. The men there stop firing as he rolls out, takes a long loop toward the north, and slows down. The attackers are apparently in contact with their aircraft.

Casey watches as the pilot turns on the landing light in the front of the intake and uses full flaps to slow himself down. Casey figures he's searching for something—probably him. Casey returns his attention to the beach and fires again at another target running toward where he saw the two figures going. The man never makes it across the break in the beach.

The MiG accelerates to make another turn and search the water. Casey puts the sniper rifle across his back and takes out the AK-47. If he is going to die in a battle with a MiG, he is going to make a full accounting of him.

He takes a spare magazine and makes sure Sereta has the other ones. Her eyes are wide with terror, but she holds them at the ready. He clears the gun of water, but suddenly something grabs his ankle and scares him badly enough to make him pass gas. Sereta gives out with a little scream and just stares at him.

"Who? What the . . . ?" he says, his speech faltering.

She's so embroiled with helping him select targets on the beach and holding onto all the things he hands her that she doesn't understand his outburst.

Casey can't feel any pain, but that only means he's operating at such a high adrenalin level that it will take a moment or two to reach his brain. He decides that if it's a barracuda attacking him, he'll pull the pin on his grenade, lob it into the water, and let the critter feed his own flesh to his fellow predators.

Now Casey again turns his attention to the MiG. Suddenly, in front of him, the water begins to bubble, and a face pops out of the water. It's a diver.

The man sees the AK pointing at him and ducks back under. He surfaces behind Casey as he brings the weapon to bear on the MiG as it makes another sweep across the water with its landing light on, and its flaps extended. One more trip across and Casey will be found out. Casey knows there is no use going under the water as clear as it is.

The swimmer surfaces behind Casey and speaks. "Whoa, marine, it's the cavalry. The UDT's here to pick you up."

Casey has never been so happy to see another American. But the boat—the boat! It's a submarine! "We've been looking for a boat. Why the hell hasn't anyone bothered to tell us the boat is a U-boat?" Casey joyously screams at the waves.

"Come toward my voice, the boat is here!" Casey shouts.

The men in the water turn and begin swimming toward him. Casey brings his full attention back to the problem with the MiG. It's finishing its sweep and starting to pull up when Casey opens up on it. It's close enough he doesn't even have to lead it much. He can hear the rounds impacting the side of the aircraft.

The smooth, whistling whine of the engine is interrupted by a *whomfm, whomfm, whomfm*. A huge puff of black smoke extinguishes the bright fire at the tail, and then the engine starts to unwind.

The aircraft stops in its upward track and banks over toward the shore. Little explosions within the aircraft that should have blown it clear illuminate the canopy, which fails to release. The MiG continues to bank over, and the pilot's seat fails to eject.

*Poor maintenance,* Casey thinks, and they watch, fascinated, as the MiG makes a slow, almost purposeful, banked flight toward the shore and impacts right where the tank and the other vehicles are parked.

There is a tremendous ball of fire along with the concussion of the MiG's bomb going off. Jet fuel ignites the whole area.

A second head pops out of the water, and the diver removes his swim mask. "What the hell was that?"

"Buck Rogers here just bagged himself a MiG," the first diver tells his buddy.

"What?" the second replies incredulously. He turns to scrutinize the inferno on the beach.

"Hell yes, I watched him do it," the first diver says. "It didn't take him but a single magazine."

"Come on, guys, go to the swimmers. They're almost exhausted, and the chief is wounded." Both divers take off in the direction of the rest of Casey's group. Casey and Sereta continue to watch the inferno burning on the beach.

*Thumper—what happened to thumper?* Casey thinks as Sereta clings to him and her ammunition canister to float while holding one of the spare magazines up out of the water.

Casey looks all around, and a long way from them, the little sphere emerges in the bright moonlight. It's being pushed along by the wind and tide. Another diver emerges from the water with a net filled with life vests. He passes Casey and Sereta vests, and they strap them on.

"Who are you, ma'am?" the swimmer asks Sereta.

"I am Sereta," she replies, holding the ammunition canister between her and the swimmer.

"Well, Sereta, darlin', I think you lost your swimming suit back there somewhere." She draws in close to Casey's side and holds onto him.

"I could not swim in my dress. I have it, and I will put it on." Casey helps her put it over her, although she is wearing an inflatable vest. He pulls the lanyard, and it inflates. She looks like a large-breasted opera singer as the vest tries to pop the seams of her dress.

"The skipper says he won't risk the sub by surfacing right here," the diver says. "There's too much light, and he thinks it will backlight us enough to make for a good target from the shore, although they look like they have their own problems." He gestures toward the fire vigorously burning the wrecked vehicles on the beach.

The other divers approach Casey and Sereta with the rest of the group. Chief Gordon is using the large empty container as a float. He looks exhausted but happy. "That was one hell of a shot, Casey, and to start out you said you didn't think you had anything to add to the group. Hell, we'd all be dead now it if wasn't for you." He stops and looks around. "And of course little Sereta too. You're really important to us."

One of the divers has a line, and as they look around, the periscope of the sub comes up not far from them.

"The captain wants everyone to get inside a loop in the line, and I'll place the lead over the scope," says one of the divers. "He'll pull us down the bay to a place where he's not backlit." The diver loops the rope around the periscope and bangs on it three times. He goes to the last man in the chain of people, and the periscope slowly begins to move away.

The rope tightens, and they're towed along through the waves. Sereta's hand has Casey in a hard grip. The periscope looks like a vertical pole pulling them along. The night under the cloud cover is so dark that you cannot see the bottom of the water now.

Casey looks across the bay and sees, to his horror, that there's a small military-type boat moving toward them. He brings it to the UDT diver's attention, and the diver bangs twice on the scope. Casey can see the lens move from the back to the front to look ahead, and the submarine slows to a stop. He's comforted by the knowledge that it is dark enough that the small boat cannot see the submarine under the water.

"Let me try . . ." Casey still has the ammunition canister he is so desperate to hold on to. He puts it in front of him and swims away from the other men. He estimates the distance and fires the AK-47. The first round impacts the water, but the rest of them hit the boat.

He flips the magazine, and this time has good range. He opens up and gives the boat the full magazine. He can hear the rounds contacting metal, along with the sound of shattering glass and the wails of wounded men. The small boat turns, and Sereta hands him the last magazine she is holding. He fires again at the retreating vessel and sees a fire break out in the center of it.

There's a tremendous gurgle from beneath them, and slowly, the conning tower of the sub emerges from the water. Sereta grabs Casey and holds him in a death grip.

"Casey, are we going to be eaten by a sea fish?" she asks him, wide-eyed in terror, having never seen or even heard of a submarine before.

"No, Sereta, it's a submarine, an underwater boat, not a fish. But it goes under the water like a fish. It's like Jonah—you know Jonah?" he says to her, attempting to calm her down.

"You mean the whale story in the Bible?"

"Yes. What happened to Jonah?" Casey asks.

"The whale eats him," she responds.

"Yes, and what happened three days later?"

"He was spit out onto the dry land and had not been eaten too badly."

"That's what is going to happen here. We're going to go down into the belly of the submarine, and he's going to take us to the naval base and spit us out."

"How do you know this, Casey?"

"God promised me this the night your mother and father died, giving their lives to save you. He promised to save you to tell the good people what is happening in Cuba."

Casey feels a tap on his shoulder and turns to see seamen from the sub. "Come on, man, give us a hand to get the chief down the shaft," he says. Bennett, Mendoza, and Brown are there to help Casey pull the chief and Sereta out of the water and onto the just barely awash deck.

He takes his pants and shirt out of the second ammunition canister and puts them on. Somewhere along the excitement, the elastic in his shorts expanded, and he lost them. He helps lower the chief into the boat. Sereta turns her back and disrobes. She wrings the water from her dress and puts it back on.

"What do we do with our weapons?" Casey asks the conning tower officer.

"Just pile them here in the conning tower chest, and if they make the trip to the base, the command will make the decision what to do with them." Casey sees that the rest of the weapons the men have managed to bring with them are piled in the chest. He tosses his unused hand grenade into the water and looks up at the heavy black cloud over them.

# Chapter 24

BOTH carbines, five of the 9mm pistols, and four AK-47s are there. He adds the sniper rifle to the heap. He doesn't put his ammunition canisters containing the documents there; he goes up and climbs inside on the ladder, taking them with him. Sereta and he are the last ones of their group to go in. A man with a knife stabs each of the vests as they come down the ladder.

Sereta's face is ashen, and Casey can see she looks as though she might want to bolt any moment. As the officer closes the hatch, they hear the hiss of air, and their ears pop.

"Get them inside and down here. The whole goddamn Cuban navy is out there and down our throats," the captain says. They hear a single *oouga* and the sound of machinery and men moving around. Sereta's grip on Casey tightens.

"Green board, Captain," the navigation officer says.

"Take us down, Mr. McNeil. Just get us under to periscope depth. How much water have we got under the hull?"

"Seventy feet, Captain."

"Crap, on a clear day you can see that deep around here. All ahead, dead slow." He turns and looks at Casey. "Christ a' mighty, son, what happened to you?" Casey is dumbfounded. Every eye in the place is looking at him. Some are grinning; some look worried. "You pick up some kind of infection? You aren't communicable, are you?" The questions come from the captain faster than Casey can answer.

"I'm okay. It's the chief that needs medical attention. You have any penicillin?"

"My corpsman is working on him. Now you and Miss . . . What the hell? We've got a woman aboard!"

The man at the sonar console speaks up. "Captain, the boat is pinging on us, and I think he's the big one with depth charges aboard."

"Christ! You and honey sit right down, now. Keep your legs out of the men's way, and don't anybody make a sound."

They all listen to the faint sound of pinging.

"New course, Captain?" the other officer asks him.

"No, let's see what he's going to do."

"He's coming up to speed, Captain," says the sonar operator. "The last time we watched him, he made twenty-one knots."

"Get me the range and an angle on the bow. Load tubes one and two; flood them and open the outer doors. I hope those old mark thirty-sevens will do the job." The sound of men moving a heavy object with a line and a pulley emanates from the front of the sub. Metal clangs, a hatch slams, high-pressure air hisses.

"Fish loaded, and the outer doors of one and two are open, Captain," a man on a phone says to the captain.

"Wait a minute!" the sonar operator exclaims. "He's not homing on us. He's picked up on the thumper. The wind and tide must have taken it halfway across the bay." A huge detonation reverberates off the hull.

"He's depth-charging already," says the captain. "He can't be within five hundred yards of the thumper. He's anxious for a kill. Come to oh three five and make it one thousand yards."

Casey hears the hydraulics and feels the boat roll some. He sees that Sereta is almost white with fear and shivering. Casey leans over to her and puts his arm around her shoulder.

"This is where the captain will shoot a torpedo at the boat coming on the water. He is going to hurt the Communists now."

"Fire number one."

They hear the sound of rushing air, and the sub rises up slightly in the front. This is followed by the high-pitched scream of small screws in the water that quickly fades.

"One away, Captain. It's running hot, straight, and normal," says the sonar operator. "Now it's homing."

The captain stands holding a stopwatch. Casey looks at his other hand; his fingers are counting down the final seconds. Five, four, three, two—there's a tremendous explosion and the sound of metal being crushed. The seaman at the sonar console, minus his headset, is also watching the captain's fingers do the countdown.

"Up scope." The captain takes a complete look around and then looks back to the front. "Damn, he's already gone! There's nothing but a black cloud of smoke in the sky. We blew him to hell. It's raining boat pieces up there. He must have had a full load of depth charges."

The captain turns and looks back to where the wreckage of the MiG is burning on the beach. "They still have one hell of a fire back there. Close up number two, and let's get the hell out of here. How much water do we have under the boat now, Mr. McNeil?"

"We have ninety-five feet now, Captain."

"Bring her up to speed, Mr. McNeil. Take the con and head us for home."

"Yes, sir." The officer, who is standing next to the sonar operator, steps over to the captain's position. "I have the con."

The captain turns to Casey. "Now then, Technicolor boy, what kind of creeping crud have you ingested or got rubbed off on you?" Casey still can't understand what he's talking about. "I'll tell you what, Mr. Disney, you and the little woman are going to get up and go aft to the diesel. Don't touch any of my men. I don't want whatever you got—swamp fever or the creeping crud or whatever—to infect any of my crew."

"Can we please have some water and something to eat?" Casey asks, pleading with him.

"You go on back, and my men will take care of you. What the hell can happen next? I'm transporting a Cuban national, and probably an underage one at that. She doesn't have any clothes or shoes, and her boyfriend is half-naked and contaminated beyond belief. No one forward knows anything, and we need to get the hell out of this water."

Casey and Sereta stand up, move past two of the men, and go aft. The smell and the noise in the engine room are enough to concern Casey, and Sereta has his hand in another death grip.

"Sereta, we'll just sit down here, relax, and wait for the men to bring us something to eat and drink." He selects the only clear place on the deck, and she sits beside him.

Sereta takes a good look at Casey and gets back. "Casey, you look like the window of the statue of the Madonna in the church in Havana!" she exclaims.

He looks at himself and sees that his skin has a peculiar blotched tone to it. Apparently, after all this time, the dye is starting to break down. He suspects the salty seawater has something to do with it. He is alternately pink, brown, and blue in places. Some places have not broken down, and there he's still the original brown color.

A seaman brings them a tray containing two apples, two oranges, a plate of french fries, and four hamburgers. *American food!* Casey thinks excitedly.

"You need water," the seaman says to them. "I'll bring you some as soon as I get the rest of the men taken care of."

"Are they taking care of the chief?" Casey asks him.

"Yes, the corpsman is taking care of him now, but he doesn't look too good," the seaman replies.

"Where are the rest of the men?" Casey asks.

"We have them forward. They're in the bunking, on the deck, and in the forward torpedo. The captain's instructions are for them not to touch anything. Are they contagious too?"

"We don't know," Casey says. There's no need to argue now. He knows it will be a failing venture. He considers that perhaps if the navy thinks they're all contaminated, it will prolong the rest they'll be able to get after they're ashore.

Casey shows Sereta how to place the meat between the halves of the bun and eat it like a sandwich. She looks on as he spreads a little packet of mayonnaise on the bread and the meat, and then he hands it to her.

"What is this I am eating, Casey? It is so good."

"It's called a hamburger. It's more or less a main ingredient of half of the American diet—that and french fries."

The captain approaches Casey. "The men forward tell me that you're the one in command. The chief has either passed out or is comatose. I don't know. The corpsman is with him. What do you want me to tell the command about you and the men?"

"Tell them that Captain King was killed, blown to pieces, and Chief Gordon was seriously injured in the same explosion of an antitank mine the captain triggered.

"The man we went out to rescue is alive and well. I assume he is; I haven't seen him or heard his whiny voice since we came aboard. The rest of the men are in as good of condition as can be expected. I don't know if we are contaminated or not. I personally don't feel any kind of fever or sickness, but you need to check with the rest of my men."

"Your men, son? What rank are you?"

"I'm an E-2 machinist's mate designated sailor in the regular navy, and you're volunteer reserve submariners from the Great Lakes. I spotted the brass plate in the main control area. I was stationed at Great Lakes for machinist mate school, and I walked around the base and saw the sub sitting in the water there. I'm amazed that you could get from there to here in such a short period of time."

"You're mighty astute, son. We're the last of a breed. We are the last of the freshwater conventional boats. They called on us because there is no way a nuclear boat could do what we did tonight." He looks over at Sereta, and something goes through his mind. He yells over his shoulder. "Davis, come here." A sailor of short stature, slightly overweight appears and stands almost at attention. "Davis, please volunteer to loan the young lady a pair of dungarees and a chambray shirt."

"Yes, sir, I'd be proud to." Davis leaves and returns with a long-sleeve chambray shirt and a pair of dungarees that look like they'll probably fit Sereta. He hands them over, being careful not to touch either Casey or her.

"Thank you," Sereta says. She smiles and takes the uniform.

"Are the divers part of your crew?" Casey asks the captain.

"Two of the four are crew; the other two are UDT stationed at Little Creek in Norfolk. I'll go and check on the rest of your men and get a message off to Com. telling them the operation is over." He starts to walk away. "Oh, you actually shot down that MiG? I mean, honest to God?

"Yes, sir. He was low and slow on full flaps, probably around one hundred eighty knots, and begging for a load of lead in his pants. It was like shooting a duck but without a shotgun."

"You had a shotgun, son. You did, and your firing at the Commies on the beach helped us pinpoint your location after the thumper alerted us that you'd made it to the water. Hearing my sonar operator yell 'Thumper in the water!' was the most joyful thing I've heard in weeks."

"What was the noise the thumper was making, sir?"

"It was thumping out 'Kilo Charley' in Morse code. That's what we were going on. There was supposed to be a password too, but your officer in charge was killed, so we knew none of the rest of you knew it. The rifle fire doubled just fine."

"How did you know Captain King was killed?"

He smiles. "I can't tell ya. It's a secret."

They finish their tray and set it aside. Sereta looks at the dungarees and sees how they open, and she demurely slips them on and quickly sits back down. She has a problem with the buttons, so Casey fastens her up. She pulls her dress up over her head and holds it to her front as Casey helps her take the deflated life vest off and put the chambray shirt on. Some of the color returns to Sereta's cheeks as she wrings the remainder of the water out of the dress and watches it disappear down a crack between the deck plates.

The sailor who gave them food returns with glasses of water. It tastes slightly of oil and chlorine. He looks appreciatively at

Sereta; it's apparent that she's not wearing a brassiere. He steps aside as the captain returns.

"You're going to be off-loaded at the close-in side of the sea wall, and you will immediately go into quarantine," the captain says. "My men and I are going to be quarantined too, but we've just replenished for the trip home, and we'll just wait it out until the time expires and then go into port.

"The only thing that really bothers me, son, is that once we get to Groton, we're to be decommissioned, and the boat is going into mothballs. I hate to see her go. She's the last boat the reserves are manning exclusively."

"Is Sereta going to be allowed to go with us? She's contaminated if we are."

"I don't know. Right now, I'd have to assume so. Son, I'd like to shake your hand, but I guess I can't. I can wish you all the luck. You're a brave man to have volunteered for the mission you took on. A funny thing—nobody will tell me what the hell this mission is all about, and I know you are sworn to secrecy."

"It's about rescuing that foreign national up forward."

The captain just shakes his head in wonder and leaves them.

Casey and Sereta lie down on the steel deck. They are seduced by the vibration and warmth, and they fall asleep cuddled together.

Casey feels someone touch him with a shoe. It's the seaman who brought the food and water. "The captain says to come to the control room. We're going to start the diesel."

They stand up and go forward, and each of the crew members they encounter pulls back to keep from touching them.

"Sit down on the deck and get comfortable. We'll be coming into port in about an hour," says the captain. "Up scope." Sereta is fascinated as the periscope rises out of the well.

The captain brings the handles down and does a quick sweep of the area. "Blow surface."

Behind them, they hear a hydraulic sound, a heavy hiss, and then a roar as the diesel comes to life. Sereta grabs Casey's arm and causes him pain.

"We aren't going to eat you, miss. It's just the big diesel that will take us into port," the captain says.

Their ears pop as the air changes, and they can suddenly feel fresh air coming down from the ventilator. Casey can tell the boat now has a more powerful engine pushing it. They watch and listen to the crew's response as the boat is maneuvered.

Once again, the air changes and their ears pop. The captain closely follows the junior officer up the ladder, and as the hatch opens, water cascades down and wets them. The sound of the diesel slows and then almost stops.

"We get to wait for our turn," the sonar operator sitting at a console says to Casey. "Old Rosy is coming in, and the admiral is aboard and has priority."

"Old Rosy? Who is old Rosy?" Casey asks.

"The carrier *FD Roosevelt*, CV 42—it's the admiral's flagship here in the Caribbean," the sonar man says.

The diesel increases thrust again, and they continue in to the pier. The shrill whistle of the tugs gives Casey an indication that they are about to dock. He looks aft and sees a light coming down another opening. He hears the voices of the men.

There is a soft crunch and a sideways roll as the sub comes against the pier fenders. Casey knows that at least this part of the adventure is over.

"All ashore that's going ashore," the voice of the captain says over the speakers. It isn't until then that Casey sees Bennett, Brown, Mendoza, and Diego. Casey follows Sereta up the ladder, so he will be the last one off.

As they step out onto the deck of the sub, they see that the pier is filled by at least a dozen vehicles. Two of them are ambulances, and another is a command vehicle with a circle of stars on little flags.

Four brawny seamen lift Chief Gordon up out of the sub in a mesh stretcher. He looks pale and is breathing hard. Casey and the rest of them are directed up the ladder. Casey completely forgets to salute the flag as he leaves because no one has displayed it. No one notices as none of the others have either.

Casey and Sereta have just a moment to talk with the chief as the stretcher is being locked down in the ambulance.

"We're going to take him directly to sick bay," the corpsman says to Casey. "After we ascertain his true condition, he'll probably be flown to Portsmouth Naval or Bethesda."

"Bye, Casey. Take good care of my bride, and keep in touch," Chief Gordon says, extending his hand. Casey wants to hug the man but knows he can't. He shakes with him, and he notices that Chief Gordon's hand feels feverish.

"Bye, Chief. You heal quickly," Casey says. Sereta reaches out, kisses the chief's cheek, and takes his hand and squeezes it. Casey and Sereta close the doors, and the ambulance disappears into the darkness.

Casey can't shake the feeling that there is something final in Chief Gordon's words.

# Chapter 25

A captain medical doctor and a first-class corpsman approach
Casey. "Are you Seaman White?" the doctor asks.

"I am, sir, except it is fireman, sir."

"All this has caught us at a particularly unfortunate time. We
have our entire sick bay full of marines and sailors who might
have been poisoned or at least gotten some bad chow. I don't have
a single bed to offer you.

"What I've managed to work out is that in the magazine area,
there are a couple of empty ammunition bunkers we can put cots
into. It won't be too bad as most of the marines are sleeping in
non-air-conditioned barracks anyway. Underground, it's about
ten degrees cooler than it is up here, so it should be bearable."

"I can sleep almost anywhere tonight, sir. It can't be any worse
than the swamp I spent nights in," Casey replies.

"My real problem is that I don't have the resources to make an
honest-to-God quarantine area to house you in. I'll make sure you
have food, water, and anything you need. If you are indeed friends
of the admiral, then we will see what else I can do for you. Where
are the rest of your uniforms and clothing?"

Casey suddenly discovers his wristwatch is gone. He assumes
it and his shorts are probably adorning the bottom of the bay they
had just come from. It doesn't matter anyway; it wasn't waterproof.
If he ever finds his sea bag, his old watch will be there with the rest
of his belongings.

"The last time I saw my sea bag was about a month ago in Kingsville, Texas, at the Auxiliary Air Station," Casey says. "Chief Gordon's wife's home was blown to pieces in an explosion that killed both of her parents. What she is wearing right now is everything she owns. As you can see, she and I have no shoes. We lost them escaping from the Communists when we came across the beach to the sub," he says to the doctor.

"I'll be back in touch with you in the morning. Right now, I have the woes of the world on my shoulders and not enough manpower to make a difference."

The corpsman beckons them to follow him. They're led to an open-top weapons carrier, and they get in. As the man turns around, they see the *Roosevelt* still being tied up. Casey hears the shrill toots of the smaller tug and watches the sub being pulled away from the pier. They waste no time concluding their operation and getting underway. Casey salutes the captain, who salutes back.

"Where do we go now, Casey?" Sereta asks.

"I don't know." He looks forward. "Driver, where are we going?"

"We're going to billet you in one of the empty ammunition bunkers just for tonight. The marines are going to be down the way quite a distance behind the range. They'll have the same facilities as you two do, but you won't be able to communicate with them. I sure hope you people are all right, Casey—is that your name? You look like hell."

They start off and are stopped by a sentry. A command car comes by with its interior lights still on. Inside Casey can see Diego. Some woman is talking to him a mile a minute, apparently scolding him. They watch the car go, and then they proceed.

The driver goes to a chain-link fence and stops for another sentry. They speak for a minute, and then he returns to the vehicle with some keys in hand. They go across the darkened area with only their blackout lights on.

"We have to do this, you know. The Communist Cubans are only a few miles down that way." He nods with his head to indicate the direction. They stop at a grass-covered earthen magazine and hop out. The driver takes the key, unlocks it, and shines a flashlight around. "It looks all right. Just go inside."

Shortly, another truck pulls up. It stops, and two sailors unload two metal bunk frames, mattresses, and a metal rig that will support the mosquito netting above them. They leave a container of some kind of juice; a metal-covered tray of food; and a small box containing toothbrushes, soap, and personal things they will need in the morning. "We'll be back in the morning, but not too soon. We have a lot of people to deal with. It probably won't be until after eight or so," one of the sailors says.

"What about blankets in case it gets cold?" Casey asks.

The driver reacts like he's forgotten something by slapping himself in the forehead. He goes back to the vehicle and returns with their bedding: sheets, pillows, cases, blankets, mosquito netting, and a pair of mattress covers. "Here are a couple more flashlights," he says. "There's a portable toilet right there." He uses his flashlight to point it out to them. With that accomplished, he gets back in and roars off into the darkness.

Casey takes a flashlight and looks around. There's a heavy table inside, and it looks like it's been used for cleaning rifles. He takes some rags lying near it and cleans it off. He opens the food container, and to his amazement, he finds quite an assortment of items. He and Sereta divide the apples, oranges, and bananas. He shows her how to assemble a Dagwood sandwich out of the cold cuts and makes one for himself. Casey slowly fills up on one, but Sereta asks for another. Casey can't believe she can hold it.

They pour juice into some coffee cups and drink. "It is sweetened by the cane, no?" Sereta asks him, drawing on the cup.

"Yes. Americans like their drink sweet," Casey replies. "Just wait until you get to taste Coke."

After they eat, he assembles the bunks. He sets hers up about three feet from his in the center passageway, between the pallet placement racks and the workbench. He helps her put the mattress into the cover and make up the bed.

The rigors of the day overcome them, and they start to go to bed. He smells himself and wonders if Sereta is as uncomfortable as he is. What he smells is the closed-up smelly, oily diesel odor of the submarine mixed with the earthy odor of fish, blood, swamp, beach, and saltwater.

Just outside the door, a pipe runs up the front of the bunker to a showerhead above a well-used pallet on the ground. He takes a look and turns it on. It belches air and spews out a rusty discharge, but then it flows clear and cool.

Casey turns his flashlight off, drops his clothes, and steps into the invigorating cool spray. In a moment, he feels her standing right beside him, the water splashing off her shoulders. Her hair smells of diesel and other old, musty submarine things. He looks up at the soap holder and finds a half-used bar of soap. He lathers up and hands the soap to her. She doesn't understand what it is. He takes it back and lathers her hair, and then he encourages her to lather the rest of her body.

"I smell like the flowers now, Casey," she says enthusiastically.

"It's Jergens. The soap has perfume in it."

"*Perfume*—it is a word I do not know." He has to chuckle; she's almost like a child learning her way around a new world she's now inhabiting.

"Perfume is the smell of flowers, only here in the soap." He takes it back and rubs his clothing and hers with it and rinses them. He gives her the soap, and she washes her dress again after smelling it.

Finished showering, they go back inside the bunker and attempt to close the door. It almost closes tight. Several rows of hooks suffice for a clothesline. Casey gives Sereta a spare pillowcase and helps her dry off. The mosquitoes make them get under the netting. Sereta's nipples point out to Casey as she sits on her cot and looks over at him.

"Are you to sleep there, and I am to sleep here, Casey?" she asks him.

"Yes, here is a flashlight if you need it; just put it under your pillow. Good night, Sereta." He hands the flashlight to her, reaching from under his netting.

"Good night, Mr. Casey. Do not forget to pray to God tonight to watch over us."

Casey goes to bed thinking about Naomi and wondering whether he will ever see her again. Sometime during the darkness of the night, he becomes aware of someone beside him. He's exhausted, relaxed, and sleeping so well that he never wakes enough to know what's happening.

\* \* \*

Casey has no idea of the time, but he sees a slim beam of sunlight containing suspended particles of dust trying to illuminate the inside of the shelter.

He and Sereta really move at the sound of a vehicle coming up the road. They both jump up and find their clothes. Sereta has been sleeping with her back cuddled up to Casey. The vehicle stops outside, and they hear the sounds of two people approaching.

"Ahoy in the bunker, are you in there?" Casey pushes the door open, rubs his eyes, and is greeted by a nurse and a corpsman in face masks, goggles, and rubber gloves.

The nurse gives Casey a quizzical look and then looks at Sereta. She has a brown stain across her neck and down her arm where they were lying together in the night. "We're supposed to take blood and urine samples. Your breakfast will be here shortly," the nurse tells them.

"I sincerely hope it includes coffee," Casey says. "I haven't had a cup of coffee in a month, and I'm already past withdrawal."

The corpsman lays out a rolled-up towel containing syringes and vacuum tubes along with cotton, alcohol, Band-Aids, and sample bottles. Casey knows what that means.

"I'll volunteer to go first so she can watch and learn what it takes to draw blood," Casey says.

Sereta watches intently as the corpsman applies the alcohol and skillfully inserts the needle. She looks to see if he winces. Her eyes widen as she sees the blood coming into the vacuum tube.

"Are you to take some of my blood too?" Sereta asks, somewhat alarmed.

"Yes, the same amount," says the corpsman. "It doesn't hurt badly; it's like a little bee sting." Casey watches as she sees the needle being inserted into her vein. She sits stiffly at attention as the blood is withdrawn and then holds the cotton swab against her arm as the tape is applied to the puncture.

"What is a urine sample?" Sereta asks. Casey leans over to her and tells her to go and fill the little bottle with pee. She looks at him questioningly but does so as the corpsman turns his attention back to Casey. The nurse listens to their hearts and breathing and does a perfunctory observation of them.

"I'm sorry things are so primitive," says the nurse. "If only you could understand how many men we have in the sick bay. We even have them sleeping in the hallways. We have one unassigned barracks full of sick men."

She pulls some papers out of a folder and hands them to Casey. "Fill these out for me, please." He looks at them and sees it's a full medical questionnaire.

"This will take more than a few minutes," Casey says. "How about we fill them in, and you come back and pick them up later?"

The corpsman looks at the nurse, and they nod their heads in agreement. "We've got to go and check on your marine buddies up the road," says the corpsman. They go back to the jeep, and Casey watches as they continue down the road and around a bend. He returns to the bunker, and Sereta follows him inside. Casey locates his ammunition canister.

"Listen to me closely now, Sereta. This is important. They want to know all about us on these papers. We are going to fill them out with your new name. You are Sereta Gordon. Chief Gordon is your husband. It is the way you will be allowed to stay in the United States. Do you understand what I'm telling you?"

"Yes, Casey, the name on the papers from the padre must be used now. I am Sereta Gordon, Chief Gordon's wife." She smiles as she says it, enjoying the sound of it.

"This little block asks if you are Miss or Mrs. That is the difference between being a senorita or a senora." He fills it in and continues.

"How old are you, Sereta?" Casey asks her.

"I do not understand 'how old,'" she replies.

"Do you know when you were born? When were your parents married?"

"My parents were married in the church at El Jiqui, and then they were taken by the nun to Havana to see the priest there.

"My father told me they walked around the city and stopped at the side door of the concert hall. The man on the stage told of a German flying ship that fell and burned in the US, and there was a war that Pope Pius was praying to stop. After that, they listened to Margarita Diaz sing like an angel."

Casey thinks a moment about history and guesses it was about the summer of 1937, when the Hindenburg exploded and crashed. There are six flies walking on the table where they are standing, and because there were eight people in the rescue party, he chooses eight as the day. He arbitrarily writes down June 8, 1938 for her birth date.

There are many of the blocks he cannot complete as he has no idea what her medical history is. She has no previous address. He enters, "Under orders, no permanent addresses." He knows that Chief Gordon was stationed at Corpus Christi, so he puts in a fictitious, military-sounding street address. He doubts they will ever check on it.

"Sereta, now you must sign the bottom. Do you know how to write cursive?"

"I do not know the cursive, but I can spell my name on the paper," she replies.

"That's not good enough. Here, take the pen and let me teach you how to write your new name." He takes the blank piece of paper from between the two forms and puts it on the desk. He pulls her close and makes her watch as he slowly forms the letters. She looks down, smiling and watching the way he forms them.

"That is me?" Sereta takes the paper and looks at it.

"Yes, and now you need to be able to write it the same way." He hands the pen to her, places her fingers around it, and guides her hand.

She's fascinated at writing without having to dip a pen in ink. He waits, and she looks at it and knows she must do better. She tries again, and he coaches as she writes repeatedly. About halfway down the page, she begins making acceptable signatures.

"Now, what I want you to write is 'Mrs. Dale Gordon.' That's your married name, and it's the one you will be using on some other forms."

Casey writes the new name, and she begins again, copying it over and over. While she's practicing, he finishes filling out his form. He signs it and has her sign her new name at the bottom of the medical form.

He looks them over and then remembers that Chief Gordon's service number is penned in at the bottom of the marriage certificate. He takes it out of the canister and carefully pulls the bottom up far enough to reveal the numbers. He writes them in on the form and holds it up for inspection.

When the nurse and the corpsman return, Casey and Sereta have filled in all the information they know. Casey hands the papers to the corpsman, who gives them a cursory look over. He hands them to the nurse, and she looks at them.

"Is there any way we can get some shoes and socks and some more clothes? Neither of us has a change," Casey asks them.

The nurse looks surprised. She glances around and sees that other than the bunks, there is nothing else in the bunker. "How did you get here?" she asks. "Where are your uniforms and clothing? Where are your shoes?"

# Chapter 26

C ASEY looks at the incredulous nurse. "We were engaged in a firefight with Russian troops and were taken off the beach in a bay about three-quarters of the way up Cuba and brought here by submarine. We had to abandon our belongings and swim for it in order to survive."

"You don't even have a cover?"

"No, ma'am. What you see is what you get." The nurse steps back and gives the problem some thought.

"I'll see what I can do for you. I'm going to approach my captain about this. This is no way for anybody to be treated, quarantine or no quarantine."

She motions to the corpsman, and they leave just as the food arrives. The two men who deliver the food are wearing surgical masks, and Casey has to stifle a chuckle at their stiffness. They come in, set down the box that contains the trays, and quickly leave. Casey sees that they have left a carafe of coffee. He knows Sereta probably will not want any, so he plans to drink all four cups by himself.

"What is this, Casey?" Sereta asks, pointing to the yellow lumps of food.

"It is scrambled eggs—from chicken."

"Where is the yellow?"

"It's stirred in; they're scrambled. And we have toast, jam, and sausage to eat with them."

Sereta waits, watching Casey put butter and jam on his toast and bite it, and then she mimics his every move. There are two pint cartons of cold milk. Casey pulls the little pointed top of one open, takes a long draw on it, and hands it to Sereta. She looks down into it and recognizes what it is. She turns it up, finishes it, and wipes the corners of her mouth with her hand. "You have a cold cow, Casey," she says. They share the second one.

Being as late as it is, Casey knows they won't be sent another meal until evening. He decides to continue with her education. They start with numbers and letters, just for him to find out how much knowledge she actually has.

*     *     *

About midafternoon a third-class WAVE corpsman drives up in a jeep and asks to come inside. "Commander Ross detailed me to come up here and get all of your sizes," she says. Sereta looks at Casey quizzically.

"She wants to measure our bodies for new clothing, Sereta."

The young woman is surprised when Sereta stands up and strips her dress up and off. She's more surprised, and a little embarrassed, when she realizes that Sereta is naked under the dress. The WAVE corpsman uses a measuring tape and, being very careful not to touch Sereta, measures her for clothes.

"Don't pull that on me, sailor. I know you know your correct sizes," the WAVE says to Casey with critical eyes.

"I've gone for a month with just barely enough food to keep me alive. I think I'm smaller than I was, but I'll give you the sizes I had when I left boot camp."

She looks more closely and sees Casey's blotchy skin. "Please don't tell me what you have is communicable; I forgot to wear my mask," the startled WAVE says when she realizes her mistake.

"The command thought we might be, but I can tell you for certain that we are not," he tells her.

"Well, what are the pink, green, orange, blue, and brown spots all over you?" she asks, looking at him critically.

"We had a reaction to some chemical we were forced to swim through during our escape, and it affected our skin." He doesn't tell her the chemical they had to swim through was saltwater.

*   *   *

The afternoon grows long, tiring, and hot. They're bored, with nothing to do other than practice Sereta's signature and talk of English and how to speak.

"Do you want to take another shower, Sereta?" Casey asks.

"Yes, I want the shower and how it makes me smell," says Sereta. They look out the door to make sure there are no other humans around, and then both drop their clothing and step into the cool, invigorating spray.

"Casey, will you like to wash me?" He takes the soap and lathers all the way down her body as she holds herself rigid. She acts like she enjoys his touch.

"I wash you now," she says as she finishes rinsing the soap from her body. "I wash all of you, but not your toro. You have to wash it."

When they are finished, they both duck back inside the bunker, leaving the door partially open for the daylight. Sereta doesn't dry herself. She's dancing around like an untamed nymph and begins to sing to herself.

"What is it you are singing?" Casey asks her.

"I don't know the song, Casey, but my body makes me sing it when I am happy. I have not sung it for a long time."

He watches her and is amazed at his own reaction. She's naked, beautiful, available, and fully a woman, and he isn't in a state of arousal. She's just something uniquely nice to be around. Her attitude is infectious, and Casey's spirits began to rise. Finally, she stops and sits down beside him on the bunk. She's slightly out of breath from her exertions.

"Casey, you are the first man other than my father who has seen me without my clothes. He said that a man had to ask his permission to come and see his daughter. I think he is hoping that

239

some rich man from Havana will come and pick me. I know that it is not to be so. There are many rich women at the hotel there."

"Don't you want to get dried off now?" he asks.

"No, when I dry, the water flowers come off my body. I will just let the sunshine make me dry."

"Let's continue to practice your signature," Casey says. Sereta takes the pen and puts the paper on the table, and he sits and watches her butt wiggle in excitement.

After some time practicing, Sereta is dry. As she is getting her dungarees and shirt on, a truck pulls up with their rations. On top is a note signed by a Lieutenant Commander Jean Ross. It reads, "Here is a surprise for you. I will be out in the morning to continue with the examination." Casey pulls the top off and finds sliced roast beef, rolls, vegetables, fruit, more milk, more coffee, and a thermos of ice water.

They sit on the bunk and share the food. Casey is surprised at how much she can eat. He sees that her ribs need to be padded with a little more flesh. Her near-starvation diet has left her in need.

"I think we need another shower after we eat," says Sereta. "It feels good to go to the bed with the cool on your body."

Casey sets the empty tray outside and starts to undress. She beats him, and it's her turn to show him she knows how to work the shower valve. They duck inside the bunker when the mosquitoes find them again.

Casey dries with the spare pillowcase and lets her do as she wishes. He sprays their netting with the little can of mosquito repellant from the kit.

"Casey, is it wrong that I want to sleep beside you?"

"No, not if it is like last night."

"I went to you in the darkness because I am lonely for my family. This place is big and dark in the night, and I am afraid."

"Come on, then, and we'll share my bunk again."

She smiles as she gets off her bunk and goes to his. "I thought you might be mad at me for being like a child in the darkness."

He pulls the sheet from her bunk and lays it in the middle of his. He gets in, and she comes to him and wraps her sheet around her. Now there are two pieces of cloth between them, just in case he becomes excited in his sleep. Once again, as he's drifting off, her hand finds his and presses it to her breast.

*   *   *

When Casey wakes, his back is a little sore from having slept in one position all night. Sereta stretches and sits up and disappears to do her morning things. Casey dresses, and she comes back inside the bunker.

"Casey, you are not to dress yet; we have not showered." He drops his clothes, and they stand and wash the night from themselves. Once again, she's her exuberant self. "I hope this does not end so soon," she says. They are dry and dressed when breakfast arrives.

Afterward, Lieutenant Commander Ross shows up and steps through the sunlit doors. She's dressed in a nurse's full formal regalia: a white nylon uniform with white nylon stockings and white shoes. She's topped with a nurse's cap bearing her rank insignia.

The sunlight illuminates her figure through the material and makes her look for an instant, as though she has nothing on. There's a white sunlit glow around her.

"It's an angel," Sereta gasps.

"I just want to check in with you and see how you're doing out here in the boondocks," she says. "I have some clothing coming for your lady, and the command has graciously looked through the lucky bag and found you a couple of uniforms of undress whites, a couple of sets of dungarees, and a pair of shoes and socks. Sorry I couldn't find a white hat.

"This afternoon I'll go and pick up your things for you, Casey, and perhaps tomorrow I can take Mrs. Gordon shopping."

Casey is surprised that she refers to him by his first name instead of his surname. "Why are you wearing the dress white uniform?" he asks.

"We had an impromptu inspection for some visiting UN clowns," she replies, slightly disgusted. "If things continue to move along as I suspect they will, perhaps we can have you out of here in another day. I'm looking at a vacant enlisted quarters to move you into, at least temporarily."

Casey and Sereta finish their breakfast with her looking on.

"I bunk in with Lieutenant Commander DeNova, and she'll be the legal advocate for Sereta when they get around to making a decision as to what to do about her," says Commander Ross.

"What do you mean 'do about her'? She's Chief Gordon's wife," says Casey.

"They've located his service jacket, but there's no record of him ever having petitioned his command for permission to marry a foreign national. Wait a minute! You're Casey White, and she is Chief Gordon's wife? Where is Chief Gordon?"

"On his way to Bethesda or Portsmouth Naval, I hope. Anyway, how many men just go and get married without their command not knowing about it?"

"I know how you feel, Casey, but we are dealing with the whole US Navy legal system now. Why did the two of you get put out here together? Did someone think you two are the husband and wife?"

"I don't know, but to be fair, the night we arrived, there was nothing but chaos on the pier. Anyway, Sereta slept alongside us the whole way across Cuba. One more night shouldn't make any difference. Is she able to get berthing anywhere else on the base, seeing as how she's being held for quarantine?"

"Someone on the base is between a rock and a hard place. I can't answer that one."

"After the medical thing is resolved, will there be a hearing about her staying on the American side of the fence?" Casey asks.

"I assume there will be some kind of investigation into her marriage. I can assume that one is being set up as we speak."

"Will I be able to be there?"

"You can ask about all this when Lieutenant Commander DeNova arrives. She's from legal. This whole area is supposed to be under quarantine except for those people who absolutely have to be in here."

"If we're quarantined, how is it that you're able to take her shopping?"

"Just between you and me, we'll have to keep it a secret. Keep doing what you're doing, and we can use that to our advantage," she says, using the term "our" in reference to Casey and Sereta, making it obvious that she has taken a personal interest in them.

A second sedan pulls up, and another woman the nurse's age dressed in officer khakis steps out carrying a briefcase. The two women greet each other. Commander Ross comes back into the magazine, again illuminated by the sunlight.

"Damn, you don't even have a place to sit down," Commander DeNova says as she pushes the mosquito netting off one of the bunks. She sits and flops her briefcase open beside her. "Hi, Sereta, I'm Lieutenant Commander DeNova. I'm going to be your legal representative when we go and talk to the command and immigration. I need to know all I can find out about you so that when the questions start coming, you won't be blindsided."

"What is 'legal representative'?" Sereta asks.

"I will speak for you in all the legal issues you don't understand. I will help you to stay here on the American side of the fence." That makes Sereta smile.

"Do you want White to hear this too?" Ross asks DeNova.

"Yes, the command is waiting for some Washington types to get down here, and he and the other guys on the raid are to be debriefed. I need him as a verifiable witness."

"Are you safe to be around?" Commander DeNova asks, looking at him critically."

"I'm as safe as a newborn baby, ma'am," he replies.

She looks at him, smiles, and then looks back at Commander Ross as she nods her head in the affirmative.

"Mary," says Commander Ross, "do you see anything wrong here?"

She looks at Ross and back at Casey and then Sereta, who is standing apprehensively. A perplexed expression crosses her face.

"I don't see anything. Is it the Technicolor tone of his skin you're alluding to?"

"No, Mary, look at the paperwork."

"You're too young to be a chief! Either that or she is too young to be his wife. What the hell is going on here?"

Casey interrupts and tells Commander DeNova the same things he told Commander Ross. It's as though a light suddenly comes on inside her head. They begin talking, and Casey learns more about the navy legal system than he ever wanted to know. The conversation continues, and the two women grow more comfortable with Sereta and him.

After a while, Commander Ross stands, smoothes her uniform, and looks around. "It's time for noon chow, and if we don't get to the BOQ soon, we'll miss it. Where are your rations?"

"We get them two times a day," says Casey. "We have enough for sandwiches for lunch, and dinner usually arrives around four."

Commander DeNova stands to go, and yet another sedan, this one with an escort, pulls up in front of the bunker. *The quarantined area is getting more crowded*, Casey thinks.

# Chapter 27

A Spanish woman wearing a blouse that matches Casey's colors steps out, accompanied by two marine escorts. Casey starts, as she looks like the same woman who did the dye job on him; she's carrying a suitcase similar to that woman's. As they approach, Casey sees that it's an older version of the woman he met before.

"Seaman Casey White?" she asks him.

"Close, but good enough," he says.

"I'm with International Outbound Environmental Services. I have some medical items I think may be of interest to you." She sets the suitcase down.

"Outbound Environmental Services—is that a euphemism for the CIA or the Cuban Expeditionary Forces?"

She looks surprised that he has a grasp on what's going on. "May I speak to you privately, Mr. White?"

"I think you can speak to all of us; this is my medical attaché, and this is my attorney." Both officers look at each other and grin at his comeback.

The woman unlatches the suitcase and opens it. She withdraws several quart bottles, a large roll of cotton toweling, and some smaller bottles.

"This is dye neutralizer. You just apply it to the skin and let it set for a minute, then use some of the toweling to remove it. The small bottles are to remove it if it causes a rash or nausea, and the others are lotion.

"After you remove the dye, take a shower with this soap and dry off. If there is any place you've missed, you can reapply or just let it grow out. Skin usually takes about eight to ten weeks to shed the color completely, and you've gone through half of that already." She smiles at him, confident of her directions.

With that, she buttons up the suitcase and the marines accompanying her open the car door and seat her. They drive away in the next couple of minutes.

Commander Ross looks at one of the bottles. She turns it around and studies it and then reads the contents label aloud. "Hydrogen peroxide suspension in salicylic acid solution, bleach suspension with organic soap, 4 percent, with an alcohol lotion base. Stabilizers and perfume less than 1 percent. For prescription use only."

"What is it, Jean?" Commander DeNova asks her.

"Apparently it's something to neutralize and remove the dye they put on him for the operation," she replies. "Mary, don't you think this is an opportune time to take Sereta to our quarters and let her try on some of the clothes donated to her?"

"I do, Jean. I'll wait for you to return before I bring her back here." They get into her car and leave the two of them studying the bottles.

"Casey, go ahead and strip and lie down on one of the bunks, and I'll try this to see whether it will do the job it's intended to do," Commander Ross says.

"How about I get on the workbench? It's a more comfortable working height. We can just put a sheet on it, and I'll get up there."

She nods in approval. "Okay, thanks, but hurry it up."

Casey's a little embarrassed to disrobe in front of her, but he does so and rests on the table. She's a registered nurse, an officer, and Casey figures she probably sees more naked bodies than she's willing to admit.

"You don't even have skivvies or a T-shirt?" She's amazed at his lack of clothing.

"No, ma'am. I lost almost all the clothing and shoes I had, not to mention my wristwatch."

Commander Ross takes his knife, unrolls and cuts a section of toweling, pours some of the liquid on the cloth, and applies it to his back. It's momentarily cool and effervescent. Immediately, the dye comes off on the towel. It leaves his skin feeling cool and tingling.

"I can see that this is going to get really messy. I need to get out of my good dress uniform. Will it bother you if I work in my slip?" she asks him.

"No, go ahead, ma'am. Does it bother you that I'm buck naked?" She laughs out loud in response.

Casey can hear the rustle of the uniform as she slips it over her head. He keeps his head turned away but peeks as she does so. She carefully folds it and lays it on the bunk, where it won't get dirty. She applies more of the chemical on his back and then his arms. The cool effervescence feels good, and he relaxes.

"God, your muscles are hard, Casey. You must be in very good shape," she says, pressing his bicep.

"If I hadn't been, I'd probably be lying dead in the middle of Cuba right now. We were lucky to get Sereta and that crybaby Frenchman out."

"Damn! This is still going to get my slip stained. I'm going to pull it off and just work that way," she says. She steps back and sets the bottle down.

"Go ahead. You'll still be covered by your half-slip, and if your brassiere is too sheer, then you can just pull the slip up over your breasts."

"How did you know I was wearing a half-slip?" she asks.

"You know I watched you come through the door in the sunlight. It made you look almost angelic."

"All right, wise guy, you just lie there and close your eyes." She looks to make sure he does it.

She continues and does his butt, legs, and feet. He peeks when he knows she can't see his eyes opening to watch her. He enjoys her touch while feeling the effervescence of the chemicals she's using.

She stands close to the table again, comes up to his head, and rubs some on his scalp. He can see the darkness of her areolae through the material of the slip and the sheer white brassiere.

"It's coming off your scalp, but it's turning your hair bright red, Casey," she says.

"Just get it uniform and I'll get it all cut off," he replies as she tries to wipe off the chemical. She wipes at his scalp but only makes his hair worse. It's red-orange now.

"Okay, turn over and I'll finish." She averts her eyes as he turns and lies back down in front of her. He can tell she's trying not to look at his manhood, which is slowly rising as she works toward it.

"Can you please stop it?" she asks softly.

"No ma'am, I'm sorry, but this is too intimate a situation. Just go ahead. Work around it and get finished. It'll go back down." She picks up the roll, tears off a section of the toweling, and places it over him. The toweling pulses with his heartbeats. She works down his stomach to his thighs. By the time she's finished his feet, she's perspiring and looks stimulated. She closes the bottle, turns around, and looks down at him.

She's standing close to the table, where his arm is hanging over. He moves it forward slowly, contacting the fabric of her half-slip. She looks at his hand coming toward her but doesn't move.

He pushes his fist forward to her and places it on the tight fabric. She still doesn't move. He looks up to see her staring down at him with a glazed look in her eyes. He reaches out and softly pinching the fabric with three fingers to bring her closer. She leans into it and lets him continue to touch her. Her eyes slowly roll upward and then close, and she draws in a deep breath. Casey can almost see the barriers falling in her mind.

"Dammit, Casey," she says in a harsh whisper. "I can lose my commission fraternizing with an enlisted man, but I've put up with so many officers who are only concerned with their own satisfaction and then jump off. Will you please try to satisfy me?

Be careful not to mess my hair up. I have to check back into the sick bay after I get done here."

She turns and removes the rest of her clothing, drags the mattress off the bunk, makes herself comfortable, and looks up at him. He pulls one of the little thin pillows down and props up her shoulders. It allows her hair to hang free but elevates her breasts toward him.

They make love right there in the partial darkness of the bunker, accompanied by the mosquitoes and the dust and dirt of a thousand men and a million rounds of ammunition. Her vocalizations resound around the hollow bunker as flies dance in the light coming in the doors.

"My God, Casey White, I've been looking for a real man to go with, but all I've been able to find have been disappointing. Pretend it's a tea bag and just let it soak for a minute."

Casey holds her hand as he looks out the door of the bunker to check for vehicles. She's reluctant to go outside, but he pulls her into the cool water spray of the shower. It shocks her momentarily, and she clings to him as he soaps her body, being careful of her hair, and then allows her to rinse herself. He carries her back inside to keep her feet clean. She takes some of the roll towels, dries herself, and sits down on the bunk.

"I guess it's way too late to ask if you can be discreet," she says.

Casey watches her, wondering why, after urging him to hurry so that she wouldn't miss noon chow, she's hesitating, displaying herself, and not dressing. "Ma'am, I have never disclosed any names of the women I have been intimate with. Your secret is safe with me. I suppose that if I wasn't discreet, it would affect me as much as you."

"Do you suppose your little sailor can come to attention and salute the nice nurse officer again?" There's an extended replay, except this time, she's more relaxed, and they take their time. As it comes to a climax, they're both out of breath and sweating, and she has the look of one who knows she's about to take another cool shower.

Once again, he carries her back inside to keep her feet clean. She finds the towels and dries herself. Casey watches her as she dons her uniform and pins her cap on. It only takes him a moment to slip into his dungarees.

"You're a sweetheart, Casey White. I've got to get back to the sick bay. Thanks for everything."

"Better than lunch at the BOQ?"

"You betcha." She kisses him, gets in the sedan, takes a comb out of her purse to straighten her hair, and reapplies her lipstick and rouge. She waves and leaves him standing there with a satisfied smile.

An hour later, Commander DeNova and Sereta return. Sereta is wearing a yellow-and-blue striped dress, shoes, and socks. She steps out and runs to him.

"Look, Casey, I look like the ladies at the hotel in Havana."

"Yes, Sereta, you look better than them," he says.

She stops then and scrutinizes his change. She seems to be a little shocked at his new appearance. Perhaps it's his red hair or eyebrows that throw her off. "Casey, you are the North Americano my father warned me about, but you aren't bad! Is my father wrong about the Americans?"

Casey reaches out and holds her hand. "He's wrong about me, and yes, Sereta, there are a lot of bad people—like the one we came down here to rescue. He didn't even stop long enough to thank us for saving him."

"I still like you, Casey White," Sereta says.

"These are all donated clothes," Commander DeNova says as she opens the rear door and takes out a suitcase. Sereta takes it from her and hauls it into the bunker. She then opens it and shows him the contents.

"White, what's with the mattress on the floor?" says Commander DeNova.

He stoops and puts it back on the bed frame. He looks over at the officer, and she looks suspiciously at him. "Commander Ross spilled some of the chemicals, and we had to move the bed to wipe them up," he says while fiddling with the bottles.

"How are you feeling. Did the chemicals work?"

"I really itched afterward and had to shower. I probably need the lotion, but I'm going to wait and see how I feel tonight before I do anything further."

"What about your two-tone hair? Aren't you a natural blonde?"

"Yes, but as soon as she tried to change it back it turned a really bad color of red. I plan just to get a buzz cut and have it all taken off when I get some money."

"I tried to get the enlisted quarters, but some chief had already claimed it. You'll have to be satisfied with this bunker for at least one more night."

"The bunker is cool in the daytime and gets cooler in the night, so much so that we use a blanket before morning. We'll make out okay," Casey says.

"That's good, White. Now I have to go. I'll personally be back in the morning. There's a scheduled meeting for all of you at ten hundred. As far as I can tell, the quarantine is lifted."

"That's a relief," Casey says. "I thought I might have to go through life as a fresco." Commander DeNova just smiles a quizzical smile. Casey can tell she's still thinking there's something he isn't telling her.

"Please be ready to go by nine. It might be a long day. It will be a full debrief with signed statements."

"We'll be ready," says Casey.

The commander gets into her car, and she disappears down the road.

# Chapter 28

A s soon as the car is around the bend, Sereta jumps into Casey's arms and hugs him.

"Look at me, Casey. I'm a lady now, not like the peasant I was."

"You can thank Chief Gordon, Mrs. Gordon."

"Yes, I don't want to forget."

The return to the bunker, and Sereta stops and looks around, smelling the air, hesitant as to what to do. She scans the entire area as if looking for something. There's a very questioning look on her face. They're interrupted by the evening meals arriving. Casey takes the tray, and the truck leaves.

Sereta is as fidgety as he has ever seen her. "Please, Casey, you look." She unbuttons and takes her dress off and shows him she's wearing slips, panties, and a brassiere. She sits on the bunk and takes her shoes off. They're standard navy issue for women, but she doesn't know or care; they're shoes, they're new, and they're hers.

"Look, Casey, I have my first new socks." She pulls off her anklets and lays them in his hands. I want to show you the—how you say—braswear now." She reaches behind her, and it takes her a minute or more to figure out the hooks. When it finally comes off, she put it in his hands. "Is it not soft and smooth?"

"Yes, Sereta, *silky* is the word, and it fits you well."

"Please wait. I am not finished." Without embarrassment, she steps out of her panties. She hands them to him and then immediately breaks down in tears. She throws herself onto him and cries her heart out. He just reaches out and holds her.

"My mother, my father, they killed them, and I could not save them. I hope it is you who killed the Communists, Casey. I prayed to God that it is you that did the judgment for God on them."

Casey is a little upset and doesn't know how to respond, or if she expects a response.

She launches into another squall of tears. It's taken this long for her to be able to grieve. She's shaking and bawling, and her nose is running. Casey reaches up, finds a clean towel, and offers it to her. She takes it and wipes her face while continuing to cry. "Look at me, Casey. You can do with me what you want to." She offers herself to him.

As appealing as she is, Casey cannot become excited; he couldn't even if he wanted to. Sereta is still shaking from her crying.

"Sereta, come here." He pulls her to him. "I wouldn't touch you, even if my body wanted me to. You're a beautiful young woman now, and you're just starting to find out what life is all about. If I go into you, I will make a baby in your body, and in nine months you will be a mother."

"What is the nine months?" She apparently has no concept of the calendar—or time, for that matter. Casey understands that life to her probably comes in seasons. Her days are marked by the rising and the setting of the sun and the phases of the moon. She obviously doesn't understand the function of her own body. He wonders what she thinks when she has her period.

"Nine months is the time it takes for the baby to grow inside a mother. You have half the baby in you, and I have half the baby with me. When I go inside you, I put my half inside you, and it makes a baby whole. Sereta, I want you to learn what life is all about long before you have a baby. You have to get an education and live in the USA and become a citizen.

"I want you to have a piece of paper that says that Sereta Gordon has gone to school and is educated. I don't know how I expect to do all this, but I'd love to see it happen. You'll be better than the women in the hotels, because you will have worked for it." He says these things gently, hoping she understands.

"You must teach me more things while we are still able to be here together," she pleads with him and tries to dry her eyes.

"Sereta, the night your mother and father died, I killed some of the soldiers who had wronged them. It was your husband, Chief Gordon, who made the big bang that killed most of them."

"Is there something that makes the big bang a good thing, Casey?" she asks, still looking for clarity.

"In this case it is a good thing, although more of the bad men came, but we could get away from them. Are you hungry enough to eat supper?"

"Yes, I like supper; it means we will soon be doing the bath again, and then we will sleep together like doves until the morning, when we see Mary and Miss Jean."

The coffee is still palatable in the carafe, and she tastes it after he puts sugar and milk into it.

"I know this coffee; my father would have it when he went to the church in Havana after the priest had given forgiveness. For him it was bitter, but mother allowed me to put milk and cane into it, and then I could drink it."

They pick the supper to pieces and end up sharing the orange Jell-O carrot salad for desert.

"Casey, you come to the shower now." Sereta waits at the door for him. Casey disrobes, and they cling together with the cool water running down over them.

Afterward, Casey pushes the two bunks together and makes the sheets cover both. Sereta has a blanket, as does he. After closing the doors and spraying the mosquitoes, she sits on the bed looking at him.

"I think you will be the best husband for me," she says, "but you do not know how long you will be gone."

"Sereta, look at me and listen. I, too, have a family. I have a mother and father like you did. They are safe in the USA. I have a brother younger than I am, and he, too, will become a sailor like me and go around the world. I still look for the woman I was to marry when the bad people in my hometown stole her and wronged me, only I could not kill them."

It takes her a minute, but she slowly understands that he is not a single entity and has commitments to other people in the world.

"Do you have a wife?" Sereta asks.

"No, Sereta, it is too soon for me to have a wife."

"But you are so old; you know of the world. Will you go back to the cane and rescue another like me or the foreigner?"

"No, Sereta, I will go on the big ships across the ocean to another land. This is what I want you to learn about. You know so little of the world beyond your father's land the Communists stole from you.

"I want you to be educated, earn a living, and be happy. If the right man comes along, and is kind, then you can marry him and have his children."

"Is this what they say love is?"

"Yes, it is like a song that comes into your head, and the song is about only one man who makes you happy."

"I learn much from you, Casey White."

He places the two pieces of mosquito netting together and pulls up the sheets for each of them. They carefully get under and nestle beneath the covers.

Once again, she lies with her back to him and places his hand on her breast. At least, this time he decides to stretch out a little more and not wake up with a sore back.

The sound of a motor coming down the road wakes them, and Casey hurriedly pulls the bunks apart. He helps Sereta dress, and then he quickly dresses and waits to see who it will be, but the truck just roars by.

The chow truck, a smaller one, comes later. The mess man on it acts like he's stepping into a leper colony. He holds his breath and offers the tray out at arm's length and hands it to Casey.

"I threw on another couple of apples, and two more milks. The oatmeal tastes like wallpaper paste this morning, so I got you an assortment of dry cereals. I'm sorry I couldn't do better for you," says the mess man in a single breath.

"We are thankful for whatever we get. Thank you for bringing it," Casey replies.

"Are you really infected with some kind of swamp fever?" the man asks him.

"No, we've been certified as completely free of any foreign organisms."

"The rumor is that sometime today there is going to be some big hearing. Are you part of it?"

"Yes, we are," Casey says.

"Let me shake your hand," the relieved mess man asks. "I heard you saved some guy from being executed in downtown Havana."

"I don't know if it's all that." *So much for secret operations,* Casey thinks. Even here, the rumor mill is rampant.

The sailor sits in his vehicle and has to wait for another truck as it goes by. Three of the marines sitting along one side jump up and wave. It's Brown, Bennett, and Mendoza. Casey waves back and wonders if they'll be part of today's debriefing.

They eat breakfast and are soon joined by Commander DeNova and a WAVE driving a second car. "I need to speak alone with Casey. We still have some legal things to work out," the commander says as she drops a pair of shoes in the bunker for him. "Sereta, you get into the car. The lady driving is First Class Monroe; she's a WAVE who will be your friend, and you are going to the beauty shop to get a permanent."

"I do not know—*permanent?*" Sereta says.

"Your hair will be like the ladies of the hotel," Casey says. Sereta's eyes and smile light up. She gets into the car, and it pulls away, going down the road in a swirl of dust.

"What do we need to talk about, Commander?" Casey turns and notices her serious demeanor.

"I had a long conversation with Jean last night, and I dragged it out of her. She confessed. My husband cheated on me while I was putting him through law school, and I really had a struggle. He was the first one I sued after I passed the bar. Coming into the navy has given me security, but working around a bunch of lawyers here in Guantanamo isn't the best place to find a mate. Now, I'm just as horny as Jean was, and by golly, we have an hour to take care of it. I hope you are as discreet as she says you are."

"I need someone to put the lotion on my back; it's itching like fire," Casey says, lying.

The commander reaches down and looks to make sure she has the right bottle as he disrobes.

He watches her as she applies the lotion to his back. She uses her other hand to undo buttons, zippers, snaps, and hooks. When Casey is ready to turn over, she's standing beside the bed. "I guess the front will have to wait," he says.

She pulls the mattress down to where it was the afternoon before and waits for him to join her.

"It didn't occur to me to ask Commander Ross if I need birth control. We didn't use any. I hope I'm not going to be a daddy."

She laughs at his concern. "The military is the guinea pig for a lot of drugs and other medical things. We're participating in the testing of new birth control pills."

"What are they all about?" he asks her while exploring what is being displayed for him.

"You get this little disc with enough pills for one month, and you time them so that the pills run out just in time for your period. You can control when it comes, and you don't have to be afraid of getting pregnant, because your body is on a hormonal schedule."

She's more experienced than Jean and works to achieve her goal. She achieves it before Casey does and then experiences a replay when he achieves his. Afterward, she holds him with her eyes closed and smiling.

Once again, it's bath time with someone who's not ready for a cool shower. When the commander steps out, her skin is pink, and she's shivering. Casey carries her inside. She dries and displays herself to him without embarrassment as she dresses. He watches her go out the door.

"Are you coming?" she asks. She looks at her watch, and they leave the bunker.

## Chapter 29

"**S**AILOR, where is your cover?"

Casey turns around and looks into the eyes of a taller shore patrolman.

"He's my responsibility, sailor," says Commander DeNova. "He's a survivor from the island. He hasn't been able to get a complete uniform, since he is on a medical hold for infection quarantine."

The word *quarantine* makes the shore patrolman step back several paces. "I'm sorry, ma'am. Please see he has a cover; it's regulation."

They go into the building and locate a large conference room on the top floor. "Casey, give me about five minutes before you come in, I don't want them to think we're together," says the commander.

When Casey walks into the room, Mendoza, Bennett, and Brown are already there in newly replaced uniforms with PFC stripes.

Commander DeNova opens her briefcase and begins sorting through papers and setting them around the table where the various men will be seated. "Take notes if you need to for purposes of remembering something, but remember, this is a closed—and, for that matter, a secret—meeting and you'll not be able to take any of your notes with you when you leave here," she says.

"Good morning, Mary. Don't you look chipper? Are you ready to kick some butt?" a lieutenant says as he approaches her.

"Don't get too fast on me, Randy. We still have to do the debrief, take documentation, get the record typed, and get it to Com," she replies pleasantly. "I hope you have all the documents I requested yesterday, and I want good notes."

"Yes, ma'am." He seems surprised by her smiling, enthusiastic response.

"We saw you at the bunker. Is yours as bad as ours?" Mendoza asks Casey.

"I don't know how bad yours is," Casey replies.

"We have critters running around—lizards of some kind. They're everywhere. We have to watch our food to make sure they don't get into it."

"I guess you must have it pretty bad, all I have to do is fight off the mosquitoes. Did you have to get checked for creeping crud and swamp fever too?" Casey asks him.

"Yeah, they came and took blood. I think they're checking us for malaria. It probably let us get a couple more days of rest, but we're to be reassigned today."

"Have you seen Sereta?" says Bennett. "We're hoping she will be here today. Maybe they don't debrief civilian rescues."

"Yes, I've seen her every day. She's being prepared for a run-in with immigration. I've been tutoring her, and I'm slated to testify on her behalf." *There's no need to let them know she's sleeping in the bunker with me,* Casey thinks.

Suddenly, the room grows quiet. Everyone takes a seat after the commanding officer walks in.

"This will be a formal hearing to find out what transpired, and each of you will have a separate response time and a chance to take your own notes," says the CO. "You men will be seated around the table." He points at the four of them, and they take places around the front table.

"All the testimony is being transcribed. If any of you disagree with any of the testimony of the man who is testifying, please stop the response and clear things up. We want accuracy here."

Casey looks over his shoulder. The room is filled with about fifty officers and senior enlisted from navy, marines, and air force, plus about a dozen men in civilian clothes.

"Mendoza, you are the first one who was recruited. Start off with the compound in Corpus Christi."

Mendoza tells of how he was approached by his platoon sergeant and told to contact the group forming at Corpus Christi. As he goes on, it becomes apparent that he's much like the rest of them. He didn't officially volunteer but was preselected based on his particular talents and abilities.

He gives his history and everything leading up to the time they were pulled off the beach by the submarine. At the end of his testimony, he reaches into his pocket and places three shoulder epaulets on the table. A sharp-eyed air force lieutenant colonel in the back steps to the front and picks them up to look at them.

"These are from the Russian forty-third Rocket Army Guards Division; these were ICBM guys." A hushed silence falls over the group.

Brown's turn is next, and then Bennett's. Casey would be the last to testify.

Mendoza has many questions asked of him while he's testifying, and as Brown and Bennett tell their story, the pieces seem to fit together, so there is less to question. The room is again surprised when Bennett takes the Russian tactical radio out of an ammunition canister he is carrying. A bespectacled civilian immediately jumps to his feet and comes forward to look at it.

"Good work, marine. It looks like we've got one of their latest."

"Let's break for chow and meet back here at thirteen hundred sharp," the commanding officer says, stopping the meeting.

\* \* \*

Once back in their places after lunch, everything is the same, except, there's a Marine Corps colonel sitting in an extra chair, placed in front, where the officers are seated.

"We can resume with you, Seaman White."

"It's machinist's mate fireman apprentice, sir. My story is basically the same as the rest. I had no special skills to add to the group except that I am a crack shot. I believe they brought me along because they needed someone who can take a bird out of the air with a rifle if the need arises."

The hearing room becomes quite still as he responds to a question about the B-25s. He reaches down, pops the top of the container open, and takes the .50-caliber casings out and places them on the table. A Master Chief Gunners mate steps up and looks at them. "These were made by Fusible-National Corporation before the start of the Korean hostilities. This is some old ammunition."

Casey continues with his take on the journey and explains in explicit detail the attack on Sereta's home and the outcome.

He starts to explain about the wedding but is abruptly stopped by an officer sitting at the table. "That will be a separate meeting with immigration tomorrow," the man says bluntly.

He explains that if it were not for her, they could have possibly failed. Some blanch when he tells them of the use of Sereta's blood-soaked rags to distract the crocodiles. He quickly mentions the severed limbs but then moves on because he thinks it might be a problem. He says that the generosity, friendship, and concealment offered at the church aided with the successful outcome of the mission.

He goes on to tell about the nights under the church and Sister Victoria's help, the meal under the pier, and the harrowing escape running down the beach. He goes into detail about the thumper and his subsequent downing of the MiG. Then he relates their rescue by the submarine and their fight to get out of the bay without getting killed.

He also brings up the quick disappearance of Diego and the fact that he didn't even thank them. When he testifies about the shooting down of the MiG, he sees the marine officer stir in his chair and say something to the officer seated beside him.

The room is then opened to general questions, and they come fast and furious. They want to know what the trucks were hauling, the strength of the men who were pursuing them, the number of tanks he had personally seen and whether they were Cuban or Russian, how he knew it was an F8U Crusader and not an enemy aircraft, and how he found the submarine. He begins to get a little tired, and they break for a stretch and a drink of water. He reaches in his container and gives Captain King's maps to the commanding officer.

Across the hall, he sees Commander Ross, and she waves as she walks past the door and down the hall past where he can see.

The meeting resumes, as do the questions, and a man in a black suit steps inside the room. The commanding officer waves him to the front. After most of the officers in the room seem satisfied by his responses to their questions, he's allowed to step back.

"All of you who aren't cleared for top secret, leave the room now," the commanding officer directs. There is a general shuffling, and about a third of the men in the room pick up their notes and leave.

Casey looks at Mendoza, Brown, and Bennett and shrugs. They don't know if they're supposed to leave. The commanding officer motions for them to keep their seats.

After the door closes, the man in the black suit stands and tells them he is from Navy Intelligence. He opens his valise with a little key on a chain. "You who are about to view these photos are reminded that this is a top-secret process, and that you are to treat your responses to it accordingly. Speak to no one about them."

He takes out photos and starts passing them, first to the commanding officer, then to the marine officer, and finally to the four team members, who are seated at the end of the table. Brown hands them to the first officer in back of him.

The first ones are of some kind of a building area dotted with numerous heavy tractors, trucks, cranes, concrete mixers, and other construction equipment. There are piles of construction materials sitting around what looks like some kind of concrete building that is under construction. In the shadows are numerous piles of supplies under camouflage netting.

"The first and second sets are from a U-2 aircraft. The next set is from a US Navy F8. We needed to get some close-up photos," the agent says.

The new set of photos shows what looks like some of the same territory but after the hurricane, and in closer detail. Three pictures are of men lying with their bodies forming the letters *K* and *C*. Three dead soldiers are to one side in the back of one picture. The last ones are round pictures taken from a periscope camera, and although the quality is dubious, they show the outline of a fire on the beach and the remains of the tail section of a MiG aircraft.

"I haven't decided if the chief in the picture is waving or giving the aircraft the one-finger salute."

Casey looks at them for a long time. Had they not done that when the aircraft was passing over, they might not have been rescued but given up as lost. Casey can make out the fingers on the chief's hand and the patch over his eye. He can tell Sereta is a female. He can see Diego just getting into position. Everything is in great detail. He realizes the pictures are how the submarine captain knew Captain King was dead.

It's a nostalgic moment for the four of them, and it becomes an indelible memory in Casey's mind. He unconsciously fingers the little notch in the top of his ear.

Casey stands and directs his remarks to the table of officers in front. "Chief Gordon was holding up five fingers in an attempt to tell you that there were only five of us left. I knew the aircraft approaching was an F-8 from having worked with them in Kingsville. We took the risk of identifying ourselves in an attempt to prove that we were still alive."

"Thank you, White. I think it's about time we break. We'll be back here at ten hundred tomorrow morning and review the transcript." They all stand, and the captain motions for Casey to come to where the senior officers are seated.

The marine colonel asks the first question. "Let me ask you, son, do you actually want us to believe that you shot a MiG out of the air with a captured weapon, while you were treading water and at night?"

Casey is somewhat taken aback. "I stood and held my hand up and swore to tell the truth, and I have done that, sir," he replies. He looks more closely, and the officer seems vaguely familiar to him. It comes to him: he is the senior officer who was there at the boot camp range the second time he shot for the assembled officers—the time he knocked the seagulls out of the air.

The officer smiles at him. "White, I want to thank you for working with my marines on this little raid into Cuba, and the support of them. We are planning a little get-together tomorrow night at the barracks. I've asked your captain for permission to have you speak to my marines. Your story would be a great morale builder. Maybe you could shoot three more seagulls for the cooks to barbecue." The marine steps forward, shakes Casey's hand, and then turns to leave the room.

"Oh yeah," he says, leaning in closely to Casey and, in a low voice, tells him, "I claimed the Mosin-Nagant as a war trophy. I thank you for it." He strides away.

"White, are you as good as your records say you are?" the captain asks him.

"What records are those, sir?" Casey asks him.

"I have your service jacket, White. Your records indicate you've been promoted to E-3. Your sea bag is being delivered to you as we speak."

"I was the top scorer at the range the day I fired, sir, and yes, I think I can do as well or better," Casey replies.

"You can't improve on 100 percent, son. What was Randy alluding to about you shooting seagulls?"

"The second day of the competition, they had run out of things to shoot at, and I took the M-1 I had, shot from the hip, and knocked down three seagulls flying about the fifty-yard line. I guess I startled some of them." The captain just looks at him, grins, and shakes his head.

# Chapter
# 30

C ASEY steps into the hallway wondering how he's going to get back to the magazine and sees Commander Ross sitting at a small table in the hall with a young woman. He walks toward them. It's Sereta. She's stunning, and he can't believe his eyes. She's had her hair cut, been given a permanent, and is wearing lipstick and rouge.

She's changed her clothes and is wearing a blouse and skirt. Her shoes are shined. She jumps up and hugs him unapologetically.

"Casey, am I not as beautiful as Miss Ross?"

"You are gorgeous, Sereta," he replies.

"Now I need to learn how to do the kiss. I saw Miss Ross kiss her friend before she brought us here."

Now it's Commander Ross's turn to blush. "Casey," she says, "we've been ordered to take Sereta to our quarters tonight to sleep. When I spoke to admin, I got the impression that somewhere along the way someone got his butt reamed big time about the two of you being together in the bunker."

"I can live with that. She needs to see how normal people live and eat and go to bed, and find out what a flush toilet is," Casey replies.

"Well, just for now let's go and get something to eat," Commander Ross says.

They go back out of the building the same way they came in, and as Casey is walking past the other little table, he reaches down and selects a white hat for himself.

"Where does the officer take her enlisted friends and wives for dinner?" Casey asks.

"We can go to the BOQ. They have a family night tonight. It is all-you-can-eat."

Sereta hangs back as they go through the doors of the BOQ. She's still overwhelmed by everything around her. They go down a steam-table line, and Sereta asks to try one of everything in the server. They notice the people in the dining area looking at Casey. *Perhaps it's my hair,* he thinks.

They choose a table in an out-of-the-way corner and eat. Casey loads up on milk and coffee. Sereta loads up again. They finish and go outside.

"Casey, I want you to wait for me here," says Commander Ross. "I'm going to take Sereta up to our room and get her settled, and then I'll come back and take you to the bunker."

When she reappears, she drives Casey to the bunker.

"Don't the sentries report on a log every vehicle that comes through the gate?" Casey asks Commander Ross.

"Yes. If you're worried about Mary and me getting caught in some kind of investigation, remember, all the records go through legal to be logged and cataloged. It's a job that everybody hates. Mary will volunteer to do it this time and modify logs containing our extra comings and goings.

"Casey, I know it looks like we're using you for our own purposes, and it's probably true. You made me feel like a real woman again." With that, she steps into the bunker and begins disrobing. Casey isn't far behind her. She's breathing hard as they together enjoy the last little tingle.

He again pulls her to her feet, and she hangs back before he turns the shower spray on and pulls her into the water.

She's pink in the light of the flashlight on the bunk after she dries herself. She stands and begins dressing. She holds and kisses him before she gets into the sedan and drives away.

Now the place seems big and empty. Something's different; someone's missing. Casey looks around, and in the back corner, he spots his sea bag!

The lock is missing, but it's packed full. He opens the top. The cut lock is packed on the top, and beside it is a replacement with keys. He looks deeper and finds that all his things are there; unexplained is the change of the stripes from E-2 to E-3. He finds a clean set of undress whites, a white hat, and, at last, his own skivvies.

He lifts the mattress off the floor and puts it back on the bunk. He pulls the sheets up, gives the mosquito netting a perfunctory spray, and beds down for the night. He falls asleep and never hears the car drive up or the doors close.

"Casey? Casey!" He's awakened by voices calling his name. He immediately shines his flashlight toward the door as it opens, and Sereta comes through, followed by Commander Ross.

"Casey, I'm sorry, but she was bawling her eyes out and could not go to sleep. She's afraid for you to be alone here. I'm going to let her stay the night, but I'll be really early to pick her up in the morning."

Sereta waits until Commander Ross leaves before she jumps into Casey's arms.

"Please, Casey, you teach me how to do the kiss, and then we go to bed." He teaches her how to kiss. The lesson lasts about a half hour before he has to break it off.

"Tomorrow will be a long day, and we need to be our best. We need good sleep," Casey says.

"I know, Casey. Let us shower now." Once again, they stand together under the cool water, being careful with her hair this time as they let the day's troubles wash from their bodies. Casey manages to get the door a little tighter than usual, but he still sprays the netting with the repellant.

She rolls immediately into his arms, snuggles back against him, and pulls the sheet around them. She guides his hand to her breast and, like clockwork, drops off to sleep. It takes Casey a little longer to get there.

\* \* \*

The sound of a car's short beep arouses them early in the day. Commander Ross pulls the big door open as they hurriedly dress. Casey helps Sereta with the hooks and buttons.

The commander gives Casey a quick little kiss as Sereta looks on, and then the two of them disappear down the dusty road. He doesn't know whether or not he should go back to sleep, but he soon decides against it.

Casey digs through his sea bag and takes a quick inventory. His pea coat is at the bottom and will have to be cleaned before he can wear it. He carefully packs everything back so that the summer things are on top.

He finds his navy-issue razor and shaves while he allows the cool water to cascade down himself. He dresses and waits for the chow truck, which never arrives.

About nine, Commander DeNova arrives, and he packs his things into the sedan. He mentions the lack of breakfast to her, and they drop by the galley.

The meeting is scheduled on the second floor, and the room is considerably smaller than the one where the debriefing took place. Sereta is already there as are legal officers and two agents from immigration. Casey brings his ammunition canister. It garners the attention of the guard at the front door, and he has to open it to show it only contains paperwork. Casey sets it at his feet in the room. Commander DeNova is seated between Sereta and him. Sereta carries a worried look, as if most of the worlds' troubles are on her shoulders. She's sworn in.

The questions start. Where did she live and how long did she live there? Where is it located? How many are in her family? Did her father and mother know she planned to marry Chief Gordon? Why did he ask her to marry him? Is she a Communist?

She relates the story she told Casey and the others about the English lessons.

"Most of the geography and references to where she and her family lived is outlined in the papers in front of you, sir," Mary tells him.

"What was your last name before you married Chief Gordon?" The room grows quiet, and she briefly looks bewildered. "Ammario," she answers hesitantly.

"Why did it take you so long to answer?" the officer asks.

"It has been a long time since I have said my virgin name," she replies.

"Who are your ancestors, starting from your grandfather and grandmother? Are they Cuban?" The younger of the two immigration agents asks.

Again, the room becomes quiet, and Sereta stands with fear on her face, trembling slightly and looking almost like she's in a trance. She's holding onto the table with her right hand, and her left is bearing down on the table for balance.

Casey looks down and sees she's wearing a small wedding band. He looks at Commander DeNova. She mouths "It's mine," and winks. It is a nice, convincing touch.

"My father's fathers name is Jean de-LeClair. He is the son of a French man who came here on a trading ship and was lost in the Caribbean in a storm. My father is the seventh of the sons of the father. Only he, another brother, and his mother survived the storm. Her name is Agnes de-LeClair. His name is Antoine LeBlanc LeClair. He died, and another man took my grandmother as a bride. His name is Bernard Le Bolde, a French man who has a German father.

"My mother's mother's name is Maria Echeverra. When my mother was born, she was called Carlotta LeBolde Echeverra before she took my father's name in the church. A judge, who knew who the real father was, changed it without the 'Echeverra'.

"She was born by the river, and when she was three, her mother was killed by the alligators in the river. Her father is a shepherd, Dela Basque, from the Basque in France. He came over here to tend the sheep. He died of the measles in Havana. Her mother is Cuban; her name is Rodriguez."

Casey can tell by the faces of the assembled men that this is getting to be really confusing for them. Sereta pauses, catches her breath, and thinks for a minute, and then continues.

"You must understand that when I was born, my father and mother did not use their last names. Everyone is known by the name they use in the fields. When the men came from the Havana tax office, they made my father get a last name.

"Since he had worked on the land so long, and the landowner did not have a son, he gave to each one who worked in the fields an equal part when he died. The men from the dictator said that terrorists have set fire to the building holding the tax records, so they collected them again that year to make sure they included everyone.

"My father couldn't think of the name he used, so he chose Delacastro, the name of the man who owned the land. The tax men were mad and told him that he owed one-half of the harvest, and that they would come and get it. They took much more than that. They also took from the other men who Delacastro had given land.

"The priest came and told them of the records, and they had to go to Havana and make a mark in the record book. After that year, they took only half of the harvest. Since then, all the other men and their families have died at the hands of the Communists or the bandits, and the Communists have taken the land and not paid for it. My father and mother were the last ones to die protecting what was theirs. I think the record of my birth is in the holy book at the church where we hid from the Communists for two days."

The room remains quiet for a moment as what she's said slowly works through each man's thought process.

"How is it that you remember the names of your ancestors but have trouble remembering your own?" The younger immigration agent asks. Apparently, his thought process is as confused as the rest of theirs.

"We do not have the parchment paper and ink to write all the names down except in the church. We use the last names only when the men come from the place in the city where they take the taxes. I have only had to use it three times since I learned what it is.

"Now I will have to remember to pray for my mother and father, who the Communists killed. The priest will put their names in the holy book in the church beneath my husband's and mine.

"I was hiding, and I heard my father cry out in pain as they tortured him, and my mother cried out and then cursed the soldiers who wronged her. She fought them as I hoped I could do, but if I moved, then they would have tortured and killed me too.

"I hope you can understand that I helped to put the bandages on my husband when the explosion took his eye. The Communists leave their death buried in the roads of my country, and they try to kill me as much as they try to kill the men who came to rescue me, and the coward Frenchman who the Americans came to rescue."

"Do you have anything that proves you are the wife of Chief Gordon?" the immigration officer asks her.

"We had a paper . . ." Startled by the question, she begins looking around her.

"I have the original document, sir." Casey unlatches the ammunition canister, carefully takes the parchment out, and puts it in front of the man. He turns it over and meticulously pulls the two pieces apart. There, written in Spanish, is the marriage document. Sereta's eyes widen, and then she smiles as Casey hands it to the officer.

"I'm not fluent in Spanish. Can you decipher it for me?" He hands it back to Casey, who in turn hands it to Commander DeNova, who is surprised to see the document.

"It's a marriage document from the Cuban Catholic Church between Chief Dale Edward Gordon and Sereta Delacastro. It's witnessed by signature of Casey White and a Victoria Garza, whom I understand is the nun at the church where the ceremony took place. I'm not able to make out the priest's name as it isn't printed and is just a signature. There is a 't-a-I-g-o' I can decipher. Chief Gordon's signature and his service number are at the bottom."

"You're a lawyer. Does this look like a legal document to you?" the agent asks.

"It looks legal to me, but you know we can't actually authenticate it, things being as they are in Cuba right now. But I'd say it's good."

"What do you think, Phil?" says the younger immigration agent to the one next to him, who is holding the rest of her immigration papers. "She seems okay to me. Let's get her papers finished and get her shipped out of here."

Phil nods in agreement.

"Can I use one of your legal people to work the papers with me?" he asks Commander DeNova.

"Yes. I'm responsible for Sereta, sir. She will be leaving with me in a few days when I move to my new duty station. You do know that all female personnel are being removed from here because of the political situation between the US and Cuba. Do you need any more of my people to testify?"

"No, but I need a permanent address for her."

"I'm being reassigned to the Pentagon and will be living in Maryland with my parents until I find permanent quarters. I'll take her with me, and she'll be staying there as part of my household. "Let me have her papers, and I'll enter my parents' home address there as her forwarding address. You can reach me through the legal system of the Pentagon anytime you need to." With that, the hearing breaks up, and everyone starts to leave.

"Is it over? Am I an American now?" Sereta asks excitedly with a broad smile and tears on her face.

"You're about halfway there, Sereta. You will be American after you take the citizenship classes and swear allegiance," Commander DeNova replies.

Sereta is all smiles, and just as she steps back to hug Casey, a shore patrolman steps inside the room. "Attention on deck," he says authoritatively.

The room comes to attention as the base commanding officer steps inside. He looks around, and his eye stops on Casey. "Stand at ease," he says. He points and crooks his finger at Casey, who hurries over to where the man is standing.

"Son, this thing between you and Colonel Strickland has blossomed all out of proportion. You should know he's the marine commandant aboard the base. He watched you shoot seagulls in 'Diego. I want you in dress whites when you get over there. I want you to make the navy proud.

"May I invite Sereta and Commander DeNova?"

"Yes, go ahead. Two more shouldn't make any difference."

# Chapter 31

"CAN I drop you over there, Casey?"

"No, I'd like the two of you to come with me."

"But this party is for you, not for us," Commander DeNova says in protest.

"You don't go, I don't go."

"Casey White, you don't turn down an invitation from the commanding officer of all the marines on the base."

"Well then, come on and let's go."

It tickles Casey the minute they walk into the lobby; the marine officers commence to hum around the commander like a swarm of drones. They are exceptionally courteous to Sereta. They take Casey by the arm and direct him to the front of the room.

"White, come and sit down." Colonel Strickland is sitting next to a smiling Captain Perry. They pull up two additional chairs for the commander and Sereta. Colonel Strickland stands up, and the room immediately grows quiet.

Behind him, two marines take three targets and pin them to the wall behind where they are seated.

"These targets are the ones White shot at the rifle range in 'Diego. I witnessed them. While it is not surprising to see a marksman do this well on three targets, I must tell you that two of these were done while he was holding the M-1 against his hip and firing doing what he calls 'hip shooting.' The one on the right is from one hundred yards, standing, with a little breeze blowing. Now I know it can be done. I want all of you to listen to what he has to say about the weapon. Look how concentric the holes are. These will be on my office wall as a reminder."

Casey stands after a polite applause. "I guess I must look like a Christmas candle up here, what with the dress whites and the red hair." A light laugh passes through the crowd. "What I should say about the M-1, is love the weapon and practice, practice, practice. Go with the intention of bettering your previous marks. Imagine the ten and two positions as the eyeballs of your enemy, and blind him and bloody his nose. If you are firing silhouette, remember to go high chest.

"I'm twenty years old and with about nine months in the service. My experience comes from having owned an M-1 since I was about sixteen and firing literally hundreds of rounds through it. My daddy was a reloader so the ammunition wasn't that expensive.

"When you are deer hunting, the deer doesn't shoot back. I learned, and you will learn in a split second, that the enemy aiming his rifle at you intends to kill you. You have to shoot first, and you have to shoot straight. You will get a gut feeling every time you go into combat. Listen to your gut. If it seems too easy or there is no danger, look again because there is always danger when you let your guard down. That is when you die.

"There is a lot to the combat I just emerged from, but because of the secrecy of it, I cannot tell you about it. The one overriding thing I did learn in this little exercise was to remember always to listen to your buddy and know where your back is."

"Let's let him enjoy his meal now, and then he can begin answering questions," says the colonel. Casey sits down, and the steward places his dinner in front of him. He eats, conscious of all eyes still on him. After he finishes, he stands, and the questions come at him again.

As Casey wraps up his answers, Colonel Strickland stands holding a manila envelope. "White, I know you haven't been able to get to disbursing and get your pay as have the marines you were on this deployment with. I talked with my men, and they decided that the fair thing to do was have each of the marines here donate a dollar to you to hold you over until you get squared away." Colonel Strickland shakes his hand and gives him the envelope. "Thank you, son, I couldn't have said it any better." He turns and leaves.

It occurs to Casey as Colonel Strickland is handing him the envelope that his buddies are not in the room enjoying the success of the operation as he is. His curiosity gets the better of him, and he opens the clasp. It is filled with bills. Inside is everything from singles to twenties. He looks up and sees Commander DeNova on tiptoe looking over his shoulder, and Sereta is beside her.

"Commander, we need to go somewhere and talk about this."

"I agree, Casey. Come on, and let's go back to the BOQ where it's air-conditioned."

"What is in the thing you have, Casey?" Sereta asks him, trying to see what the folder contains.

"It's money, Sereta, apparently a whole lot of it."

"It's American dollars?" Sereta asks as a smile breaks out on her face.

"Yes, Sereta. Come on. Let's go and see how much the golden goose left in our nest."

Commander DeNova drives them to the BOQ, where they choose an out-of-the-way corner in the back of the lobby. A steward approaches, and the commander orders them Cokes.

Casey opens the folder and pours the contents out on the table. "We need a quick tally," he says. "I'll start with the twenties; you take the tens and, Sereta—look here, see this picture of George Washington? You take all of them and put them into a nice little stack."

The steward comes back and looks wide-eyed at all the bills Casey has on the table. He sets the Cokes down, and Casey simply takes one of the fives and hands it to him. He smiles in appreciation and starts to withdraw.

"Bring us refills in about fifteen minutes, please," Casey asks the steward.

Immediately, Casey and the commander pick up their drinks, tilt them up, and take a long pull on the sweating bottles. Sereta watches to see how it is done and follows suit. She pushes back, coughing as the Coke burns her nose. They laugh, and she takes another smaller pull on the straw, and this time, she enjoys what she tastes.

"This is the American Coke?"

"Yes, Sereta," Casey replies. "Welcome to the drink that keeps America afloat—after coffee, that is."

"It is good. I think I will be a good American." It takes them some time to arrange all the bills of the same denominations in neat little piles. The odd ones are two fifties. Casey sets them aside.

"Commander, I know there must be someone here in contact with the civilian population. Can we give these one hundred dollars to someone and buy rice for the church that fed us and perhaps replace the donkey cart Chief Gordon destroyed with the hand grenade?"

"I'll see what I can do. Now, how much is there in each of the piles?" She holds a pen and a napkin.

The final tally is just over twenty-five hundred dollars.

"My god, I've become an entertainer. Commander, do you realize how many marines there are aboard the station right now?"

"I think we should downplay that information as something the enemy could use, Casey. Another thing you need to do is to mail Colonel Strickland a thank-you note; don't make it too sweet, and just thank him for this effort."

The steward returns with more Cokes, and Casey takes his, nurses it, and enjoys the moment.

"Commander, I know that Sereta doesn't understand about money and the things she needs to know. Can I give her enough to keep her in spending money until she can get hooked up with whoever is going to be paying her the dependent's portion of the chief's monthly pay?"

"That's a mighty fine gesture on your part, Casey. Yes, I think she needs funds to keep her going until we can get her settled in. If she has spending money, then it won't put a crimp in mine if I need to do something."

"Do you want any of this?"

"Casey, you've been the one bright spot in my life in this last, rather dull, portion of my time here at Guantanamo. I don't need any of your money. What I'd like you to do is put it into the bank before someone decides to relieve you of it."

"Good idea, but how do I get my money out of a bank here if I'm about to be moved?"

"The bank is only a branch of a national bank, and you can get your money anywhere you need it in the continental US."

She drives Sereta and Casey to the branch bank, and Sereta opens an account, as does Casey. There is a little confusion over Sereta not having any ID, but the account gets opened anyway after Casey again proffers the marriage license with Chief Gordon's serial number on it. He gives it to Commander DeNova for safekeeping.

"Casey," she says, "did you realize you've not checked into the transients' barracks, and you don't have a bed for tonight? You can't go back to the bunker."

"What do you suggest?" He's surprised by her realization.

The commander looks up at him. "I'll ask for a roll-away to be put into our quarters, and we'll smuggle you into the room. The only thing I can't be too sure of is what you'll be able to do in the morning."

On the drive to the parking lot, she locates all the sentries and then parks almost next to the side door. She goes inside accompanied by Sereta. Shortly, she comes out the door again and signals for Casey to run. He makes it to the hallway, runs to the stairway, and bolts up the stairs two at a time. He goes down to the third door, jumps inside, and as quickly closes the door and lets out a sigh of relief.

"Is he a fourth for bridge, or are we really tempting fate tonight?" Commander Ross asks Commander DeNova and Sereta when they come in the door.

"Put him in the head and close the door. I think I hear the steward coming down the hall with the roll-away bed," says Commander DeNova.

Casey quickly goes into the bathroom and shuts the door behind him. After the voices stop, he comes out and looks at what will be his bed for the night. It's in the middle of the room opposite Sereta's pull-out couch. They talk over the events of the day, and eventually it grows late, and they turn off the lights.

"No hanky panky tonight now," Commander DeNova says, watching Casey disrobe and pulling the sheet up over him. Sereta, clothed in short pajamas, watches him get into bed.

Commander Ross comes across the darkened room and sits down on the bed. "I have orders to Bethesda Hospital and will be leaving here on the same aircraft as Sereta and Mary. Casey, thank you." Commander DeNova comes down the hall and replaces her. She pulls the top of the sheet down and buries her bare breasts against him.

"Thanks for everything, Casey." She disappears back down the hallway to her room.

Sereta wants to know if she gets a good-night kiss too. Casey gets up, goes to her bed, and kisses her good night. She holds him down and pulls her covers away.

"You touch my breasts too, Casey." He unbuttons her top, gently lays it aside, and runs his hands up her breasts. He cups and holds them and gives the nipples a little roll between his lips and tongue and kisses each one. Sereta lets out a little surprised "Oh!" He kisses them again and returns to his bed. The night closes around him, and when he wakes, Sereta is cuddled with her back to him.

They hear an alarm clock go off, and Sereta jumps out of bed and goes back to hers.

Commander DeNova is dressing as she comes through the door of her bedroom. "I'm going to check with personnel. I think they might wonder where you are. I'll just keep your sea bag in the sedan until we find out where you're supposed to report."

"Do you want me to stay up here?"

"No, housekeeping will be up on this floor soon, and we can't take that chance. Go downstairs, and I'll drop you off at the galley. You can take your time getting breakfast, and I'll come by later."

"Good-bye, Commander Ross," Casey hollers down the hallway. She comes out of the bedroom to the living room.

"Wait, I may not be able to get away from my job to see you off." She stands close and kisses him while Sereta looks on.

Casey waits until after Commander DeNova leaves, and he looks out the door to see if the way is clear.

"Casey, you leave without telling me good-bye?" He puts his arm around Sereta, and she kisses him and lingers against him as long as she can. He steps back, lifts her gown, kisses each breast, and watches her nipples extend. "Good-bye for now, Sereta."

Commander DeNova brings the sedan around, and Casey jumps in. She drops him off at the galley. Afterward, he finds the exchange. The barbershop opens, and he's the first patron there. The barber eyes him suspiciously. "High and tight," Casey says, "and if that doesn't get all the color off, then keep trimming until you do."

The barber starts at the back of his neck and takes the clippers up over his head, and everything comes off. There is enough new growth that the red hair is mostly gone.

"What can you do about my eyebrows?"

"I have some stuff here that might do it." He reaches down and withdraws a small bottle. He pulls a brush out and applies some of the liquid. It's cool as it evaporates. The barber takes a mirror and gives it to Casey for his appraisal. Now his eyebrows are blond-red, not bright red.

He steps out of the door and sees Commander DeNova coming down the hallway. "Personnel was about to mark you up as being AWOL," she says. "I straightened them out. Nice haircut. It should last you about three or four months until you have to do it again."

"What did you find out about me?" he asks her.

"Ships come down here for readiness training, and some dock overnight and then go out in the morning. The ship you're assigned to is currently somewhere off Cuba now, going through the routine. They will be coming back in this evening, and you will have to report aboard then."

"What happened to my shore duty status at Kingsville? I still have about half a year to go there."

"That's all been canceled. You can kiss that shore duty good-bye and say hello to sea duty."

"It looks like I've got a day to kill until I can check in," Casey replies, rather dejectedly.

"There's a small library you can go to."

"No, I think I'm just going to look around until the time to check in. What about my sea bag?"

"It's not going anywhere. I'm going to come down and see you off this afternoon. I'll meet you at the piers. If you go to the head of the piers, there's an office in a little shack that has records of all the ship arrivals and which moorage or pier where they will be tied up."

She gets into the sedan, and Casey starts looking around for a base directory. He knows what he's looking for will probably be in the administration building.

One of the offices houses the Cuban liaison. Casey walks to the second floor and finds the door. He immediately recognizes the liaison's name as one that Commander DeNova consulted about sending the rice to the church.

He recognizes Casey as he steps in. "Welcome, Senor. It is good to see you. Has your little Cuban girlfriend left for the States yet?"

"I don't know. I've sort of lost contact with her. How are we coming on the deal with the rice?"

"I wanted to tell her that the Cuban authorities allowed the church people to go to Sereta's home and get her parents' bodies. They blamed their deaths on the bandits. They are buried in the churchyard in El Jiqui.

"I have made inquiries, and there is a dealer who will guarantee that five fifty-pound bags are put on a fishing boat, and it will go up the Bay of Pigs and be unloaded at the fish pier. From there, some of it will go by donkey cart under a load of straw to the churches. The man who will deliver it demanded more money to do the job. However, I am at a loss as to where the extra money is going to come from."

"How much more?" Casey asks.

"Fifty for the boat, and fifty for the donkey cart."

Casey stands up, takes out his wallet, and puts one hundred dollars on the table. "The donkey cart isn't Horatio Pena's, is it?"

"No, but he was almost caught by the Russians when they did a sweep of the whole valley. Now no one is safe there anymore. All the people who lived in the northern part of the valley have been moved to the south. They have been deprived of their land, and it will be bad for them for a while until they can get settled again. They are being allowed to rebuild some of the huts and the homes in the town where the fish are taken off the boats."

"I remember the place. Look, thank you for all you've done." Casey stands and shakes the liaison's hand and leaves the building. He wanders the base for a while just looking around. During his walk, he sees Mendoza jogging toward him. "Where are you headed?" he asks.

"I can't stop right now, Casey. I need to get to admin and pick up my orders. I'm being stationed down here for the next year. Bennett and Brown are both going to the Fleet Marine Force. They left for Morehead this morning. I talked to Commander DeNova, and I have her address. I'll write as soon as I can." With that, he runs off toward the administration building.

Casey hits the galley for early chow and dawdles for almost an hour, and then he makes his way down to the piers. Out in the channel a large, haze-gray ship makes the final turn. He goes to the little shack and finds that the USS *Monrovia* APA 31 will be tying up at the end of the pier, and she will be in shortly.

He goes through the gate, presents the sentry his ID, and recognizes the sedan parked along the waterfront. He walks to it and knocks on the roof. The rear door opens, and to his pleasant surprise, he finds that Commander Ross is with them. She isn't Snow White now; instead, she is in khaki.

"Hi, Casey," says the commander.

Sereta smiles at him and waves from the opposite seat. She gets out and goes around to him. They all watch as the ship grows nearer and when it's close enough to see the men on the rails, they all go to the pipe fence.

Casey leans there watching until Commander DeNova comes to his side and tells him she needs to talk privately with him. They move down the rail a distance.

"Casey, you know I'm going to go to Bethesda and take Sereta with me to see Chief Gordon. Who do I tell him the father of her baby is after four or five months or so when Sereta starts showing?"

The question makes Casey step back. "Commander, Sereta is a virgin. I haven't touched her. Nobody touched her since the day we pulled her out from under the pile of sugar cane in the hut where she was hiding from the Russian soldiers."

"What? You were sleeping together in the bunker." Commander DeNova has a severe, disbelieving look.

"I promise you, ma'am, I did not touch her. I did not have sex with her. Ma'am, she's just a sweet, innocent, virginal young woman who's loved being rescued. I have seen her naked and have, in fact, showered with her, but I have not had sex with her. I have had sex with two women in the bunker—one who blew my mind, but that must be kept a deep, dark secret."

Commander DeNova blushes with embarrassment, and she steps back to reconsider her thinking. She is flushed and sweating slightly, and she wets her lips. "You don't know how much I was dreading this conversation, Casey. I'm so relieved. Thank you for being responsible."

"As for those other two alleged women who may or may not have had sex there, you can mark off any threat of pregnancy, because they allegedly are using birth control pills. Now tell me, what deep, dark secret keeps your eyes so brooding? Did you lose someone you wanted to be with a long time ago?"

"It wasn't a long time ago, but yes, I lost someone I love. I just have to make up my mind that there's nothing I can do to change anything and get on with my life. I'm not going to be ready for another long-term relationship for quite some time."

"Oh, by the way, I talked to the Cuban liaison, and he told me to tell Sereta her parents were buried in the cemetery at El Jiqui."

# Chapter 32

Plumes of steam and a series of blasts from the whistle announce the ship's arrival as the tugs place her along the pier.

"I need to make sure you have my family's address. Do you?" Commander DeNova asks him.

"Yes, I took it and put it into my sea bag. We need to get it out of the trunk now."

They walk back to the sedan, and the commander unlocks the trunk. As it opens upward, she steps up to him, buries her breasts against him, and gives him a long good-bye kiss.

"Casey, please keep in touch with me, or if you can't, then tell me that you can't so I'll stop worrying about you," she says with big doe eyes.

"I will, Commander. You and Commander Ross really helped me get past a bad place in my life." He retrieves his sea bag, and she closes the trunk. Commander Ross gives him a handshake but then decides a kiss is in order and gives him a quick one.

Sereta, on the other hand, is almost tearful. "Casey, I know I cannot have you for my husband, but you must tell me where you are sometimes, and I will look it up on the map to see."

"Sereta, you go and do the things that will make you the American you want to be. Learn the language well, go to school, and learn of our ways. Let the commander give you advice, and later look for a job doing something you love to do, and you will be a good citizen." He holds her and kisses her a long one, and tears form in her eyes. She reluctantly lets him go.

He picks up his sea bag and walks through the gate to the ship. He has to wait for a while for the men coming down the gangway. Once he can get up the gangway, he salutes and hands his orders to the officer of the deck.

"Damn, another snipe. When are they going to send some more deck apes? I need men." The crusty old boatswain mate chief stands behind the officer of the deck, mouthing off. "Take your sea bag down the outboard passageway and wait for someone from engineering to get up here."

He looks down and waves at the three of them, who are still looking up at the ship. He's thinking about the commander's conversation. It occurs to him that it's well past the nine-month range after his coming together with Naomi. He knows he's a daddy; he just wonders how many times over. And he is also thinking about Belinda.

A seaman in dirty dungarees comes down the outboard passageway carrying a bale of rags on his shoulder. It's cut open, and some of the rags start dropping. Casey is looking out at his trio on the pier when the sailor stops beside him and looks to see where Casey is looking.

"Man, look at the cute little greaser in the striped dress. I'd like to—"

He never gets to finish his sentence. Casey jerks a rag out of the bundle and drops it at his feet. As they stoop down to pick it up, he stands up quickly and drives the back of his head into the man's nose. He recoils back and hits his head on a stanchion holding the overhead. His eyes roll upward, and he's out like a light.

"Something's happened to this guy," Casey says to the trio on the quarterdeck, and he points back to where the man is lying on the deck. The chief looks down at him. On the pier, Casey watches his trio run back to get in the sedan and leave.

"Perkins, you dolt, what have you done to yourself now?" says the chief. He goes back to the quarterdeck, picks up the phone, and requests a corpsman.

In short order, the duty chief from engineering comes up to the quarterdeck. "Damn, another machinist mate. When are they going to send me some boiler tenders? Come on, son, and I'll take you down to M division."

Casey dutifully follows the chief through a hatch and down a ladder. The first thing Casey notices is the heat. It's much too hot to be comfortable. He follows the chief to the engineering berthing, and he throws his sea bag on the bunk the chief designates to him.

"Get changed into dungarees," says the chief. "You'll probably have the watch."

A first class appears. "Hi, White, I'm Greene. I'll be your section leader."

"It's nice to meet you, Greene." Casey extends his hand, and they shake.

"Come with me, and I'll show you the engine room." Casey follows him down the equivalent of two stories of steps to the main control. He can feel the heat and humidity further surround him as he descends. The chief is down there and looks up at them.

"I have a new man for you, Chief," Greene says.

"See that he gets broken in for the steaming watch, and make sure he has the mid watch. I need the rest of the gang to get as much sleep as possible. We only have two more days of this shit left; then we can go home." The chief doesn't offer to shake hands with him.

Casey doesn't have the slightest idea what the chief is talking about. They go down to the lower level, and Greene shows him the freshwater evaporators, refrigeration compressors, lube oil pumps, the main turbine engine and reduction gear, shipboard generators and electric board, and, finally, the bilge pumps. Casey looks at a thermometer on the bulkhead; it reads 135 degrees. Next to it is a five-gallon cooler. It's full of jungle juice, or in the parlance of the uninitiated, navy-style Kool-Aid. Alongside it is a salt pill dispenser.

"Have you ever been aboard ship before?" asks Greene.

"No, my navy time began at an air station. I have no idea why I'm here now, but being as it is, I'll do the job."

"Good, I don't need another slacker. Stay away from the goof-offs—I won't even tell you who they are; you'll be able to pick them out of the lineup at quarters. Come on, now, and let's find the chief engineer. Oh, by the way, you have the mid watch."

Casey follows him back up the ladder to the main passageway and to the engineering office. It's only one hundred degrees up here.

"Lieutenant Ireland, this is E-3 mm-designated Casey White. He has no sea time and is already an E-3 with about eleven months' service time." Casey sees that the engineering officer has his service jacket open on his desk. He isn't smiling, and he eyes Casey suspiciously.

"White, you must either know something that none of the rest of us knows, or you have a friend in the office of personnel. I've got E-2s here with over two years' time in service that would jump at the chance to be promoted. What gives with you?"

"I honestly don't know. My division officer came to me and told me that my name was on the list for the test, and I took it. I guess I must have scored high enough to get promoted. One other thing, sir, I think I might have qualified for third-class also." Casey is secretly happy about the promotion, having not actually taken the test.

"Nobody gets a crow that soon, White. You gotta know somebody," the officer says with a snarl.

"I'll keep my nose clean and do my job and prove myself to you," Casey replies.

"Well, White, we have a little problem with you. We have been undergoing underway training for a month now, and we are in the last two days. If the team comes aboard tomorrow morning and finds a new man, they will run your ass through the meat grinder, and you won't know our engineering procedures from shit, and they will chop our ratings down.

"Pursuant to that, I will have my ass in a wringer with the old man. So do you know what I'm going to do? I'm going to hide you out for two days until the inspection teams finish with us, and we are on our way home."

Casey doesn't know if that is good or bad, but it's what he'll have to live with. He stands the mid watch and meets Hindsman at four hundred hours as he descends the ladder two minutes after his watch begins. Hindsman looks surly and wants to know who Casey is.

Casey introduces himself. Hindsman ducks the handshake, takes the engineering sheet, and enters readings before he even sees what is actually happening. Casey quickly leaves the area. He's found one of the screw-ups.

At the top of the ladder, he encounters Chief Carnes, who tells him to go directly to chow and report back to the engineering office. As soon as he reports to the office, the chief takes him up on the boat deck and introduces him to a "papa" boat; it is a thirty-six-foot, diesel-powered, plywood, ramp front-landing craft used by the marines when storming the beach.

"Take this sack and get under the canvas," Chief Carnes says. "Lie down and keep quiet for the day. When we come back into port, I'll come and get you for chow."

Casey takes the bag, ascends the ladder, and slips under the canvas top. Inside the well deck of the boat are an old, nasty-looking mattress and a pillow used by the seamen who repair the boat. They're so oil soaked that if lighted would burn like a highway flare.

It isn't as hot as the engine room, but it has a sticky, stinky canvas smell he knows will permeate his clothing.

He again stands the mid watch, gets two hours' sleep before having breakfast, and falls into ranks with the rest of M division at quarters. Some of the men standing there don't even know he's aboard.

The second day passes, and on the third, the captain comes on the speakers again and congratulates everyone for the work they put into the training. He tells the crew that the ship will be getting underway as soon as refueling is completed. That doesn't take but the next half hour.

At a break before they have to go to the engine room, Casey wanders topside to the pier side and looks out one last time, hoping against hope for a glimpse of someone on the pier waving up at him. All he can see are Dixie cups and the far silhouette of a US Navy R-5 taking off for who knows where. He wonders if his "girls" could possibly be on it.

Once again, he has that little gut feeling of being alone. Morale is high the first time he goes down to the engine room and meets all the machinist's mates he'll be working with. Right away, he gets a feeling of jealousy from some of the men who have been aboard for a couple of years and haven't earned promotion.

When the ship clears the breakwater, the skipper again announces to the crew that, after some exercises in the Atlantic, the ship will be going back to Norfolk for some needed repairs and that the Christmas holiday will be broken up into a period of two weeks. The first group gets Christmas week off and will return that weekend. The second group will have the New Year's week off.

Chief Carnes, the chief responsible for the engine room who was standoffish with Casey when he first reported, becomes more open and talkative with him. Casey apparently proves to him that he can be trusted and is dependable.

\*   \*   \*

The *Monrovia* makes the turn into the Norfolk channel, and all hands are required to appear topside. The pier is a blaze of color, and the smell of perfume wafting up almost takes Casey's breath. It is Casey's first liberty call. He finds his way to the main gate and waits for the Hampton Boulevard city bus to arrive. When he gets off in front of the Navy YMCA downtown, the street is a sea of white hats.

*So this is shit city.* Casey wonders when he will see his first "sailors and dogs keep off the grass" sign. He goes back to the Navy YMCA and gets a room. It's on the fifth floor and is as tiny as a large broom closet. It does, however, have a clean bed, and that's what he wants. He goes back down to the lobby and looks at the church directory; there are no Alfeta churches listed. *Great!*

Back on Granby Street, Casey starts looking for a camera shop. He finds one right in front of him—Acme Camera. He recalls Acme being the brand the coyote used in the road runner cartoons. He goes inside, looks at several cameras, and finally decides on a 35mm single-lens reflex model. Now he'll have to learn how to use a good-quality camera. This is no Brownie. He decides to learn how to use it before he returns to Westriver on leave, so he can impress his dad and mom.

\*     \*     \*

The bus pulls into the parking lot at Westriver, and Casey looks around. Nothing has changed—except that there is about a foot of new snow on top of the existing three feet. He goes across the street to the depot and looks around. He drops a dime into the pay phone. His dad answers.

"Casey! Hello, we didn't expect to see you until tomorrow. I can't come and get you because the car is snowed in. You will never get a cab after a snow like this. Are you dressed warm enough to walk it?"

"Yes, Dad, what is it, twelve blocks? All I have is an AWOL bag to carry, so I'll be there in about half an hour." He hangs up and starts walking at a brisk pace. Almost up the hill, he discovers he isn't dressed all that warm. It only spurs him to walk faster.

At the corner of Seventh Street, the city didn't even try to push the drift of snow; it's higher than a man's head. He follows someone's footsteps around it and realizes they are probably his dad's as they go right up to the back door of the house. He steps inside the back porch and walks right in. Nobody in this little burg locks their doors.

His dad is all over him. He's not one who usually hugs, but he does this time. Mom gets hers next and there is a cup of coffee and her two hands helping him remove his snow-filled oxfords. Casey's dad wants a full accounting of all his adventures while he's changing the little Christmas tree bulbs, looking for one that's burned out.

Casey knows the navy answered one of his father's letters while he was in Cuba, but he knows that he can't even mention that. He tells his parents of his life on the airstrip in Kingsville and all the airplanes he actually saw. He tells them he transferred to the ship because they trained him in a shipboard trade, and he wasn't doing that type of work on an airfield. His dad seems to agree with that.

He digs down into his AWOL bag and takes out his new camera. His dad looks at it and holds it like it is some kind of a prized gem. "What happened to your ear? It looks like a little notch at the top of it is missing?" his dad asks him while examining it.

"I got it caught up on a sharp piece of one of the aircraft we were servicing in Kingsville, and I couldn't get across the field because of all the jet traffic, so it was a couple of hours before they could put a stitch in it."

Made up on the spot, that lie would have to suffice. Dad wouldn't like to hear that an enemy sniper nearly took his head off with that round. The evening grows late. Casey tells his parents good night, goes upstairs to his room, and looks out the window. It's all iced up, and he can't see through it. He unfastens the latch and opens it. The moon on the snow makes the landscape look almost like day. There is no Ford sitting down there, and Naomi invades his dreams.

"What are you up to today?" his dad asks.

"I need to go downtown and pick up a few things. I think I'll look around and find out if any of the guys made it back home for Christmas."

Casey goes into the Walgreens, sits at the soda fountain, and orders a cherry Coke phosphate. It tastes like the ones he used to have, but something is different. He finishes his drink and goes to the post office. There is no one there. He opens the little mailbox just to see if he remembers how to do it.

Through the back window of Westriver Wholesale Retail Supply, he sees Mr. Herman sitting at the general manager's desk. Mr. Herman doesn't look up, and Casey doesn't do anything to gain his attention.

He walks across the street and goes to the front of the little weekly newspaper with the intention of reading past editions to find out what the birth announcements proclaim. It's dark, and the door is locked. He wonders if his dad kept any back copies, or if they were strawberry mulch now.

He drives to Arlene's house and knocks. A light is on in the back, and he can see her coming toward the door. She opens it, squeals, and hugs him.

"Casey, come in and meet someone." She takes his hand and leads him to the kitchen. There's a man sitting there that he vaguely recognizes.

"Casey, this is Richard Spencer, my ex, my fiancé, the man who I am going to marry again." The man stands and extends his hand.

"Glad to meet you, Casey."

"Likewise, I'm sure." He's starting to get bald in the back and has combed the hair over to hide the fact.

"When are you going to quit the phone company, Arlene?" Casey asks.

"I already have. We're just going to wait until after the Christmas season and then move down to the valley, where Richard's job is."

"What do you hear from the rest of the old gang?" he asks, fishing for information about Belinda and Naomi.

"I haven't heard anything about Naomi, but Belinda gets to stay overnight about once a month. Her husband was transferred to the Agriculture Headquarters in Laramie, and from what I hear, it's quite a promotion for someone so young. He's going to college there, and Belinda is too.

"You should see her beautiful little twin girls, Casey. They are adorable." That information shocks Casey, and it takes him a minute to catch his breath.

\*     \*     \*

Christmas morning breaks bright and sparkling. The sunrise across the hills makes the snow glisten. Casey's mom pulls the drapes open to allow the sunshine to help heat the front room.

They wait until his brother comes down from his room before serving breakfast.

"How's the job going?" Casey asks his brother.

"Not too bad if I don't get many truckers that want me to install their own oil. I get a nickel for every can I sell."

"How's school coming?"

"Not too bad. I don't bother anyone, and they don't bother me."

"What are your plans after next year? You'll graduate, and then what?"

"Right now I don't have any plans."

Casey has only one chance to corner his brother and ask if he's heard anything about Naomi. He has not. It's as though she disappeared off the face of the earth along with her family.

At one point, Casey finds himself alone with his mom. "What seems to be the trouble, Casey?"

"I don't know, Mom. Everything seems the same, but it's different. Nothing I do or see makes me feel like I'm happy to be home. I think I've outgrown this town. I don't know where my town is, but it isn't here."

"I understand, son. I know you lost someone, and there is nothing you can do about it. My best suggestion to you is to move on and make your life somewhere else. Keep in touch with us. I know you like to write letters. You can keep doing that, and I'll keep writing back."

"Whatever ever happened to old man Herman?"

"Casey, you'd not believe the scandal. They're taking money and stock out of the store and using them for their own purposes, but nobody seems to know what those purposes are. I think the state might still be investigating it. The night he was attacked, he lost some of his personal parts and the big toe from his foot."

"I thought Mr. Herman owned a great big chunk of the business."

"Yes, apparently, but they were doing it and not paying taxes on it somehow. They received a huge fine, and old man Milner had to retire. Mr. Herman took over his job, and Lloyd is the manager of the men's department now. I don't know who the new man is, but I think he is someone from the Alfeta church in Salt Lake. I think they sent someone here just to look out for things."

"Where's the card that Belinda promised to send for Christmas? Did anyone else send cards?" Casey's mom thinks for a minute and then goes to the front room and looks over a pile of Christmas cards. She drops the one with the Salt Lake City return address behind the box and brings the rest of them to the table so that Casey can read them. About halfway down is a card from Belinda with a picture of her and Johnny with the twins.

He looks at the picture. The twin girls have their mother's hair and facial features. Belinda dominated in the gene pool this time. In the picture, Johnny is holding one, and she is holding the other. They look happy.

Casey remembers every detail of the night they made love in the bed at the store. He wonders whether he will ever find out about Naomi. He remembers that rather vividly also.

After supper, he goes downtown and confirms his return ticket. He's been hoping to take a plane or train, but they're all booked up. He should have thought about that before he left the ship.

As he passes the alley in back of Westriver Supply, he sees the local cop doing the nightly shakedown. He waits a few minutes and then drives through the alley and stops right behind Mr. Herman's window. He jumps out and retrieves his lug wrench from his trunk. He pops the window open, tosses a large chunk of snow onto the seat of the chair, slams the window shut, and quickly leaves the alley.

\* \* \*

The following day, Casey's parents take him to the bus station and say good-bye a little after five. The sky turns from winter's overcast light gray to steel gray. It's the sure sign of a winter storm. The sterile scent of snow is in the air.

He watches them grow smaller as the bus pulls away. The wind blows the snow off the bluffs as they transit along the frozen Green River.

Just beyond Rock Springs, the weather takes a turn for the worse. The once gray sky turns black, and the snowflakes start to hit the windshield. They're like little sleet pellets, and they bounce off as they hit. Farther on they change into snow, and soon the wind starts kicking up.

The bus is soon in a serious ground blizzard. There's no oncoming traffic, and the road is snowed over. Casey can see a dozen automobiles behind the bus, which is breaking a trail for them. The bus slows to about forty-five, and Casey leans forward, looking at the road, trying to help the driver.

It turns out to be the so-called one-hundred-year blizzard. He ends up riding four different busses, and the trip takes over forty-eight hours from the time he boards the bus in Westriver. It's afternoon when he reaches Norfolk.

# 33

T HERE aren't any drunken sailors going back to the ships this early in the evening, and it's a cold walk down the pier where the ship is tied up. Casey walks up the gangway and gives the quarterdeck his papers.

"You know you are a day early checking in."

"Yes, the weather was bad, and I thought I should get on a bus early and not be late checking back in. I ended up traveling on a bus for forty-eight hours anyway."

"Well, get a bite to eat and hit the rack; you have the mid watch tonight."

After steaming to pick up marines at Morehead City, North Carolina, Casey is amazed watching the men come aboard; he sees all the equipment it takes to keep a fleet marine going. All three forward holds are converted to a huge berthing space. That's where they will live. Three decks down beneath the marines is the storage for all their eight-inch howitzer ammunition. It is not only for the *Monrovia* but also the entire amphibious group. That's all six ships.

\* \* \*

It's getting to be a long two-week passage going across the Atlantic. Once topside, Casey can go up on the aft end of the third deck, look out, and see the ships of the squadron, which seem to be taking turns playing follow-the-leader.

Thirteen hundred hours rolls around, and back in the engine room the messenger comes down the ladder and tells Casey the engineering officer wants to talk to him. He takes a minute to straighten his uniform and goes to the office. Lieutenant Ireland is sitting at his desk, frowning, and motions for him to step inside.

"Close the door behind you, White." Casey finds a chair opposite the man. The officer looks up from studying a stack of papers. Then he lays them on the desk and looks directly at Casey, studying him. "What is it with you, White? Do you have a friend in personnel in Washington? I'd really like to know who's looking out for you." His tone is almost angry.

"I don't know who, if anyone, is looking out for me, sir," Casey replies honestly.

"How do you explain this, then?" Lieutenant Ireland takes the top paper from the stack and hands it to him. It's a list of men on board who are approved to take the third-class test for machinist's mate.

"I don't understand, sir," Casey's a little upset by the officer's attitude.

"You have to be nominated by the command. When the papers went in, you weren't even aboard the ship."

"Did it come from my last command and is just catching up with me, sir?"

"White, you don't even have much more than a year in the service. I've got men in the engine room right now who have been aboard two years that are still E-2 and haven't had the opportunity to take the E-3 test."

"Isn't it supposed to be based on performance?"

"I don't think that's it, and you're presumptuous to think you are better than they are. I can kill this if I want to; I just won't allow you to go and take the test when the documents come aboard," Lieutenant Ireland says.

"Have I done something that disqualifies me to take it?" Casey asks him.

"Hell yes! You don't have the time in rate you need."

"Apparently someone else thinks I am able to handle the responsibility, sir," Casey replies.

Lieutenant Ireland stands. "Right, and I'd like to know who is looking out for you."

"The answer I must give to you, sir, is that if you look in my personnel jacket, you will find a notation at the bottom of the security documentation page annotating the fact that I've had a top-secret security clearance. It was pulled only because I was assigned to sea duty and am not required to have it anymore.

"I must inform you that after this conversation, I am by law required to inform my contact at the Navy Department in Washington that you've made a demand of me to divulge information to which I have been sworn to secrecy. All I can tell you is that I was involved in a secret, covert military action and survived it."

Lieutenant Ireland lets his jaw drop slightly. "You're shooting straight this time, aren't you White?" Apparently, Casey's little outburst has made the man back down from his dominating attitude.

"What happens if you take the test and fail or don't pass with a mark high enough to get ranked on the promotion list?" he asks Casey.

"Sir, then I wait until the next time around and get to try again," Casey replies.

"Go back to work, White. I need time to think about this."

Casey knows Lieutenant Ireland will try to contact someone in Washington to find out what's going on. The thing that amazes Casey is that he himself doesn't know what's going on. He has no knowledge of anyone promoting him. He wonders if Brown, Bennett, and Mendoza are being treated the same way.

The first port of call—Naples, Italy—is two days out. All the divisions are called to quarters, and the hospital corpsmen give the standard lecture on sexually transmitted diseases and tell them that every man is required to pick up a package of condoms at the quarterdeck before going ashore. The rest of the two hours is spent acquainting the troops with the local customs and where they can visit and what is off limits.

Because of the draft of the ship, they cannot go into the inner harbor and tie up at the sea wall. The *Monrovia* has to anchor out and run liberty boats for the crew. The following morning, the ship receives mail from a helo drop. It takes the post office all morning to sort through it. It's an accumulation of almost a month's mail.

While they're at morning quarters, Chief Carnes tells the men he'll allow them to take their mail down to the engine room and have an hour or whatever time it takes them to read it. He asks them not to make a big thing of it. *If you want to make men happy that is the way to do it,* Casey thinks.

When Casey is at last handed his mail, he receives a pile the size of a large loaf of bread, with a rubber band around it. He takes it and sits down in front of the forced air vent on the steps going to the lower level. The usual noisy chatter in the engine room dissolves into silence broken only by the throb of the equipment and the *zzzzzip* of letters being opened.

Casey looks through the pile and begins assembling his letters from home in order by date. He sets the newspapers aside to be read at his leisure. The next-to-last letter he turns over has a Virginia address on it. Commander DeNova promised perfume on her letters. There is none here. He reads.

Casey, I'm sorry to be the one to tell you, but Chief Gordon passed away on 15 January of massive infection and pneumonia. He was laid to rest in Arlington Cemetery after a one-week wait for the ground to defrost enough to open the grave. It's been really cold here in Washington.

I accompanied Mrs. Sereta Gordon to the services, and she really was the grieving widow. I guess she did feel some real attachment to the chief. None of Chief Gordon's previous wives turned up to muddy the water. It was an impressive funeral, what with the firing of the rifles and the folding of the flag.

We went to the Washington National Cathedral, and she wanted to know if it was where the pope lived.

I had to explain to her where we were, and it only drove her to study my globe at home.

She is starting to realize how large the world really is. She was surprised to find out how small Cuba is compared to the USA. While we were looking at the globe, I knew the group was in the Mediterranean. They usually make Naples the first port of call.

I've purchased a home outside Washington in Virginia, and it takes me about twenty minutes to get to the Pentagon. Sereta claims the basement (at her request) as her home. She pays me rent and has learned to do housekeeping. She actually makes supper for me some nights when the menu isn't too complex.

She likes to eat at the Carol's Hamburgers about half a mile down the road from the house. To start with, she had trouble accepting the concept of going everywhere by car. When the carhop came out the first time and took our order, it really confused her. She likes to go in, sit at the little tables, and eat. I guess it makes her think of being in some hotel in Havana.

She has access to the bus line, and it's a half-hour ride with only two transfers to her citizenship classes. She is doing very well.

I am dating a navy captain in the security group, and we are contemplating marriage. I have to get him over his last little bit of reluctance actually to ask me. He is four years older than I am. He is a very gentle lover. Need I say more?

Please continue writing and tell me about yourself and how you are doing. I won't let Sereta know about your letters as I know you don't want to get involved with her.

I spoke to Jean Ross. She's working at Bethesda and has some really crazy shifts. We saw her after the funeral when we stopped at the hospital to pick up Chief Gordon's personal effects. I read his personnel jacket, and he has a very impressive record. I don't know if you know this, but he's the recipient of a silver star. If there was some kind of trouble around the world, he was a part of it. It's a shame the way he died. As far as I can find, he has no other living relatives.

I'm sure you are busy, and this is too long as I can go on and on.

With all my love and affection,
Mary D.

Casey reads the letter several times and then carefully puts it back into the envelope. He looks at the last envelope in the stack and realizes it's from home but has been forwarded to him. Inside is the Christmas card from Belinda and Johnny Stephenson. His mom sent it on to him. He opens it and finds a copy of the picture he saw at home. Now he has his own copy.

He has the strangest feeling looking at the picture and knowing that the kids in it are his flesh and blood, although they don't exactly look like him. Belinda dominated in the gene pool this time. He decides to keep up with them as long as possible. He's still hoping somehow to hear something about Naomi.

The chief returns to the engine room. "All right, men, we've killed an hour and a half. Let's turn to and get this dump cleaned up now."

The afternoon passes uneventfully, and Casey takes his mail out to the fantail and finds a clear, wind-free place to sit down and read. He opens the letters in order of the dates and gets a feeling for life at home. He also looks through some copies of the little local newspaper that have been sent to him.

Casey feels a presence above him and looks up to find Brown looking down at him. "Brown? What in the world are you doing here?"

"I'm not taking my life in my hands coming back here, am I?" he says, looking around at all the black shoes casting angry looks at him.

"No, I'll protect you. Have you been aboard since Morehead?"

"Yes, I'm surprised we didn't find each other sooner." Brown sits down and holds out a letter to Casey. "Read."

Casey takes the letter and reads the return address. It's from Commander DeNova. He doesn't say anything about the letter she sent him. He opens it and finds that it reports the death of Chief Gordon. She gives the short version of the news, deleting any reference to Sereta other than the funeral.

"I'm sorry to see him go. He deserved better," Casey says. to Brown. "At least he was able help get Sereta out."

"I know. I hope she tells Mendoza and Bennett. If I ever get to Washington, I'll have to make a trip out to the grave and have a look around," Brown says.

"Me too, I might make a project out of it sometime. Speaking of Washington, weren't we supposed to be invited to some grand thank-you, kiss-my-ass, and go-to-hell party affair in the capital city and have it hosted by the pres himself?" Casey asks Brown.

"That's what the project officer promised us, but you know about politicians and promises. I've got to get back to the hold now and get my rifle cleaned for inspection. I'll try to see you sometime on the beach." He taps Casey on the shoulder, turns, and leaves the fantail.

"What are you doing allowing a jarhead back here with the rest of us black shoes," one of the first-class electricians arrogantly asks Casey. He's apparently trying to start something.

"He's my brother," Casey replies casually.

"Oh." That stops any confrontation that might arise.

Casey picks up his mail and has to chuckle. He's a blond, and Brown has black hair. He wonders if the first class even looked beyond the uniform. *What is it with some people?*

Back in his bunk, he starts a letter to Commander DeNova and makes sure to enter her address in his address book. He tells her that Brown is aboard the ship, and they talked about Chief Gordon. He asks if she has Mendoza's and Bennett's addresses.

\*   \*   \*

Thirteen hundred hours rolls around the following day, and back in the engine room, the messenger comes down the ladder and tells Casey the engineering officer wants to talk to him. He takes a minute to straighten his uniform and goes to the office. Mr. Ireland is sitting at his desk frowning and motions for Casey to step inside.

On his desk is a set of sealed orders. He hands them to Casey and waits for him to open them.

"Go ahead, White. Make me feel good and let us know what old Uncle Sam has in store for you." Casey hesitates and then opens the letter, knowing that he won't get out of the office without doing so. It's short and sweet.

"It says to have my sea bag and all personal effects together and appear at the fleet landing in the morning. There will be a sedan waiting for me. The command is notified and will comply. I'm under transfer orders." It's all Casey can do to stifle a grin. He is getting off this tub. He hands the letter to the officer.

"Okay, White, get out of here!"

Casey meets the chief in the passageway. "Do you really know what's going on, Casey?" the chief asks him as they walk along.

"I don't really know, Chief, but I took part in a covert operation, and I believe this might be some kind of follow-up on it. I personally thought I'd be part of the gang for the rest of my enlistment."

"Well, I wish you the best." The chief extends his hand, and Casey shakes with him.

The engineering officer makes sure Casey has the mid watch. Casey can do it standing on his head the frame of mind he's in now. He tells no one about his transfer and doesn't bother to attend morning quarters after chow.

He finishes packing his sea bag, goes to the quarterdeck, and waits for his turn to depart. He looks down the outboard passageway and, to his amazement sees Brown walking up with his sea bag packed. They immediately know their orders do, in fact, have something to do with the operation—but what?

# Chapter
# 34

T HEY'RE able to get aboard the second boat with the officers, and when they step off the boat at the fleet landing, there's a sedan waiting for them. They give the driver their identification. There are no other passengers.

"Where are we headed, driver?" Casey asks him.

"You don't know? You're going to the air station and on to Paris." Brown looks at him, and they wonder where this little jaunt will ultimately take them. After being shuttled off to the MATS section, they fly to Paris aboard a US Navy R5.

Finally, when it's their turn, they land and taxi up to the terminal maintained by the American consulate. They have no idea of who, where, how, or when, so they step into the terminal, take seats, and wait.

Fifteen minutes after most of the other passengers are gone a dapper little man dressed in a three-piece tweed suit with a bowler hat approaches them. "Are you White and Brown?" he asks with a chuckle. Apparently, the names seem funny to him. White is dressed in dress whites, and Brown is in brown uniform. He extends his hand. "I'm Harold Bogsworth. I work on the foreign relations staff at the embassy. I'm supposed to take you there. You'll be berthed overnight tonight, and then you'll go on to wherever it is the ambassador has set up."

They follow Harold to a waiting Citroen sedan with diplomatic plates. They try to follow along as he points out various sights along the way. A marine guard allows them to pass through the gates, and the sedan drives around to the side entrance. A porter comes out and removes their sea bags from the trunk, and they follow him as he walks down the hall to a small elevator.

They ascend and go down another long hall. Harold quietly knocks on a door, and shortly someone unlocks and opens it. Casey recognizes Mendoza, and Bennett is looking up from the couch.

Usually sailors and marines don't hug, but this time, there is hugging all around. It's a mini family reunion. All that's lacking is Sereta, Chief Gordon, and Mr. King. Reality has to set in sometime, and for a moment, it's solemn.

They all have sea stories of the past months. Mendoza and Bennett are just as mystified as Casey and Brown as to why they've all been brought here.

*       *       *

They're awakened the next morning and served breakfast, and an embassy staff member tells them of the coming day's events. They'll be driven to the Du Bois's family estate outside Paris for a meeting with the family of the man they rescued.

*So this is the payback for all the time we spent rescuing the little bastard.* Casey notices all his marine buddies are sporting lance corporal stripes.

A marine in full dress opens the door, and the ambassador steps in. The ambassador sits with them and attempts to inform them of diplomatic protocol.

"This man is the French ambassador to Spain, so he will be accorded the same recognition as any other ambassador. His son will also be in attendance." Casey hopes that will be the case as he really wants to tell the arrogant little SOB a thing or two.

The destination is a large, walled and gated four-story residence at the end of a long, tree-lined driveway. There are dogs roaming in the outer portion of the estate, and they have to go through another gate before they can get to the house.

The limousine pulls up in front, and a uniformed doorman opens the door for them. He appears to be immediately impressed with the marines in full-dress uniforms, but not so much with the sailor in dress uniform. They go across a huge entry and are led up a set of stairs to the second floor. The doorman pauses and opens the door. It is semi-dark inside, only being illuminated at their end.

The American ambassador leads the group inside, and the occupants turn, acting as though they are looking to see who's intruding on their privacy. The five of them step inside and immediately see Diego sitting on an elevated chair, dressed in what looks like silk pajamas with a scarf tied around his neck. Seated by his side is a young woman well along in her pregnancy.

Behind them on the wall is what appears to be a family portrait. Casey notes there are three young men in the picture, not just Diego, but Diego is the one who looks different from the rest of them.

"Please let me introduce the family to you, gentlemen," says the American ambassador. He turns and starts with the French ambassador, whom he apparently knows.

"This is Albert Laurent Du Bois the fourth, the Ambassador to Spain, and his lovely wife, Camille Blanch Du Bois. You already know Diego; around here, they call him Francoise. Beside him is Arnaude Rousseau." They all do a little bend that could be taken for being a bow if not so stiff.

"We're pleased to meet each one of you and to thank you for what you did for Francoise," the ambassador says.

Casey notices an air of suspicion, or perhaps disdain. *Apologies can be painful,* he thinks.

"Will you please come and join us for lunch?" the ambassador asks. They all file out the door behind the family and walk back down the long hallway to a dining room that can seat over one hundred. A single table is set up for them.

They're seated. The meal is served, and the ambassador proposes a toast to the four of them. He never refers to the two

307

people missing who gave their lives to save the little pimp with his arrogance showing so loudly.

Up to this time, Diego has not said a single thing, nor has his mother or the woman with him. Casey starts to get a little upset about this. He starts to stand to give a toast, but the ambassador catches him by the leg under the table and makes him desist.

Finally, Diego stands and speaks in French. They wonder why he's doing so, and the interpreter relays what he says. Apparently, he cannot apologize or thank them in English. Dessert is served, and after the dishes are cleared, the French ambassador stands. At the opposite end of the room, a waiter wheels a table into the room. On top of it are four gifts, wrapped and tied up with pink ribbons.

"I know we can never thank you enough, but please accept these as a small token of our gratitude," says the ambassador. Casey and the rest untie and open their boxes. Inside each is a Beretta shotgun. The French ambassador is smiling and waiting for someone to say something. Casey stands and thanks them for the presents, although he's wondering why the decision was made to get them shotguns.

Diego finally speaks up in English. "I thought that since you were army men, you could use an additional armament." Casey's buddies stiffen at being called "army" but let it pass. "We will make arrangements to have them shipped to your individual homes in the United States. I believe the ambassador said that you are unable to keep personal arms in your respective duty stations." It's all Casey can stand, and he takes the opportunity to speak. He's still standing, and he addresses Diego.

"Diego, we missed you on the pier in Guantanamo after the submarine dropped us off, and we didn't get to say good-bye. Please tell us something of your life after our little adventure in the countryside of Cuba."

Diego looks a little surprised by Casey's question. "I was picked up by mother"—he drags the word *mother* out with just a little disdain in his pronunciation—"and we journeyed back here to France in the style I am accustomed to. I had to relearn good table manners and various social graces as I lost some of my refinements in the jungle. Now that Arnaude has joined me here, I have reestablished my rightful place in French society." He pauses and looks at Casey and the rest of them to see what effect his response is having on them.

"Have you been to the chapel and prayed for the two men who gave their lives affecting your rescue and who are now memorialized in Arlington Cemetery?"

A shocked look passes through the French ambassador's family. Diego apparently forgot to tell his family of a marine officer giving his life helping him escape from Cuba, or of a wounded chief.

"Has your half brother been told you are safely home?" There's no answer, only a negative shake of Diego's now bowed head.

Another almost imperceptible movement goes across the family's faces once again. Casey knows he has hit a nerve. *Old Mom will be drilling him tonight to see how much of the family's skeleton is out of the closet.*

The American ambassador stands and announces they have scheduled a sightseeing tour. It's getting late, so they must be getting started. They're escorted through the house and seen off at the front door. Once inside the Citroen, the men break out into laughter.

The ambassador turns and looks right at Casey. "What was that all about?" he asks.

"One hot, mosquito-buzzing night, Diego let it slip that the president is his half brother." A look of surprise he cannot mask crosses the ambassador's face.

"My God, man, now I have a lot of apologizing to do. I hope you haven't told anyone else of this!" He looks into the eyes of each of the men present.

"No, none of us have. I guess we didn't consider it important enough to tell anyone. I don't think it even came up in the official debrief afterward." Inwardly, Casey chuckles, and he knows his fellow conspirators are doing likewise, as they watch the ambassador's reaction.

"You must promise never to divulge any of this to anyone," the ambassador says in a demanding tone.

*        *        *

The following day, they're taken on a tour of Paris along with a busload of other American tourists. Casey can only wonder what's next.

That evening they're called to the ambassador's office, where they meet a navy commander carrying orders. Casey opens his file and finds he will be going stateside to a destroyer in Norfolk. It's presently in the navy yard in Portsmouth undergoing an overhaul. *At least, I won't be returning to that rust-encrusted amphib*, he thinks. Brown and Bennett will be going back to the fleet marine force but not to their present group. Mendoza is given orders back to Guantanamo. *Go figure.*

They're booked on a commercial flight to Washington, DC, where they'll go their separate ways. Casey tells the officer he would like to have leave once he arrives in DC. After a phone call, it's scheduled.

The flight back stateside turns out to be somewhat nostalgic when they realize it might be the last time they'll see each other. Afterward, they all agree to give Mary copies of their new addresses and try to keep in touch.

# Chapter 35

C ASEY watches them take off for Norfolk, and he then looks into his little pocket directory, finds Mary DeNova's number, and calls it. He has to try again later in the afternoon, and she finally picks up.

"Hi, Commander, I'm stateside again, and in Washington. I have about a week to sightsee."

"Casey, what a pleasant surprise. I just put Sereta on a Greyhound bound for Florida for a meeting with some relatives of hers. Why don't you come here? I'll fix you dinner, and we can talk over old times. This is ironic; I just mailed you a letter yesterday. You probably won't get it until you get back to your ship."

"I'm going aboard a different ship, Commander; it's a destroyer out of Norfolk.

"Well, where are you coming from, and how in the world did you get off the ship you were on?" she asks excitedly.

"It's a long story. The four of us met in Paris and went to the French ambassador's home for a halfhearted thank you for saving Diego's skinny little ass. There's more to the story I'd like to share with you."

"Casey, I can't wait. I'm looking at the bus schedules for the airport. When you get downtown, you'll have a few blocks to walk from the Greyhound terminal. Catch a local bus; it stops about two blocks from here."

"Good, I'll be there as soon as I'm able." Casey takes down the information and hangs up the phone. It turns out to be almost three hours to get from the airport to the bus stop two blocks from where she lives. He finds the residence set back in a little court.

She meets him at the door, still in her uniform. She apparently wants him to notice she's now a full commander. Acting very formal, she opens the door and allows him in. Once inside, she quickly shuts it, grabs him as he drops his sea bag, and gives him a firm hug and an intimate kiss. They cling together a minute, and then Casey follows her to the dining room.

"I'm sorry I didn't have anything made up for the occasion. I'll feed you leftovers tonight," commander DeNova tells him.

"That's okay. It'll be better than the meal the Frenchman served us. I can't get past eating something that crawls on the ground." She goes to the kitchen and brings out what looks like freshly prepared rib eye, vegetables, and mashed potatoes, followed by ice cream.

"Where did you say Sereta went?" he asks her.

"She's been looking around for relatives and found some she thinks are cousins on her mother's side. I'm a little skeptical, but she insists, and it will do her good to get out on her own and learn about the world. Would you like the nickel tour of the house?" She leads him through the house, pointing out various things. It's a nice home she's managed to put together.

As they go down the brightly painted basement stairs, she says, "This is all Sereta's domain." The basement has a Latin flair, in that the paint is a bit bolder than in the upstairs. In her bedroom, a diary sits on the nightstand. The first hanger in the closet still suspends the dress she wore the day she emerged from the cane pile in the hut. It's carefully laundered, repaired, ironed, and hung there as a reminder of where she's come from.

"Does she ever wear the dress?" Casey asks her.

"No, I have never seen her in it. I think she's saving it for some purpose unknown to me. Now come upstairs and let's get a drink and talk over old times. You've been pretty good about keeping me informed, and the rest of the guys have too. Oh, by the way, I have all their letters for you to read if you care to."

"Yes, we had a pretty good time telling sea stories at the embassy one night," he says. He follows her back up the stairs. "How often do you see Jean Ross?" he asks. They go to the front room. The commander disappeared and returns with a box of letters from the marines. She pops the cork on a bottle of wine.

"She's a full commander too now, by the way. I see her perhaps once a month, or any time we can get together. She's dating a scientist she met at the university. He's about four years older than her, and he works for the Smithsonian. Kind of like the guy I am engaged to." She studies him for his reaction.

"Good for you. Did you finally find a guy who fulfilled all of your criteria?"

"He fulfills most of it. He's a full captain and about four years older than me, like Jean's guy is to her."

"Is he a lawyer like you?" Casey asks her.

"Yes, dammit, but he has a different take on life than my former," the commander replies, knowing the why of his question.

"How long do you have before you can retire?"

"About eight years, but I've been thinking about going into the reserves if I get married."

"If you get married?"

She sets her glass down, turns the light off, and scoots over beside Casey on the couch. He doesn't know where she's going with this, so he chooses to sit and let her make the moves. There's a long silence as they finish their wine, and Casey then sets their glasses down beside the arm of the couch.

The commander turns the lamp on and displays her left hand. The engagement ring's stone is huge. She carefully takes the ring off, places it back in the small box she has in her other hand, turns the light off, and nestles closer. "Casey, I would very much like to reenact the day we made love in the bunker, if that's okay with you."

Casey stands, and she pulls his jumper off over his head. He can feel her hands shaking as she carries out her seduction. In the bedroom, she flips the bolster pillows on the floor and pulls the top covers off. The bedroom is totally black except where light from the living room filters in.

"Come to my voice, Casey, and let's reenact." Once again, he does as she requests. She's fantasizing, and he's not about to mess up her dreams.

When they finish, she seems to be content to keep holding him; and after a while, they fall asleep. Sometime in the very early morning hours, she wakes him. "Casey, did you ever have a chance to live out a fantasy like I just did?"

"Does it bother you that you did it with a man other than the one you're supposed to be marrying?"

"This is my bachelorette party. I know he has one hell of a party planned for himself. Besides, I removed his ring. I'll bet you couldn't guess that my underwear is the same I was wearing the day we first made love."

"What is your intended's name?"

"Dennis Ekland is his name. His father is Ekland of Ekland, Romanno, House, and Penn. They're one of the oldest firms in DC." Mary looks for a reaction.

"That's great. Now I'll know who is suing me for alienation of affection."

"Casey, I've continued to fantasize about you since the first time you touched me. You didn't realize how horny I was that evening we were standing by ourselves at the pipe fence when you went aboard ship, and I couldn't do anything about it. I knew we could never be together, so I just made my dreams around you. I think Jean fanaticizes about you too; she as much as admits it to me."

*Here I go again,* Casey thinks.

"What happened to you, Casey? The first time I saw you in the bunker, you looked like a lost soul. If it hadn't been for Sereta, I think you might have gone over the hill. You really liked having her around, and I can't blame you. She is a real inspiration."

"Let me tell you my story, apparently we have time." Casey starts to tell the commander his life history. The only thing he leaves out is the stealing of the wallet and the shooting of Mr.

Herman. She's incredulous about some of the story of the religious cult, and his sexual escapades seem to interest her. He wonders if she thinks he's bragging or lying.

The jangling of the telephone awakens them. The commander reaches over and answers. She leaps up to a sitting position on the bed. "Oh God, Captain, I'm down with the flu or some kind of bug. I was going to call in, but I fell back asleep. I'm sorry. I can come in if it's important." Casey hears the distant voice tell her to stay home and not come in and infect the rest of the office.

They spend the better part of the day making love, talking, and eating piecemeal from the refrigerator. About four thirty, Casey goes to the front hall to get clean underwear, and as he looks out the front door window, an expensive sedan pulls up in the driveway.

"Mary, someone's outside!" He picks up his sea bag and clothes and runs down the hall with them.

"No, don't go that way. Take it to the basement and get into Sereta's closet next to the bed, and be very quiet." She parts the drapes and looks out the side glass. "It's Dennis. He's probably worried about me and came to check. He might stay for a while, so you'll have to be patient, be quiet, and wait." Casey takes his clothes and his sea bag down the stairs and pulls the closet doors open. He gets inside but leaves the one door open a crack so he can see the hallway and the stairs.

He hears the front door open, and heavy footsteps come down the house hall above him. The bedroom is located directly above where he's hiding, and he hears the conversation between the captain and the commander.

The captain is solicitous and concerned about the commander's sleep-deprived and reddened eyes. She assures him she has everything she needs and tells him he shouldn't stick around and get whatever she has. He overrules her and decides he'll stay for a while just in case she needs something.

Casey braces for a long stint in the basement. He wonders whether the captain will find the wine glasses he left in the front room beside the couch. He quietly sits on the floor, and as time begins to wear on him, he looks up and remembers where he saw Sereta's diary. He manages to get it off the nightstand and carefully looks to see if she has anything set against it or beside it, so he can return it like he finds it.

The one thing that catches his eye is his name mentioned in the writing. Sereta still has a thing for him. He finishes it and looks for something else to entertain himself.

At last, he hears the two upstairs talking again. The commander had fallen asleep, and the captain had prepared her some soup. She thanks him, and he lets himself out.

Casey looks through the curtained basement well windows and sees the car turn to drive away. He waits for a while, and finally, the commander calls down to him to come out. She's in a short nightgown and tells him to go to the bedroom.

"Does it bother you that I haven't dressed?" she says temptingly. "Come on." Casey follows her, and it becomes another all-nighter. Her bachelorette party is a two-day affair.

\*     \*     \*

The following morning, she holds him and snuggles, reluctant to let the thing she's building in her head go until the very last moment.

"Casey, do you think this helps you to forget all the life you left behind when you joined the navy?" She apparently remembers most of what he has told her during their two days together.

He just smiles an appreciative smile as she calls work again to check in and then makes them lunch. She offers directions to the bus stop but then decides she doesn't want the neighbors to see him coming out of the door.

He puts his sea bag in the trunk of the car in the garage and lays his head on her lap as she backs down the driveway. She's allowed her skirt to creep up her thighs, and Casey just lies there enjoying the accommodations.

"Where are you headed now, Casey?" the commander asks him.

"I think I might cut this leave short and hope I can get some time off after I check in."

"Casey, whatever you choose to do, let me know. I'm getting worried about Sereta mooning about you all the time. Perhaps it's time to have a sit-down conversation with her. She's become a wonderful housekeeper and a quick learner. She's leaning toward learning law. She aced the high school equivalency test, and early next year, she'll be getting her diploma."

Commander DeNova pulls the little ring box out of her pocket and puts the engagement ring back on her finger. Casey slams the trunk, and she gives him a departing kiss and drives away. He goes inside the terminal and finds a bus schedule.

\* \* \*

The trip south reminds him of the return from home before, and he watches the passing Virginia countryside.

Instead of checking into the transient barracks at the naval base, he chooses to catch the tunnel bus to Portsmouth and ends up at the main gate of the shipyard.

The security there is more stringent than at the naval base, but Casey finally passes inside the gate. He walks several blocks to find the docks and the ship. He is amazed to see her high and dry alongside another destroyer. If not for the newly repainted hull number 724, he wouldn't know which ship was his.

"Give you a hand?" A third-class machinist's mate behind him offers to help him carry his sea bag across the narrow bow. He looks down; it's a long way to the bottom of the dry dock. He salutes the colors and hands his orders to the chief on the quarterdeck.

"Looks like M Division is getting another one," says the chief. "Garrity, can you give him a hand finding Mr. Roberts? I think he's still aboard. Welcome aboard the *Laffey*, sailor."

"Thank you, Chief." Casey shakes hands with him. Garrity shows Casey to the M Division berthing quarters, which is considerably smaller than the quarters he left behind on the *Monrovia.*

He finds an available bunk, flops his sea bag on it, and follows Garrity up to the engineering office. Sitting inside an incredibly narrow little office is a tall, dark-headed officer with lieutenant bars on his coat. Casey hands him his orders, and he opens them and reads.

"It says here you've been promoted to third class, White. Why are you still wearing E-3 stripes?"

"I've been in transit for quite a while with two different shore duty stations and no seagoing rating badges at the tailor shops, and I haven't been able to get them changed." It is all news to him. He won't, however, complain about the promotion.

"I need another third in the after-engine room. White, that's your new duty station. We meet at o eight hundred hours. It will be the first time all the men are together there for quarters. We only moved here from the barracks barge today. Your arrival is well timed."

Casey follows Garrity back to the bunk room, and he opens his locker and pulls out some work shirts. "Does anyone on the ship do sewing as a pastime to make a few bucks?"

"You're looking at him. I charge a dollar a shirt, but I don't do dress uniforms."

Casey hands the shirts to Garrity and follows him down to the after-engine room. He looks around and sees powder all over. "What is the white powder all over the decks?"

"It's just asbestos; we had to do a main engine tear out of the lagging on the turbines because some yardbird failed to make the right entries in the maintenance logs."

*   *   *

Casey awakens with the bugle and begins his first day's tour of duty aboard a destroyer—or, in his mind, a ship that can go fast enough to create its own breeze. Another plus is that the ship sparkles under several new coats of paint.

\*　\*　\*

The first night Casey has liberty, he goes downtown to the telephone office where there's a courtesy phone bank for the use of servicemen who want to call their families. He gives the operator Commander DeNova's number, and shortly he hears her answer the phone. The first thing he asks is whether she can talk freely without fear of someone hearing her conversation.

She tells him Sereta is attending her classes and her soon-to-be husband is attending some kind of meeting and will not be coming to her home until late. They talk for half an hour, and Casey tells her of his promotion and the conditions aboard the ship. He's eager to go to sea just to see how conditions will be aboard a fleet destroyer. The commander agrees that he should get to Washington as soon as he's able.

\*　\*　\*

On a clear, cold Tuesday morning, Casey walks into the bus station in Washington. He eagerly looks around for his greeters. Failing to see anyone he knows, he goes inside and waits, thinking they're probably caught in the holiday traffic. He calls the house, but there is no answer. Now he's growing concerned.

He finds a city bus schedule and leaves for Commander DeNova's home. He grows more apprehensive as he approaches the door.

# Chapter 36

T HE house is dark except for a single light in the rear. He rings the bell and steps back.

"Casey!" Sereta pulls the door all the way open, reaches out, and drags him inside. She pulls him to her and kisses him. He's overwhelmed but kisses her back.

"Is anything wrong?" he asks. "Mary's supposed to pick me up at the bus station."

"I'm sorry, Casey. I was in the shower, and I didn't get out in time to catch the phone. I tried to answer it."

"Where is Mary?" Casey asks her.

"She got a call from Captain Ekland's mother. Captain Ekland's father had a heart attack, and they had to go and see whether he will die or not."

Now he's really concerned. "Have they called back home and told you anything else?"

"No, she said it will take them several hours to get to the home, since they moved from the old house. I was to contact you and tell you not to come if you didn't want to. I did not know how to call the ship and talk to you, so you had to come anyway."

"Where did they have to go to the hospital?" Casey asks, continuing to try to find out what she knows and how it might affect him.

"Here. See, Casey. I wrote it down."

It takes Casey a moment to figure out that it says, "Johns Hopkins." Sereta then takes his hand and pulls him along with her to the kitchen table, where she begins to serve supper. The phone number of the Ekland residence is written down; Casey knows no one will be there. He has to chuckle, as Sereta still writes her *d*'s backward like big sixes.

"How soon do you think we'll be hearing from Mary?" he asks her.

"I hoped that we could already know how bad the heart attack was and perhaps talk of happier times."

For some reason, Sereta is not at all relaxed around Casey, but she makes her movements close to him as though she wants to touch him. She straightens the table and returns things to the cupboard. "Casey, please let us go to the living room, and I will show you the pictures," she says. She takes his hand and leads him. She draws a file from the bookcase and hands it to him. It contains the history of her coming to Washington.

Commander DeNova is a thorough documenter. Several pages in, there are pictures of Arlington and a picture of Chief Gordon's cemetery plot and the headstone. Along with it, in a plastic folder, are papers that have a hospital logo on them. Casey reads them and sees she's kept them as a memento of him. On the next pages are two pictures of the commander and the chief in the hospital room. He looks drawn and pale.

Sereta leans over his shoulder as he looks through the album, and she narrates as he turns the pages. When he finishes the album, she reaches behind herself and draws out a small package gift wrapped in Christmas-themed paper. "I got something for you, Casey." She hands it to him and waits. He opens the present and finds a wax-paper-covered box containing several sticks of sugar cane. Does that ever bring back memories! It makes him smile.

"Where in the world did you find these?"

"I shop in the Cuban market in DC, Casey. I know it will please you."

"I'm sorry I didn't bring you anything."

"You are my present, Casey. I want to see you for a long time, and now you must tell me of the things you have seen while across the ocean in Europe. Mary says the pope is in Italy. Did you get to see him?"

"No, Sereta, he lives in the Vatican in Rome, and we didn't get anywhere near there. I did, however, go to see Diego and his family in France."

At the mention of Diego's name, Sereta wrinkles her nose and frowns. "He is a bad man and not worth the death of anyone to save him," she replies.

It's getting close to eleven when the phone finally rings. Sereta jumps up like she's shocked. She takes the call and then waves for Casey to come to the phone. He takes the receiver.

"Casey, it's Mary. I'm sorry we couldn't be there, and I apologize for not being able to contact you. I hope I didn't make you wait at the bus terminal too long. I'm calling from a booth in the hospital cafeteria. Dennis is up in the cardiac care waiting room. We haven't heard anything from the doctors, although several of the nurses have been out to tell us that they just barely managed to save him. He's on life support, and they want us to wait around until he's stabilized before we make any decisions.

"I don't know how much sleep we'll be getting tonight, but you go on and take the front bedroom across from our master bedroom. I left a little Christmas gift there in the headboard for you."

"Do you have any idea when you'll be coming home?" Casey asks her.

"I don't know, Casey. I'll try to give you some indication of how things are coming along as soon as we find out something. If it gets into the morning hours, I plan to get a roll-away bed and sleep here. They have them in the critical care units for that purpose."

"How is Dennis taking it?" he asks her.

"He's a nervous wreck. All the firm partners are in contact, and two of them are planning to come up here."

"Is there anything I can do from here for you?"

"Casey, have the conversation with Sereta and let her know that you're not the man for her. I can't say what is in your mind, but I get the impression that you still have feelings for the little girl you lost back in Wyoming. You need to work that out as there has not been enough time."

"I'm about to broach the question, commander. I hope I can do it correctly. You didn't tell me that she's become so Americanized. She's gorgeous. She shouldn't have trouble finding a husband."

"I've got to go now, Casey. The phone number for the nurse's station on the cardiac wing is on the notepad in the kitchen. You can call it and ask for one of us. They won't allow the line to be tied up, but I will just call you back. I love you, guy. Take care."

Casey hands the receiver back to Sereta, who was listening to the end of the conversation.

"No! Casey, she says she loves you. How?"

"Relax, little one. It is like a brother loves his sister or a child loves his mother."

"Oh, that is good. Now let me show you the house and my room that I painted with Mr. Dennis's help." She stands and beckons him to follow. He's seen the house but pretends to look interested as Sereta shows him each room. He has some very good memories of the master bedroom.

Sereta is fascinated by flush toilets and has to flush one to show him. They go down the stairs to her domain. She explains how each of the colors she's used on the walls has a meaning to her.

"I wanted to make a picture of my mother and father, but I don't know how to do the painting, and I cannot describe to anyone how they looked."

"Why is the back of the closet black?"

"It is the bunker where we slept together, Casey. Some nights I open the doors, go to bed, and pretend I am there with you, sleeping with the mosquitoes biting at our ears." She stands beside him, holding his arm.

"Casey, you come with me now, and I will show you." She takes him by the hand and leads him to the bathroom. "Look, Casey, this little plastic wheel is birth control pills. It is in the middle with half gone." Her hand is shaking slightly, and her voice is edgy.

"Please, Casey, look on me like the bull and use your toro with me, please. Can you not smell that I need you like the cow that waits for the bull in the pasture? I long to have you make me a woman. I am tired of being a little girl waiting for some peasant to come from the field and roll with me in the grass." She takes his hand and physically drags him back to her bedroom, where she closes and locks the door. Her free hand starts working on her dress.

"Please, Casey, you watch now." She begins to disrobe, catching the dress zipper and expertly unfastening her bra in a single movement. She drops the top of her dress, and her breasts blossom out. The blush that's starting to form on her chest emphasizes the color of her skin. A good diet has done wonders for her.

"Please, Casey, you come now, please, for me." He steps farther into the room, and she knows she's won.

*What a gorgeous woman,* Casey thinks. She isn't the fearful little girl he shepherded across Cuba to get to the United States.

"Take off your uniform, Casey, and come to the bed with me."

Casey quickly disrobes, and Sereta's eyes follow his every move. "Please come now," she says. "I don't care if the priest says to wait."

"Sereta, are you sure?"

"I have asked for forgiveness from the priest. He thinks you have already made me a woman."

The lovemaking begins. "Oh, it is good as I had hoped," Sereta says softly. "Please, Casey, do it like the bull and make me cry out like the cow when she puts her tail to the side and he makes her sing the happy song after they are through."

This is a new experience for Casey. Right away, Sereta begins making little chirping noises. The end comes with a thrill, and then Casey tries to relax.

"Oh, Casey, do not let it end yet. I am so happy to have your half of the baby inside me now."

"It won't be a baby, Sereta. The birth control pills will take care of that."

"I know, Casey, but you did put it inside me and make me cry out in joy. Is this how it ends, or can I have more? No wonder the cow goes singing across the grass swinging her tail and has to get a drink. Now I don't have to ask the Holy Father for forgiveness, because I am no longer a virgin."

"Now it's my turn." He leads her into the bathroom and turns the shower on. He doesn't have the heart to do it all cold, so he waits until it is slightly warm and then draws her in beside him. It's almost like she's singing while she holds him. They shower together like they did at the bunker.

It's getting late at night, and Casey decides to go back up and at least mess up the bed so it'll look like he occupied it. "Sereta, Mary told me to sleep in the bedroom across from where she sleeps. I need to go and sleep in the bed, so she won't know we made love down here." He pulls his skivvies on and wanders up the stairs to the bedroom. Sereta follows him to make sure he isn't leaving.

"Casey, I will go to my room, and you come soon as you can. I want to sleep with my back to you like in the darkness of the bunker. We will open the closet doors."

She turns and goes as Casey sits down on the bed and looks for the present Mary left. He rummages around and finds a small box wrapped in Christmas-themed paper in the headboard of the bed. He pulls at the ribbon and opens it. The box is from a jewelry store. He carefully opens the top and finds, folded compactly, some notebook paper covered in a hand-penned script.

> Casey, I don't know how to start this, but you should know that you are my all-time hero. I had just come away from a terrible legal mess with my first husband and yet another failed romance with another lawyer. The men I dated at Guantanamo were a disappointment. I was as low mentally and desperate as I can ever remember having been. I could have been the one going over the hill.

The night I made Jean confess to me what had come about between the two of you, I wanted to go and just kill something. Then I decided that what she got, I could have also. I don't know what you thought of me or us, just another piece or a notch on your gun perhaps, but it changed my whole outlook. During that encounter and afterward, I knew I needed you again. I remember never having had an orgasm with my husband, and I had two during those two times we were together.

In the very short while I had to know you, my outlook concerning the male gender positively changed. I knew there must be a good man out there for me somewhere. When you visited the last time, you reassured me of your intention to be just a friend, even if you did deprive me of almost two nights of sleep. What I received from you, I cannot begin to describe. My body still feels those nights of passion.

Unwrap the little ball of tissue and please accept this as a token of our friendship. I know that our lives will never be together as I have made other arrangements for mine. I hope you can find someone for you. I have your address, and I might share a photo or two. Dennis is going to be a dad.

Love,
Mary

Casey wonders how or where she intended to give it to him. He unwraps the little ball of tissue and finds what must be the old engagement ring from her first husband. The rock is modest, with two very small diamonds on the side, and Casey wonders immediately how he can have it reset into something a man might want to wear. He knows the wedding band Sereta wears is the match to it.

He sits for a while, contemplating, and decides not to mess up the bed. He returns to the basement after he wraps the ring up and puts it into the pocket of his coat. Sereta is sitting on the side of the bed, and when he comes back into the room, she stands and turns to him.

"Look at my dress, Casey. I am too much woman to fit in it now." She's wearing the dress she had on when they rescued her. The fabric is stretched tightly across her breasts now. The button at the breast level is popped open, exposing her, and the skirt rides up because it's too tight across her hips.

"Casey, watch please." She nudges the buttons, and her breasts leap out to him. She lifts it over her head, turns, and lies down on the bed where they made love.

"It is as you first saw me Casey. I have no panties or brassiere. I have no socks for my feet, and I had to lose my shoes on the beach as you did."

"You are beautiful, Sereta."

"Please, Casey, you come and make my body sing the song again. I do not know the English to tell you how I feel when you do it, but it is like nothing I ever felt before. It is better than the sweet chocolate the priest in the church in Havana gave to us when we were children. I want to stand now and dance."

Sereta runs down the hall and begins singing the song again. The phone rings, and she comes running into the bedroom. She lets it ring a second and third time while she manages her racing breath.

She picks up and listens for a moment. "Yes, Miss Mary, I will go and wake Casey in the bedroom." She lays the phone down and beckons for Casey to follow. She prances up the stairs, making noise, and he very quietly ascends the stairs and follows her back to his room. The little lighted princess phone is in the same recess of the headboard where he found the ring. He picks up and tries to sound sleepy.

"Yes, Mary, hello."

"Listen, Casey, I need to tell someone . . . Dennis is in the hospital now too. They said the stress of his father's heart attack is a contributing cause. They said he has palpitations, or something like that. His heart is racing too fast for his body, and they had to get him some medicine to get it under control. He's been placed in cardiac care three beds from his father. Casey, I don't know what to do."

"Do you want me to come to where you are?"

"No, Casey, I just wanted to hear your voice and make sure that you and Sereta are okay. I need to be the strong one here and work through this."

She asks him about the meal, whether he's opened the gift, and whether Sereta is too much of a bother to him. She tells him of food available for the two of them that she had planned to fix for them as soon as he arrived and for the following day or two. She continues on to tell him of the medical assessments of both her future father-in-law and her future husband. Casey listens patiently. After a while, she runs out of talk and apologizes for having held his ear captive for so long.

"Mary, I'll remain here as long as I can. I have a few days I can kill before I have to go back to the ship."

"Okay, Casey, thank you. I'm going down to the cafeteria to get something to eat and look for a book to read to keep my mind off my problems. Love ya, bye."

Casey hangs up, and when he turns around, Sereta is standing in the doorway, beckoning to him. The next encounter lasts longer than the initial one. They fall asleep on the bed with her nestled back against him with his hand on her breast. The closet doors are open, and the night-light makes just enough light for them to see it.

\* \* \*

Casey awakens to Sereta's voice. "Casey, I will make breakfast with the hen's eggs and toast." She makes them breakfast, and while they're eating, the phone rings again.

Sereta answers. "Yes, Miss Mary, I will go and look for a pen." She lays the phone down and finds a little notepad in the drawer.

She writes items on the list as they are dictated to her and then hands the phone to Casey.

"Casey, I need you to do me a huge favor," says Commander DeNova. "Make sure Sereta packs seven days' worth of clean clothes along with what I told her of my clothes. Can you please get the Mercedes out of the garage and drive her to the law office in DC? She knows the building, and the address is inside the gray suitcase anyway. Park the car in the garage. I've already made arrangements for the attendant to be on the lookout for you.

"Take Sereta to the bus station in a taxi and put her on the bus to Baltimore. Call me and tell me when she's arriving, and I'll be there to pick her up. I need her up here. I know this isn't fair to you, but will you just do it and then go back to the ship? I know it'll cut your leave time short by a couple of days, but this is the best way to handle it.

"Sereta will be available to help me up here, and we can get Dennis back home. We'll be staying in the Eklands' house, and I'll be looking out for Mrs. Elkland. Sereta is so good with her, and I can leave her there to do the little things she needs."

"Mary, I'll do whatever you need," Casey replies. "I'll get things going on this end and call you when we get to the bus station."

Sereta shows him where the suitcase is stored in the basement. He watches Sereta take clothing from the closet and pack. He closes the case, and they take it to the master bedroom. He gets to rummage through Mary's closet while he picks the items she's requested.

The suitcase is full by the time he snaps it closed. He wonders how long it will be before the family arrives back here.

He convinces Sereta she needs to take some of the food, and they make sandwiches. They clean the kitchen and then go to the garage. Casey takes a moment to familiarize himself with the Mercedes. He's ridden in it once and paid attention to Jean's operation of it, so he feels comfortable driving it.

Casey knows Sereta is about to cry, but she holds it in. There is a long silence, and then Sereta speaks. "Casey, I want you please to listen. Mary tells me that I cannot marry you and still be Mrs.

Dale Gordon with the survivor money and the hospital from him. I want you for my husband, but it is not to be. You still look for the one they took from you. I will be a single woman but continue to love you. I will work for Mary and Mr. Dennis, and my life will be as an American single woman."

A cold wind blows through the basement parking lot as they take the suitcases out of the trunk and find the elevator to the main level. "I have to be a strong woman, Miss Jean tells me, and now I start," Sereta says.

They go to the street and hail a cab. It's a short ride to the bus station, and after finding the schedule, Casey finds a phone and calls the commander. The hospital desk will not allow Casey to talk to her in the cardiac unit and can't connect him to the room. He doesn't know what other numbers to call.

He buys a ticket to Baltimore and accompanies Sereta on the trip. The entire way up there, they snuggle together, and Casey wonders what is going through her mind. When they arrive, she becomes a strong woman again. Casey finds directions to the hospital and puts Sereta in a cab, and that ends that. "Tell Mary hello for me, Sereta," he says, "and let me know how things work out."

"I love you, Casey White," she replies, and she kisses him good-bye. He watches the cab disappear down the street as emptiness creeps in like a fog around him. He goes to the ticket agent and gets a bus back to DC.

*     *     *

Casey books a room at a cheap hotel about two blocks off the mall. In the morning, he takes a tour bus to Arlington Cemetery. He finds the visitor center attendants helpful, and after walking quite a way in the snow and cold, he manages to find Chief Gordon's grave site. It's a plain white marker like all the others, and Casey spends a few solemn but chilly moments there. An hour later, he finds a bus headed for Norfolk. He still has the taste of Sereta's kiss on his lips.

\*   \*   \*

Bright and early on the second Tuesday morning in February, the *Laffey* teems with yardbirds and a heavy hiss sounds as water is admitted to the dry dock. All the engineering personnel are in the propulsion spaces to watch for leaks. There are none, and after a day of lighting off and getting things warmed up, they're pulled out of the dry dock by a little yard tug and turned loose in the Elizabeth River.

They make a short run of only five days to make sure everything is as it should be. They pass the engineering phase of the refloat and become the first of the US Navy's old WWII destroyers to have undergone the FRAM II (Fleet Rehabilitation and Modernization) conversion. They return to port that Friday, and Casey's mail finally catches up with him.

# Chapter 37

T HE next Monday marks a new set of operational requirements, and the *Laffey* ends up in the North Atlantic in some severe weather conditions. Casey feels quite frightened as he watches the inclinometer on the bulkhead in the engineering office swing over to thirty-nine degrees, knowing that beyond forty-five is unrecoverable.

The old refitted destroyer shakes off the storm like a trouper, and after everyone aboard thinks they might die, it feels as though some huge hand of God just reaches down and grabs the ship and makes it stable.

They enter the ice-free harbor at Argentia, Newfoundland. Casey goes topside and looks aft. There's a seawall built out of huge stones that protects the inner harbor. They stay there a week, replenishing and replacing the life rafts washed overboard and lost to the storm. *Hurricanes are tough, but you really have to experience a raw northeaster if you want to sea-story about bad storms*, Casey thinks.

Operations resume like before once Casey is back in Norfolk. He makes more friends at the old stone church and more or less quits running with the gang aboard ship. Most of them are married anyway and usually just want to go home and be with family.

It's in this time frame that Casey sews on his second-class crow. He had taken the exam earlier but had no idea how well he'd done for some time. The results are a pleasant surprise. The award ceremony is scheduled and carried out between two operations while the ship is in port replenishing.

One afternoon when Casey is coming out of a downtown theater, a shore patrolman jumps him and tells him, in no uncertain terms, to return immediately to his command. The city is running special buses. No fare needed, he boards one.

Rumors are rampant, and Casey quickly makes his way back to the ship. He cannot get any concrete information from the quarterdeck, but as he looks around, he sees three destroyers already getting underway. The one sitting outboard of them has singled up the lines and is waiting for the XO.

Casey dresses in dungarees and goes to the after-engine room. Civilian workers on the pier are working to disconnect shore power as the pressure in the boilers is almost built up to where they can get underway on their own steam.

All of the after-engine personnel available are working to get up vacuum on the mains, so they can respond to engine-order commands.

The steam-powered turbo generators come on-line, and Casey hears the shore power disconnect with a loud pop. They contact the bridge after they achieve twenty-five inches of mercury and can answer all engine-order bells.

They're ready to steam, but no sailing order comes. The chief divides the men and lets half of them go topside. Individually, they come back down and report that some destroyer or another is getting underway. Waiting is probably one of the hardest things an adrenalin-charged sailor can do. Casey stands watch until about midnight, when he's relieved.

The skipper comes on the speaker and announces that they will not be getting underway but are to stand watches just like they are underway. *Damn!* thinks Casey. He's ready to go. The only thing they need to do is pull back the locking lever of the main engine jacking gear and go. There is more waiting, and no more explanations come forth.

Two yard tugs pull them out from the pier, turn them around, and place them at the head of the pier. There's more time spent waiting and no explanations. Finally, around o six hundred hours, the skipper gets on the speaker and tells the crew that there are Russian missiles in Cuba aimed at the United States and there is a fleet blockade of Cuba going on.

The reason *Laffey* hasn't sailed is that it is the designated so-called "court of last resort." If the first Russian missile is launched, all the captains and admirals and senior officers at CINCLANTFLT will come running down to the pier and board *Laffey*, and they will steam like hell down the Chesapeake Bay to the Atlantic Ocean before the first nuclear bomb detonation.

Casey smiles thinking about a 375-foot destroyer with over sixty senior and flag officers aboard. Who would be in command? He wonders if the navy employees aboard the base were let go. It wouldn't matter anyway; if one nuclear explosion goes off, no one on earth will survive. The president told the Russian premier in a telephone conversation that the United States would initiate a full retaliatory response if a single missile was launched toward the United States or the fleet. Thinking about it, Casey realizes that's over twenty thousand bombs of all sizes and that's just on the American side.

They sit at the pier for two weeks with a fuel hose attached, pretending to be going somewhere. Finally, on the following Monday, they're allowed to stand down but still cannot go any farther than the little gedunk at the end of the pier to have something to eat just to change the monotony.

Casey begins to think of the holidays and wonders what he should do about leave. The last two Christmases were total busts, and he doesn't want to go back home and have another disappointment. He decides he'll just spend his time off here in Norfolk. He's made acquaintances with enough people at the old stone church that he'll have somewhere to go at Christmastime.

Christmas comes and goes. When Casey looks through his mail, he finds a card from Belinda and Johnny and another from Arlene, who has married her former husband in a ceremony in a little chapel in Las Vegas. The two are living out on a ranch in the desert, miles from civilization, and south of Salt Lake City.

Toward the bottom of the stack is a heavy envelope from Mrs. Dennis Ekland with no street or city in the return address. He opens it and looks at the picture within. It is of the wedding. The commander and her new husband are standing in front of the rest of the wedding party with the groomsmen on one side and the bridesmaids on the other. She is obviously enjoying every minute of it. Behind her and Dennis is the rest of the wedding party, with Sereta in back of them. The picture sets off a wave of melancholy in Casey. He wishes he could have been there. There is a letter included.

Dear Casey, This is the last time I will be in touch with you. I have my marriage to think about now, and I know you don't want Sereta, so I think it best if we just break the connection. I want you to know that there is no way I will ever forget the good times we had together.

Sereta is continuing her night school studies and babysitting while we are at work. Dennis wants me to get out of the navy and go to work for the firm. This I plan to do, but I will continue in the naval reserve until I can retire.

We're moving from my little house to another in Maryland. It's larger, with more bedrooms, and it has a full basement that Sereta will co-opt and make her own after we get several more walls up and painted. I've lost contact with all but you and Brown, and I haven't heard from him in six months. I know the marines deploy, and it is hard to maintain contact with anyone not stateside.

Jean is married now, transferred to California. I think she is in line for a promotion. I can't think of her married name right off the top of my head.

Casey, go and find someone right for you and get on with your life. You are a great person and should not have any problem finding someone. The past is the past. I love you and will until I die.

All my love,
Mrs. Mary Ekland

Casey rereads the letter a half-dozen times and realizes it's really over. Now he'll concentrate on his life and his life only. He looks through the stack, finds several letters from home, and reads them. The last one is from his brother, who has gone into the navy to dodge a draft notice.

*       *       *

Monday the ship is hauled into the yards for some changes and then back to the main side for more electronic equipment to be installed. The quarterdeck watch comes looking for him. There is a high-priority message in the engineering office for him.

# Chapter 38

$C$ ASEY puts his things away and goes to find the engineering officer. He ends up knocking at the door of the officer's quarters. Lieutenant Mack is sitting at the table reading, and when the steward tells him, Casey is waiting, he tells Casey there is a letter. It is some kind of naval message that has not come through the post office. Lieutenant Mack opens it and reads it. Casey is being ordered to appear at the Pentagon in some kind of hearing room on Monday morning.

He's given TAD orders and a stipend to pay the expenses incurred for travel and lodging. After the Paris thing, Casey has grown weary of this method of informing—or not informing—him of what's happening. The duty disbursing office personnel are still there and Lieutenant Mack has them cut orders for him. Casey rises early, before reveille, and departs for downtown. It's around five in the morning when he arrives at the Greyhound station and catches the first bus out.

The trip to Washington is getting to be boring for Casey, but he tolerates it once again. He steps off the bus at the Pentagon and takes a long, cold walk across several parking lots. He then follows the crowd into what he takes as the main entrance. He provides his identification to the marine guard behind the desk and digs his TAD orders out of the AWOL bag he's carrying. It's thoroughly searched. He asks for directions to the office where he is to report.

"That's here," the marine tells him, turning to point to a map of the building. "Don't use this main passageway to get there; it's too crowded this time of day. Go inside to the next ring and find the elevators here, and go up to the third floor here, and the office should be somewhere around this area."

Casey walks, looks, and avoids anyone who appears as though he is looking for an enlisted man to pound on. He's never seen so much brass in all his life. After he finds the elevator and steps in, all he sees are senior naval officers. He rides the elevator up to the fourth floor. He notes his mistake and tries to get back aboard. He waits until the elevator comes up with another load and gets back on, and it descends to the first floor. *This is beginning to become a challenge.* He waits as the elevator returns from the basement.

He's going to get to the third floor some way. He positions himself right in front of the door as it opens. There in front of him is Commander DeNova—or Ekland now. She stands with a very startled deer-in-the-headlights look and tries to keep her composure.

She starts to say Casey but manages to get White out. She's pulling a little four-wheeled cart that takes up some of the space and apparently annoys the brass standing at the sides of the elevator.

Casey notes her greeting and replies. "Good morning, Commander." The door closes, and the car rises to the third floor. Casey steps off, and she attempts to follow, but one of the little wheels is not cooperating. Casey takes hold of the handle and helps the commander pull it off the elevator. The door closes, and she looks at him.

"Casey, what in the world are you doing here?"

"I don't know. I have orders to report to some hearing room up here, for what I don't know." He shows her the paperwork.

"That's Admiral King's office. That's where I'm headed," she replies with a questioning look.

Casey takes the tongue of the little cart and pulls it along for her. They wind their way through several hallways and then into a reception area.

"Hi, Francine," says Commander Ekland.

"Good morning, Commander, and good morning to you, White. It's good to see you here so soon. The admiral has another appointment this afternoon and wants to get your business completed first."

Francine stands and goes through a door and reappears momentarily. "The admiral will see both of you now."

Commander Ekland looks surprised to hear that, and Casey follows her into the office. The man standing behind the desk in the office is without his coat; it's on the back of his chair. Casey notices that his resemblance to Captain King is astounding. Now things are starting to make sense.

He extends his hand. "Welcome, welcome, White. It's been a long time since I saw you shoot at 'Diego, and I've been anxious to make your acquaintance." Casey steps warily forward and shakes his hand and then finds a seat. His mind is working overtime wondering what's happening.

"Commander, do you have my files for me?" the admiral asks.

"Yes, Admiral King, they're all here. I had to go to the basement to find them. When they're returned, someone will have to sign—and please remember to scratch my name off the sheet, so I don't have to track them down and restore them." She turns to go.

"Commander, is there somewhere I can speak to you after the admiral is finished?" Casey asks her.

Admiral King looks at Casey and then back to Commander Ekland. "Do you two know each other?" he asks.

Casey looks at her and sees she's uncomfortable with the question. "Commander DeNova—uh, Ekland—was the legal counsel for the Cuban girl who married Chief Gordon. I witnessed on her behalf before I was stationed aboard ship."

"Yes, White, I know all about you. Now I've got another piece of my puzzle. Sit down, Commander. I'll have Francine call your boss and tell him that I've co-opted your services for an hour or two." He keys the button on the intercom and tells Francine to call

Commander Ekland's boss. He then opens a little file cabinet on wheels with his security key.

"White, the reason I had you come up here is that I'm about to retire. I want to put a final stamp on this case and put it to rest somewhere where nobody will have reason to open it again. I have letters from all your commands wondering if you aren't getting some kind of special preference, which I am going to destroy. And yes, you are.

"Captain King was my son, and I appreciate everything you did for him and the group. The president was a personal friend of my father, and he's the one who ordered the rescue of Diego Du Bois, his half brother. I don't know how the political ramifications of his being captured by Castro and his henchmen would have worked out, but I'm sure it would not have been in favor of the United States. That's why it was important that we get him back.

"I'm sorry the president came to the horrific end that he did, and his family will have to learn to live with it. What I've been doing for you and the rest of the marines is my attempt to repay you for what you did. I know the president can't, and I know his family won't. I watched you come off the USS *Mero* hoping the report of my son's death was mistaken. I couldn't approach you because I had been sworn to secrecy by the president himself.

"Do either of you have any idea what happened to the little Cuban girl who married Chief Gordon? I know she isn't in Miami, or we would have found her before now."

"Yes, Admiral," says the Commander. "She is currently living with me and is at this very moment babysitting my son. She's an American citizen now, by the way."

A look of surprise crosses the admiral's face, and he scrutinizes her. "We've been looking for her for a couple of years now, and all this time she's been living right under our noses."

"What is it that you need of her, admiral?"

"Nothing, really. I just wanted to talk to her and find out why she chose to marry the chief when she did. I hope you can convince her never to disclose any of the circumstances of her getting to come here."

"I think I can honestly say that she was in love with the man and he with her, and they chose to make the best of a bad situation. It's a tragedy Chief Gordon was wounded and subsequently succumbed to his injuries. She was heartbroken and a lost soul for quite a while. If it hadn't been for the group, some other close friends, and me, she might have ended up in a bad situation."

Casey sits there listening to her explanation and knows she is smoothing the way for the case to be put to rest.

"How much of the history of the raid do you know, Commander, and how did you come about your knowledge? It was, after all, a covert operation."

"I was legal counsel to the men on the raid. We had to take transcription at the debrief. I have knowledge of bits and pieces Sereta told me one night while she was reliving the loss of her parents and her husband. I don't know the legality of what happened, and I just decided to put it all out of my mind. I haven't spoken to anybody about it, nor will I."

"White, do you intend to stay in the navy, or will you be getting out at the end of your enlistment?"

"I plan to get out, sir. I don't think it is the environment I want to live in. I'm from Wyoming and love the snow and cold. The navy places me in an engine room, where in the normal summer, the working temperature goes to one hundred thirty-five degrees. I can't stand the heat, so to speak, so I'm getting out of the kitchen."

"I'm sorry to hear that, White. One thing I can do for you, since you are not staying, is help you get a decent job. I have some friends in the Norfolk area, and I'll hook you up with them. I've done it for Sergeant Brown. He'll be getting discharged about the same time you are."

"What are Bennett and Mendoza doing, sir?"

"They will re-up—or already have. I don't know for sure." The conversation stops for a minute as the admiral looks at the contents of the little file. "Is there anything you'd be interested in seeing in here before it goes away forever?"

"Captain King's map, is it in there?" Casey asks. Admiral King reaches into the cabinet and fishes out the weathered-looking book. He hands it to Casey who thumbs through it to the page showing El Jiqui and pulls the page out of it. Casey folds the page in fourths and places it in his wallet as Admiral King and Commander Ekland watch.

"Is there anything else, Commander, White?"

Casey thinks about it and then decides to let sleeping dogs lie. "No, sir. I remember the aerial photos the man displayed during the debrief quite vividly. I remember most of the trip across the island. I wish there was some way to bring Captain King back, but you and I know that isn't possible. I'd like to kick little Du Bois's arrogant ass one time, but that too won't happen. I think it's a good move just to let it rest. How about the submarine, Admiral—did it get mothballed?"

"Yes, the freshwater conventional and most of the other conventional, for that matter, are out of service now. Wait a minute, White. Here's something that might interest you." He leans down, extracts a manila folder, and breaks the seal on it. "Commander, you have your top-secret classification, don't you?"

"Yes, Admiral, I was the lead on the ReciproCal rocket engine scandal. Two of us in the office worked that one."

"Good. White, I know you are not currently top-secret qualified, but because you are part of this, it shouldn't take you long to figure things out." He pulls the sheaf of papers from the folder and spreads them across his desk. He reads the papers for a moment and then gives Commander Ekland several sheets and hands a small batch to Casey. Casey's is a report on a program started by the intelligence officers who interviewed them at Guantanamo.

Casey reads that the Soviets think the gunfire from the sea the night Casey was in the water came from some kind of submarine-launched, radar-guided weapon controlled by the submarine. They couldn't figure out any other way to account for every one of the men being systematically picked off from the water. They were unwilling to believe that one of their MiGs could be shot down by anything but a radar-controlled gun.

Casey openly laughs, and Commander Ekland looks at him wondering what can be that funny. "I've been called a lot of things in my life," says Casey, "but never a submarine-launched radar-controlled gun."

"White, it gets better. Read on past the third page down at the bottom." Casey thumbs through the papers and reads the paragraphs at the bottom. The agency followed up on the smoke-and-mirrors operation and found a Soviet agent in the research department of a university developing the advanced radar to be fitted on future ships."

"This stuff really gets deep once you're involved, doesn't it, sir?" Casey says.

"You have no idea, son, and I'm happy to be leaving it to the younger generation."

Casey hands the papers back to the admiral and looks at Commander Ekland. She appears to be curious about something. "Casey, you actually threw enemy body parts to the crocodiles? Why would you do that?" she asks.

"Sereta and I were still on the other side of the swamp from the rest of the group as the crocodiles were returning. I guess I was operating at such a high adrenalin level that I would have done about anything to get the two of us across that water.

"As it turned out, we just barely made it before a couple of the big ones got wise to what I had done. I make no apologies for what I did. In my mind, it was warfare. We both managed to get back to civilization because of what I did."

"I'm not condemning you, Casey. I'm just amazed that you would have thought to do anything like it under the circumstances." She hands the papers back to Admiral King. He puts them into the envelope, initials the little tab on it, and reseals it.

"Oh, one other thing, Casey. Since I saw you shoot that day at the range, can I assume that it was, in fact, you who shot down the MiG fighter?" Admiral King asks him.

"Yes, it wasn't a difficult shot. He was looking for me or some kind of radar and gun in the water, and he had extended to full flaps, slowing him down to around one hundred eighty knots so that he could utilize his landing light to search the water.

"He was broadside to me, and I just unloaded a magazine of rounds on him. I never expected him to roll over to where the tank and the communications vehicle were on the beach, but the resulting explosion cleared out most of the guys who could shoot at us, and it really facilitated our escape to the sub."

"Boom," Admiral King says with a smile on his face. "I guess that's probably it, unless the commander has any more questions." He looks at her, and she shakes her head. "Good call, White. Commander, is there anything I can do for either of you before I retire?"

"Put in a good word about me to my boss. I've married the man I wanted, and my life and career are on track."

"You mean Dennis. Yes, he's a good man. He has good contacts throughout the area and will go a long way." With that, the admiral stands, extends his hand, and shakes with Casey. He doesn't release his grip but instead pulls him close and wraps his arm around him in a big bear hug. "Thank you for everything you did, son." He releases his grip.

"Francine, we are finished in here. Can you get someone to return the security case to the basement so that Commander Ekland doesn't have to?" Casey and Mary leave the office and go down the hall together.

"My God, Casey, it's so good to see you. Casey, the reason I had to break it off with you is that I'm still infatuated with you, or at least the image I have of you, and this past meeting didn't do anything to diminish my feelings.

"I'm a married woman with a child now, and I still have images of us together those times in the bunker and that week you came to visit. You're the reason I chose to move when I did and not let you have my forwarding address. We needed a larger house, and you just sped up the process."

"Commander, how is Sereta getting along now, I mean after you got back from Baltimore? She was pretty upset when I dropped her off to go to the hospital."

"Casey, I guess there are some things I should tell you. When we got back home from Baltimore, Sereta and I had a long conversation about us and things in general. She admitted to me that she seduced you while the two of you were together at the house. She said the reason she kept her dress hung up down there was as a constant reminder to her of that goal.

"Now that she has achieved that, I believe she has moved on. She has her high school diploma and is enrolled in night studies at George Washington University. She told me she wants to learn law. She babysits my son Dennis in the evenings if we have to go somewhere. She is very good with babies."

"Do you hear often from Jean?"

"Oh, that's another thing, Casey, Sereta somehow knew that Jean and I had sex with you at the bunker. She seems to have a great sixth sense about that, or a good sense of smell, I don't know which. I think that might have been one of the reasons she wanted to seduce you, so she would be on an equal footing with us."

"Mary, I think I've been the odd card in this deal. I never wanted to hurt anyone; all I want to do is get on with my life. I still carry a special place in my heart for you, and of course for Sereta. My goal now is to finish up my enlistment and go somewhere and start my life over again and see if I can make something of it."

"I've got to get back to the office, Casey."

"Okay, Mary, it's nice to know I'm appreciated." Casey stands, and the commander pulls him behind a door and hugs and kisses him. He kisses her back, and they hold on and look into each other's eyes for a long moment. "There, that should give you a couple more fantasies to operate on," he says.

She smiles at him. "Good-bye, Casey, let's meet again in twenty years and have a good laugh about all this." She walks from behind the door and disappears in the flow of people in the passageway. He turns to leave, but a heavy hand takes his wrist and holds it.

345

He attempts to pull away, but it holds on. A rather ruggedly built naval officer stands and looks him in the eye. "Do you know the penalty for fraternization with an officer, sailor?" he says with a snarl.

"Do you know the penalty for not kissing, hugging, and telling your mom good-bye before you're deployed to Southeast Asia?" he answers.

The officer looks at him and then toward the doorway Mary went through. He releases Casey and sits down, looking a little embarrassed.

It takes Casey a little longer to find his way out than it did to find his way in. The bus service to the Greyhound station is miserable. He walks across the mall to the same hotel he used the last time he was there. The following morning, he returns to Arlington Cemetery and takes pictures of Chief Gordon's grave site. He plans to make copies and send them to the rest of the group. He wonders how or where Captain King will be remembered.

After another five miserable hours getting back to Norfolk, Casey goes to the YMCA and gets a room, knowing that the ship is at sea, and he'll have a two-week hiatus until it returns. He buys a paper and starts looking for addresses of car dealers and real estate agents. During the two weeks, he opens a new bank account, buys a new van, and finds a house out in the suburbs. He has no intentions of returning to western Wyoming and the Alfeta quagmire.

\*　　\*　　\*

After quarters the next Monday morning, he's called to the executive officer's office. The XO has his personnel file open upon the desk. He asks Casey point-blank if he intends to reenlist. The man's bluntness surprises him, but he relaxes and tells him that it's his intention to become a civilian come the first part of January.

"May I ask why you have made your decision to leave the service?" the XO asks.

"Yes, sir, I'm from Wyoming, and before coming into the navy, the hottest temperature I ever encountered was on one Fourth of July when it got up to one hundred degrees. The humidity was still around 40 percent. The ship I was on before coming to *Laffey* had an engine room that stayed around one hundred thirty-five degrees and almost 90 percent humidity while we were in the Caribbean. I have never grown used to the temperature and humidity."

"I appreciate your candor, White. The ship is getting ready to go to the Med, and I need to know how many men we will have aboard when we go."

Lying in Casey's personnel file is a letter addressed to him. On it is inscribed "for your eyes only." The XO hands the letter to Casey and stands. Casey leaves the office, returns to the engine room, and finds a quiet corner where he can read the letter.

The letter is on Admiral King's personal stationery, and it introduces him to the woman who chairs the head of civilian personnel at the naval base.

# 39

O N the tenth of the month, as a newly minted civilian, Casey
finds himself at the personnel office. The following Monday,
he finds himself at the fire station at Dam Neck, a little naval
facility in Virginia Beach. His new life begins.

Two weeks later, he encounters Brown coming out of the
public works offices. He's started work on the base the same day
as Casey.

\* \* \*

Casey has always liked to take vacations in the spring or fall when
the weather is cooler. It's mid-September of 1967 now, and he's
looking forward to his time off. He muses about all the changes
he's incorporated into his once-stripped van while he drives
home. He's modified it with a small sink, stove, and refrigerator.
It has a couch that folds out and becomes a double bed. The van
is insulated and has a small heater. There's enough room beneath
the bed for his dog Bofus to lie down on the carpeted floor and
sleep. He's found a campsite he likes in the Blue Ridge Mountains
in North Carolina, almost in Tennessee.

Casey acquired Bofus one afternoon after reading about a
dogfighting ring being broken up and animal rescue needing the
dogs to be adopted. Bofus was the result of one of the participants
experimenting and trying to create a bigger and more ferocious
combatant. His gene pool consisted of German shepherd, black

Labrador, Saint Bernard, and chow. This experimentation yields a large, powerful, but friendly dog. It was the intent of the breeder to break these animals mentally before they fought. Bofus's training had only just begun, and Casey's handling of him made a gentle, loveable pet of him. However, Bofus did not react well if anyone raised a hand as if to strike him.

\* \* \*

Casey arrives home in the old 1953 Dodge pickup he uses to go surf fishing at Cape Hatteras. It's the trusty vehicle he uses just to drive the twenty miles to work. He picks up the fishing rod he wrapped the previous evening during a slack time before going to bed, and then he punches the remote for the garage door and waits for it to finish rising. With a click of the tumbler, he unlocks the van and tosses his fishing rods into it.

Now all he has to do is to get breakfast, clean up, and finish packing. The morning paper is on the front porch, which surprises him; it's usually on the lawn or the porch roof. It's huge, full of sales advertisements. He picks it up, takes it inside, and tosses it toward the overstuffed chair. It bounces, opens and falls on the floor. The advertisements flood out of it into the open doorway.

He retrieves the front section and reads the headlines just before a tail-wagging wet-tongued dog attacks him in greeting. He gets down on the floor and rubs the dog's upturned tummy. He then picks up the paper and reads the front page. It's a follow-up on the USS *Forrestal* fire.

Below the fold, the paper tells him that the government is convicting half a dozen of the coconspirators in the Alfeta conspiracy and bigamy trial in Utah. Several more are due to be tried. When he turns to the next section, the picture fairly leaps off the page at him. It's Naomi Samuelson, one of the people who witnessed for the state's evidence and helped convict many of the current crop of criminals. He reads about the events that unfolded during the various trials.

Naomi divorced her husband and turned over to the FBI the contents of the family safe in the basement—documents she'd been copying for years. No, she couldn't testify against her husband—or ex-husband, as was the case—but she could testify against the rest of them.

The divorce settlement gave her the house, car, bank account, and several other properties. She retained custody of her son, and another adopted son. Her ex-husband is one of those still being investigated on a charge of procurement for murder, and there's a $1 million bond holding him in jail. The evidence against him is overwhelming.

One of the defendants, an already-convicted murderer, testified he was involved in everything from beatings to arson to forced slavery and prostitution. What bothers him now is that Utah still uses the firing squad to execute murderers.

Casey finishes the page, rolls the newspaper up, and tosses it into the van, planning to pick up the advertisements and throw them in the trash when he locks up. When he gets to his destination for the night, he'll finish reading the articles. It usually takes him two days to get to the little hideaway campground in the mountains.

He pulls the van out onto the driveway. Now all he has to do is to finish breakfast, load a few incidentals, and go. He goes out the back door to see if there are any more vegetables he can take along from the garden. He's already made an agreement with LJ, his neighbor lady, to watch his place while he's gone.

Casey hears someone at his front door when he steps back into the kitchen. He puts the vegetables down and walks toward the front with Bofus leading the way. He looks out the still-open front door and sees a car parked along the curb.

Now his interest is really kindled. It looks just like the one he had when he was a kid. It's even the same color. It has the expensive nylon wide white sidewall tires on it. He couldn't afford to put those tires on his when he had it. He can see even the upholstery is the same. He decides to check it out before he leaves for the mountains if it's still there when he's ready to go. He wonders where the driver is and goes out the laundry room door and looks around. Seeing no one, he returns to the kitchen and prepares breakfast.

"Bofus, you stay here and look out for the front." He pats him on the head. The big dog turns and goes to his special corner behind the living room chair. Casey hears the low bark and the growl that Bofus always uses when a stranger approaches the house.

"Hello, anyone home?" he hears someone call out.

Casey walks across the living room and sees the woman is holding the storm door closed with her foot to keep Bofus from coming out. He looks up and can't believe his eyes.

"Naomi?!"

"Casey!"

"Oh my God!" they both blurt out at the same time.

Now it's all they can do just to get the door open fast enough. They pause only a second to look at each other, and then they almost become one as they embrace, kiss, and melt together. A trail of clothing from the door down the hall to the bedroom soon lies hurriedly discarded. There's no bedroom light, only the squeak of the bed as both bodies fall together on it.

Their initial passion sated, they're still locked together, but now aren't engaging so vigorously. They're covered with sweat and haven't covered themselves with the sheet.

"Naomi, I can't believe it. How in the world did you manage to find me?"

"Casey, I've been working with a private detective for over three years, digging up evidence for my ex-husband's trial. Finding you was easy for him when he got to investigate some money that came to the East Coast. He sort of threw in your file as a thank-you for all the business I was giving him."

"Naomi, what came of our night behind the Hansens' barn? Do we have a child?"

"Yes, Casey, that is one of the things I've been so anxious to tell you. Our son, Matthew James Samuelson, was born almost a week premature. I plan to get his name changed as soon as I figure out what mine will be. Another thing I need to tell you is that both of my parents are dead now. Mom died in childbirth giving life to what I think is probably your son. She wanted him named Casey but wouldn't tell me what happened."

"Naomi, that is one of the things I need to explain to you."

"No need to do that, Casey. I found out about the contract she had signed with the Alfeta church. It guarantees her they will have to provide her a home until her youngest child is eighteen. The doctors told her not to have any more children after Donnie was born. I am the only relative the baby has, and I took him home from the hospital and I am raising him as my child."

"Eeeeek, Casey, what the . . . ?" Naomi almost screams and then realizes it's the dog smelling her. She turns over, and he puts his front paws up on the bed.

"Casey, call off your beast and tell him I'm a friend."

"He knows it, Naomi. If you made an overt move to harm him on the front porch, we'd be calling the ambulance now, and I'd be calling the insurance agency."

"Who or what is he?"

"He's a rescue dog and good watchdog, aren't you, Bofus?" He woofs and steps down from the bed, wags his tail, and returns to the doorway. "Go guard the front door, Bofus." He turns and looks at Casey to make sure he wants him to do what he's said. Casey points. "Front!" The dog disappears down the hall.

"Naomi, wait a minute, continue with the children, where are they now?"

"Casey, my husband was illegally married to two other women, and he fathered children with both. When the authorities started looking into his marriages, he spirited them away. He was going to take my children, but I beat him to it. I took them to eastern Wyoming, and they are with Belinda and Johnny."

*This plot is really thickening now*, he thinks, remembering his night with Belinda in the store and her resulting pregnancy.

"Come on, Casey, as many times as we can, we have a lot of time to make up." Naomi feels like she can just eat him alive she's so happy. They continue for most of the morning, only pausing to eat and drink and share a shower. Naomi continues to tell Casey of her life.

He hears Bofus coming back down the hall and looks at his watch. It is almost noon. He can't believe the time has gone by so quickly. Looking out the window, he sees there is an approaching thunderstorm.

"Naomi. Let's get dressed and get some lunch, and I'll feed Bofus and then we can sit and talk. It's so ironic. I was all ready to leave for the mountains just before you arrived."

"Casey, I can find all my clothes except my panties. Where can they have gotten to?"

"Just go ahead and get the rest of your things on, and we will look for them as soon as we get back to the front room," Casey tells her.

"Oh gosh," says Naomi. "I should go and close up the car. It looks like it's about to rain." She dashes out the front door, goes to the Ford, rolls up her window, retrieves her purse, and locks the car. She comes back inside to the kitchen clutching her little purse, where Casey is still looking for her panties. He triggers the remote and closes the overhead garage door.

Casey hears Bofus give a little bark and a deep growl; he sees strangers carrying sticks. There's a crack of lightning and a roll of thunder as big drops of rain began hitting the walk.

Bofus starts a heavier growling. That isn't good. Casey hurriedly goes to the hallway off the kitchen and looks out the window. He just manages to catch a glimpse of a man carrying what looks like some kind of automatic weapon.

Through the front door glass, he can see another approaching. They're dressed in black, which can only mean that they intend to harm anyone who gets in their way.

"Naomi, come on!" Casey takes Naomi's hand and starts toward the back. There's a loud crack, and the lock on the back door disintegrates into a mass of small pieces of shrapnel.

Casey drags Naomi back to the kitchen where he reaches up and gets the phony box of cornflakes. He quickly returns to the stairs and pulls Naomi along up the steps past Bofus, who's now watching the intruder in the front. His hackles are raised, and he is giving a deep, throaty attack growl. He tenses but remains on the landing.

"Casey, they've come to kill me," says Naomi.

"Who are they?"

"I don't know. Probably, some of my ex-husband's goons. He's involved in a lot of killings and the torching of homes. That's one of the reasons he is in jail right now."

Casey pulls her along into the room over the garage and closes and locks the door. His heavier guns are downstairs in the bedroom and the bathroom. The little .22 automatic he keeps in the phony box of cornflakes is all he has time to get. He slides the file cabinet against the door but knows that it will only slow down the assailant.

"Naomi, come here and let me put you up on the top shelf of the bookcase. It's wide enough to partially conceal you." Casey listens and can hear one of them directly below them in the hall from the laundry room. The second one is coming in the front. He can hear the squeaky board in the doorway coming from the front room.

There is a bark and a growl and the sound of a body hitting the floor and then a shot and a man's scream and a dog's yelp. Casey knows they have killed Bofus. He makes sure Naomi is well seated on the top shelf of the bookcase, and he looks around for something to protect him.

He goes to the back of the room where he is finishing it off and gets behind the stack of Sheetrock. It should be thick enough to stop any bullets. All at once, the floor is torn up with a trail of bullets fired from the lower hall. Had he not moved, Casey would have been hit. He listens, and someone is coming up the steps to the hall.

Casey looks up and in the almost-dark room, he can see Naomi squirming around and looking in her purse.

Casey knows from experience that rounds are usually fired horizontally at about chest height. He squats behind the pile of Sheetrock that remains from the wall job. All at once, the doorknob is blasted across the room, and he looks up to make sure Naomi is okay. The eight thickness of Sheetrock stops the bullets before they can hit him. Naomi is lying with eyes filled with terror. Casey wonders how he can resolve this.

"Come out, whore child of the devil," says the assailant. "I have come to deliver you to your eternal punishment. I will allow you only a minute to make peace with your pagan God, and then you must step out, and I will send you back to the devil."

Casey can't believe what he's hearing. His memory flashes back to him. He looks around to where the boxes were shoved up into a pile when he put up the Sheetrock. He looks for the boxes his dad sent from home. He quickly discards several of them.

"Pray that the devil doesn't consume your flesh," the man says.

Casey senses that another round is about to come through the door. He flattens himself out on the floor. The next dozen rounds make more little dots of light appear through the door. The assailant audibly releases the magazine and installs a new one.

Casey sees the box he's been looking for right in front of him. He pushes the stack over, flips the top off, reaches inside, and finds the gun he shot Mr. Herman with. Now, if he can only find the pocket with the cartridges in it. He pulls his coat out and fishes around in a pocket. He flips it over and feels inside the other one. He quickly loads the two .22-caliber cartridges and positions the chamber so that they'll fire on the first and second pulls of the trigger.

Casey looks up and sees light coming through the holes shot by the aggressor and knows the ones in the middle that aren't showing light are where he is standing. Casey raises himself up on his elbow, reaches up as high as he can, and aims the gun toward the center of the door. He rapidly fires both rounds.

The gunman gives out a surprised "Gah!" and Casey hears first the gun then the man fall to the floor. Then there's silence.

Casey is reluctant to stand up yet, so he just remains where he is. He looks up and can barely see Naomi on the top shelf. All at once, the door is riddled with another round of fire. The gun doesn't make a regular bang. Instead it makes a spitting noise. Casey knows that this is a new, well-silenced weapon.

"Your time has arrived to meet the devil," says a voice on the other side. A heavy boot kicks the door open and forces the file cabinet back. "Devil children, now you must die. You have killed the emissary of God and must suffer the consequences." The assailant continues to force the file cabinet back and push the door open. He steps inside the room, uncertain exactly where Casey and Naomi are.

"Prepare to die," Casey hears him rant as he clicks the safety of his automatic off.

"Donnie? Is that you, Donnie Stryker?" Casey can't believe she would give herself away like that.

"Speak to me, daughter of the demon master, so that I can put you out of your earthly misery."

"Donnie, it's me, Naomi, your sister. Why do you want to kill your sister?"

"You have sinned against the earthly plans of the highest and must pay for your blasphemy." Donnie has an idea where she is now and turns the muzzle of his weapon upward.

As Donnie's muzzle swings around toward her, Naomi produces the little snub-nosed .38, closes her eyes, and pulls the trigger six times as fast as she can. The bullets find Donnie's face, and the force on his body throws his weapon backward. His reflex fires a single round.

It isn't over yet. Casey hears yet another person coming up the stairs. He takes a quick peek above the pile of Sheetrock and draws himself up to his haunches. The man is at the top step but doesn't have his weapon pointed directly at him. He pops up and empties the little .22 at the man. He hits him with all nine rounds, and the man teeters at the top of the steps and falls backward down them.

Immediately, there is the sound of running feet as a spray of rounds penetrate the outer hall floor. Casey hears the clip hit the floor and another being inserted, and the bolt being pulled back, and another assailant appears at the top of the stairs. He crouches and walks forward.

Naomi looks down and is shocked as she sees what she's just done. Casey looks out the door and sees another man coming up the stairs. *If I can just get to the dead man's weapon,* he thinks. But there's no way he can get past the opening of the door.

Donato Montovi, a man wanted by the federal government for interstate flight to avoid prosecution for murder, steps into the room. He turns the light on, looks around, and finds Casey.

"Get up and get over there," he says in a heavy Brooklyn accent. He looks up and sees Naomi on the top shelf. Her dress is pushed up, and she's without her underwear. "Hey, lookie here at the little lady. She's offerin' me a shot of dirty leg. I think I'm gonna get some pussy before I leave here today, and you, Mr. White, will have to watch me get it. I might have to leave her a few bruises too."

Naomi rolls over and points her gun at him. He can see it is empty and laughs.

"Ya gonna just yell bang, bang?"

"Is this what you want?" She throws the empty revolver at him, and he ducks. It's the distraction Casey needs, and he launches himself across the area to where the dead man's gun lies. Naomi catapults off the shelf and falls toward Johnny. Her body is above his weapon, and she manages to deflect it downward as he closes his finger on the trigger. He fires the entire magazine into the floor.

Casey grabs the other gun and pulls the action back to make sure it's loaded, but he finds it has stovepiped. The round is stuck in the fully upward position, jammed tight. Casey jumps toward Johnny, intending to use the gun as a club, but Johnny is extraordinarily strong and simply pushes Casey aside.

Donato stands up and points his weapon toward them. "Now ya die, ya gentile fools." An embarrassing click sounds as the firing pin falls on an empty chamber.

Casey, Naomi, and Donato jump as a new voice shouts, "Police! Drop the weapon. I repeat, drop the weapon!" Johnny spins and raises his weapon toward the approaching police officer. The policeman's revolver speaks five times as quickly as he can pull the trigger. Johnny staggers back from the fusillade and flings the weapon aside as he falls.

Three shots ring out from yet another location. The policeman fires his sixth round as he pitches sideways and falls. The little hall closet door opens, and a man steps out. He's holding another of the weapons the other assassins were carrying.

"Four saints have joined the maker in glory, and I am here to finish what is ordained," the new assailant says. "The pawn of the devil I have vanquished, and I will now complete what God has ordered for the ones who will incarcerate the true believers." He steps over the fallen policeman and slowly walks forward.

The new gunman never hears the dog dragging himself up the stairs on three legs. Bofus leaps and hits the man in the back. He locks his huge jaw around the back of his neck as he leans forward. Bofus holds on, grinds, and shakes, trying for a kill. Casey can hear bones being crushed.

The man screams in pain and tries to pull the dog off his neck. Casey launches him at the assailant and takes hold of the weapon and pushes it down against his stomach as the assailant squeezes the trigger. Casey can see the bullets exiting his lower body and feet; there is bone and blood in the blast. The would-be killer's foot and leg are mercilessly torn to shreds until the weapon runs out of ammunition.

Casey quickly finds the one weapon he knows is loaded and points it at the man. He throws the cylinder open on the police officer's revolver and checks the load. There is one unfired cartridge remaining.

"Drop the weapon! This is the FBI! Drop the weapon!" Casey looks up and sees that a huge man wearing a bulletproof vest and a shirt with FBI proudly displayed on it is wielding a Thompson submachine gun and advancing toward him.

"I'm the homeowner. I'm the one you came here to protect," Casey says.

"Drop the weapon, and we'll consider it."

Casey puts the gun down, steps toward Naomi, and sits on the floor with her. In a rush of emotion, they break down into tears.

The FBI agent steps over Bofus, who is looking up with big, brown pain-filled eyes. The agent cautiously enters the room. Casey watches him go to the back of the room to a secure position and bend down to speak into his radio. "The situation is neutralized. All stand down. There is an officer down, and we need medics, stat. All units do a sweep of the entire premises and report back to me."

When Casey looks up, the room fills with every kind of law enforcement officer he can imagine. They seem to come out of the woodwork. The FBI agent helps them to their feet, and a paramedic leads them down the stairs and through the kitchen.

Casey and Naomi want just to sit a minute, but the paramedic insists that the house is now a crime scene, and that they need to follow him outside. They step over the bodies of the fallen assassins, go outside, and climb into an ambulance, where the paramedic checks them over. All they've suffered are scratches, splinters, and bruises. Casey and Naomi hold each other and cry tears of relief.

"I need someone to get my dog attended to," says Casey. "He's been shot, and I know he's lost a lot of blood."

"Please relax. Animal Rescue is on the way," says the paramedic. "You need to thank your neighbor and some guy from a private detective agency; they're the ones who saw the attackers coming and made the first call to the police."

"My God, Casey, I'm sorry I brought all this on you," says Naomi. "All I wanted to do was find you and see if we could pick up our lives like we planned back in 1960."

"Naomi, I knew my life was restored the instant I saw you at the front door. I wanted things to be just like they were between us." Casey turns to a nearby policeman. "Can we go back in the house now?"

"No. As of now, you both are in protective custody. We have a secure house to take you to."

The FBI agent approaches the couple with a police sergeant, and for the first time, he smiles. "We need both of you to come with us to the station and give us statements. The man your dog took out is Stanley Simplex; he's on the agencies' wanted lists, and there's a substantial reward for him. I don't know what the reward is for the others, but I think you might get something out of this to mitigate what they put you through."

"Can I please get my house closed up and put the car into the garage?" Casey asks.

"Casey, bring me my little blue suitcase out of the back seat." They allow him to back his van in, and then he sits behind the wheel of the little Ford, and a flood of memories come back to him. He carefully parks it inside and closes the door. He wonders who found his little treasure behind the glove box.

The detective escorts them to police headquarters where they're put into separate rooms and questioned for what seems like hours. Casey finishes before Naomi and waits in the hallway for her. He notices that the thunderstorms are over as he drops coins into the coffee machine and receives a cup. He then realizes how hungry he is. Naomi finally appears and rushes into his arms, and they just hold each other.

The chief detective comes out of the office. "Come with me to the car now," he says. He nods to another man, and they go out the front walkway into the twilight street. Casey wonders how they'll be able to go by car. The street beyond the blocked-off entrance to the parking lot is flooded with news media.

A black Cadillac is parked across the street from where they are leaving. The back door opens, and a tall man steps out. It's unusual for a local to be wearing the kind of overcoat and floppy hat he has on, and it catches the interest of several of the officers who have followed Casey and Naomi outside. When the tall man spots the couple, he moves toward them, walking with a little limp. He stoops slightly and quickly opens the coat. The front sight of what appears to be an automatic weapon catches on the cloth. He quickly tries to level it but is unable to get off a round as the night shatters with the shots of over a dozen officers.

The man goes down in a bloody haze of impacts from the rounds hitting him. The front car door opens, and the driver launches himself out of the door and goes prone on the street. There's stone silence as several of the officers approach the bloodied form on the street. Others take the driver into custody. Apparently, the police's work is not yet completed this evening.

A crowd of reporters and camera crews try to force their way through the police line but are stopped short of the scene. The camera lights illuminate the street, and the air pulsates with the pops of flash bulbs.

One of the officers kneels down, rolls the man over, and pushes his gun away as Casey and Naomi approach, and she steps to where the body is relieving itself of its vital fluids and viciously kicks it.

"Matthew, you stupid bastard, you never knew when to quit," Naomi says, fairly spitting her words at him.

"Is this the felon we've been seeing all the bulletins on?" the officer asks her.

"Yes, it's Matthew Samuelson, my ex-husband and fugitive from the law. I guess now the million-dollar bail he paid will be enjoyed by the government, and by God, I claim the reward for him."

Casey and Naomi are guided to an awaiting helicopter behind the operations building, and they duck inside and take off before any of the press can figure out what's occurring. It's the first time Casey has flown above the city. The lights are coming on, and the streets below seem to have a festive air.

\* \* \*

The next few days flash by in a haze of appointments for Casey and Naomi, with various factions of law enforcement interviewing them. The press is kept at a sizeable distance at first, but they eventually move in and take long-range shots, trying to get exclusives for their particular venues.

After a week and a half, Casey begins to tire of the whole thing. That night, they're unceremoniously and secretly pulled out of their original safe house and taken to another.

Chapter
40

Two agents accompany a woman up the sidewalk to the house, and after her briefcase is checked, she's allowed to enter. The door closes, and once again, Casey is face-to-face with Mary Ekland. She hands him her card.

"I hear you need a lawyer. I told them you contacted me, and I agree to be your council."

"Excuse me, Naomi, I need to hug this lawyer." Casey steps up, and he and Mary find themselves in each other's arms. She kisses him once, smiles broadly, and then moves back to take a long look at him and Naomi.

"Mary Ekland, meet Naomi . . . what's your last name now?" Casey says, stumbling over his words.

"Naomi, I guess I owe you an explanation," says Mary. "I've known Casey since his navy days in 1960, at Guantanamo Bay, Cuba. We've been buddies off and on forever, it seems. He's actually the biological father of my oldest son. I told him I was on birth control pills at the time. My two younger boys I made the right way." Casey steps out of the way for Naomi to shake Mary's hand. Mary has a sly grin on her face at Casey's reaction to her statement.

"I'm happy to meet you, Mary. I'm Naomi, with the bad reputation. I think I'm going to reclaim my maiden name, Stryker, but I'm hoping it won't be for long. Casey and I go back too. We, in fact, go back to the fifties; he helped me create my son before I was forcibly sent away to endure the marriage from hell. It's taken me all this time to catch up with him. Now I have him, and he's not getting away."

They go to the kitchen, and as they sit down, an officer interrupts them. One of Mary's paralegals is here with some paperwork for her. Casey can feel his heartbeat as he goes to the front door. Standing there is a beautiful Sereta, with tears in her eyes. He beckons her to come in, and she reaches out and hugs him. The astonished look on Naomi's face appears again.

Sereta approaches Naomi. "I've known Casey since before he met Mary. He rescued me in Cuba and made it possible for me to become an American. He is the biological father of my son." She stops and looks Naomi up and down. "You are the one my Casey has loved all these years, and now you have him back from where they took you. You are beautiful, and I am happy for the both of you."

Naomi's eyes begin to water. She's overwhelmed by the unfolding events, and tears stream down her face.

"Casey," says Naomi, "when we're finally able to get back to the car, I drove halfway across America to return to you, I will show you a file I put together after I discovered some things about you." Now Casey is the one who looks astonished.

"I've been doing a yearly class history, and you were a naughty boy after I was kidnapped and forcibly married off to that felon. You were really angry and working at revenge, and I've suspected all along that it was you who shot Mr. Herman the night the eighteen thousand dollars disappeared that he was using to pay off assassins, two of which were going to eliminate you and your family." That little disclosure perks up Mary's and Serta's ears.

"I'm happy that when Mr. Herman languished after a stroke, the authorities gained some valuable information from him before he died. He never did let Belinda, the girl he calls his daughter, know who her real father is, and I think it's because of all the intermarrying. They couldn't question her mother because she disappeared shortly after with two of her children. I think she is living with relatives somewhere in Missouri or Illinois, if she isn't dead."

"Naomi, I think I know who Belinda's father is," says Casey. "I found out the day the widow lady allowed me to peruse the marriage records in the courthouse. It's Thaddeus Milner, Mr. Herman's boss at the feed store. He's some kind of high priest in the Alfeta church, and he needed a place to hide his daughter from his second marriage when the authorities looked into his dealings back in the forties."

"Casey, tell me truthfully now, is there anybody else stirring in the gene pool I should know about, or will you have to think about it?" Naomi asks.

*　*　*

It's almost another week before they can return to Casey's house. Casey calls work and finds that since federal authorities are holding them, he isn't being charged leave. His boss knows he'll need some time to unwind, and all Casey has to do is tell him when he gets home. His vacation leave will start then.

When Casey and Naomi return home, they can see someone inside the house. The policeman with them steps ahead of them, his hand hovering over the handle of his revolver. He cautiously opens the door, and there, amid scrub buckets, is LJ, Casey's next-door neighbor, cleaning the house. She turns and smiles. Raring to go behind the inside screen door is Bofus, anxious to get to Casey while carrying his prized pair of panties in his mouth.

End